A Knight's Vengeance

CATHERINE KEAN

Jewel Imprint: Sapphire
Medallion Press, Inc.
Printed in USA

passions, while Fane must fight the demons of his own haunted past. The secondary characters, from the servants to the peasants, are finely drawn, too, and serve to bring this tale to life."
— Romantic Times BOOKclub Magazine

"Dance of Desire is one of the reasons I love Medallion Press so much."
— The Romance Studio

♥♥♥♥♥ FIVE HEARTS!
"Catherine Kean's novel *Dance of Desire* is an excellent debut novel making it a must read for 2005. It will capture you, it will put you under its spell, and it will make you want more by this author."
— The Mystic Castle

"DANCE OF DESIRE is a perfect blend of character and plot driven storyline. This reviewer could not put it down. Ms. Kean is a gifted writer that will deliver a timeless classic for any book lover. Run to buy *Dance of Desire* and find a book worth getting lost in."
— Love Romances

"Intrigue and passion drives *Dance of Desire*, debut author Catherine Kean's compelling novel, from the first page to the last. This impressive new book ranks right up there beside veterans of the genre. Readers will be pleased with the ease with which the plot advances through the action of the story. Not to mention the characters are easy to like. Superb debut for Ms. Kean!"
— A Romance Review

"*Dance of Desire* is a well-rounded story with a pace and tempo that will keep you on the edge of your seat, a suspenseful plot and characters that evoke your emotions. Enjoy this sensual medieval tale."
— Fallen Angel Reviews

"One of the best historical romances this reviewer has ever read! *Dance of Desire* will definitely stay on the "keeper" shelf."
— Romance Divas

DEDICATION:

For my dear friend Alicia Clarke, who loved this book
from its very first draft. Your friendship and endless
encouragement are very special to me.
Thank you.

ACKNOWLEDGEMENTS:

So many people graciously shared their enthusiasm and kindness each step of my writing journey.

For fabulous, insightful critiques and editing suggestions, I thank many times over my friends and awesome critique partners Nancy Robards Thompson, Teresa Elliott Brown, and Elizabeth Grainger. I don't know what I'd do without you!

My sincerest thanks also to my friend Cheryl Duhaime, who never fails to say, "I can't wait to read the rest;" to my dad, David Lord, who read and made suggestions on an early draft; to my mother, Shirley Lord, whose nurturing, creative soul runs rich and deep; to my sister, Amanda Lord, who read this story at least twice and gave constructive feedback.

Most of all, I must thank my husband Mike, who supported my quest to become a published author. His generous heart bears the hallmarks of a true hero.

PROLOGUE

Moydenshire, England, 1174

"Father," Geoffrey de Lanceau moaned. Wrenching his gaze from the dark outlines of the horse and animals nearby, he knelt beside the man sprawled on the stable's filthy straw.

The metallic scent of blood seared Geoffrey's nostrils. In the feeble torchlight, his father's face bore the waxy pallor of death.

Tears blurred Geoffrey's vision. His mind whirled with memories of flaming arrows. Thundering horses. His father's agonized roar as a sword slashed his chest. Biting down on his hand, Geoffrey fought the sobs that tore up from his belly.

Outside, the wind wailed past the stable's walls. The lone torch inside hissed and spat. Light glimmered on the silk surcoat crushed into the straw. The embroidered garment, symbol of his family's noble heritage, was soiled and torn.

Helplessness welled up inside Geoffrey like boiling pitch. As the acidic taste of bile filled his mouth, he curled his hands into fists.

He would not fail to save his father.

He had rescued his sire from the siege and found refuge. Now, he would save his father's life. He would prove himself worthy to be the son of Edouard de Lanceau, a knight whose heroism had been lauded in *chansons de geste* and praised in the king's court.

Until the king branded Edouard a traitor.

Until the king ordered Lord Arthur Brackendale to besiege the keep at Wode and kill Edouard.

Confusion and fear snaked down Geoffrey's spine. His sire was not a traitor.

"Geoffrey?" The rasped voice sounded pitifully faint.

"Please, lie still." Geoffrey pressed his palms to his father's stained shirt. Fresh blood oozed between his fingers. "Need a healer. Poultices. Must stitch the wounds—"

"No . . . time," Edouard whispered.

Geoffrey trembled. "Do not speak. Save your strength. The Earl of Druentwode—"

"—will protect . . . you now . . . as his own kin. I would do . . . same . . . for his sons."

"Nay!"

Edouard's mouth twisted into a pained smile. "Promise me . . . you will care for . . . your brother."

"Live! You *must* live. Thomas and I do not want to be orphans." Despair lodged in Geoffrey's throat like a stone. "When Mother died, you swore we—"

"Promise . . . me."

With a choked cry, Geoffrey wrenched his hands away. Panic and anger swarmed in his belly like flies. "Do not die a traitor. *Live*, Father. Prove Lord Brackendale's siege was wrong. Prove you did not betray our king."

Anguish shimmered in Edouard's gray eyes. "Ah, my son."

The tender words clawed at Geoffrey. "I cannot make the vow." The tears he had tried so hard to hold back streamed down his cheeks. "I cannot wield a sword. I have no armor. I am naught but a *boy*."

"Not boy." Edouard groped for Geoffrey's hand and squeezed it. "You are heir to the de Lanceau estates. I ask you again—"

His father's tone held urgency. With a shuddered sigh, Geoffrey nodded. He curled his small fingers into his sire's and held tight. "I promise. 'Tis a vow sealed in blood."

Edouard groaned. Gasped. His breath expelled on a rush, faded to a gurgle, then . . . only the wind's eerie shriek.

"Father?" Geoffrey looked down at his sire's pale, lifeless hand. In the shadows, animals stirred.

Rats scurried across the fouled straw, eyes bright in the torchlight.

"*Father?*" Geoffrey's voice rose to a wail. He freed his hand and blinked away tears. Screaming, he slammed his fist against the dirt floor.

With trembling fingers, he reached out and closed his father's sightless eyes.

Geoffrey sobbed, shoved to his feet and staggered to the doorway. Rage and grief burned like hellfire in the pit of his stomach. "I will avenge you, Father," he cried toward the night sky shrouded with fog. "God's holy blood, I will avenge you!"

CHAPTER ONE

Eighteen years later

"Love potion, dove? An elixir ta ease yer lonely heart?"

"Not this day, thank you." Lady Elizabeth Brackendale strolled past the one-eyed peddler waving flasks and vials. As she sidestepped a mound of manure, she sighed. Love potion, indeed. Her heart's afflictions could not be cured in that manner.

Behind her, she heard the voices and booted footsteps of her lady-in-waiting and two armed guards. What a nuisance the men-at-arms were, an unwelcome reminder of the perilous future.

Elizabeth shivered, skirted two men arguing over a spilled crate of onions, and walked further into the crowded market square. She would *not* spoil this rare, glorious day that her father had allowed her to leave Wode's fortified walls. She would *not* worry about the lord rumored to be plotting vengeance against her sire, a rogue named Geoffrey de Lanceau.

Her father would deal with him.

Tipping her face into the breeze, she inhaled a waft of ripe vegetables, wood smoke, and horse. Ahead, men unloaded cartloads of cloth and spices, jugglers performed for a laughing crowd, and merchants hawked their wares. What a glorious mélange of smells, sights, and sounds. How she had missed her visits to the market.

Apprehension, cold as bone fingers, trailed down her spine. If only battle were not looming in the days ahead. If anything happened to her father . . .

She shoved the thought aside. When necessary, he would summon his armies, crush de Lanceau, and peace would again rule Moydenshire. Her father could not fail with Baron Sedgewick of Avenley and his armies at his side.

Baron Sedgewick. Her betrothed.

In seven days, her husband.

Fluttering strips of cloth lured her toward a stall. Blinking away tears, she paused and fingered a blood red ribbon. Resentment flared, sharper than her worry. She could not wed the baron. She *would* not! How could she marry and leave her father's side with de Lanceau still a threat? How could she marry a man she did not love, but loathed?

She must persuade her father to break the engagement.

Or, she would find a way to escape it.

"Three pieces of silver? I suggest you reconsider."

Recognizing the voice, Elizabeth dared a sidelong glance. Mildred Cottlepod, her gray-haired lady-in-waiting, scowled at a hunchbacked crone who sold healing herbs. Elizabeth's gaze slid to her guards who leaned against crates of squawking chickens, and pointed to the jugglers who boasted of an impossible feat.

Onlookers shouted bets. Coins clinked.

The guards laughed and reached for their money purses.

Elizabeth sucked in a breath. Could she slip away? How wondrous, to elude her guards' watchful gazes for a while. Since de Lanceau had taken up residence in his crown-awarded keep two months ago, they had become her permanent shadows.

Heat stung Elizabeth's cheeks, and her fingers tightened around the ribbon. She was a grown woman, not a witless simpleton who needed constant supervision.

No harm would come to her in this peaceful town protected by her father's fortress. Without her guards hovering nearby, mayhap she could think of a way to convince her sire to annul the betrothal.

And, she could choose the thread she needed to finish the embroidery on the orphans' chemises and shirts, for she had promised the nuns she would be donating gifts of clothes and sweetmeats to the children. Her lips flattened on a painful, buried memory. She would not forget the thread, or the promise she made, one year ago, when her mother and infant sister died.

"Ye like it, milady?" said a gruff voice.

"Pardon?" She swung around, and came face to face with the stall's proprietor.

He jabbed a grubby finger at the bit of silk in her hand.

"'Tis lovely." She dropped a silver coin into his palm, far more than the ribbon cost, but no doubt he had a wife and children to feed. He flashed her a toothless grin. She smiled back and glanced at her guards. They were engrossed in the bet.

Lifting up her bliaut to keep it out of the dirt, she darted into the market square.

A thrill rippled through her. Freedom, at last.

The merchant who stocked the nicest thread was just past—

"Milady." A man's voice carried over the *honk, honk* of geese flapping to get out of her way.

Had the guards seen her?

Ignoring the shouts and *clop* of hooves behind her, she sidestepped a puddle and quickened her steps.

"Milady, look out!"

Elizabeth whirled around. A wagon laden with wooden casks rumbled straight for her.

The driver yelled for her to get out of the way. He jerked hard on the horse's reins. The wild-eyed beast tossed its head, snorted, and refused to obey its master's command.

Elizabeth lunged to the side, expecting to feel the stinging weight of the animal's hooves. A muscled arm snaked around her waist. She shrieked an instant before she was yanked to safety. The cart hurtled past.

Elizabeth coughed. Waving her hands, she tried to disperse the dust that burned her eyes and clung to her cloak, hair and skin. Her legs wobbled. She prayed the stranger who had saved her would not release his hold, or she would topple face first on the ground. She closed her eyes against a wave of dizziness.

"You fool. Were you trying to get yourself killed?"

Her coughing subsided. She recognized the deep, rich voice that had called out moments ago. *Fool?* Who would dare to chastise her so? She, the daughter of Lord Arthur Brackendale.

Equally annoying, she had sagged into the stranger's arms like a swooning maiden. Her cheek pressed against his warm chest.

Elizabeth took a steadying breath, calmed by the rhythmic *thud* beneath her ear, the pulse of life. This man did not deserve her anger, but her gratitude. He had risked himself great harm to save her from a painful death.

"Kind sir, I owe you my thanks," she said.

His arms, curved around her waist, relaxed. He must have sensed her strength returning. "A moment more, and you would have been crushed beneath the wagon's wheels," he said. "A pity, indeed, if such a fair damsel were broken like a child's toy."

His breath stirred the hair at her forehead. Goosebumps shot down her arms. She did not like the sensation, or the trace of humor warming his voice.

"I did not see the wagon," Elizabeth said.

"Nor did you heed my warning."

He spoke in the same tone as her father when he told her of her betrothal, but her sire had gentled his words by insisting the arrangement was for her safety, to ensure she and Wode never fell into de Lanceau's clutches. She scowled. Her whole life it seemed of late was governed by this rogue de Lanceau.

She tipped up her chin. Her savior was a tall man. Shoulder muscles stretched his gray wool tunic. She steeled herself against his enticing, musky scent. "You are bold to speak to me in such a manner."

"Not half as bold, milady, as you appear to be."

Elizabeth groaned, for he spoke true. Her hands curled into his tunic. The ribbon poked between her fingers.

"Or half so bold again," he continued with a velvety drawl, "as if I had stolen a kiss from your sweet lips."

Her breath caught in her throat, trapped like a robin in a hawk's talons. She wrenched free of his hold. The ribbon slipped from her grasp and drifted toward the ground.

"You would not dare kiss me."

The stranger chuckled, and Elizabeth glared up at him. Her gaze locked with eyes the color of cold steel. Magnificent, captivating eyes, framed by dark lashes. His gaze glinted with amusement. And challenge.

Unease shot through Elizabeth. Where were her guards?

The stranger's stare did not waver. His eyebrows arched with unquestionable arrogance, and her heart beat like a frantic bird's wings. Why did he not lower his gaze and show her due respect? He must realize her position. Her sky blue gown was tailored to the latest court fashion and sewn from the finest English wool, unlike his plain, homespun gray tunic and hose.

"You are a fool to challenge me," she said, hoping to hear the loud roar that signaled the end of the jugglers' act.

The stranger smiled. "*I* am the fool? I did not run into a wagon's path." His grin widened to reveal straight, white teeth without a spot of decay. "Mayhap your attention was claimed by more important thoughts, such as the whispered endearments of an eager suitor?"

She gasped, aware that curious townsfolk gathered around them. Insolent knave. How dare he mock her before an audience, and her father's people? "Do you not know who I am?"

"A lady, forsooth." His gaze traveled the length of her cloak. "Come to market to buy a pretty trinket?"

Pride warmed her voice. "My father is lord of the keep which stands upon yonder hill, and the lands surrounding it for many leagues."

Surprise and anger flashed in the man's eyes. "You are Brackendale's *daughter?*"

She had expected awe, not the fury and stark pain that ravaged his features. He looked wounded, cut to his soul. She wondered at the source of his anguish, even as the emotion vanished and his lips thinned into a bitter, controlled smile.

Over the crowd's murmurs, she heard shouts and the thunder of approaching footsteps.

"Your faithful guards, milady."

Elizabeth smothered a relieved sigh. "Good. My father will enjoy meeting a rogue who thought to kiss me."

"Alas, I must miss that meeting, and bid you good day."

Without warning, he caught her fingers. He bent at the waist, an elegant movement better suited to a chivalrous knight than a knave, and shiny brown hair fell over his face. Light as a feather, his lips brushed the back of her hand.

Heat skittered across Elizabeth's skin, spiraled through her arm, and pooled in her belly. The odd sensation was both exciting and frightening.

She yanked her fingers free, and he smiled.

"Until we meet again, milady." Without the slightest attempt at a bow, he turned and strode into the crowd.

A hand clutched Elizabeth's arm. "By the blessed Virgin," Mildred said, wide-eyed, her wrinkled fingers at her throat. "Are you all right?"

Elizabeth nodded. Her flesh still tingled, as though his mouth continued to ply its sensual wickedness upon her.

Indeed, her whole body tingled.

"The man who saved you—"

"A rogue." Elizabeth glared at her guards. "Find him."

Drawing his sword, one of the men-at-arms hurried off

in pursuit. The other bellowed for the throng to disperse.

As Elizabeth forced her breath to slow and fought the heat in her cheeks, the stranger's parting words spun through her mind.

Until we meet again, milady.

Were the words a promise? Or a threat?

❈ ❈ ❈

Geoffrey de Lanceau leaned against the mildewed wattle-and-daub wall of Totter's Ale House, his arms crossed over his chest and his gaze on the lady. He had easily eluded the guard. In his childhood, Geoffrey had scampered through Wode's narrow streets and alleys many times, and he had not forgotten them.

The matron fussed over her charge like a hen clucking at a chick. The lady's hands clenched into fists, her chin thrust up, and even from a distance, he saw the spark of her eyes. A willful damsel. She did not like to be scolded, even if she deserved a tongue-wagging.

He cursed under his breath, for his palms still burned where they had pressed against her slender waist, holding her, so she would not crumple into the offal at her feet. Her honey-eyed scent clung to him, as damning as the scorn in her voice.

Of all the things he had expected this morn, it was not she. He had come to Wode to study his enemy, to learn from the folk who frequented the market, to find Lord Brackendale's weakness. He had not anticipated that weakness would fall into his arms in the form of a fragrant, tempting woman, whose blue eyes, lush mouth, and beauty could tempt the most pious man to commit sin.

He dismissed his ridiculous interest. She was the daughter of the man responsible for his father's death.

He intended to destroy Lord Arthur Brackendale.

A shuffling sound came from behind him.

Geoffrey's senses snapped alert. Warning hummed in his veins. He grabbed the dagger in his belt and whipped around.

His friend and fellow knight, Dominic de Terre, stumbled out of the shadows of an open doorway. His chestnut brown hair, cut short at the nape, looked damp and tousled. His cheeks were ruddy, and he grinned like a besotted fool.

Geoffrey blew a breath and lowered the knife. "Dominic."

"A bloody Turk could have charged up behind you, and you would not have heard," Dominic said with a good-natured chuckle. With his hand, he stifled a belch.

A flush burned Geoffrey's cheekbones. Surely he had not been that engrossed in watching *her*. He shrugged off the sting of embarrassment and sheathed the dagger. "I heard you well enough. Still, I am glad 'twas you, and not a drunken brute."

"Aye." Dominic's gaze darted to the putrefying piles of vegetables and manure beside him as though they might suddenly transform into fly-covered demons. "'Tis common knowledge back alleys hide the worst thieves, pickpockets, cutthroats . . . even vengeful lords plotting to claim keeps." When Geoffrey frowned, Dominic laughed. "Milord, what had you so captivated?"

Geoffrey snorted. "I was *not* captivated."

"Ha! You stared into the market like you spied a chest full of silver. Or a wench eager for a tumble."

"Wrong on both accounts."

"Not a wench?" Dominic's brown eyes widened. "Mayhap I do not know you as well as I thought. You once boasted quite a reputation with the fair sex."

"Enough! Tell me, what did you learn?" Geoffrey glanced back at the market, in time to see a scrawny urchin snatch a joint of meat from the butcher's stall.

Dominic plucked straw from his tunic's cuff. "It seems you visit Wode at a fortuitous time. The men in the alehouse were most willing to chat once we had shared a few rounds of brown ale. The miller complained of all the sacks of grain he must grind so the castle's chief cook can prepare the wedding feast—"

The butcher's roar carried above the buzz of voices. The boy fled, clutching his prize to his chest, and vanished into the crowd. Elizabeth turned, a look of surprise on her face. Sunlight played over the black curls at her brow and wove highlights into the glossy braid falling to her waist.

Geoffrey remembered the soft brush of her hair on his sleeve. He shoved the thought from his mind. "Wedding?"

"Brackendale's daughter's. She is betrothed to the notorious

Baron Sedgewick. They are to be married on the town church's portico in seven days."

Geoffrey's eyes narrowed. So there was a suitor. As he watched, unable to wrest his gaze away, she halted the butcher's angry pursuit of the urchin. With a smile and a few words, she put something into the butcher's hand. Coins.

The lady had a heart, unlike her father. How ironic that a lord who could cut down a man in front of his young son could sire such a compassionate daughter.

Clenching his jaw against the foolish and unwelcome sympathy, Geoffrey said, "The marriage will never happen."

"'Tis a clever union. Brackendale's estates border Sedgewick's. If either lord should die, the marriage allows the holdings to merge and create the largest estate in all of Moydenshire." Dominic waved a hand in the air. "Yet, even more important, Brackendale gains a powerful ally."

A growl burned Geoffrey's throat. The sound echoed in the wounded reaches of his soul, the place that would only heal when he had vengeance. "As I said, 'twill never happen."

Dominic arched an eyebrow. "King Richard rewarded you well for your valor in the Crusades, but surely you do not expect your small estate or your new position as lord of Branton Keep to have any influence upon this wedding."

"You underestimate me."

Dominic shook his head, as though he reasoned with a stubborn child. "Milord, you have lived at Branton for only two months. The fortress is in disrepair. Your wealth and position are insignificant compared to Brackendale's or Sedgewick's, and you have neither the money nor the armies to challenge them to battle." His mouth eased into a wry grin. "Admit it. Until Pietro sends the profits from the silk trade in Venice, you must watch how you spend every bit of silver."

"'Twill not cost me one bit," Geoffrey murmured, shoving away from the tavern wall, "if we have the right pawn."

"Pawn? Now we speak of chess? I thought—"

"I mean the daughter."

Geoffrey tilted his head toward the market. Dominic scanned the throng until, at Geoffrey's nod, his gaze alighted on Elizabeth. She stood peering down at the wagon-churned dirt. She seemed to be searching for a lost treasure. Her ribbon?

Followed by her guard and lady-in-waiting, she walked on a few paces, her strides fluid and graceful.

Dominic whistled. "'Twas a wench, after all."

Geoffrey dragged a hand over his jaw. He tore his gaze from the shimmer of pale silk at her ankle.

"A rare beauty, is she not?"

A rough laugh burst from Geoffrey. "The lady is a spoiled, haughty little—"

"For the spawn of Lord Brackendale, I believe that is a compliment." Dominic's eyes sparkled.

"'Twould not matter if she were buck-toothed, bow-legged, or ugly as sin." Geoffrey clenched his fists against seething bitterness and anguish. "She is Brackendale's flesh and blood. I vow he would move heaven and hell to ensure her safety."

The mirth vanished from Dominic's features. "Milord?"

"Wode *will* be mine, but without unnecessary expense or bloodshed." Geoffrey swallowed the vile taste flooding his mouth. Over the course of a lifetime, he had witnessed more killing than any sane man could bear. He would never forget the slaughter—of innocents and warriors alike—that had stained the ground at Acre crimson with blood. He would not forget his brother's sacrifice.

Nor would he forget the last, strangled breath that marked his father's passing, or forgive his dishonorable death.

An armed man elbowed his way toward the lady. The second guard. Soon, word of the morn's mishap would reach Brackendale, and if he cared half as much about his daughter as Geoffrey suspected, the town would be swarming with men-at-arms. He must not be captured.

Not now, when revenge would soon be within his grasp.

"What do you intend?" Dominic asked.

Silent laughter swirled up inside Geoffrey. "By this afternoon, Brackendale will receive word of fires in the village of Tillenham. Devastating blazes, rumored to be set by my hand."

Dominic scratched his head, a nervous sound. "A ruse, I trust?"

Geoffrey nodded. "A diversion."

"And the daughter?"

She abandoned her search for the ribbon, and her entourage urged her to leave. She shook her head and pointed across the market. As she walked, sunlight and shadow skimmed over her, outlining her slender figure, her swaying hips, and her bottom's fetching curve.

A primitive, sensual hunger roused in Geoffrey's gut.

Vengeance would be delicious indeed.

"Through her," he said, "I shall exact my revenge."

CHAPTER TWO

Raising her bliaut's hem, Elizabeth hurried up the fore-building's steps toward Wode's great hall. Her father's voice boomed into the torch lit passage, and her pulse quickened. The guards had told him of the market mishap. He did not sound pleased.

Ten more steps and she would reach the hall. What pleasure she had enjoyed as a little girl, counting each step aloud as, hand in hand with her father, they made their way up. He had been patient and forgiving when she muddled her numbers.

He would not be so forgiving of her running from her guards and falling into the arms of a randy rogue. Nor would he be pleased that, despite the wagon incident, she refused to leave the market until she had bought thread.

As she climbed the next step, she swallowed hard.

Whatever happened, she would not regret her much needed purchase. She had vowed to donate the garments, and she would see her commitment through.

She also would not be blamed for her rescuer's boldness. *He* had spoken of a kiss, not she.

His voice reverberated in her mind and the skin across her breasts prickled in a peculiar manner. A fit of nerves, no doubt. She brushed away the memory.

Footsteps echoed ahead. Someone descended the stairs. She edged toward the wall to allow room to pass, and a young man loped into view. Aldwin, her father's squire, whose corn-silk blond hair always looked tangled from bouts in the tiltyards.

"Milady." A relieved grin warmed his features. He caught her hands, and warmth flooded through her. "Your father is in quite a rage," he said, his tone hushed. "I heard what happened. Are you all right?"

Dear Aldwin. His friendship had helped her through the anguish of her mother and baby sister's deaths, and she adored him as if he were her own brother. He, in turn, never failed to be overprotective. Elizabeth smiled. "I am fine."

Terse conversation drifted down from the hall.

"Your father has ordered half the garrison into town to catch that rogue. Your sire intends to join the hunt soon. That man might have saved your life, but if he had dared to kiss you . . ." The corner of Aldwin's mouth tilted upward. "Did I tell you I have become an excellent shot with the crossbow?"

She laughed. "Four times. This afternoon, I hope to watch you shoot some targets."

Afterward, they could retire to the secluded bench in the garden. While she embroidered one of the children's garments, he might lift her spirits with tales of knights rescuing damsels and vanquishing evil. How she hoped he would agree. His stories always took her mind off the matters weighing upon her heart.

Aldwin squeezed her hands. "I am to go with your father. Later, I will be pleased to show you my target skills."

She nodded, but could not stop her smile from slipping.

In the dim light, the squire's face reddened. "I do not wish to disappoint you, but I must obey your father's orders. With the threat of de Lanceau—"

"I know." She sighed.

Aldwin's gaze turned earnest. "Milady, do you realize I have honed my prowess for you? Until that son-of-a-traitor is dead, I fear you will not be safe. I have sworn upon my honor—indeed, my life—that I will always protect you."

His words were soft, but echoed the passion of the chivalrous knights in his tales. As his voice faded, she stared up at him. She wondered if he referred to more than de Lanceau.

Aldwin had never tried to discuss her upcoming wedding with her. Yet he was a man of fierce convictions.

His thumbs caressed the backs of her fingers, and she fought a shudder. If she confided how much she hated her betrothal, would he see her as a damsel in distress and do all within his power to save her from her plight?

Desperate hope soared within her. If he agreed to be her protector and help her flee Moydenshire, then she would not have to marry Sedgewick. She would also be safe from de Lanceau.

Once her father had crushed that treacherous rogue, she could return and marry a man of her own choosing. A knight as noble as those of the *chansons*.

A man she loved.

Her belly knotted. Such a plan meant deceiving her father and angering him, but she had no other choice.

She met the squire's concerned stare. "Aldwin, I—"

Footfalls sounded near the top of the stairwell. "Where is she? Does she ignore my summons?"

At her father's roar, Elizabeth yanked her hands free. Under her breath, she cursed her foolishness. How could she have considered discussing such a matter now? She must not risk her budding plan's success, or get Aldwin into trouble.

Keeping her voice low, she said, "I *must* speak with you. This eve, in the garden?"

Curiosity lit Aldwin's eyes, and he bowed. "I will see you anon, milady." He brushed past and pounded down the stairs.

Elizabeth squared her shoulders, drew a calming breath, and hurried up the last steps. As she entered the hall, the tap of stone under her shoes became the crunch of dried herbs and rushes. Wood smoke hazed the chamber, but she made out her father's tall figure, hands clasped behind his back, pacing the floorboards. Nearby, her guards stared down at their feet.

Her father glanced up. "Elizabeth." He dragged a hand through his silver-gray hair. Tension lined the corners of his eyes, and guilt pinched her. She had not wanted him to worry.

She crossed the distance between them, but a throaty rumble drew her gaze to the lord's table. The balding man seated there might long ago have been called handsome, but now his features were bloated by excess.

His mouth slid into a lecherous grin, and he wiggled his fingers. "Beloved."

The knot in her belly twisted. "Baron Sedgewick."

She had not expected to see him today. Was this another surprise visit, in which he would try to woo her?

"I brought you a gift. I hope you like it." He held up a delicate hair comb, studded with gemstones.

"Thank you." Revulsion for him pressed upon her like a granite slab, yet she graced him with an elegant curtsey.

She straightened, and his tongue flicked over his lips. He tossed aside the comb and slurped his wine, then reached under the table and groped at his bronze silk tunic, stretched over his stomach. His hand kept rummaging. She looked away.

Shivers crawled over her skin, colder than when she had overheard the servants whispering of Sedgewick's perversions and cruelty. *Malicious gossip started by a former lover,* her father had said. *Pay it no heed.* Could there be truth to the rumors?

"Daughter." Her sire hugged her, and, with a sigh, she leaned into his reassuring warmth. He pushed her to arm's length, and frowned down at her. "You look pale. Are you well?"

She forced a smile. "Aye."

"Thank God," Sedgewick muttered.

Her father's mouth flattened. "What possessed you to flee your guards? Why were you so senseless, when you know of the dangers from de Lanceau?"

Frustration welled up inside her. "Why, every day, must I be accompanied by guards? 'Tis ridiculous, Father. De Lanceau is no threat so close to Wode."

"You were almost run down by a wagon."

She smothered a groan, and hoped he did not suspect the poor wagon driver of trying to do her harm. "'Twas an accident."

"Was it?" His fingers curled into her sleeves, and he seemed to struggle for patience. "Accident or not, think, Elizabeth. What might your rescuer have dared to do, if the guards had not run to your side?" She tried to speak, but he thrust up his hand. "I love you, and I will not risk your safety. You will accept your guards and obey them."

She gnawed her lip. Still, after all these years, his angry voice made her tremble. "Father—"

"You are all I have left."

His anguished words tore at her. The little girl inside her

cried, and Elizabeth's head dipped in a nod. "I will obey."

"Good." He released her and turned on her cowering guards. "See that my orders are carried out. I want to depart as soon as we have eaten. Go!"

The guards darted for the stairwell, just as young women rushed into the hall with wooden boards of bread and platters of food. It was too early for the midday meal to be served, Elizabeth noted, but it seemed her father had arranged for him and the baron to dine. As the maidservants hurried past, the scent of spiced sauces and spit-roasted fowl wafted to her.

"Come." Her father gestured to the lord's table, where the servants set the fare. "The baron wishes to eat before we join the search. No doubt you are hungry too."

She would rather eat cow dung than share another meal with the baron. Yet, if she refused, she risked not only offending him, but her father. She must not arouse their suspicions.

Forcing herself to take poised strides, Elizabeth walked through the sunlight filtering in through the high overhead windows and crossed to the table. Sedgewick's greedy gaze skimmed over her before riveting to her breasts. His eyes gleamed, as though he imagined trailing his fingers over her naked skin and examining her breasts' weight and feel.

Her cheeks flamed. He ogled her as if she were as valuable as a king's ransom and as delectable as a cream pastry. Had he looked at his previous three wives that way, all of them deceased?

She slipped into the vacant chair beside him, and the baron grinned. His chipped teeth, stained from the wine, had shredded food caught between them. Shoving aside his wine goblet, he leaned in close. "My love, you look most fetching in that gown." His thigh nudged hers under the table. "'Twill be a long seven days till we are husband and wife."

She choked. She grabbed the nearest wine goblet and took a gigantic gulp.

"Careful." His sweaty hand smothered hers. "I could not bear to see your life endangered again this day."

As the wine scorched its way down to her stomach, she freed her fingers and dried them on the tablecloth's edge. 'Twas the same hand the rogue had kissed. Sedgewick's kiss could never be as thrilling, or as competent.

Her skin warmed, and with shocking clarity, she recalled the glint of her rescuer's eyes. Brilliant, secretive eyes. He seemed far too clever a man to be apprehended by her father's guards.

Sinful heat coiled through her to the tips of her toes. What would his kiss have been like? She imagined his eyes darkening to a smolder, and his lips pressing over hers. He would kiss like the heroes in the *chansons*. Her belly swooped.

The chair beside her creaked as her father sat. She blinked away her thoughts and fought a blush. How foolish to swoon over that arrogant stranger, when she would never see him again.

Her father smiled at her, then asked the flushed chaplain,

who had only just emerged from the stairwell, to bless the fare.

Sedgewick piled a day-old bread trencher with the dishes that smelled of ginger, cumin and fresh rosemary. "What can I tempt you with, love?" He dangled a greasy bit of game hen between his fingers. "You must keep your strength for our wedding night"—his eyelid dropped in a wink—"and if your womb is to swell with my son."

Elizabeth waved away his offering and grabbed the goblet, grateful for the wine's numbing warmth.

Just as she set down the vessel, cool air whipped over her ankles. Bertrand de Lyons, Wode's captain of the guard, strode out of the stairwell. He crossed to her father, bowed, and handed him a rolled parchment.

"A messenger gave this to one of the guards. 'Tis urgent."

"Urgent?" Her father wiped sauce from his chin, then cracked the wax seal between his fingers.

Bertrand turned and handed her a scrap of faded linen. "Milady, for you."

Elizabeth frowned. She was not expecting any deliveries or messages. She set the little parcel on the table and opened it.

Her ribbon!

She had thought it lost for good. Who had found it? Who had returned it? She gently brushed it free of lingering dust.

"*God's bones.*"

Unease plowed deep within Elizabeth. She had never

heard her father speak in such a tone.

Her sire's lips were pressed into a line. His blue eyes blazed.

"Father?"

"Fires have burned the harvest at Tillenham." His hands shook. "The wheat, barley, and rye are destroyed."

The meat in the baron's fingers fell with a juicy plop.

"The message bears the Earl of Druentwode's signature. He begs for my help. He writes that whoever started the fires made sure naught would be left but ashes."

"Who would be so pitiless as to burn the year's crops?" Elizabeth whispered.

The baron's eyes bulged. "You do not think—"

"De Lanceau." Arthur snarled. "For weeks, I have heard rumblings that he was spying, gathering an army, and plotting revenge against me. Now, he has issued his challenge."

"If he wishes to stake his blood claim to Wode, why did he set fires in a town two days from hence?" Sedgewick's chin trembled. "The man is a hero of the Crusades. He knows how to fight and win. If he wanted to defeat you in battle and reclaim Wode, he would bring an army and spit at you through the portcullis. Would he not?"

"I will wrest an explanation from him."

A desperate wail lodged in Elizabeth's throat.

"Do not worry, beloved," Sedgewick crooned. "I will fight at your father's side. I will not allow wretched de Lanceau to win." He tried to take her hand, but she pulled away. Her stomach lurched, and she pressed her arm across her middle.

Her father's fist slammed down on the table. Goblets and platters rattled. "I refuse to be threatened by an idiot who believes he has claim to what the crown awarded to me." He glared at Bertrand. "Summon the knights and foot soldiers. We ride to Tillenham at dawn."

"Father, nay."

For a moment, tenderness softened her sire's gaze. Then his eyes hardened with ruthless determination, and she glimpsed the battle-seasoned knight who, eighteen years ago, had besieged Wode on the king's orders and wrested it from a traitor.

Her father was no longer a young warrior. Over two score years old, with joints that pained him on winter evenings, he had not fought in armed combat in years.

De Lanceau was a crusading hero fresh from war.

Elizabeth's heart ached, the pain as awful as the day she lost her mother and sister. Tears pricked her eyes.

"Come, Daughter. You have not lost faith in me, have you?"

"Of course not." She clasped her sire's weathered hand and smiled through her anguish. "I know you will triumph."

He nodded. "De Lanceau will realize his folly."

Fear shivered through her. "Please. Be careful. I could not bear to lose you too."

Her father's gaze clouded. He withdrew his fingers and shoved his chair back from the table, the squeal of wood against wood echoing her silent scream.

"If de Lanceau believes I am a weak old man, he is very much mistaken. He wants a bloody battle. He shall have one."

CHAPTER THREE

Elizabeth awoke from a fitful dream. Someone pounded on a door down the passage. She grumbled, rolled over in the cozy tangle of bedding, and shoved a pillow over her head. Could the matter not wait until morning? It seemed only moments ago that she had fallen asleep.

After helping to organize her father's departure yesterday, and her extra duties overseeing the keep's routines, she had rested little in two days. She had crawled into bed last night, her body numb with fatigue, but sleep refused to come. As she lay staring at the fire lit trusses overhead, battle images charged through her mind.

She worried for her father, and Aldwin, who had ridden at his side. She had not been able to speak with him before he left, and visions of her and the baron standing side by side in Wode's chapel, reciting wedding vows, haunted her. How sinful, that a part of her hoped Sedgewick would not return from battle alive.

The hammering persisted, loud even through the downy pillow. A door creaked open. Mumbled voices sounded in the passage.

"By the blessed Virgin."

At Mildred's shocked cry, the sleepy fog flew from Elizabeth's mind. She tossed aside the pillow and sat up in her dark chamber.

A terrible chill ran through her. Her father was dead.

She shoved aside the sheets and coverlet and slid her legs over the bed's edge. The fire had burned to embers, and the wooden boards were cold as hoarfrost against her bare feet.

Teeth chattering, she yanked on her leather slippers and groped for her woolen robe. Tears threatened, but she blinked them away. She did not know for certain her father had died. She must be strong, and not succumb to worry and despair.

A knock rattled her door. "Milady!" Urgency rang in Mildred's voice.

Abandoning the robe, Elizabeth stumbled to the door and pulled it open. In the light of a tallow candle, Mildred's face looked ashen, her eyes huge. Her unbound hair, spilling down over her shoulders, glowed white.

"What has happened? Is my father—?"

"De Lanceau!"

Elizabeth's breath caught. "*What?*"

"De Lanceau is inside the keep. Young Jeremy counted

at least ten men, all armed. They hid in the miller's wagon."

"The delivery for the wedding," Elizabeth said. Fraeda, the chief cook, had ordered extra flour to be baked into pastries, pies and tarts for the nuptial feast, and had requested the delivery be made early this morn.

Panic clutched Elizabeth's innards like a fist.

"They took control of the kitchens right after Fraeda sent Jeremy to fetch salt from the storerooms. The poor lad fled out a side passage. He came to warn us." Mildred tugged on Elizabeth's sleeve. "You must hide."

"Hide? Like a frightened animal?" Anger crackled in Elizabeth's veins. She clenched her shaking hands into her shift. "This is my father's keep. I will not cower to a traitor's son."

Mildred shook her head. "Your sire would want you safe."

"I will warn the men-at-arms."

"Milady—"

"Wode will not fall to de Lanceau." As Mildred's mouth opened, Elizabeth said, "Please, do not argue with me. I will not be swayed." Softening her tone, she said, "Find my mantle. Hurry."

Muttering under her breath, the matron hurried to the linen chest at the end of the bed. She pushed off the pile of children's clothes and embroidery thread, lifted the lid, snatched up a knee-length black wool cloak, and set it about Elizabeth's shoulders.

"The air is cold, milady. Will you be warm enough?"

"Aye."

Footsteps echoed in the passageway.

Elizabeth's pulse raced like a spooked horse.

Mildred grabbed the edges of the mantle together and struggled to secure them with a gold brooch. Firelight flashed off the ornament's scrolled design.

Images of another desperate moment flashed through Elizabeth's mind. Her mother's screams. Her sister's wails. Her mother's hand falling limp and the brooch's weight falling into Elizabeth's palm.

"Hurry!" she pleaded.

Mildred exhaled a shaky sigh. "'Tis fastened."

Elizabeth shoved her hair under the mantle's hood, drew it over her head, and darted into the passage. The wall torches sputtered and cast eerie shadows, but she smothered the anxiety surging inside her. She must reach the stairwell.

"Sweet lady," she heard Mildred whisper. "God be with you."

❖   ❖   ❖

Geoffrey knew each of Wode's corridors as though he had never left the keep. His strides quickened as he approached the lord's solar, the spacious chamber where he had been born and where his mother had died from fever when his younger brother, Thomas, was scarce one year old.

The familiar, musty odor of the passage stirred a host of memories: boyish pranks played on the scullery maids; afternoons spent collecting stones and chasing Thomas through the maze of torch lit corridors, laughing and yelling at the top of his lungs; the siege.

Geoffrey fought a maelstrom of fury and hurt so overwhelming, he wanted to roar in agony. He ground his teeth, resurrected the iron wall around his soul, and forced himself to concentrate on his task.

His father had not deserved to die in disgrace.

Lord Brackendale would suffer for his misdeed.

He saw candlelight in the doorway on the left. A plump, gray-haired woman in a linen shift shrank back into the shadows.

A smile twisted Geoffrey's lips. Lady Elizabeth's lady-in-waiting. Mildred, if Dominic's information were correct. She had been in the market that day. She seemed to remember him, for her eyes flared and her hand flew to her mouth.

As his gaze shifted to the open doorway, his jaw hardened. The fact that Mildred stood waiting for him was very telling.

The lady had been warned.

Geoffrey halted before Mildred. Her white-knuckled hands tightened around the candle. She shivered. He could not tell whether 'twas from his stare, or the cool, pre-dawn air.

Nor did he care.

Hands on his hips, he strode into the chamber. His gaze traveled over the opened linen chest, the heap of garments and thread on the floor, and the mussed bedding. He placed his palm flat in the center of the bed and fought to ignore the linens' sweet fragrance. *Her* scent.

The bedding was still warm. She had not gone far.

Turning on his heel, he glared at Mildred. "Where is she?"

"W-Who?"

"Do not toy with me, *Mildred*. You know of whom I speak."

Her face blanched. She clearly had not expected him to know her name. Yet she held his gaze. "Milady is not here."

Geoffrey growled deep in his throat. He crossed the chamber, his boots rapping on the floorboards. "I will ask you but one more time. Where . . . is—"

A shout rang out in the corridor. Geoffrey strode to the doorway, aware of Mildred's shuddered sigh behind him.

Dominic appeared in the embrasure, his brow beaded with sweat. "Milord, Viscon saw the lady heading for a stairwell. She is trying to reach the bailey."

Triumph coiled inside Geoffrey. "Excellent." He signaled to the armed men awaiting his order. "Troy. Paul. Bring the matron. We will meet you at the stairwell."

Dominic frowned. "We intended to take only the lady."

"Mildred will ensure that Brackendale's daughter cooperates."

"Milord, is that wise? 'Twas cramped in the wagon with ten of us. To find room for two mo—"

Anger flared inside Geoffrey, hot as burning oil. "Do not question me in this. Go!"

Dominic hesitated, then nodded and hurried away.

Geoffrey arched an eyebrow at Troy and Paul, and tipped his head toward Mildred. "Now."

"I will not go with you." She retreated from the two advancing men, step by step, until she hit the whitewashed stone wall. She lashed out with the candle, but one of the men knocked it from her. Snuffed out, it rolled away under the bed.

Cursing, she struck out with her arms and legs. The men grabbed her wrists and restrained her.

Mildred panted. "Tell your idiots to release me, de Lanceau, or I shall scream."

"Do not waste your breath. I would regret ordering the guards to knock you senseless. Yet I will, if you try to scream or refuse to do as I bid."

"Harrumph! You do not frighten me." She inhaled.

Geoffrey softened his voice to a lethal murmur. "Do you wish harm to come to your lady?"

His theatrics had the desired effect. The color drained from Mildred's face. "You . . . you *monster*. I will never let you harm Lady Elizabeth."

"She is far more valuable to me alive and well."

Mildred's lips pursed. "Pah! You would tell me all kinds of lies to get your way, you thick-skulled, swine-bellied—"

Geoffrey walked out the door. "Bring her."

✤ ✤ ✤

Her breathing ragged, Elizabeth stumbled to a halt and pressed her hand against her pinched side. Footfalls echoed in the passageway behind her, and she wondered if they belonged to her servants, or de Lanceau's cohorts.

Wraithlike shadows, surrounded by torchlight, grew across the walls behind her. She imagined the men's jeers and coarse laughter when they trapped her.

A man who burned the harvest had no mercy.

De Lanceau would not show compassion for his enemy's daughter.

A scream burned Elizabeth's throat, but she swallowed the cry. She must not yield to fear. Her father and the castle folk depended on her.

She must not allow de Lanceau victory.

Forcing herself back into motion, she ran into an adjoining corridor. Through the wall torch's hazy smoke, she spied the entry to the stairwell. Relief washed through her like a spring rain. When she reached the inner bailey, she could shout the alarm. The door was at the bottom of the stairs.

As she entered the stairwell, her mantle's brush became amplified to a whisper. The tap of her slippers echoed. The musk of damp stone enveloped her. Her mind roused images of hideous, fanged ghouls slithering out of the cracks in the mortar. Shuddering, she squashed her imaginings and pressed on.

Darkness descended with her. The torches further down

had gone out. Biting her lip, Elizabeth reached out to find the wall, and her palm skidded across mildewed stone.

Had her father not ordered the servants to keep the stairwells lit at all times?

For a panicked moment, she started to turn back.

She could not. She must secure the keep.

Her foot slid down to the next step. Almost there.

Only a few more steps to go.

A scuffling sound came from behind her.

She froze. Someone else had entered the stairwell.

She held her breath. Waited. Listened.

Whoever followed tried to be quiet, but had difficulty judging the stairs' width.

A hand bumped her shoulder.

Elizabeth shrieked and bolted forward into the darkness. Her pursuer swore. Her right foot slipped out from beneath her, and she fell. Her head and right arm slammed against the wall.

Dazed, she struggled to stand. She righted herself.

Her pursuer grabbed for her again.

She must reach the bailey.

Her ankle twisted on an uneven stair. Her legs crumpled. She cried out, felt the weightlessness of air beneath her, and landed at the bottom of the stairs.

Elizabeth moaned and struggled to sit up. The stairwell filled with light, voices, and the rasp of drawn weapons. She pushed the mantle's hood from her eyes. Squinting in the brightness, she saw armed men walking in from the adjoining corridors. She did not recognize any of them.

Dread screamed through her. She scrambled to her feet.

A tall man strode toward her.

She gasped, for she would never forget his handsome face. Memories of his embrace and wicked words had lived on in her illicit daydreams since the day he saved her life. "*You!*"

"Geoffrey de Lanceau." He smiled and took her hand. "At last, Lady Elizabeth, we have the pleasure of a proper introduction."

Geoffrey watched the emotions play across her pale face: shock, anger, and fear. Her hand, clinging to his, shook before she wrenched her fingers free. He let her go. He allowed her the momentary illusion of freedom, as a falconer would indulge his favorite bird before calling it back to his arm and slipping the hood over its bright eyes.

She held his stare, and he steeled himself against her beauty. He had remembered her eyes were blue, but now, offset by the dark mantle cloaking her head and body, they were the color of a summer sky.

Her cheeks pinkened, and her gaze narrowed to a frosty glare. All hint of vulnerability had gone. Again, he looked upon the composed woman he had rescued days ago.

"I regret I could not reveal my identity at the market," he murmured. "I could not risk you telling your sire."

Rage glittered in her eyes. "A wise choice, since I would have done so. Where is my father? What have you done with him?"

A smug grin tilted Geoffrey's mouth. "He is on his way to Tillenham, I believe."

"To capture you. You set the fires, did you not? He accepted your challenge." Her eyebrow arched. "Were you afraid to fight him, after all?"

Fury snapped inside Geoffrey like a cracking whip. She called him a coward. Years of anguish and resentment rammed against the wall of control around his heart and threatened to shatter it into thousands of pieces.

He balled his hands into fists. He would be foolish to lose his calm now, as she well knew. She had insulted his pride and prowess in front of his men, no doubt to provoke him into rash action. How clever of her, but futile. "Your father and I will fight soon, milady. When we do, I shall win."

Her expression shadowed with wariness. Geoffrey anticipated a biting reply that her sire would trample his bones into the ground. Yet, at that moment, crimson liquid dripped onto her shoulder. Blood?

He frowned. "Dominic, a torch."

Elizabeth jerked her head to the side, but Geoffrey was faster with the light. The curls at her brow covered a scrape that bled down her hairline and gleamed on the rise of her strong checkbones. She would need a healer. He stifled a pang of remorse, and wondered if she had any other injuries.

The mercenary at her back snickered, and Geoffrey shot him a foul look. Viscon had rushed the lady down the stairwell, an unnecessary risk since she could not escape, and she was wounded. He would not receive all of the coin promised to him as payment.

Geoffrey handed the burning reed back to Dominic. "I did not intend for you to be hurt, milady."

She snorted, a sound of disgust.

"You may think me many things, but I am not a brute." Geoffrey reached for the dagger at his belt. She flinched, but to his surprise, did not retreat. He lifted his wool tunic, took his shirt's hem, and slashed a strip of linen. After sheathing the knife, he reached up to dab her temple.

"Do not touch me."

The venom in her voice drew his gaze to her mouth. Her lips were so near. Lush. How would she react if he tipped up her chin and kissed her, as he had teased that day at the market?

Was he *mad*?

He lowered his hand and gestured to the dirt-smudged mantle. "My shirt is cleaner than your garments. Take the cloth."

She shook her head. "I do not want your pity."

He believed her. Hatred sparked in the air between them like invisible lighting. As grunts and mutters echoed from the opposite end of the passage, and the two guards hauled Mildred forward, he shoved the linen at Elizabeth. "Tend to the wound, or I shall do it for you."

She looked at him, hard, then snatched up the cloth. She wiped her face. The linen stained crimson.

Mildred shrieked. "Oh, milady. You are wounded."

"'Tis only a scratch," Elizabeth called back.

Geoffrey watched, unable to tear his gaze away, as with stiff movements, she pulled back the mantle's hood. She eased her hair free. Lustrous as black silk, it tumbled over her shoulders and fell to her waist in a riot of curls.

He caught the scent of flowers. Desire thickened his loins.

Curse her!

He turned away, angered by the appalling weakness of his flesh. "We shall tend your injury later. Dominic, bring her."

"I go nowhere with you."

Geoffrey halted. He had anticipated a struggle, but not a refusal spoken without the slightest tremor. He spun on his heel and faced her. She swallowed and, while she held his gaze, she clasped her hands together.

So she was afraid of him, after all.

"You will come." He growled. "Now."

"My father's servants are loyal. They will not allow you to take me from this keep against my will."

"Indeed?" Geoffrey chuckled. "'Tis astonishing what a few bits of silver can accomplish when placed in the right hands."

"Bribery!"

Her indignant cry sent satisfaction tingling through him. He resisted the urge to taunt her more. Later, he would have all the time he wished to toy with her. He looked at his men, drew a breath to give the order to move out.

Her laughter stopped him. "Are you not aware we were forewarned of your arrival? By now, the captain of the guard and all the men-at-arms will know of your intrusion." She smoothed her mantle with casual disdain. "You are probably surrounded."

Geoffrey frowned. Did she speak true?

Then he remembered the boy. "You cling to foolish hope."

Her irritating smile did not waver. "I do not think so, *Lord de Lanceau.*"

Her mocking use of his proper title scratched down his back like claws. "If you refer to the boy, Viscon captured him on his way back from your chamber. The lad will not be warning anyone of our presence here."

Her smile vanished. Desperation shimmered beneath her lashes. Her pulse beat hard against her throat's milky skin. "What have you done to Jeremy? Did you . . . kill him?" Revulsion darkened her voice.

Geoffrey's gut tightened. At last, he had found leverage to make her obey. As long as she believed him capable of such a deed, she might comply. For that reason, he did not answer her.

"You killed a defenseless child?"

He shuddered inside and forced the words through his lips. "Killing is a consequence of war, is it not?"

"How could you? Jeremy was only eleven years old."

Before Geoffrey could step away, her right arm moved. Her fist flew toward his face.

He trapped her hand in mid-air. The smack of skin against skin echoed like a thunderclap.

He locked his fingers through hers, crushing the blood-stained scrap of linen between their palms. She gasped, and her cheeks drained of color. He held her arm immobile. She tugged. Swore. He waited until the blazing intent faded from her eyes, before he lowered her hand to her side. When he released her, the linen dropped to the floor.

She stumbled back, cradling her arm to her chest.

"Remember the boy, before you are as rash again."

"Why?" she demanded. "Will you kill me as well?"

❖   ❖   ❖

As soon as she had spoken the words, Elizabeth regretted them. Her stomach clenched with a pain worse than her bleeding head or hurt arm.

The man standing behind her shifted. Mildred screeched.

Tension buzzed in the smoky air.

If only she could take back what she had said. Yet she would not back down from de Lanceau's glare. His eyes had darkened to the hue of a winter storm.

He stood so near she could have reached out and run her fingers over his jaw's day-old stubble. His scent taunted her, a blend of leather, horse, and a masculine essence all his own.

"I have never harmed or killed a woman," he said, his breath hot on her forehead. "Nor would I find any pleasure in doing so. But I warn you, do not force me to prove it." He turned to his men, strode toward them, and gestured to the man named Dominic. "Take the matron to the wagon. We will escort the lady."

Armed men moved toward Mildred.

Elizabeth exhaled on a trembling rush. She had to stop de Lanceau. Whatever plan he had for her, she would not be a part of it.

She fought her wound's discomfort and looked around. A pock-faced oaf blocked the stairwell behind her. She recognized him. Gareth Viscon. A mercenary. A soldier who had once fought for the king and would now lend his sword arm to any man who paid him. Her father had once hired him to ferret out a band of murderous outlaws living in a nearby wood.

Viscon grinned and picked at his dirty fingernail with a knife, and she looked away. She would never get past him. Her gaze shifted to the men with drawn swords standing in the corridor to the left. She could not bolt past them, either.

The bailey door was just yards away.

She *must* reach it.

She glanced at Mildred, now surrounded by guards and struggling to wrench free of her captors. Elizabeth tipped her head to the door. Mildred's eyes widened. She winked before beginning to fight in earnest.

"Swine! I demand you release my arms at once. Ouch! I shall have bruises upon my flesh on the morrow." She huffed. "If you do not stop, I shall—"

Elizabeth ran. Her fingers tensed, ready to yank open the door. She would scream with such force, her mother and sister would hear her in heaven.

De Lanceau still had his back to her.

She shoved past two startled guards. Her feet pounded on the stone.

"Milord," a man yelled.

De Lanceau spun around.

In one smooth lunge, he blocked her path.

She skidded to a halt, an instant before their bodies would have collided. Her mantle and shift swirled about her legs. Her breath rasped between her teeth, and in desperation, she looked toward the door.

"You will not escape, milady," he said.

Faint voices emanated from the stairwell. Two women talking. Servants checking the torches, Elizabeth realized with a burst of hope.

In hushed tones, de Lanceau snapped orders. A man yanked open the bailey door. The scream flared in Elizabeth's throat, but before it broke free, Viscon grabbed her from behind. His arm slammed around her and knocked the air from her lungs. His scarred hand clamped over her mouth.

She clawed and kicked, but her clothing twisted around her legs. Her foot hit his shin. He grunted, grabbed her injured arm, and wrenched it behind her back. Pain shot up into her shoulder, and the passage around her blurred. As she slumped against him, Viscon dragged her through the doorway.

The cool air, as startling as river water, snapped her agony-fogged mind alert. Dawn's golden haze had not yet warmed the sky, and the inner bailey was blanketed in darkness. She squirmed, jerked her head from side to side to dislodge Viscon's hand, and dug her heels into the dirt. Viscon hauled her toward a horse-drawn wagon waiting near the kitchens.

Men pushed Mildred up into the wagon. The matron shivered, hugged her arms across her bosom, and crouched in the far corner.

Viscon released Elizabeth's arm. Before he took his hand from her mouth, he grabbed her hair and jerked her head back. He waved his dagger under her nose. "Ye make so much as a whimper, milady, and I will slit yer throat. Understand?"

He sounded so savage, Elizabeth nodded.

From somewhere behind her, de Lanceau muttered a curse. "Easy. Put the knife away. Get her in the wagon."

The mercenary spat an oath. He released Elizabeth and shoved her up into the wooden cart. Clutching her mantle to her shaking body, she staggered to her feet.

She would yell for the guards.

The wagon rocked, and Viscon leapt up behind her. He must have guessed her intent, for his eyes glinted. He looked from her to Mildred, unsheathed his knife and pushed it up inside his sleeve.

He strode closer, and Elizabeth's mouth went dry. The shrill cry refused to emerge.

His hand closed on her shoulder, and he shoved her down to the floor. He squatted beside Mildred, the knife's leather-bound hilt visible.

De Lanceau's low voice came from nearby. "I will ride up front with the driver. Dominic, keep watch on the women."

Elizabeth felt Geoffrey's stare upon her. Salvaging a last tattered shred of bravado, she raised her chin and glared at him standing beside the wagon.

His mouth twitched. "On the floor."

Mildred gasped. "You cannot possibly expect my lady to—"

Geoffrey strode from view.

Viscon grabbed Elizabeth's hair and shoved her face down against the filthy floorboards coated with flour. She flattened her hands against the wood and tried to rise, but the men crowded in. They trapped her hair and clothing beneath their boots. A rustle sounded overhead; then a sour-smelling tarp settled over her and Mildred.

She heard muffled voices, one sharp with annoyance. Someone reached beneath the tarp and shoved a soft linen shirt in her face. It smelled of *him*. After dropping de Lanceau's garment, the hand disappeared.

A moment later, the wagon creaked into motion.

Elizabeth jostled from side to side. Her cheek bounced against the boards and, with a grudging sigh, she spread out the shirt for her and Mildred, and laid her cheek upon it.

The wagon rumbled on, gathering speed. Each jolted movement sent pain shooting up Elizabeth's arm. Her head throbbed.

She squeezed her eyes closed. She would *not* cry. She would not give de Lanceau the satisfaction. Under her breath, she prayed the wagon would be stopped and searched at either of the two gatehouses.

The cart did not slow. The wheels drummed on the wooden drawbridge, then gritted on the dirt road beyond the keep.

Anger and determination blazed through her. She would escape. She would foil whatever scheme for vengeance de Lanceau had begun.

Above all, she would never let him harm her father.

CHAPTER FOUR

"Stop here." De Lanceau's terse command carried over the *clop* of hooves and the wagon's rattle.

Elizabeth raised her head a fraction. The crunch of dirt changed to a hiss. The wagon had veered off the road and into grass.

After a while the jostling slowed, then stopped.

Mildred groaned. "My body is one big bruise."

"Mine too." One of the men trapping Elizabeth's hair moved his foot, tugging on her tresses, and she winced. "Barbarians."

The pressure eased from her hair and clothing. The wagon swayed from side to side. The tarp shifted and was hauled away.

Elizabeth squinted in the sudden light. The sun had risen well into the sky. She sucked in the fresh morning air and fought the dizziness that threatened to overwhelm her. She would not succumb to the beckoning darkness.

Gritting her teeth, she pushed herself up to sitting, shoved hair from her eyes, and looked around.

The ruffians now stood in the waist-high grass. Several guarded her and Mildred, while others moved off to keep watch from a distance. They were all armed.

The wagon rested at the edge of a meadow. A glassy stream meandered through the field of wildflowers and grasses before it disappeared into a forest. There was no sign of a road.

Movement drew her gaze to two men striding toward the willows that grew near the stream. She recognized de Lanceau and Dominic. They headed toward horses tethered in the trees' dappled shade. De Lanceau's dark hair glinted silver-blue in the sunlight and hung in waves over his tunic's shoulders, and she cursed herself for paying him the slightest heed.

The man was a rogue. Worse than a rogue.

He did not warrant her attention.

"Are ye goin' to sit there gapin', me foin lady, or do I come in and get ye?"

Viscon's fingers clamped around her wrist. The guards standing a few yards away chuckled.

With a loud "oomph" Mildred rose to her feet, her tresses a wild tangle. "Let go of her. This boorishness is unacceptable."

"Ye too, ye fat old hen," Viscon sneered. "Out. De Lanceau wants ye ta stretch yer legs. While ye can."

Proving he would get their cooperation one way or another, Viscon drew his dagger with a slow, deliberate rasp.

Recalling that blade waved in her face, and his earlier threats, Elizabeth rose to her feet. He looked disappointed— he obviously had hoped for a fight—then shrugged and released her.

Mildred climbed out. Elizabeth gripped the splintered edge of the cart and stepped down to the ground. Her stomach did a sickening turn. Daisies swam beneath her feet. As she pitched forward, Viscon chortled.

Mildred rushed over. Her arms went around Elizabeth's waist and propped her up. "Can you stand, milady?"

"I . . . I think so. Aye, the dizziness has cleared."

The matron's worried gaze shifted to Elizabeth's brow. "Does the gash hurt?"

Elizabeth nodded. The headache had returned with a vengeance, and her arm throbbed as though goblins hammered at her flesh. A cool breeze whispered through the grass and swirled over her bare ankles, and she shivered.

Mildred, too, was shivering. When she began to fuss over Elizabeth's bloody hair and cheek, Elizabeth caught her wrinkled hands. They felt like slabs of ice. "You are chilled. Here, take my mantle." Elizabeth unpinned the gold brooch and pulled the cloak from her shoulders. She ignored the men's mutters and stares.

"Milady! You cannot stand before these ruffians wearing only a shift."

Disquiet flooded through Elizabeth, but she shook her head. "I do not want you to become ill. My clothing is not indecent, and I doubt de Lanceau's men will harm me. If they wished to do so, they had the chance earlier."

"But—"

Lowering her voice, Elizabeth said, "You must stay well, so we can escape."

"Are you certain you do not need its warmth?"

Elizabeth resisted the urge to hug herself. "I am."

With a grateful sigh, Mildred pulled the garment around her shoulders.

Fingering windblown hair from her cheek, Elizabeth glanced across the meadow, to where de Lanceau and Dominic stood beside the horses. They were taking items from the saddlebags.

A chill skittered through her. The mantle had given her an added layer of armor against de Lanceau's heated gaze, but now . . .

She shook off her thoughts. She would not drain her strength by worrying. She must focus on escape.

Mildred fastened the brooch beneath her chin and rubbed her palms together. "Ah, for a hot draught of mint and nettle." Her gaze slid to Viscon leaning against the wagon, then to the other watchful guards. "Why has de Lanceau run off? The least he could do is offer ointment for my lady's wound."

The mercenary picked at a sore on his face. "'Is where-abouts are no concern of yers."

"Oaf!" Mildred turned her back to him. "Come, milady. Let me wash the grime from your face. Then I can examine the cut."

Sliding her left arm through the matron's, Elizabeth whispered, "On the way, mayhap we will get a chance to flee." They started for the stream, flattening a path through the grasses dotted with poppies and cornflowers.

"Oy!" a guard called.

"Where do you think you're going?" another shouted.

Elizabeth wrinkled her nose. "Ignore them."

Mildred chuckled. "I shall."

Irritated voices rose behind them. Grasses crunched as the men followed. Elizabeth quelled the urge to run. With her wounds, and the guards so close, she and Mildred would only get a few paces before they were caught.

A little later, however, they might have the perfect opportunity to elude their captors.

Ignoring her pursuers, Elizabeth slowed her strides to a graceful walk and pretended she had no intentions of fleeing. As she approached the stream, she slipped her arm from Mildred's, raised her shift's hem, and stepped down to the bank. The earthy scent of mud and sun-warmed pebbles rose up to her. Silver-bellied minnows shot out of the glimmering shallows.

Tucking her shift between her knees, she bent to wash. A bedraggled woman stared back at her.

How wretched she looked. Her hair was streaked with flour. The dried blood on her cheek enhanced the dark smudges beneath her eyes, and her fine linen shift, embroidered at the cuffs and neck with delicate flowers, was creased and stained. Anger and humiliation blazed through her, and she plunged her hands into the water and rinsed her face.

Mildred crouched beside her, tore a strip from the hem of her shift and dipped it into the water. "I will be careful, but this may hurt."

Elizabeth stood. Shutting her eyes, she steeled her nerves against the press of wet cloth. She paid no heed to the approaching footfalls.

"Come away from the water," a guard snapped.

"Did you hear something, milady?" Mildred asked with a disdainful sniff.

Elizabeth smiled. "Naught but the wind's pleasing sigh."

The guard swore. Another spoke in a tone fraught with concern, and Elizabeth resisted a giggle.

More footsteps approached.

"You can tell that rogue de Lanceau we have no intention of cooperating with any of you," Elizabeth said, not opening her eyes. "Tell him I think he is an idiot. If he has even a mote of intelligence in his addled head, he will release us."

"You may tell me yourself."

Elizabeth's eyes flew open. De Lanceau stood above her

on the bank, his hands planted on his hips. In one fist, he held a scuffed saddlebag.

"Well?" he said.

Her cheeks flamed, but her soul would roast in hell before she would allow him to best her. She turned to face him. The abrupt movement set the meadow spinning before her eyes, and she blinked twice before he came back into focus.

His mouth tightened. "You wish to speak with me?"

"You heard every word. I have no wish to repeat them." With an annoyed huff, she flicked her hair over her shoulder.

A muscle ticked in his jaw. His expression darkened, and her breath jammed in her throat.

With agonizing slowness, his heavy-lidded gaze dragged up her torso, across her shift's embroidered front, to her face. Her skin prickled. Heated. Burned, as though his fingers, not his gaze, had swept over her.

He stared at her with fierce intensity. A look that suggested he saw every swell and curve under her shift.

She forced herself to exhale, and crossed her shaking arms over her breasts. His stare should not fill her with a strange excitement.

"I heard your words," he murmured. "Foolish words, spoken in haste. But then"—his gaze skimmed over her again—"you seem to have a talent for foolishness."

Elizabeth's belly somersaulted. She wondered if he referred to her giving Mildred the mantle, or the market incident. How shameful, that she still remembered his body's warmth pressed against her, and that she had once dreamed of his kiss.

"Come away from the water, before you slip and fall in, and I have to rescue you again."

She drummed her fingers on her forearms. "I do not take orders from ruffians."

He arched an eyebrow. "You wish me to come and get you?"

"I most certainly do not."

"We have a long journey ahead of us, and will be leaving soon. There is food and drink at the wagon." He opened the saddlebag. "I brought ointment for your wound."

Elizabeth turned her back on him. She did not want his fare, or his ointment. She thrust up her chin, tried to walk away, but found her right slipper stuck in the mud. She tugged her foot. It came free with a *pfffrrttt*, the sound of hearty flatulence.

Laughter erupted behind her. Elizabeth fought the mortified giggle welling in her throat.

"I suggest you eat," de Lanceau said, his tone lightened by a chuckle. "We leave when the horses are ready."

She glared at him over her shoulder. "Where are you taking us?"

"You will know soon enough."

"Branton Keep?"

His expression clouded with wariness.

Elizabeth smiled. "I heard King Richard had granted

you that run down old fortress as a reward for your bravery in the Crusades. How ironic; you return the king's gratitude by kidnapping the daughter of one of his loyal lords."

De Lanceau scowled.

"'Twill not bode well for you when the king learns of your actions. You will find your keep under siege for the same reasons your traitorous father was attacked years ago."

He drew a hissed breath. "You have a bold tongue, milady, and know not what you speak of."

"And you, sirrah, are an idiot to provoke war with my sire."

De Lanceau stared at her across the muddy ground. The sensual heat had vanished from his eyes. Now, he looked angry enough to throttle her.

Fear whipped through her. She had spoken without forethought. Yet she had held true to her heart, and would never relinquish faith in her father.

De Lanceau's voice became a rasp. "You are unwise to speak of matters you do not understand. You are an even greater fool to taunt me. Fall into the water. Eat or not eat. I do not care."

He shoved a small earthenware pot into one of the men's hands, slung the saddlebag over his shoulder, and stalked off.

Elizabeth blew a sigh. She uncurled her hands, flexed her numb fingers and resisted the impulse to watch him walk away.

"We should use the ointment and eat the food he has

offered," Mildred said, her tone soothing. "If he is taking us to Branton, we shall not reach there till nightfall."

"I would rather starve." As Elizabeth spoke, her stomach gurgled.

"You cannot best de Lanceau if you faint from hunger."

Elizabeth sighed. She could not escape, either. She took Mildred's arm. The matron snatched up the ointment pot and they headed back to the wagon.

De Lanceau stood with several of his men, adjusting the bridle of a gray destrier. He looked up, but Elizabeth refused to meet his narrowed gaze. She swept past him and surveyed the food set out on a blanket on the wagon's lowered edge—bread pitted with stones, and wedges of yellowed cheese, to be washed down with mead from a battered pigskin flask.

Her stomach whined, and she loosed a silent groan. At least when Fraeda baked bread she picked the bigger stones out of the flour to spare one's teeth.

Mildred popped open the pot and sniffed the contents. With a finger, she scooped out some of the greasy yellow ointment.

"Sit on the edge of the wagon, milady. This smells vile, but 'tis all we have."

Elizabeth sat. As Mildred dabbed at her temple, Elizabeth broke off some bread, nibbled the crust, and watched a butterfly flit through a cluster of daisies. Under other circumstances, she would have loved this pretty spot perfumed with wildflowers.

As Mildred pressed on a tender spot, Elizabeth winced. She sensed de Lanceau's assessing stare, and smothered another groan.

The sooner she escaped, the better.

✦   ✦   ✦

Geoffrey gave his destrier an affectionate pat on the neck before starting toward the wagon. Wariness shadowed Elizabeth's eyes. She brushed breadcrumbs from her lap and rose from where she sat beside Mildred on the wagon.

So he made the lady uneasy. Good.

Striding past her, he grabbed a slice of the coarse bread. As he bit off a piece, she moved away and stared toward the forest. The breeze blew her shift against her body. The sheer fabric clung to her figure, and mocked him with its filmy drape, light and shadow.

He didn't want to gape like a randy green squire, but he couldn't help himself.

The cloth outlined all of her woman's curves. Her glorious black tresses curled down over the swell of her breasts and tumbled to her slim waist. How foolish, that he wanted to run his fingers through her hair, to savor its scent, to feel its shiny weight in his hands. As he stared, drawn by the sunlight playing over her tresses, she brushed strands off her throat.

His loins stirred. She was a magnificent creature.

She was Brackendale's daughter. Forbidden.

A tiny stone slipped down his throat.

Choking, he groped for the flask, raised it to his mouth, and took a sip. The mead was warm. Sweet as a virgin's first kisses. As sweet as Elizabeth's lips.

He wiped his mouth with the back of his wrist, and cursed his mind for wandering where it should not.

Elizabeth took another step, and Geoffrey frowned. She swayed a little. It clearly took effort for her to keep her balance. She cradled her right arm.

Unwelcome guilt tore through him. In the Earl of Druentwode's tiltyards and on Acre's bloodstained battlefields, he had seen enough wounded to recognize physical injury. She had hurt more than her forehead when she fell.

He gripped the flask and chewed more bread. He would see her wounds healed, but would *not* feel sorry for her. The lady had enjoyed a privileged life, without the slightest want or need, and had done so because his father had died.

His honorable sire had never deserved to be named a traitor.

He had never deserved to be slaughtered.

Geoffrey forced himself to swallow the mouthful. If he shut his eyes, if he allowed the despair and memories to surface, he again felt his father's icy fingers gripping his own, and smelled blood-soaked straw . . .

"Have you finished with the mead, milord?" Mildred asked.

Geoffrey's eyes snapped open. He quelled a violent tremor, and glanced at Mildred. "What?"

"A drink, if I may?"

He tossed her the flask and looked back at Elizabeth. She bent to pick a flower. By abducting her, he could well end up with his head lopped from his neck. Yet he could no longer live the bitter lie which had haunted him since he was ten years old.

He could not find proof to exonerate his father—and by God, he had tried—but the simple truth remained. His sire had wanted him to rule the de Lanceau legacy, the lands granted to his proud Norman predecessors by William the Conqueror, and passed down through the oldest male sons.

And so he would.

By force and cunning, Wode and all its lands would be his. He would have his inheritance, and revenge.

A grim smile touched his lips. No one would stand in his way. Above all, Brackendale's daughter.

Grasses rustled behind Elizabeth, and she tensed. Moments ago, she had sensed de Lanceau's brooding gaze upon her, prowling over her body in a manner that shot goose bumps over her skin. She had ignored him and hoped that, like an irritating wasp, he would be distracted and go away.

A futile wish.

"We leave now," de Lanceau said. His voice held command and a warning not to disobey.

Elizabeth refused to look at him. Her hands tightened around the cornflower she had turned in her fingers. She had heard him order the men to water the horses at the stream, but had not expected to be departing so soon.

She tried to think of some way of escape.

Without success.

Her pulse thudded against her ribs. If she had any hope of eluding him, she must act now.

Gathering her reserves of courage, she turned and faced him. He stood with his hands on his hips, his hair tousled by the breeze. His flinty gaze told her he expected her to do as he ordered.

Elizabeth stole a glance at the shadowed forest. One could get lost in those woods.

An idea flooded into her mind. A brilliant idea.

Why had she not thought of such a request sooner?

Smoothing all excitement from her voice, she asked, "May I have a moment of privacy?"

Suspicion glinted in his eyes, but then he nodded. "Be quick about it." He summoned two armed men and thrust a hand toward the forest. "Do not let her out of your sight."

Elizabeth started toward the trees. When she marched into the shade of outlying ash and birch trees, and headed for a patch of blackberry vines fringed with ferns, the men shouted. "That is far enough."

"Very well," she said. "Will you turn your backs?"

The guards looked at each other. "Lord de Lanceau—"

Laughing, Elizabeth pointed to the surrounding shrubbery, a tangle of bushes, nettles and vines. "Where can I go? Up a tree like a squirrel?"

The men exchanged frowns, shrugged, and faced the meadow.

The breeze gusted. Leaves rustled overhead.

Elizabeth bolted. As she hurtled through a patch of tall ferns, she came upon a worn deer trail.

A branch snapped beneath her slipper.

Shouts rang out behind her.

The wound at her temple throbbed. Dizziness threatened to blur her vision.

She must not stop running.

She dodged low-hanging branches. Jumped raised tree roots. Twigs grabbed at her shift like gnarled fingers. The linen pulled taut. Tore.

Her pursuers were gaining ground. Their harsh breaths sounded louder than her own.

Her lungs burned.

She stumbled on a root. Slowed for the barest instant.

A guttural roar exploded behind her. A hand grabbed her arm and spun her around. A hard body slammed her against an ancient oak. She kicked. Clawed. Fought the blackness that threatened her consciousness.

Smells seared her nostrils. The churned loam. The musky

tree bark. The male essence of the rogue trapping her.

He caught her wrists. "Be still!"

De Lanceau's voice sent fear blazing through her veins, and an element far more dangerous. She stilled. His hands dropped from her, but he did not ease away. His thighs pressed against her hips. His chest crushed her breasts. His breath rasped over her flushed skin.

She shuddered.

"What were you thinking?" he growled. "You would never have outrun us. Were you hoping to break your neck?"

Her whole body quivered. "Release me."

"You will not escape me, milady. Not until I have vengeance against your father." His mouth formed a wicked smirk. "Mayhap not even then."

CHAPTER FIVE

"Get on the horse."

Elizabeth's blue-eyed gaze hardened, and she crossed her arms over her tattered shift. "Nay."

Geoffrey looped his destrier's reins about his knuckles, and looked at her standing beside his horse. Two scarlet spots stained her cheeks, yet she stared back at him without as much as a blink. Her furious blush had not dimmed since he hauled her out of the forest and set her between his horse and the wagon, curtailing any more attempts to escape.

He narrowed his eyes, willing her to yield, yet her glare did not falter. Irritation swelled within him, hot as the desire he was struggling to leash. He had only to look at her, and her fragrance, the crush of linen against his hands, the warmth of her quivering body, hummed anew in his blood.

He squashed the foolish, inconvenient lust. "I do not

offer you a choice."

"How dare you demand further indignations of me? I shall *not* sit with my legs dangling either side of that beast."

"You fear your modesty will be compromised?" When her lips parted on a shocked gasp, Geoffrey chuckled. "Next time I abduct a lady, I will remember to bring a side saddle. I do not have one now, so you will ride like the rest of us." He smiled his crooked smile that, through the years, had swayed countless women's hearts. "Unless you prefer to walk?"

Elizabeth huffed and looked away. "Rogue."

"At last, you concede." He grabbed the drab woolen cloak draped over the destrier's saddle and tossed it to her. She let it crumple at her feet. He shrugged and tightened his horse's girth. "Put it on."

"If I do not?"

Her insolent whisper pricked his thinning patience. "If you do not," he said, "I shall be forced to heap further indignity upon you. I may dress you in the cloak myself, even if I must wrestle you to the ground and hold you down to accomplish it. You will make an even more fetching sight with flowers and grass in your hair." He gave the leather strap a firm tug. "Mayhap I should summon Viscon, and let him take care of the matter."

She sighed, a sound of reluctant defeat. He cast her a sidelong glance, and watched her pick up the cloak. His gaze skimmed her dirty face. She looked exhausted. Fragile.

As she drew the yards of brown wool over her shoulders,

fresh blood glinted on her brow. In her idiotic dash for freedom, she had reopened her wound.

He cursed a stab of pity, and lashed his leather bag to the saddle. He had no wish to coddle her on the journey.

Not when in the secluded forest, his blood had heated, his loins had hardened, and his mind had turned to less noble, but far more pleasurable, ways to slake his revenge.

He had intended for her to ride with him, where he could keep close watch on her, but the thought of her enticing body brushing against his . . . Aye, 'twould be wiser if she did not ride with him, after all.

The *thud* of hooves brought his head up. Troy led his horse, a sway backed blue roan, to a halt beside the wagon's spoked wheel. "The men are ready, milord."

"Good. The lady will ride with you."

In the midst of adjusting the cloak, Elizabeth stilled. Her eyes widened, and she glanced at his destrier. "I thought—"

"Troy has more patience than I. He will sit behind you and keep you from falling off." Biting the inside of his cheek, Geoffrey added, "Since you cannot ride astride."

Her color deepened. "Why you—"

"Milady!" A cloak draped over one arm, the matron squeezed past the roan's hindquarters and set her hand on Elizabeth's shoulder. "I tried to attend you sooner, but that miserable Viscon would not allow it." Her gaze traveled over Elizabeth and her face pinched. "My poor lamb. What wretched garments we are forced to wear. I pray they are not infested with fleas, and do not bring you out in a rash."

The matron shot Geoffrey a withering glare. His lips twitched. She thought to intimidate *him?* He had clashed swords with bloodthirsty Saracens and triumphed.

He raised his brows.

"Harrumph!" Mildred picked up the cloak, shook it out with a perfunctory snap, and fastened it over the black mantle.

Over glinting gold.

Warning tingled through Geoffrey. He had forgotten about the brooch. "Wait."

He stepped forward and parted the cloak's edges with his fingers. The matron squawked and swatted his hand, but he managed to unfasten the ornament. It dropped into his palm.

"Nay!" Elizabeth lunged forward, but Troy caught her arm. She cursed and struggled.

Geoffrey rubbed the intricate scrolled pattern with his thumb. The metalwork was of superb quality, a masterful blend of gold and artistic design.

"Give me my brooch." Hurt and anger rang in Elizabeth's voice.

He wondered what the ornament meant to her. Mayhap one of her adoring suitors had given it to her, or Sedgewick.

Or even her accursed father.

Elizabeth stretched out her hand, palm upturned, fingers curled like a water lily's petals. "Give it back. I demand it."

Words ground between Geoffrey's teeth. "Demand? So

you can use it to bribe one of my men and escape?" His fingers closed around the shimmering gold. "I think not."

"'Tis mine!"

He locked his heart and mind against her shrieks. He would not return the brooch. By doing so, he could jeopardize his victory, and he had waited too many years for revenge.

Geoffrey turned his back to her and slipped the gold into his bag. "Troy, get her on the horse." Over her indignant cries, he shouted, "Paul. Viscon. Bring a horse for Mildred. Be quick about it."

✤　　✤　　✤

The roan stumbled. Elizabeth pitched forward, then back against Troy's chest. Her breath expelled on a groaned "oomph." The cursed nag seemed to find every one of the road's potholes and raised stones.

Elizabeth straightened and drew back the edge of the cloak's hood which shielded her face. Viscon rode on her right, his scarred hand braced upon his knee, his saddle creaking like a hangman's noose.

Shuddering, she recalled the gleam in de Lanceau's eyes when he had spurred his destrier up alongside her several leagues back. He had ordered Mildred and Paul, riding on her left, to the back of the entourage. No doubt he had done so to separate her from her one ally on the journey.

Fury had whooshed through Elizabeth like a summer

fire, for she had indeed planned to conspire with Mildred to leave clues behind—a dropped shoe, or even a torn bit of shift. When de Lanceau had addressed her and asked if she were all right, Elizabeth had stared off at the fields and refused to answer.

His rough laughter mocked her. "Watch her," he had told Viscon in a tone cold enough to freeze stone. "If she draws attention to us, or escapes, you forfeit your payment."

Elizabeth sensed the mercenary's gaze dart over her now like the flick of a serpent's tongue. "Keep yer head down," he snapped.

She dropped her chin, but only until his attention slid from her to a dog bounding through a field dotted with clusters of bundled sheaves. Raising her lashes, she looked through the haze of dust and floating dandelion spores to where de Lanceau rode ahead with Dominic. They spoke in low voices, their words punctuated by occasional laughter.

Both had donned concealing cloaks, as had the guards. The easy sway of de Lanceau's hips proved he was comfortable riding a horse. She scowled. Of course he was. On Crusade, he had galloped headlong into battle against the Saracens.

He had become a hero.

He was no hero now. He was a man robed in deceit. He kept his horse to a walk, adding to the illusion they were a convoy of unhurried travelers. The farmers and peasants they passed on the road would not suspect him of kidnapping their lord's daughter and spiriting her off to his wretched keep.

Elizabeth fought the sting of tears, and glared at de Lanceau's back. Knave. She could never replace her treasured brooch. Would he return it, or keep it as part of his cruel revenge?

She could not bear to think of never wearing the beautiful ornament again.

Viscon grunted and swatted her cloak's sleeve. "Head down."

De Lanceau swiveled in his saddle, his expression wary. She dropped her gaze to the roan's tangled mane and bit back an unladylike oath.

As the day wore on, she shifted in the saddle to ease a cramp in her thigh. Twice, de Lanceau took bread and mead from his saddlebag and passed it back to her and his men. Twice, Elizabeth refused. Her bottom hurt. Her arm pained. Her head ached so much that her stomach churned, and she could not have swallowed the food if she tried. Hugging her arms across her grumbling belly, she tried to forget the mead's tempting scent and her parched mouth.

Swollen clouds blackened the afternoon sky. As raindrops splattered on her hood and shoulders and peppered the road with dark spots, de Lanceau barked an order to quicken their pace.

She burrowed into the cloak's folds. While the garment provided her with an extra layer of warmth, it did not stop the water from soaking through. Her shift plastered to her skin. The road transformed into a sheet of mud. Ahead, de Lanceau and Dominic huddled against the driving rain. Their chatter and laughter ceased. Over the gusting wind and *clip-clop* of hooves, she heard harsh commands to keep moving.

Her teeth chattered, and she pulled the cloak tighter around her body. Dizziness courted her, and tempted her to close her eyes and yield to soothing darkness.

It seemed only a moment later that a hand shook her.

"Milady." Troy's voice sounded distant. "Wake up."

"Mmm?" She forced her leaden eyelids open and pushed wet strands of hair from her cheek. As the smells of horse and wet earth flooded her consciousness, she blushed, mortified to find she had slumped against Troy's chest.

She sat up, and froze. Twilight had fallen. Ahead, a fortress perched on the edge of a natural rock incline. Silhouetted against the sunset's vibrant reds, oranges, and gold, the stone walls looked black as midnight. The squared keep thrust up past the crenellated curtain wall like an ugly dragon rearing its head, and a water moat curled around like a tail.

Branton Keep looked a forbidding place. She had no wish to ride into de Lanceau's lair, but her body screamed for an end to the day's ride, a change of clothing, and a hot, tasty meal free of flies and lumps.

As they clattered through the streets of the town nestled around the fortress's wall, villagers peered out of their wattle-and-daub homes. De Lanceau spurred his horse to a canter, and the other men did the same. As they approached the massive wood and iron portcullis, locked under the gatehouse, he

shouted to the sentries in the watchtowers. The wooden drawbridge thumped down over the moat, the portcullis winched
up with a squeal, and the inner wooden doors opened.

Flickering reed torches lit the inner bailey. Men emerged
from straw-roofed buildings, some young, some old and battle hardened. They smiled and, as de Lanceau reined his
horse to a halt, welcomed him with cheers and handshakes.
His face eased into a boyish grin, and an odd pang gripped
Elizabeth. She looked away.

Troy slid down from the roan and led it through the
crowd toward the stables. She struggled to calm her pulse.
What would happen to her now? The boisterous chatter
around her swelled, and she laced her clammy fingers together over her lap. She must keep her wits about her. Any man
who tried to harm her would learn she was the daughter of a
powerful lord, and would regret his actions.

As Troy slowed the mount near the stables, the noise
seemed to rise again. She glanced over her shoulder. De
Lanceau had dismounted and stood watching her, his gaze as
keen as a predatory hawk's.

He handed his destrier's reins to a stable hand. "Will you
need help getting down from the horse, milady?"

His words hummed with challenge. She shoved back the
soaked hood, and, ignoring the icy rainwater trickling down
her arms, shot him the frostiest stare she could muster. "Not
from you."

She stretched her stiff legs and prayed for ladylike grace

as she drew one leg over the front of the saddle. Despite her bravado, she winced.

De Lanceau muttered under his breath. He shrugged out of his wet cloak and drab tunic, tossed them to a servant, and headed toward her. The sea of men around him parted.

A tremor shook her. He could not mean to help her himself. The thought of his hands upon her—

She should not stare at him. 'Twas not proper, but she could not seem to wrench her gaze away. His common garments had concealed a black tunic, a garment that rivaled even her father's costliest clothes. The damp cloth molded to de Lanceau's chest, outlining broad swells of muscle. Exquisite filigree embroidery accented the collar and cuffs. Light glittered off the gold thread. How he dazzled.

As he neared, his jaw taut with purpose, she jolted her exhausted body into motion.

"Lady Elizabeth!" Troy cried. "Wait."

She held the edge of the saddle, turned, and slid down.

The instant her slippers touched the slick, hard-packed ground, her legs collapsed. She clawed for the saddle. "Oh!"

Arms swooped around her from behind. De Lanceau's embroidered cuff brushed against her wrist. He drew her back against him, supporting her weight with his. Her bottom pressed against his thighs. Her cloak tangled about his legs.

Awareness hurtled through her. She squirmed, tried to pull away, but dizziness thwarted her. She sucked in a breath, ripe with the scents of man and sweaty horse, and fought to clear her whirling mind.

Potent, invisible tension unfurled in her belly.

His breath stirred her hair. "Can you stand?" Next to her ear, his voice sounded unsteady.

She nodded.

He pushed her away, and turned her to face him.

"Does your arm still pain you? What of your forehead?" Concern glinted in his eyes.

Drawing herself up to her full height, Elizabeth refused to acknowledge the slightest gratitude for his compassion. He had abducted her as part of his plan for vengeance, and no doubt intended to use her as leverage against her father.

De Lanceau did not care for her well-being.

"I am fine," she said.

His laughter grated. His eyes darkened to steel gray.

Elizabeth gnawed her lip. He *knew* she lied, but if it took every last bit of her strength, she would not admit weakness.

"For a moment," he drawled, "I thought you looked pale and unwell." His smile turned lazy and, as his gaze traveled over her sodden cloak, her breath settled like a rock between her ribs. "I would hate to think my prize had been damaged during the day's journey. Your value to me might be lessened, Lady Elizabeth, if that were so."

She swallowed. She scrambled to find words with which to battle, scathing remarks to wound and scar.

Yet she was so very, very tired.

Darkness beckoned. She closed her eyes, unable to resist.

The bailey's noise faded to a drone.

A hand caught her elbow. Steadied her, though she did not realize, until then, how close she had been to collapsing.

"Troy, escort her to her chamber."

When Elizabeth opened her eyes, de Lanceau had gone. He stood across the bailey, speaking to an old woman drawing water from the well. Elizabeth strained to see past the stable hands crowded around the other riders, to see what had become of Mildred, but Troy set his hand in the small of her back and urged her toward the keep's forebuilding.

She stepped inside. The dank air smelled of cheap tallow candles and a century of secrets.

Her strides stiffened. De Lanceau intended to throw her in his dungeon. A shiver rippled through her, and she steeled herself to face rats and iron shackles. Yet Troy led her up into a cramped, winding stairwell. At the end of three flights of stairs they came to a chamber. A short, plump maidservant with wide brown eyes and hair the color of honey stood inside. She turned as they approached. After setting down a stoneware pitcher, she dipped in a timid curtsey and hurried out.

Troy motioned for Elizabeth to enter.

She paused on the threshold, held back by a sense of misgiving. "Whose chamber is this? Why have you brought me here? Tell de Lanceau I—"

Troy shoved her forward, mumbling an apology. The door thumped closed. A key grated in the lock.

"Troy!"

Elizabeth fisted her hands and hammered on the door. He did not answer. She yanked on the iron handle, twisted and turned it, but the metal refused to budge.

With a furious sigh, she spun away from the door. Her fingers shook, yet she managed to shed the cloak. It slapped into a heap on the floorboards. She ignored the ache of bruised muscles and stalked around the chamber. If there were a way to escape, she would find it.

She threw open the window's wooden shutters. A wrought iron grille barred the opening, and held firm when she gave it a good tug. She slammed the shutters closed.

Turning on her heel, she crossed to the high oak bed near the door. The worn sheets had been patched in places, as had the woolen blankets. They would not hold up if she ripped them to shreds and braided them into a rope. Desperate laughter bubbled in her throat. Since she could not squeeze past the grille, that plan had no merit anyway.

Her belly did an anxious turn, and, steadying herself, Elizabeth leaned against one of the bedposts. Her palm brushed rough wood. Glancing down, she saw the post had once splintered. The clumsy repair was the work of an apprentice rather than a skilled carpenter. She smiled. If she exerted enough pressure, mayhap she could snap the post again. She could use it to batter down the door, or, if that failed, knock senseless whoever next came into the chamber.

Linking her hands around the mended wood, she pulled, hard. The joint held firm.

Defeat wailed inside her. Refusing to listen, she crossed to the dust-covered trestle table and the bedside table set with candles. Neither held items that might aid her escape. Not even a book to hurl at a guard and distract him, while she dashed for the door.

De Lanceau had planned well.

Elizabeth slumped on the bed's edge. The ropes squeaked and sagged. Her eyes burned and she bit back a defeated sob.

She would *not* cry.

Lying on her side, her cheek pressed to the pillow, she stared at the opposite wall. She should remove her garments before she got a chill or soaked her blankets. Yet all strength had drained from her body.

Her eyelids drooped. Wretched de Lanceau. He had not sent a bath to ease her aching muscles, wash her wounds, and scrub away the wagon's filth. He had not offered her a meal, lumpy or not. She wrinkled her nose. The pillowcase, no doubt stored before it had dried, smelled sour; and the linen scratched her skin.

Her eyes closed. Elizabeth fought the ever-present dizziness. She must not rest. She must not sleep.

She must find a way to escape.

❖   ❖   ❖

Geoffrey stood in the chamber doorway and listened to Elizabeth's rhythmic breathing. Hers was a sleep of sheer exhaustion, free, for now, of emotional distress and memories that gnawed at one's soul until it bled.

How he envied her.

His leather boots creaked as he crossed the threshold. Moonlight slipped in through the cracks in the shutters and painted the room in an ethereal, silvery light. The maid-servant Elena had left a candle burning beside the bed, but he did not need its light to see. Still, he did not snuff the flame.

Softening his strides, he approached the bed. He stared down at Elizabeth. Studied the beauty he had snared.

Willful damsel. She had surprised him today with her defiance, but in the end she had only made the journey more difficult for herself.

She lay on her back, her hair tangled across the pillow, the bedding tucked about her shoulders. She had not stayed awake long enough for Elena to bring food or water to wash. The damsel had not even roused when the damp clothes were stripped from her body. When Elena had applied the last of the healing salve he had saved from the hospital at Acre to Elizabeth's temple, she had moaned, but not awakened. Not once.

His gaze skimmed over her cheek, brushed by moon-light. Did his eyes trick him, or did she look ill? Frowning, Geoffrey bent over her. Her lids were the color of cream above the dark fans of her lashes. Her mouth formed a gentle pout, innocent of the biting words she hurled at him at every opportunity. Elena said the lady had no fever, but he set his hand on her forehead to see for himself. Her flesh was warm, pulsing with life, but not hot.

She stirred. Sighed.

He jerked back, and his face stung. He hoped he had not woken her. What would he say?

If he tried to leave the chamber now, he would wake her for certain.

Still as a tombstone, he counted his throbbing heartbeats. Waited. Her head drifted to one side, and her breathing slowed.

Relief whooshed through his body. He should leave and tend to the other matters demanding his attention this eve.

Yet the delicious warmth of her skin shimmered on his palm.

He longed to touch her again.

Caution blazed through him. Still, his traitorous fingers trailed a feather-light path down the side of her face. How smooth her skin felt against his, and as soft as the silk hawked in the crowded Venetian markets.

Her warmth curled up his hand. Reminded him, with arousing potency, of how good she had felt in his arms.

He ground his teeth and drew away from the bedside.

She had found a weakness in him. How he hated her for it.

The candle extinguished on his coarse oath. He could not afford weakness. Not when years of anguish and rage had led him to this pivotal point, and victory was so near.

This beauty was his enemy. He admired her boldness, but he would not let her weaken him. Not through desire.

He turned and strode to the door.

Lady Elizabeth Brackendale would never touch his soul.

CHAPTER SIX

Through a sleepy haze, Elizabeth became aware of two people speaking. The man's voice seemed familiar, but she did not recognize the woman's.

"Milord, the head wound does not appear deep," the woman said in hushed tones. "'Twill be clearer once I wash away the dirt and blood."

Elizabeth's groggy mind stirred. Who had been injured?

"Troy told me she faded in and out of consciousness."

Concern poked at the fog smothering Elizabeth's thoughts. Troy? She recognized the name, but could not remember from where. Why did her thoughts seem as dense as cabbage pottage?

"Poor dove. She will have a mark on her brow for a few days, I vow."

The man sighed with displeasure. "What of her arm?"

"'Tis not broken, but the bruises may cause her discomfort."

A breeze wafted against Elizabeth's cheeks. Fabric rustled. She dragged up the strength to raise her lashes.

A warm, wet cloth pressed against her temple.

Pain!

She gasped. Her eyes flew open.

"Do not fret, my child." An old woman hovered at the bedside. Her black habit and white wimple enhanced her round face wizened by sun-bronzed wrinkles. Her smile offered trust.

Elizabeth licked her dry lips. "Who—"

"Lie still. Let Sister Margaret finish her work."

The rumbled command swept the last slumberous cobwebs from Elizabeth's mind. Memories of the previous day flooded back to her, and her stomach tightened.

She turned her head on the pillow. Geoffrey de Lanceau leaned against the doorway, his leather-booted legs crossed at the ankle. He wore a burgundy wool jerkin and black hose, and looked refreshed and clean despite their long journey but a short time ago. He had even shaved. With his squared jaw bare of stubble, he looked even more arrogant.

Her gaze flew back to Sister Margaret. Did the nun know that de Lanceau was a kidnapper? It seemed not. Sister Margaret's gentle smile did not waver as she rinsed the bloody cloth in a bowl on the side table, and dabbed again at the wound.

"Ouch!" Ignoring a wave of nausea and dizziness, Elizabeth pushed herself up to sitting. Yet she did not lie atop the bedding as she remembered, but was snug inside it.

The linen sheet slid from her shoulders. A draft cooled her throat. Her *bare* throat.

Someone had removed her shift.

She squeaked and snatched at the bedding.

De Lanceau chuckled. With lazy strides, he strode to her, his boots thudding on the floorboards.

The nun glanced at Elizabeth. Puzzlement shone in the woman's eyes before she shook her head and picked up the bowl. "I must fetch clean water. I shall return in a moment."

As the door clicked shut behind the nun, Elizabeth clutched the blankets to her naked flesh.

"What ails you, damsel?"

A blush stung her face. "How dare you?"

"Dare I what?" He dropped down on the edge of the bed. The ropes creaked and groaned, and she bobbed up and down like a child's ball. With effortless grace, he crossed one muscled thigh over the other and seemed oblivious to her frantic attempts to keep hold of the bedding, though she guessed from the mischievous glint in his eyes that he knew of her predicament.

She shot him an icy glare. "Where is my shift?"

His grin, a slash of straight, white teeth, made her belly flip-flop. "Ah, I remember now. That filthy, ripped bit of linen? The one you wore yesterday?"

"Aye," she snapped.

"I told Elena, the maidservant, to send it to one of the town peasants. He could use it for scraps."

"You *what?*"

De Lanceau's brow furrowed into a frown. "Should I ask Sister Margaret to treat your hearing too?"

"I hear as well as you." Elizabeth choked back a shriek. "My shift could have been mended with a needle and thread. You had no right to give it away."

De Lanceau flicked a speck of lint from his hose. His gaze locked with hers. "'Twas not worth salvaging. The esteemed Lord Arthur Brackendale would not want his daughter to be seen wearing such an inferior garment."

Anguish lanced through her, but she stifled the hurt. She would not stoop to his challenge and fight to defend her father. Her sire was a brave, loyal, noble man, and when he learned of her abduction, he would lead his army to Branton and squash de Lanceau like an annoying bug.

"By your own admission, you are a thief as well as a rogue," she said in a cold voice. "'Twill cost you many coins to replace my shift with one of equal quality. Yet you will, since *you* are responsible for its ruin."

His brows arched. "Am I?"

"You are."

He laughed. A warning. He flattened one hand on the bedding and leaned on his extended arm, bringing his broad torso nearer to hers.

She shivered, but refused to shrink back from him. She would not be threatened by his nearness. His mocking words had failed to defeat her. His intimidation would not either.

His tanned fingers splayed on the patched blankets. His hands were beautiful. Callused, weathered, yet nobly formed. She remembered his fingers closing around her mother's brooch, and resentment swirled within her like a gathering tempest.

Had he taken the ornament to sell it? The gold would fetch a good price, more than most merchants earned in a year. With its proceeds, he could hire an army to fight her father.

She must get the ornament back.

"The brooch you took from me," she began.

He shrugged. "The trinket?"

"'Tis *not* a trinket."

His gaze bored into hers. "Why is it important to you?"

Elizabeth looked at her white-knuckled fingers. If he knew how she cherished the brooch, he might ensure she never got it back. By admitting how much it meant to her, she gave him another means to taunt and wound her.

Yet, if she did not speak out, how could she hope he would understand or return it?

Tamping down an inner cry for silence, she said, "It belonged to my mother."

"I see."

"She gave it to me before she died." Elizabeth looked up at him. "I ask that you return it now."

His mouth flattened. "I cannot."

"*Why?*"

"As I said before, I will not risk you using it to bribe a servant. You are an intelligent and resourceful woman. You would use any means to escape me."

"I give you my word."

"Your *word?*" He laughed. "You think I am foolish enough to trust you?" His gaze clashed with hers, then slid down to her shoulder peeking above the blankets. Dangerous promise blazed in his eyes. "I will not risk losing you, before I have had revenge."

Wariness screamed through her. He stared as though he saw through her flimsy shield of sheets and blankets.

Someone had undressed her as she slept.

Had he?

Shock snatched the air from her lungs. Heat scorched across her skin. The indignity. The horror. The thought of his hands upon her as she slumbered, oblivious—

Words, rough as stones, ground between her teeth. "Who removed my shift?"

De Lanceau grinned. "Who do you think?"

A chill raked down her spine, yet she must ask. "Did you?"

He shook his head, and his silky hair slid over his shoulders. "Elena has nursed the sick and aged for years and tended you well. She told me you did not stir once." His smile turned crooked. "If I had been so inclined to undress you, damsel, you would have awakened. And you would remember the experience."

"Why, you lewd, vile—"

The bed ropes creaked. He leaned toward her. Closer. Closer. Blue flecks darkened his irises, yet that was not half as unsettling as the blackness of his pupils. Or the intoxicating, soapy tang that surrounded him.

He paused, his face a mere hand's span from hers. "Beware your insults, my dear lady." His words rubbed over her nerves like gritty sand. "Remember, your fate lies in my grasp."

Did he expect her to cower like a terrified girl? In her mind, Elizabeth condemned him to eternal torment in Purgatory. "I do not fear you, and do *not* call me your lady."

"Why not? You are my prisoner. You are secured like a dove in a stone cage. You are indeed my chattel."

"*Chattel?*"

"As lord of Branton Keep, I command all who live within these walls, including you. My blood is as noble as yours, milady. I will speak to you with respect, and, in turn, you will address me with the honor I am due."

Stunned laughter bubbled up inside her. Honor? He was a thief, a rogue, and a traitor's son. "Never."

"Tsk, tsk. You will not win my favor with that answer."

Her breath exploded from her lungs. "Your *favor?* You arrogant, thick headed—"

He lunged. Before she could scoot sideways, he caught her chin. She shook her head, tried to jerk free, but he pulled her forward until their noses almost touched.

His glittering gaze bored into hers. Where his fingertips touched, her skin tingled. Burned.

Her pulse thundered.

Awareness hummed. He was her avowed enemy, but also a man. A bold, handsome, determined man.

Why had she taunted him?

His eyes lightened with the barest smile. "Now, I ask you again. Will you show me due courtesy?"

By sheer willpower, she said, "Nay."

"I can make you say 'my lord'."

His thumb traced her jawline. Oh, God, that one, gentle touch was enough. Her skin throbbed. Her body began to wilt like a parched flower, like a besotted maiden's in the chivalric tales. His touch devastated like a lover's kiss.

Nay, his kiss would shatter her.

He seemed to sense her thoughts, for he looked at her mouth. He stared as though her lips were a feast, and he was starved.

She fisted her hands into the bedding. "Release me."

"Why? You have not done as I bade." His thumb paused, then started to caress her neck with light strokes.

"Stop."

"Say 'my lord.' Two simple words. Then, I will cease this sweet torture."

"You cannot sway me." Squeezing her eyes shut, she prayed for fortitude. "You are knave, a rogue, a criminal. I will never show you the respect that—Ohhh!"

His chuckle rumbled like a cat's purr. "Aye?"

A moan burned for release. Would she have to yield?

Three knocks sounded on the door before it creaked open. Relief flooded through Elizabeth.

Shuffled footsteps echoed, then a gasp. "Lord de Lanceau?" Sister Margaret's voice quavered. "Shall I wait outside? I . . . I do not mean to intrude, but soon, I must return to the abbey to settle the accounts and—"

De Lanceau growled under his breath. "I will hear you say it, damsel." His hand dropped away. "Come, Sister."

He uncrossed his legs and rose from the bed.

The ropes shifted, settled, and Elizabeth exhaled. She had won a reprieve. For now. She slumped back against the pillows, cocooning herself in the bedding.

In quiet tones, he spoke with the nun. She appeared bewildered and a little frightened, but as he continued, gesturing with his hands, the worry left her eyes. She nodded.

Elizabeth scowled. Whatever he said, he had gilded the truth to suit his purpose.

De Lanceau smoothed the front of his jerkin. "Milady, Sister Margaret will finish tending your wounds now."

"'Tis a pity you must leave," Elizabeth said. Hope sparked within her like a greedy flame. If he quit the chamber, she could tell the nun of the kidnapping. Mayhap Sister Margaret would even relay a message to—

De Lanceau's laughter prowled into her thoughts. "I will wait here until she is done. I will not have you delaying her work, or telling delusional tales. A knock to the head can cause all manner of imaginings."

As Sister Margaret strolled to the bed, Elizabeth pursed her lips and stared at the mortared wall. He might have thwarted her for now, but she would not yield to defeat.

Not now.

Not ever.

❖ ❖ ❖

Geoffrey escorted the nun out of the chamber, shut the door behind him, and guided her down to the great hall. He ordered a maidservant to fetch the wooden chest from his solar. Once she returned, he withdrew a small bag and pressed it into the nun's hands. "Thank you. I pray my donation is welcome."

Her fingers closed around the bag and the coins inside clinked. Her eyes widened. "Milord, 'tis too much."

Geoffrey shook his head. "The sisters do good work in this land. I vow the abbey has need of the coin, as you have started feeding the children who beg in Branton's market."

A smile spread across the nun's face. She bowed her head, patted his arm, and then shuffled off toward the forebuilding.

He tucked the chest under one arm and watched her leave, an odd sensation warming his belly. He had indeed been generous, more so than he could afford. Yet, when he had sent a messenger to the abbey, seeking a healer, she had come right away and had not plied him with awkward questions.

Blowing a sigh, he glanced across the smoky hall to the leather bound ledger, quill and ink he had left earlier on the lord's table. He skirted the dogs curled up near the hearth, stepped onto the dais, and dropped into his high-backed chair. He pushed the chest aside. The shy maidservant set a jug of ale before him. He nodded in thanks, then opened the ledger.

The crisp pages, marked with lines of black ink, whispered as he fingered through them. In the blended scents of cured parchment, ale, and smoke from the fire, he caught a memory of Elizabeth's fragrance. His brow creased into a scowl. He flattened his lips and glanced over the rows of numbers, accounting of the recent purchases of wine, spices, grain . . .

He wondered what Lady Elizabeth was doing now. Did she march about the chamber, damning his name? Had she wrapped herself in her blankets, one hand holding them together while she paced and plotted her next verbal battle? What a glorious sight she was when her eyes blazed blue fire.

He tapped the ledger's edge. By now, Elena should have delivered the lady's meal and clean clothes. A laugh tickled the back of his throat. He wished he could have seen the lady's face when she spied her new garments. Ah, wickedness.

He blinked, and the ledger came back into focus. Sunlight slanted further across the scratched oak table. The day passed. Once he had settled the accounts, he must ensure he and his men were prepared to confront a furious Lord Brackendale.

That day would come. Soon.

Geoffrey snatched up the quill, braced an arm on the table, and leaned his head on his hand. He began to add a row of numbers. Anger simmered. He should not waste moments thinking of *her*, when vital details demanded his focus. He was not starved for a woman's attentions. The lady was no more than a means to change fate and, at last, avenge that night years ago.

"Milord." Dominic stood at the opposite side of the table, his hair snarled and coated with dust, his tunic damp across the chest. No doubt he had been in the tiltyards.

Geoffrey lifted his cheek from his numb hand. How had he not heard Dominic approach? Pointing to the chair beside him, he said, "Come. Sit."

A wry smile tilted Dominic's mouth. After scraping the chair back, he sat. "You looked leagues away. You were not mulling over the accounts."

"Nay," Geoffrey muttered.

Dominic's gaze shadowed. He linked his hands together and rested them on the table. "Do you have doubts?"

"Of course not. Our plot is unfolding the way I had hoped."

"Then what troubles you?"

"Naught." Geoffrey sipped his ale and swirled the lukewarm, bitter liquid on his tongue. He would not be coaxed into revealing his musings on the lady. He picked up the ale jug and offered Dominic a drink, but his friend shook his head and chuckled, an all-too-familiar, knowing sound.

The jug landed back on the table with a *clunk*.

"Milord, I have known you long enough to know your moods"—Dominic grinned like a well-fed cat—"and when you speak false."

A groan dragged up from deep within Geoffrey. What had he done this time to give himself away? Hold his mouth at an angle? Squish his eyebrows together?

"Will you tell me what weighs upon your mind, or must I resort to more devious measures?"

Despite his friend's good-natured teasing, fury heated Geoffrey's blood. He resisted a snide reply. Loyal, trusted Dominic did not deserve his scorn. "If you must know, my thoughts were of no consequence."

Dominic snorted. "You insult me. Do you believe that after visiting your hospital bed every day for months and months, and coaxing you back to the world of the living, I have no idea what eats at your soul?"

The residual ale soured in Geoffrey's mouth. "You visited me because you expected me to die. You felt obliged to offer me succor until my spirit left my body."

"There were other reasons, as well you know."

Geoffrey's words emerged as a growl. "As I told you long ago, and many times since, you are not indebted to me for saving your life at Acre."

"Not once, but twice. I *do* owe you. That is why I worry about your well-being."

Geoffrey gave a brittle laugh. "It seems you are the one with doubts, my friend."

To his surprise, Dominic did not refute the statement with a jest and a lopsided grin, but nodded. "Rage is a dangerous ally. I hope in the coming days you will not act with rashness, and will consider the consequences of your vengeance. You are a good man. I have no desire to see you lose your head."

"My father was a good man. He should not have died a traitor. Thomas, too, did not deserve his fate." Geoffrey's fingers tightened around his earthenware mug. "My brother deserved to be a scholar, as he dreamed."

Geoffrey downed a long draught of ale. The anguish had not dimmed, even after eighteen years. The invisible wound hurt ten times worse than the Saracen blade which had plunged deep into his chest and left as proof a brutal scar.

"You cannot change the past," Dominic said, "but—"

"You believe I am mad to return to England and seek what is mine. I should release the helpless, suffering Lady Elizabeth, forget revenge, take Veronique to Venice, and earn a fortune from the silk trade."

"Eloquent words. In part, they are true." Dominic smiled. "Yet the lady does not seem helpless or suffering. She is a woman of astounding courage."

Geoffrey's rage flared, and became so intense, he almost choked. "I look into her haughty eyes and know all the luxuries she enjoyed because of my father's sacrifice. Father bled to death in a stable. A *stable!* I owe it to him to demand revenge."

Regret softened Dominic's gaze. "Milord—"

"Brackendale will soon learn his daughter is missing. He will receive my ransom note, and demand my head. If he and the baron attempt a siege or challenge me to a battle, my men must be prepared."

"Sedgewick may have ridden with Brackendale to Tillenham. He may not yet know of his betrothed's abduction."

Geoffrey spat an oath. "Sedgewick could not find the sharp end of a sword if it poked him in the arse."

Dominic laughed, the sound vibrant in the quiet hall. "Still, he has the power to rouse a formidable army. His and Brackendale's forces will outnumber yours."

Wiping a drop of ale from the side of his mug, Geoffrey nodded. "I have not forgotten. I am not afraid."

Uncertainty clouded Dominic's gaze. "You asked me to scribe the ransom missive."

"If you will. Your letters are far more patient than mine. I will not have Brackendale misinterpret my demands." Geoffrey paused. "Yet if you would rather not—"

"I will write it. When do you wish to send it?"

Geoffrey leaned back in his chair and stretched out his booted legs. "In a few days. First, I want Brackendale to agonize over his daughter's fate. Then, in exchange for her return, I shall demand my rightful inheritance as Edouard de Lanceau's first born son."

With his finger, Dominic traced a deep mar in the

tabletop. "Will you ask for Brackendale's life, too?"

"I shall not have to. When he raises his sword to me in combat, I will not spare him." Geoffrey imagined drawing his sword in that delicious moment, and his fingers curled and uncurled. His palm warmed with the imagined rub of leather, and the weapon's slashing weight.

'Twould be a sweet victory.

Dominic frowned. His gaze shifted to the ledger. "There is also the matter of Viscon. Will you pay him to fight for you? He has already demanded a high fee for his part in the abduction and, I might add, has bedded down with one of the maidservants and made no move to leave."

Geoffrey waved away Dominic's disapproval. "I do not like the man either, but I have asked him to stay. His price is no greater than others of his profession."

Exasperation gleamed in Dominic's eyes. "Where will you get the silver? Have you received payment from Pietro?"

At mention of the Venetian merchant, Geoffrey smiled. He would forever be grateful that Pietro had befriended him when he was in the care of the Knights Hospitallers, at a time when Geoffrey wished each night for death. Pietro had introduced him and Dominic to the riches of the Eastern silk and spice trades.

Aye, and Pietro had shown Geoffrey that every man had his price. When it came to his mistress.

Or his daughter.

"I do not expect the profits from the silk shipments till

the first frosts. I have some silver in my coffers. I also have this." Geoffrey drew near the wooden chest, flipped open the lid, and withdrew Elizabeth's gold brooch.

"By the saints." Dominic picked it up and held it at his eye level. Sunlight gleamed off the delicate design. "Where did you get it?"

"Lady Elizabeth."

Dominic whistled and weighed the gold in his palm. "Worth a fair price, I vow."

Geoffrey grinned. "Enough to pay several more mercenaries."

"The brooch seems of an older style."

"It belonged to the lady's mother. When the lady first asked after it, I thought she missed a pretty trinket. Then I looked into her eyes, and—"

Dominic eyed him with fascination. Did he expect some kind of profound confession?

Geoffrey snapped his jaw shut. He would *not* admit compassion for her. "I do not care if 'tis important to her. Now, it belongs to me."

"You should return it." Dominic's fingers brushed over the design. "If you kill Brackendale and seize his lands, she will have naught. The coin from selling this brooch would provide her an income for several years, at least until she finds a husband."

"She is betrothed to the baron. He will provide for her."

Dominic's mirthless laughter cut into Geoffrey's thoughts.

"I doubt Sedgewick will still want her, when she no longer comes with a large dowry."

Geoffrey resisted a stab of guilt. He would *not* care for the damsel, or cripple his ambitions with concerns for her welfare. Not when revenge was so close.

Over the crackling fire, he heard the patter of footsteps. He glanced up, and saw Elena. She looked tired and flustered, and he realized she had come from Elizabeth's chamber.

He beckoned Elena over to the table.

She curtsied. "M-Milord?" Her face looked pale.

"How is the lady?"

"She would not eat." Elena stared down at her fingers, which were linked tightly together. "She refused. S-She said she cared not for lumpy gruel."

Geoffrey downed the last of his ale and dried his mouth with his hand. "You left the fare with her?"

"Aye, but I do not think she will eat it." Elena's hands shook. "I helped her dress in the clothes you sent for her, but she almost ripped them to shreds. She shouted and cursed like a wild woman."

He remembered well the heat of his captive's eyes, and her stinging words. "What did she say?"

The maid drew a breath. "She . . . well, she did not re-spect your generosity, milord."

"Go on."

"She said you provided the gown of a *strumpet*."

Geoffrey chuckled. Dominic hooted and slapped his

palms on the table, and Elena jumped, her gaze wide as a startled hare's.

"Did you borrow from fair Veronique's wardrobe?" Dominic asked.

"I dared not risk her wrath. I took a spare gown from one of the maids." Geoffrey dried his eyes with his cuff, yet Elena did not curtsey and take her leave. "There was more?" he said.

She looked about to wilt in fright.

"For God's sake," Geoffrey snapped. "What?"

"She . . . she . . ."

"Tell me!" He did not mean to shout, but from Elena's demeanor, he guessed the lady made another demand on his patience. She rankled him more than he ever imagined possible for one of the fairer sex, who had been in his company for less than a full turn of the sun.

"She demands . . . a bath," the maid squeaked.

"*Demands?*" Dominic sounded astonished.

Geoffrey scowled. "Does she, now?"

"I told her she needed your permission, milord, for the water must be heated and brought up from the kitchens, but she insisted."

Biting back his fury, Geoffrey jerked his head in dismissal. "I will deal with the lady. Tend to Mildred, then help prepare the evening meal."

Elena dropped into a quick curtsy and scurried away.

"The next few days will be full of adventure, milord,"

Dominic said with a grin.

"I do not think so." Geoffrey shoved his chair back with such force it crashed to the floorboards. He stepped off the dais and stormed across the hall, dried rushes and herbs crunching under his boots. The sleeping dogs scrambled to their feet and darted under a table.

As he climbed the stairs to her chamber, his blood boiled.

The damsel would learn her lesson.

CHAPTER SEVEN

Pacing the floor of her tiny chamber, Elizabeth brushed her hand over the gown Elena had helped her into, a plain garment fit for a serving wench, not a noblewoman. "Knave," she muttered as she walked. When she next saw de Lanceau, she would ask why he deliberately insulted her by sending her common clothing.

Her irritated gaze settled on the rough-hewn wooden door warmed by morning sunlight. If he had chosen the garment to torment her, or bend her to his will, he would soon learn she would not be manipulated or coerced.

She spun on her heel, and her leg pinched. With gentle fingers, she massaged the spot, and winced, for every muscle in her body screamed from yesterday's horseback ride. Her limbs were stiff as a wooden doll's.

Reaching her arms over her head, she stretched and

groaned.

A soak in steaming water perfumed with rose petals, lavender, and herbs, like the splendid baths Mildred arranged for her at Wode, would remedy the aches and pains.

Yet de Lanceau did not seem a man to care about a prisoner's wishes. Most of all hers.

Worry gnawed at Elizabeth. She wondered what had happened to Mildred. She hoped the matron was all right, and being shown the courtesies due a woman of her aging years.

When asked about Mildred, Elena had refused to answer. De Lanceau must have forewarned her not to divulge any details, and it seemed she took her duty to her lord with utmost seriousness. Elizabeth's attempts to chat with the maid had won her a shy, guarded "aye" or "nay," and no more. The conversation had dwindled to tense silence.

When asked to relay the request for a bath, Elena had looked about to faint. "I will ask, milady," she whispered, and had sped from the room as though chased by a feral boar.

What kind of demon was de Lanceau to instill such fear in his maidservants? Uncertainty shivered through Elizabeth, but she swept it aside. Since she had not seen him since Sister Margaret's visit, she could not have communicated her wishes except through Elena.

A bath was not such an onerous demand.

Elena had opened the shutters, and a breeze blew in the window and stirred Elizabeth's unbound hair. She walked forward, drawn by voices and the *clang* of a blacksmith's hammer from the bailey below. Sunshine spilled over the stone embrasure and cast the grille's pattern onto the marred floorboards.

Elizabeth linked her fingers around the wrought iron. The sun's warmth felt wonderful, and she leaned forward to soak in all she could.

Beyond the fortress's curtain wall, a river meandered through wheat fields. At its deepest, the water looked as blue as her favorite bliaut. Giant oaks with gnarled roots lined the water's edge. Swallows lifted from the boughs of one of the trees, looped and danced in the breeze, then disappeared in the direction of the distant, mist shrouded, blue-gray hills.

Elizabeth dropped her brow to the cool metal. What she would give to be a bird, with the freedom to soar wherever she desired. She would spread her wings, slip through the grille, and fly to a place where fear, death, and the past could never touch her.

Somewhere beyond the hills, her father and Aldwin rode toward Tillenham. They would reach it soon. Worry nagged at her again, and her fingers curled tighter around the bars. Did they know of her abduction? Did they know she was imprisoned at Branton?

If only there were some way to get a message to them.

Or escape.

A pair of robins hurtled past the window. They dove into the bailey and over the curtain wall, then raced back past her window. She laughed, wriggled her hand through the grille, and stretched out her fingers. One of the birds alighted on the ledge outside and studied her with its head cocked to one side.

At that moment, the door to her chamber opened. She glanced over her shoulder. De Lanceau stood in the doorway.

The robin flew away.

Withdrawing her hand, she faced him.

His expression was controlled, almost bland, but she sensed his seething rage. His gaze raked over her, from her hair to her bliaut's hem that grazed her calves, and his lips curled in a faint grin.

He strode forward, slamming the door behind him.

Anxiety settled in Elizabeth's belly like a lump of ice.

She was alone with him.

He halted near her, leaned one hip against the side table, and folded his arms across his jerkin. "You are well?" he asked, his words crisp yet polite.

"As well as I may be, under such conditions." A silent groan burned inside her, for her frazzled nerves had betrayed her. While she wished to convey her outrage and disdain, she did not want to infuriate him. Then he might never grant her a bath.

She also had no wish to repeat their earlier confrontation. Her skin still tingled where he had touched her.

"You feel mistreated?" His eyes darkened to the color of wet slate, and his gaze shifted to the bandaged wound at her temple. "How so?"

Unease ran through her, but she squared her shoulders and met his stare. "For a start, I am not used to being attended by a stranger. Mildred is my lady-in-waiting, and has been since I was a girl."

"Elena is skilled."

"She is, but I prefer Mildred's help."

He shrugged. "You cannot have it."

Anger and concern thickened Elizabeth's tone. "How do I know she is all right? If you dare mistreat her—"

"No one has harmed her. She is being held in another part of the keep, and is fine."

Elizabeth crossed her arms to stop them from shaking. "If I could see her for myself, my worries would be appeased."

He leaned farther back on the table, into a bright splash of sunlight. "You will see her soon enough."

"When? The day my father batters through the gates and rescues me?"

De Lanceau's jaw hardened, as though she tested the frayed boundaries of his temper. "The day my demands are met and I choose to release you, if not before then."

A defiant reminder of her father's military might sizzled on her tongue, but before she could say one word, de Lanceau shook his head. "I will not discuss your freedom. I was told you had grievances. Is your concern for Mildred the sum of them?"

Elizabeth shot him a glare. "Not at all. Elena tried her best, but could do naught with my hair. She could not even run a comb through it, 'tis so matted with grime. The jug of water provided me is enough to wash my face and hands, but no more, so I cannot complete my morning bath." She sucked in a breath. "My bed linens also smell sour, and the dust in this room is thicker than mud in a pigpen."

"I see." His words held menace. Yet, in her ramblings, she had outlined good reasons why he should allow her a bath. She must persist until she had his answer.

"I am sure you will agree that my well being would be improved by a hot bath. I trust Elena relayed my request to you"—Elizabeth sweetened her tone in a deliberate show of respect—"*my lord?*"

His gaze sharpened. "She did."

"And?"

"And, milady, you have no right to make demands of my servants."

What sort of answer was that? He had not agreed to the bath, but he had also not refused her one.

She waited for him to continue. Drummed her fingers on her arms. Swept hair from her shoulder. When he still did not reply, but watched her movements like a hungry hawk, she sighed and threw up her hands. "Well? What is your answer?"

"I am considering your request." He glanced at his fingernails, then back at her. "Elena mentioned to me you had another matter of concern. The gown?"

Elizabeth pressed her lips together. How clever of him

to change the subject without agreeing. Well, she would ask him again, before their talk was done. "You have given me peasant's clothes, milord."

Did the light playing over his face trick her, or did his eyes spark with mirth?

"I feel a draught at my ankles." She gave her skirts a brisk shake. "The sleeves do not cover my arms. You know as well as I that only a strumpet would bare this much flesh for all to see. 'Tis appalling."

"I find the bliaut most fetching."

Heat scalded Elizabeth's cheeks. The rogue tried to appease her with flattery. Yet she could not suppress the thrill that coursed through her, right down to her toes.

Shame crushed the pleasure. She should not savor the honeyed words of her father's sworn enemy. "If you like this gown," she bit out, "'tis all the more reason for me to hate it."

His smile faded. "Milady." Warning hummed in his voice.

She ignored an inner prick of caution and welcomed a rush of scorn. "You insisted before on courtesy and honor, yet you dishonor me with this gown. 'Tis clear you do not respect me. I shall never respect you, you despicable rogue!"

His face darkened with a lethal scowl. He straightened away from the table. "Beware. I may exact an immediate apology from your lips."

Elizabeth thrust up her chin, even though her insides had turned as soft as pudding. She should not have insulted him, and let her pride and embarrassment overrule her common sense.

Tiny shivers started in her belly. De Lanceau was lord and master of Branton Keep. As his hostage, she had no rights or privileges. Naught stopped him from beating her if he so desired. He could throw her on the rack, have her tortured with hot irons, or lock her in a small, lightless cell without food or water for days.

He could rape her here in this room.

No one would stop him.

He took a step toward her. His boots creaked.

Elizabeth's pulse lurched.

"So, you dislike my choice of garments." The dangerous silk of his voice wrapped around her, threatened to ensnare her, and she fought the urge to step away.

Her nervous gaze dropped to his jerkin, the color of fine Bordeaux. She doubted even her father could afford such magnificent material that looked as soft to the touch as lamb's wool. "You picked this gown on purpose. You intended to humiliate me."

His heel scraped on the floor as he took another step forward. "Would you prefer to go without clothing?"

"Of course not." She did not like his nearness, but she also would not show cowardice and retreat.

"You should be satisfied with what I have given you. Grateful, even."

"*Grateful?*"

He nodded. His hair, curving past the edge of his collar, gleamed like polished oak. "When I came to Branton, I found it in disrepair. 'Twill take months to bring it to the standard to which a spoiled lady, like you, is accustomed."

Chills rippled through her.

"Vast structural repairs must be done or this keep will crumble into a heap of stones and mortar. I need a full retainer of servants, which I do not have. There are far too many tasks for a few hands, yet I still provided you and your lady-in-waiting with a warm bed, clean clothing, food and drink." His lip drew back from his teeth. "I even paid a healer with my own coin, little that I have, to tend your wounds."

"W-Why are you telling me this?"

Promise smoldered in his gaze. Promise of . . . what?

He smiled, but warmth did not touch his eyes. "Mayhap I should have sent you to the dungeon instead. 'Tis a foul place, the perfect home for spiders, rats, and *vermin*." His tongue curled around the word and Elizabeth shuddered. "'Tis damp and cold even in the heat of summer. Unlike this chamber, which you hold in such contempt."

De Lanceau took one last step and halted in front of her. His gaze raked up the front of her bliaut. "Aye, you have much to be grateful for. Most of all, that I have not unleashed my fury and sought your body to appease me."

Elizabeth gasped. She stumbled back, but his hand caught her left wrist and held her firm. She struggled, but he pulled her toward him until her breasts brushed his jerkin. Fabric whispered where their bodies touched.

He smelled of bitter, earthy ale. Of man.

Trembling, she stared up at the seductive fullness of his lips. "Milord."

"You think to apologize?" His breath fanned against her forehead. "Too late, milady. You have taxed my restraint once too often with your waspish tongue."

With a strangled cry, Elizabeth broke free of his grip. She whirled and bolted toward the trestle table.

De Lanceau's laughter chased her. Pace by pace, he stalked her down the table. She scooted ahead of him, her bottom pressed against the table's edge. Her hands skidded on the dusty surface. She tried to dart past him, but he thwarted her escape.

Her fingertips scraped against stone, and, with a horrified jolt, she realized she was against the far wall.

Trapped.

A wicked smirk on his lips, de Lanceau towered over her. He crowded her back into the corner.

His palms slammed on the wall either side of her head.

"Tell me," he murmured against her hair. "Are your only assets the lands you bring to marriage, damsel? Or, are there other reasons for Sedgewick to covet you as his betrothed?"

"I do not know what you mean." She flattened back against the cold stone, one hip squeezed against the end of the table.

"You will."

"Please, let me go."

His fingers tangled into her hair. "You should not have provoked me. Any woman with any sense would have realized I am not a kind or patient man."

His thumb tilted up her chin.

He meant to kiss her.

Elizabeth jerked her face away. With gentle but firm movements, he twisted her hair around his hand until she had no choice but to look at him. "Nay," she choked. "N—"

His mouth crushed down over hers.

The kiss tasted of anger. His lips branded hers with the essence of ale. His tongue lashed. In all her years, no man had ever kissed her.

No one had dared.

She shrieked and clawed and scratched at his jerkin. The fabric softened her blows. Grinding his hips against hers, he pinned her flush against the wall. Where they touched, the heat of his body scorched.

Elizabeth squeezed her lashes shut. His scent enveloped her, and her head reeled. Somehow she must endure this torture. She must maintain a prudent detachment until he lost interest or she wriggled free. With a strangled sob, she let her hands fall to her sides.

She sensed tension warring within him, the desire to crush her spirit with his strength. Yet he did not. His kisses slowed, gentled, and as his tongue flicked into the corner of her mouth, she gasped. The skin across her chest tingled, a similar sensation to when he had kissed her hand in the market.

An unfamiliar ache blossomed inside her.

He nibbled her bottom lip. Taunted. Coaxed. Dared her, with the glide of his mouth and tongue, to meet his sensual challenge.

A muzzy haze clouded her mind and in her mind, she wept in self-reproach. He knew of the tremors running through her body.

Tremors not due to fear.

She moaned. Her lips parted. Despite the warning shrilling inside her, she began to kiss him back.

He growled. The pleasured sound stirred a primitive hunger. Molten heat flooded through her like sunlit water surging across glistening sand, slowing to a swirling eddy, and then returning a moment later on another cresting tide. His tongue slid into her mouth, and she sighed.

He released her hair. His fingers caressed her neck, and then slipped down her shoulder blade.

His palm brushed her breast.

She stiffened. Shock slashed through the haze of wondrous sensation, then indignation. De Lanceau meant to do more than kiss her.

As he had no doubt planned, she had melted under his onslaught like a lusty tavern wench. He could not conquer her will, so he would subdue her body instead.

This man was her sworn enemy.

She betrayed her father by wanting de Lanceau's touch.

Resentment drowned her last glimmerings of pleasure.

De Lanceau hesitated. He lifted his lips from hers and stared down into her face, his heavy-lidded gaze intense.

Protecting her bruised arm, she braced her palm against his chest and shoved with all her might. She kicked his shins and scratched with her nails. He swore, yelped, and she broke free.

Elizabeth darted behind the bed. "You *rogue!*" With the back of her wrist, she scrubbed her mouth, desperate to erase the taste and feel of him.

"I did not hear you protesting a moment ago." He dragged a hand through his mussed hair and glared at her.

"You will pay for your boldness. My father will see you punished."

De Lanceau's eyes glinted like steel. "Consider what happened fair warning, damsel. Next time, you will not escape unscathed."

CHAPTER EIGHT

Geoffrey strode into the hall, his clipped strides shattering the near silence.

Dominic glanced up from where he sat by the hearth. "The first adventure, milord?"

With a savage roar, Geoffrey slammed his fist down on a trestle table. Stoneware mugs bounced into the air with a dissonant *clink*. The scullery maids setting out bread for the evening meal shrieked and glanced at one another. He scowled in their direction, and, after frantic curtsies, they disappeared into the stairwell.

Aware of Dominic's grin, refusing to acknowledge it, Geoffrey grabbed a mug, sloshed in some ale, and downed it in one gulp. The drink cooled his burning throat.

Every muscle in his body felt taut as a drawn bowstring. Because of her.

Dominic rose from a carved oak chair. He raised an eyebrow and his gaze dropped to the scratch marks on Geoffrey's jerkin.

"What happened?"

Geoffrey swore. He did not use the vulgar oath often, but he embellished it with other expletives.

Chuckling, Dominic shook his head. "Send the ransom demand now. If the lady is that much trouble, you are best rid of her."

A silent bellow exploded inside Geoffrey. He wished the solution were that simple. His blood pounded with a need that only a woman could assuage. In the musty hall, tempered by the tang of old rushes and smoke, he still smelled Elizabeth's perfume that clung to her skin and hair.

He had gone to her chamber intending to frighten her and subdue her into respect for his authority. The moment he strode in and saw her gilded by sunlight, he longed to kiss her. She was stunning, a woman who would tempt him wearing naught but rags.

His fingers had itched to plow into her hair and feel its silk. Her bewitching blue eyes had challenged him to taste her, woo her, and coax back the radiant smile which had faded when she turned from the window and saw him.

He should never have given in to the urge to taste her lips. He should have guessed the experience would be as frustrating as her sharp tongue.

She was the daughter of his enemy, the man responsible

for his father's death. Forbidden.

He was a fool to crave her.

Geoffrey released his breath on a hiss.

"Take my recommendation," Dominic insisted. "Send—"

"We keep to the original plan." Shrugging tension from between his shoulders, Geoffrey stalked toward the solitude of the hearth. He sprawled in one of the chairs facing the fire and cursed; his carelessness with the mug had caused a slosh of ale, which soaked his thigh.

He did not glance up when Dominic sat in the other chair. Logs had recently been added to the blaze, and the flames crackled and shot sparks across the tiled hearth. Geoffrey leaned his head back, closed his eyes, and stretched his legs toward the inviting warmth.

Ah, for a moment of quiet.

In the space of three heartbeats, he sensed a powerful feminine presence stroll into the gap between the chairs.

The rustle of silk identified her, along with the scent of rosewater. Veronique. He would never mistake the signature fragrance of the vixen who had shared his bed for the past two years. She wore only the attar of the prized Damask rose brought into England by Crusaders on their return from the East. She considered any other oil inferior.

Veronique strolled past and a heady waft of perfume filled his nostrils. The scent teased, aroused a host of wanton memories. He raised his eyelids a fraction and watched the enticing sway of her hips. Yestereve, he had heard the maids whispering of the rosewater baths she ordered at least three times a week, and how she slapped servants for pouring water too hot or too cold.

One merchant in the town of Branton stocked oils to her exclusive standards, and a few weeks ago, she had wanted him flogged for sending fragrance she did not like. Geoffrey had refused. She, in a pique, had brushed the oil into her chestnut tresses and then tormented him with the sleek strands late into the eve.

That he permitted such extravagance was almost beyond reason. That he gave her a firm hand in his household was almost beyond belief.

Almost.

As his gaze traveled up Veronique's curvaceous figure, outlined by a scandalous bliaut of red silk, he understood.

"Good day to you, Veronique," Dominic said.

Her voice husky, she answered, "Dominic." Pausing at the hearth, she stretched her hands toward the warmth. "Milord."

Firelight played over the expensive fabric and her long hair, worn loose as Geoffrey preferred. Turning her head, she met his stare. Her eyes narrowed in a bold perusal of his body, and his desire flared.

Ah, she was a beauty. Her dark brows were slim and arched, her nose small and rounded, her mouth painted crimson. Yet he did not mistake the cunning that glittered in her amber eyes. Sometimes, when her gaze settled on his face, Geoffrey felt she could read every thought that flashed through his mind.

He experienced that sensation now as Veronique smiled. His flesh remembered her skilled touch, and he flinched.

"Veronique," he murmured.

"I saw Jenna in the kitchen. She thought you might have need of me." Her words were smooth and heady, intoxicating as a strong liqueur. "I pray, milord, Jenna was not mistaken." She turned, enough to silhouette her body against the fire-light and display her bosom stretched taut beneath the silk.

Geoffrey dragged in a breath. The invitation could not have been clearer if she had written it on the floor in blood.

Did she realize how his body craved release?

"Jenna spoke true," he rasped.

Triumph glimmered in Veronique's eyes, bright as the blaze behind her. She dropped to her knees before him and trailed slender fingers up his right calf. He shivered. With artful strokes, she caressed his corded leg muscles through his hose. After easing his knees apart with her body, she ran her palm up to his thigh.

Dominic cleared his throat and took a noisy sip of his ale, a reminder that what took place in the hall was public spectacle.

Geoffrey caught Veronique's hand, stilling the movement.

Her lashes flickered down, concealing a glimmer of disappointment. "Milord? What—"

Setting aside his ale, he linked his fingers through hers.

He drew her to her feet, and grinned at the flush of anticipation that warmed the chalky layer of flour dusted over her face. With a curt goodbye to Dominic, he led Veronique up the wooden staircase to his solar.

Sunlight fingered over the coverlet on the massive bed set against the wall. Without breaking his stride, Geoffrey led her across the room and pushed her down on the mattress, crushing her body beneath his. His limbs tangled with hers, a passionate contrast of black and red. He kissed her with fierce hunger.

He had to unleash his need, or it would devour him from the inside out.

"Geoffrey," Veronique moaned against his lips. "Ah, Geoffrey."

Elizabeth had made a similar sound. With stunning clarity, he remembered the moment she had surrendered and opened herself to him. When, with hesitant thrusts of her tongue, she had begun to kiss him in return.

Confusion muddied his desire. He shoved thoughts of Elizabeth from his mind and brushed his lips down Veronique's perfumed throat. She would assuage his need. She always rendered him weak, gasping, and slick with sweat, the last time the night before he left for Wode.

From their first tryst in a farmer's field outside the fair at Bruges, with stars glimmering in silent witness, Veronique had proved herself mistress of his body. She, unlike other wenches, had not cringed at the sight of the hideous, puckered scar that ran down the side of his chest, a permanent reminder of the battle wound that almost killed him. Lusty, creative, she had given him pleasure and he had offered her a life far richer than that of a poor cotter's daughter.

His jaw tightened on a shudder. He wanted Veronique to shatter him with pleasure now, to vanquish the tension coiling in the pit of his stomach.

With feverish urgency, Veronique guided his hands to the ties that fastened her bliaut. Between one slippery kiss and the next, the red silk slid to a pool beside the bed, followed by her chemise. Breathing hard, Geoffrey pulled Veronique into his lap. She straddled his legs. He smothered her gasps with his lips and buried his hands in her hair.

Skeins curled between his fingers and around his wrists. Her hair felt coarser, heavier, than Elizabeth's tresses. He inhaled and savored the scents of rosewater and willing woman.

Elizabeth's fragrance had been as arousing.

Why did the damsel plague him so? *Why?*

She meant naught to him.

Closing his eyes, he willed himself to recapture his need for Veronique.

Her throaty laughter blew over his ear. Squirming against him, she skimmed her hand down between their bodies. She lifted his tunic's hem.

Before she could release the points of his hose, he shoved her back and caught her hands.

"You are in a mood to dally?" she purred. "Pray tell, how

do you wish me to tease you?"

"Nay," he muttered.

Veronique's lashes lowered on a delighted smile. "You shall tease me." Pressing her palms flat, she arched back and lowered herself to the coverlet. She spread her hair across the bed, into the gleam of sunlight. "Come." She dragged her toes along his thigh. "I await ravishment."

Forcing Elizabeth from his mind, Geoffrey leaned forward and trailed his fingers over Veronique's smooth, naked belly.

He shook. Cursing, he balled his fingers into a fist. He rose from the bed and strode to the window, his ragged breaths echoing in the silence.

"You do not want to couple with me, milord?"

Geoffrey heard incredulity in Veronique's tone, underscored by anger. Self-condemnation and disgust seared his throat and threatened to choke him. He well understood her scorn.

Indeed, he could not explain his thoughts.

He could never tell Veronique that when he looked into her face, the eyes staring back at him were sapphire blue, not amber.

And the hair splayed across his coverlet in wild abandon shimmered like black silk.

❖   ❖   ❖

Elizabeth stood resolute until the door banged shut, and then flung herself on her knees beside the bed. She clasped her trembling hands together. Bowing her head, she recited an urgent prayer for forgiveness.

She should not have allowed de Lanceau to kiss her. He was a villain, a rogue without honor. The astonishing sensations she had felt were no more than clever manipulations by a man familiar with a woman's body.

Of her own free will, she had kissed the knave who had kidnapped her, imprisoned her, and who no doubt intended to barter her for Wode.

Even worse, she had enjoyed it.

"How could you?" she whispered. No one must ever learn of her weakness moments ago, most of all her father. She imagined his expression when he realized her betrayal, for that is how he would see the kiss, and her vision blurred with tears.

She would not allow de Lanceau to kiss her again.

Drying her eyes with her sleeve, Elizabeth stood. Her gaze fell upon the water jug and earthenware bowl on the side table. Her mouth still felt swollen from de Lanceau's wretched kisses. After pouring a little water into the bowl, she scrubbed her face and lips with her fingers, and then rinsed her mouth to wash away the lingering taste of his ale.

A soft knock sounded on the door. The key scraped in the lock and the door opened, admitting Elena.

"Milady." The maid bobbed in a shy curtsy and offered

a trencher laden with bread and roasted quail, a mug, and a jug of wine.

Behind her, the door creaked most of the way closed.

It did not shut.

Excitement glimmered inside Elizabeth like rekindled embers, and she wiped her fingers on her gown. If she were quick, she could dart by Elena, throw open the door, and run past the startled guards outside.

She must escape, for she would not be held captive to de Lanceau's sensual wickedness.

Elena crossed to the trestle table, and Elizabeth ran.

"Milady, stop!"

Two steps. Three. Elizabeth grabbed for the iron handle.

The door slammed. The lock clicked.

"Nay!" She pounded her fists against the wood. A frustrated sob welled inside her. Laughter and male voices rumbled in the corridor beyond, and then faded.

Blinking hard, Elizabeth whirled away from the door.

Her fingers knotted together, Elena stood by the food set on the table, her gaze fixed on the floorboards. "Please. You will feel better once you have eaten."

Elizabeth scowled. She would feel better when she was free.

The overcooked quail did not look at all appetizing.

Storming back to the water bowl, she said, "Return the fare to the kitchens. A hungry child may have my portion." Twisting her hair into a coil, she lifted it atop her head and splashed water down her flushed throat.

"Lord de Lanceau ensures all the keep's children are well fed." Elena sounded worried. "'Tis foolish not to eat."

Elizabeth sighed. She did not care to argue. "Very well. Leave it."

The maid nodded and hurried across the chamber. Glancing over her shoulder, she rapped on the door. It opened a fraction, and a guard grunted his consent before Elena slipped out and the door shut.

Elizabeth poured a mug of wine, slumped on the bed's edge, and pulled at a frayed bit of blanket. De Lanceau must know sheer boredom was a form of torture. At Wode, she never sat idle. If she were there now, she would be overseeing the servants and making sure the daily tasks were done. In quiet moments, she would embroider one of the orphans' chemises or shirts.

Resentment burned inside her. De Lanceau prevented her from finishing her task, and she had never once failed to do as she promised.

She sipped her drink, and wrinkled her nose at poorly-aged wine. Her temple throbbed. Setting aside the mug, she lay back on the bed. If only she could have one of Mildred's poppy tonics and enjoy the oblivion of sleep.

Her eyelids grew heavy. Yet, when she closed her eyes, she saw de Lanceau looming over her. His gaze smoldered with the thrilling intensity she had witnessed before he kissed her.

Her lips tingled.

Rolling onto her side, she pressed her face against the scratchy pillowcase.

The next time she attempted escape, she *would* succeed.

❖　　❖　　❖

A sliver of moon gleamed like an ivory tusk in the night sky beyond the window when Geoffrey disentangled his limbs from Veronique's and rose from the bed. She stirred, mumbled a few incoherent words, and then turned over with a rustle of bedding.

Standing in the shadows, he stared down at the satiny curve of her arm draped atop the coverlet. At last, she slept. He had not made love to her. While fury blazed in her eyes, he had explained he was more tired from the previous day's ride than he had first thought.

"You speak false, milord?" she had asked, her voice tight.

"I do not." Exhaustion ached in every bone and muscle in his body. Of that, he spoke true. After a silence, her anger diffused to grudging acceptance and she allowed him to take her in his arms. He had coaxed her under the coverlet and had lain with her, his clothed body nestled behind hers.

He watched the steady rise and fall of her shoulder. Guilt tore through him as his lust stirred anew, the urge to drive hard and fast into her voluptuous body.

Would she deny him now, if he asked her to make love?

He doubted so. After wringing a gasped apology from his lips, she would take him inside her with the eagerness he had come to enjoy, anticipate, and expect.

For the first time in years, that was not enough.

He muttered a soft oath into the darkness. The lady had addled his brain. She interfered with his lovemaking, and now she influenced his judgment.

The moonlight's pale glow revealed his boots lying beside the bed, and he bent to retrieve them. In all his years, he had never encountered a woman quite like Elizabeth Brackendale. Why did she intrigue him?

Elizabeth lacked the sophistication of a wench who knew the power of her own beauty, but she held a power over him just the same. Veronique used her fingers, tongue and body to stir him to passion. Elizabeth had but to challenge him with the toss of her hair and barbed words, and his blood ignited like liquid fire.

Tension tightened his gut. Such comparisons were pointless. The lady was a temporary burden. No more.

Taking care to prevent the leather from creaking, Geoffrey pulled on his boots and then quit the solar, pulling the door closed behind him with a faint *click*. His footsteps echoed in the stairwell and when he stepped out into the torch lit bailey, he breathed in deep to clear his mind.

He would not lose sight of his purpose.

As he exhaled, his breath formed a white cloud. Change was in the air. The cool summer night foreshadowed winter's chill.

The wind gusted and tangled his hair like an invisible hand as Geoffrey began to walk the bailey's perimeter. A guard on the wall walk hailed him, and Geoffrey called out a gruff greeting.

He turned to retrace his steps across the uneven ground. A sound, the scrape of a boot heel, warned him he was not alone. Someone concealed in the dark shadows, where light from the flickering torches did not reach, watched him.

His disquiet shifted into warrior alertness. "Reveal yourself," he ordered.

Dominic materialized, garbed in a brown wool cloak. His mouth eased into a sheepish smile. "Good eve, milord."

Geoffrey massaged stiffness from his neck. He wondered how long Dominic had watched his pacing, and how much his clever friend had gleaned from it.

"I am surprised to find you here, milord. I thought you would be enjoying the warmth of your bed and fair Veronique."

"I could not sleep."

"Ah. Lady Elizabeth."

"'Tis not so," Geoffrey snapped.

Dominic winged an eyebrow. Geoffrey wished that by some miracle, the breeze would blow, snuff out the torches, cloak the bailey in darkness, and shield him from his friend's scrutiny.

"May I point out that the lady came into our care yesterday morn? Since that time, you have acted like a demented boar."

Geoffrey snorted. "Far better a boar than a *weasel*."

"I was not spying on you, but looking at the moon. I drank one too many mugs of wine with the evening meal, and fresh air is known to calm the temperament." His tone lightened. "Which is why you are here."

Setting his hands on his hips, Geoffrey half-turned and stared up at the moon's bluish outline. He would not be snared into admitting his idiotic yearning for the lady.

He sensed Dominic's gaze sweeping over his profile, and turned his face away.

Dominic chuckled. "The lady causes this restlessness?"

"The *lady* . . ." Geoffrey said between his teeth. "When I am in her presence, I wish to throttle her."

"You desire her. She is stubborn and spirited, aye, but also quite lovely."

"She is Brackendale's daughter."

Dominic shrugged. "Unfortunate for her, but not her fault."

With stiff fingers, Geoffrey flicked wind-tousled hair from his brow. "Lady Elizabeth is a pawn, a means to win my revenge. In a few days, she will no longer plague me."

Burying his hands into his cloak, Dominic tilted his head to one side. "Tell me, milord. Do you suffer any guilt?"

Geoffrey laughed. The sound vanished on a blast of cold air. He should not feel remorse for the way he had treated Elizabeth. Nor would he regret one mean-spirited word he had spoken to her, or forcing her to kiss him. Not when his father's death demanded retribution from Lord Brackendale.

"I suffer no guilt," Geoffrey said. His voice caught and betrayed him.

He thrust his face into the wind, even though it stung his cheeks and eyes. His heart throbbed, and he welcomed the familiar anguish. He would win the loyalty of the people who once paid homage to Edouard de Lanceau. He would rule the lands that by birthright he should have inherited. He would build the cloth empire of which he had dreamed, and set the once-revered de Lanceau name on the tongue of every noble and fat-pursed burgess in England.

Then, they would not call him the son of a traitor.

The lady would not stand in his way.

Dominic sighed, and the sound was echoed in the wind's hiss. "Mayhap you should reconsider your relationship with her."

Suspicion lanced through Geoffrey, nurtured by his friend's mischievous smile. "Dominic—"

"Why not treat her as the titled lady she is? Show her courtesy, instead of trampling her wounded pride."

Geoffrey choked on his indrawn breath. "*What?!*"

"That would be too difficult?"

"I should be civil to *her?*" Geoffrey spluttered. "I am not the one who—"

"Aye?" Dominic's eyes glowed.

"She is a prisoner, not a guest," Geoffrey snarled. "What will you suggest next? Five maidservants to see to her whims? Jugglers and dancing bears to alleviate her boredom?"

Dominic shook his head. "The servants have sworn

allegiance to you, and know the lady is your hostage. She and Mildred cannot escape. 'Twould be generous of you to let her out of her chamber."

"You are mad!"

"It could do no harm."

"No good can come of it either." Geoffrey kicked at a stone, and it rattled into the shadows near the curtain wall.

"If she must stay confined, give her entertainments—books, games, or a lute. She has naught to help her pass the days but visits from you and Elena. Her only solace is to plot escape and invent new insults to hurl at you."

"I will think on what you said. Now, I wish to return to my bed. Unless you have more weepy tales of the lady's plight?"

Dominic smiled his knowing smile. "Nay, that is all."

✦   ✦   ✦

As the solar door closed, Veronique dug her fingernails into the coverlet. Anger burned her mouth dry. In all the years she had loved Geoffrey, he had never deserted her late in the eve.

Tonight he had rejected her seduction.

Tonight he had abandoned her.

Kicking aside the bedding, she flung herself onto her back and stared up at the darkened ceiling. Cool air swept over her bare skin, another reminder Geoffrey was not there to warm her.

She remembered two nights ago, when he stood naked

and aroused before her, his body a rippling length of toned, corded muscle. He had wanted her then. Veronique smiled and shuddered at the memory of his body straining over hers. Of his hoarse cry as his seed pulsed into her. Of his satisfied kiss.

She would not allow him to cast her aside.

Geoffrey de Lanceau was hers.

With a husky laugh, Veronique stretched her arms over her head and curled her toes into the feather-filled mattress. She would sob, sulk, and seduce, whatever she must to keep him hers.

She would stand at his side when he ruled Wode.

She would share his power, fame, and the profits from his cloth empire.

For all the nights she had spread her thighs for him, she deserved a share of his wealth.

Much later, footsteps thudded outside the door. Veronique pulled the bedding under her chin, curled onto her side, and closed her eyes. The door creaked open. Fabric rustled, boots and garments dropped onto the floorboards. As Geoffrey climbed in beside her, the mattress sagged.

"Mmm," she moaned. Feigning a sleepy stir, she rolled over to snuggle against him. By sheer force of will, she resisted a smug smile.

Geoffrey de Lanceau was hers.

CHAPTER NINE

"He *what?*"

"Milord asks that you join him for the midday meal."

Elizabeth turned from the window, where she had been watching the robins glide on the breeze, and stared at Dominic. A gust of wind blew hair into her eyes and she tucked the ringlets behind her ear, wondering as she did so why de Lanceau would ask her to dine with him.

By now, Elena and the guards must have informed him of her attempted escape yesterday, which made his request even more suspect.

Frowning, she studied Dominic. His soft brown eyes were the same hue as his straight, silky hair. She steeled herself against his compassionate smile and the overwhelming burst of hope she might be allowed out of this dreary room. Her gaze traveled over his brown wool tunic, hose, and scuffed boots caked with mud, mayhap from a morning of swordplay near the river. If she had hoped to discern a motive for the invitation, she found none.

"You will pardon my suspicion," Elizabeth said, "but I cannot believe your lord wishes for more of my company."

Dominic's pleasant smile did not waver. "My role is to bring the message, milady. Yet the idea must have more appeal than being locked in this tiny room all day. Alone."

He sounded eager for her to accept. Did she really have a choice in the matter?

What a perplexing predicament.

The green wool gown swirled as she moved to the trestle table and pointed to the bread and cheese Elena had brought earlier. "If I were hungry, I would have eaten the food your lord sent to me."

"Ah, but 'tis more than a meal." Dominic spread his hands wide. "He has made a concession. A truce, if you will."

"A *truce?* How ridiculous." She crossed her arms and cast him what she hoped was a lofty dismissal.

He chuckled. "Milady, he asked me to be sure to convey the full extent of his message."

"Mmm?"

"If you dine with him, he will grant you the bath you desire."

Elizabeth's hands fell to her sides, and elation welled up inside her. She had washed her skin and hair as best she could with the jug of water, but a bath would be wondrous.

If she kept her wits about her during the meal, she might also discover a way to escape. "I accept."

Dominic grinned. "Good. Now, if you will please come with me, milord awaits."

As Elizabeth crossed to the door, memories of her last encounter with de Lanceau flitted through her mind, and she hesitated. She had no way of knowing if his intentions today were honorable, and did not trust him as far as she could spit.

Anxiety smothered her excitement like a blanket tossed over a fire. He had roused sinful sensations in her body with his kiss. Mayhap he meant to deceive and then seduce her, as part of his cruel revenge.

A chaperone, however, would ensure he kept his hands on his food.

His fist raised to rap on the door, Dominic glanced back at her. "Milady?"

"I will not dine without Mildred."

His gaze shadowed. "Milord did not include your lady-in-waiting in his invitation."

"Then tell your lord I refuse. I shall indulge in a bath after my prompt and efficient rescue."

She pivoted and marched back to the window.

A groan came from Dominic. "No wonder milord has behaved like a mad boar."

Elizabeth blinked. A mad boar? The image that filled her mind was too delicious to ignore. She pressed her hand to her lips and giggled.

A muffled sound erupted behind her, and she looked at Dominic. He was laughing too.

"Very well, milady. I shall send Mildred to join you, though milord will not be pleased with me."

"Thank you."

After a brisk nod, he knocked twice on the door. The key rasped in the lock, the wooden panel swung open, and he motioned for her to follow.

She walked out into the dank corridor. Two broad-shouldered guards armed with swords and daggers moved away from their posts outside, and fell into step behind her.

Their boots rapped on the floor. The sound mirrored her heart pounding against her ribs. Elizabeth held her head high, walked with years of tutored poise, and pretended she took no interest in her surroundings. She prayed the guards did not suspect she was memorizing as much detail as possible and counting the number of paces and turns in the passage. The details might be crucial when she escaped.

Flickering reeds, locked into iron brackets along the wall, illuminated the passage. The flames cast eerie shadows across the mildewed stone.

Ahead, the corridor turned and merged into another passage that seemed less gloomy. Woven tapestries portraying campaigns of Charlemagne hung on the walls. Although they were grayed by dust, Elizabeth guessed that if the weavings were taken down and beaten with a wooden paddle, the colors would be as vibrant as the day the wool was dyed and spun.

Daylight brightened the corridor ahead, which echoed with laugher, cheers, as well as the clatter of crockery; and ended in a wooden landing overlooking the keep's great hall.

Elizabeth squinted through the hazy smoke into the room below. The hall looked enormous, though not as imposing as Wode's. Sunlight streaked in through horn windows, splattered with bird droppings, positioned at opposite ends of the room. Trestle tables ran along two of the four walls. A meager assortment of men-at-arms and servants sat awaiting their food.

A stout, gray-haired woman flirted with the men and kicked aside the hounds at her feet as she set ale jugs on the tables. The third wall boasted a fireplace as tall as a man, and twice as wide. The fourth, a scarred table on a raised stone dais.

De Lanceau sat at the head of the lord's table. Through the smoke, his gaze met Elizabeth's, and she stiffened.

The instant she stepped onto the landing, he saw her.

Glancing past her shoulder, he nodded. The guards motioned for her to follow Dominic down the narrow stairs. As Elizabeth descended, she became aware of the curious stares that followed her, and the sudden hush.

With an encouraging smile, Dominic ushered her toward the dais. Dried rushes and herbs crunched under her shoes. In the silence, the sound seemed as loud as snapping branches. She clasped her sweaty hands and fought the warmth stealing into her cheeks.

As she neared him, de Lanceau's gaze sharpened. "Milady."

He could not have looked more of a rogue. The lustrous silver thread embroidering his collar matched the glint of his eyes. His skin looked tanned against the white linen shirt. Her gaze dropped to his mouth, which shimmered from his last sip of wine. A quiver shot through her. She would not be able to eat one bite without thinking of his kiss.

She did not want him to catch her staring. "Milord." Because she wanted that bath—and *only* for that reason, she told herself—she graced him with a stiff curtsey.

Surprise lit his gaze. He drank from a goblet, then dragged his thumb over his lips. "You accepted my offer. I was not certain you would."

"I was not certain myself, until Dominic promised Mildred would accompany me."

His mouth pursed. "Mildred?"

Dominic stepped forward. "I had to sweeten the arrangement, milord. I agreed her lady-in-waiting could dine as well."

De Lanceau's brow darkened with a scowl. Elizabeth expected him to order swift punishment for Dominic. To her astonishment, the rogue gritted his teeth and bared a smile that looked almost painful.

"Well, milady. Since Dominic has taken it upon himself to honor your request, I would be remiss not to see it done. Guards, fetch Mildred."

She heard the men behind her turn and stride away. Hushed conversation resumed in the hall.

De Lanceau stood and gestured to the chair beside him. "Come."

The thought of sitting next to him and suffering his attentions for the whole meal tied Elizabeth's stomach into a knot. Yet there were other vacant chairs at the table. Mildred would soon arrive to chaperone.

Elizabeth squared her shoulders and forced aside her reluctance. She would have the bath he promised. If she must pacify the rogue for a short while, then so be it.

She nodded to him, stepped up onto the dais, and sat in the chair to his right. Tension seemed to ease from his posture. He called to the serving woman to bring more bread, and with effortless grace, lowered himself into his chair. The scents of fresh air and leather wafted to Elizabeth, and his nearness stirred memories of his body's heat pressed against hers. She bit down on her lip.

A blush threatened, but at that moment, the gray-haired woman waddled toward them and set down a wooden board of grain rolls.

"There ye are, milord. Plenty for ye and the lady."

De Lanceau grinned, and the serving woman's face reddened. "You are as kind as you are beautiful, Mistress Peg."

His smile, warmed with genuine affection, took the harshness from his features. He no longer looked forbidding, but handsome.

Elizabeth wrenched her gaze away.

Peg's blush deepened. "Ye tease, milord." She giggled,

dipped in a curtsey, and then stomped away, shouting orders to the maidservants delivering food as she went.

A tantalizing smell reached Elizabeth. She sniffed and tried to identify the meaty scent.

De Lanceau reached out to the table's edge and pulled over a filled trencher. Stew. He set the food between them.

Her knotted stomach lurched. He had not started to eat, though as lord of the keep he would have been served first. He had waited for her. He intended to share his meal with her and honor the custom between noble lords and ladies.

She was going to be ill.

He must have sensed her thoughts, for he pushed the fare toward her. She glanced at the braised meat and vegetables swimming in gravy. The sauce looked greasy and lumpy, but she did not care. Her stomach rumbled in an unladylike fashion, and she cringed.

Geoffrey slid a small silver eating dagger toward her. "Hungry?"

Denial buzzed on her tongue, but her helpless gaze fell again to the stew. Her stomach ached. Her fingers itched to grab the knife, spear a chunk of meat, and stuff it into her mouth.

"Elena tells me you have not eaten much in two days," he said. Elizabeth watched his lean fingers break apart one of the rolls and tear it into bite-sized pieces. She had never seen such wondrous bread, flaked with oats and seeds. Choosing a soft morsel, he dipped it in the rich broth. "Is that true?"

"Aye."

"'Tis foolish to starve yourself," he murmured, toying with the bread. "If you refuse to feed yourself, I will have to find a way to make you." His gaze flicked up, and he looked at her. "Is that what you want?"

"Of course not."

He lifted the soaked morsel to her lips. "Then eat, or I will make good my promise."

Elizabeth stared at the tempting mouthful. Gravy ran down his fingers and dripped onto the tablecloth, but he made no move to wipe it away. She tasted a biting refusal that would no doubt irk him as much as his stern words had irritated her.

But the stew-soaked bread smelled so incredible, she could not refuse.

She bit down on the morsel. Her lips closed around his fingers, and, as his skin brushed her bottom lip, awareness shot through her. She jerked back.

He smiled and lowered his hand to the table. "Good?"

Elizabeth wiped the corners of her mouth and tried to sound nonchalant. "Aye, though not as tasty as the stews Mistress Fraeda prepares at Wode."

"How is Wode's fare better?" His tone was mild, almost detached, but she sensed his displeasure. For a moment Elizabeth regretted baiting him. Yet she could not deny a thrill of satisfaction that she had struck a nerve in his dark heart.

"Well," she said, watching him dip more bread, "Fraeda

adds handfuls of fresh herbs to her cooking, such as sage, rosemary, and basil. Each morn she cuts what she needs from Wode's gardens, then tells the scullery maids how each herb should be prepared for a particular recipe." Keeping her voice light, Elizabeth added, "Mildred is responsible for our extensive herb patch. She redesigned Wode's gardens after my father took control of the keep."

De Lanceau frowned. "Redesigned them? How?"

"She increased the number of vegetable beds. The layout is much prettier." When de Lanceau's gaze darkened, Elizabeth shrugged. "I believe Fraeda puts bay leaves in her stew, and a few sprigs of rosemary. It does make a difference." She parted her lips and took more bread from him.

"I see," he muttered.

She chewed, and he stared at her mouth a long moment before glancing away.

"The rich flavors therefore cannot be achieved," she said, licking her lips, "if Branton lacks a garden and herbs."

"We have both."

"You do?"

He nodded. "'Twould take a healer to tell weed from herb, though. The garden has not been tended for years."

"Oh." Elizabeth slapped her hand to her mouth to stifle a belch, and her stomach released such a growl she was certain the entire hall had heard. The mongrel licking up scraps under the table pricked up its ears and looked at her.

De Lanceau sighed. "Eat." He snatched up the silver

dagger, stabbed some meat and held it to Elizabeth's lips. When she gobbled that bite, he offered another. "Chew with care, damsel, or you will end up with a bellyache."

The trencher was half-empty when murmurs rippled through the hall. Mildred hurried toward the table, her gray braid swinging to and fro.

"Milady," she called and waved.

Elizabeth lunged to her feet. She jumped down from the dais, ran to the matron, and embraced her. Held tight in Mildred's arms, tears filled Elizabeth's eyes. How she had missed Mildred's harrumphs and her gruff affection.

After a moment, Mildred held Elizabeth at arm's length. Her green eyes shone. "What a wretched bliaut. You look so wan."

"I am well," Elizabeth said, proud her voice did not waver.

A hand touched her shoulder, and she turned to find Dominic at her side. His smile seemed strained, and she looked past him to the lord's table.

Fury blazed in de Lanceau's eyes.

"Milady," Dominic murmured, "please return to your place."

Aware of castle folk gaping at her, Elizabeth choked back a surge of anger. "I was greeting Mildred. I have not been permitted to see her."

Dominic nodded. "True, but 'tis best not to bait a dragon, if you understand my meaning."

She did. With a sigh, Elizabeth stalked back to the

dais. Mildred's shuffled footsteps came a few paces behind. De Lanceau's stare never wavered, and Elizabeth fought the awful tightness in her chest. De Lanceau was a fool if he overreacted to such a trifling matter.

She had just set one foot upon the dais when Geoffrey motioned to Dominic. "See the matron has what she needs."

With obvious reluctance, Dominic pointed to a place at the table's opposite end.

Elizabeth's eyes narrowed. She and Mildred were to be separated? "But —"

"Sit," de Lanceau growled.

Elizabeth curled her fingers over the carved chair back and thanked the saints that the furniture came between them. "Milord, I insist. Mildred is my lady-in-waiting." In a deliberate gesture of humility, Elizabeth met his gaze, then let her lashes flutter down. She doubted the rogue had a decent bone in his body, but she would try and appeal to his honor. "Mildred has been in my family's service for years. She is like a mother to me. 'Tis right that we dine together."

"Is it?" His tone was cold. "I agreed she would share a meal at this table. I did not agree you would sit beside one another." He signaled for Mildred and Dominic to pass.

Elizabeth glared at him. "You thoughtless—"

His hand snaked out, seized her wrist, and pulled her down into her chair. Cursing, Elizabeth struggled to rise.

His palm pressed upon her thigh. She froze.

The warmth of his hand permeated the thin gown. His

fingers shifted, a mock caress. She recoiled as though stabbed with a knife.

He grinned like a hawk ready to devour its cornered prey. "Now, where were we?" He brought more stew to her lips.

"I am no longer hungry."

"Nay?" He did not sound at all surprised, and his tone resonated with amusement. "Since you have finished, you will serve me."

"I think not."

"'Tis common courtesy," he said and tossed bread into his mouth. When she crossed her arms and refused to obey, his fingers skimmed over her hip.

Elizabeth stiffened. How shameful, that he would caress her in such a way, and for all to see. His lazy smile proved he knew just how wrong his actions were. "Remove your hand."

"You did not say please." With his tongue, he plucked a dripping morsel from the dagger's tip. "Were you not taught to be polite, when you learned your ladylike duties?"

"My ladylike duties," she said between clenched teeth, "did not include entertaining rogues."

He grinned as he chewed, his teeth a slash of dazzling white. With his dark hair tangled around the shoulders of his white shirt, he looked wild. Predatory. Wicked. *"Entertaining?"* His tongue rolled over the word with such sensual appreciation, tremors raked through her. "What delightful possibilities."

He had twisted her words to imply far more than she

intended. Elizabeth's hands shook. She must destroy his deliberate misconception. Now. Or he might test her mettle in front of the entire hall.

"You mistook my meaning, milord," she said.

"I wished you to return the noble courtesy I showed to you, and you refused." His gaze locked with hers in frosty challenge. "You may despise me, but I am still due a measure of respect."

An unspoken message flashed in his eyes. She would not get her bath, unless he was satisfied.

Elizabeth grabbed the closest piece of bread and jammed it into the stew. *Respect?* He had not earned it, not when he took pleasure in provoking her anger, humiliating her, and denying her the slightest privileges.

For all he had done to her, she should dump the trencher's contents in his lap.

For one exquisite moment, she thought she might. Yet, if she did, he would refuse the bath. She sighed and forced her anger to cool. Soon, the meal would be finished.

Geoffrey's fingers lifted from her thigh and brushed the back of her wrist. The pressure on her skin was gentle, but she did not mistake the warning.

"I do not like mangled bread."

Looking down, Elizabeth saw the bread was indeed becoming the same consistency as the gravy. She frowned, annoyed he had chastised her, but when she looked up, a grin curved his lips.

Wrenching her hand free, she thrust the bread in his face. He took the bite, but with agonizing slowness. His gaze never left hers as he ran his hot, slick tongue over the tips of her fingers and sucked the morsel into his mouth.

She shuddered. "I hate you." The words slipped out before she willed them.

"Of that, I have no doubt. More bread, milady."

Again Elizabeth fed him, repulsed yet also excited by the ritual's intimacy. She tried not to watch him eat, but his lips were so well formed, his profile so handsome, 'twas hard not to.

After several more mouthfuls, he slid the eating dagger toward her. "Now, some meat."

Her fingers closed around the smooth hilt. The blade looked sharp. "You dare to place a weapon in my hand?" she said, unable to conceal her astonishment.

"You are no fool, and I give you fair warning. Threaten me, and I will prove your idiocy before every man, woman and child in this hall."

He would indeed. She skewered a round of carrot with the knife and had just raised it from the trencher when she smelled perfume. Rosewater.

"Veronique," Geoffrey murmured.

The skin across the back of Elizabeth's neck prickled. Once, he had spoken to her in such a tone. When he had held her in his arms in the market. When he had not known her name and teased her for a kiss.

"Milord," said a sensuous feminine voice. Elizabeth looked up. The woman dropped into an elegant curtsey before de Lanceau.

Veronique's coral silk bliaut fanned out around her on the rush-strewn floor. The gown, shorter than the undergarment, revealed a chemise so delicate, it looked woven from spider webs. A coral-colored ribbon wove through the braid coiled about her head.

As Veronique straightened, the exquisite cut of the gown became evident. The fitted sleeves flared below the elbow and were accented by shimmering embroidery in patterns of diamonds and squares. The same design rimmed the squared neckline.

Pinned in the center of the embroidery, between Veronique's breasts, was a gold brooch.

Elizabeth's breath became a painful gasp.

Her mother's brooch.

Anguish pounded in her veins. Rage clouded her vision until the hall became an angry red blur. Hatred boiled.

She heard Veronique titter. "So this is Brackendale's daughter. Not much to look at, is she?"

Elizabeth shot to her feet. The knife, warmed by her skin, molded to her palm. Warning flared in Geoffrey's eyes, an instant before she pressed the blade against his neck.

"I want my mother's brooch. Refuse and I will plunge this dagger to the hilt."

❈   ❈   ❈

As the knife jabbed his flesh, Geoffrey grimaced. Her eyes wide, Veronique stepped back several paces. Shocked castle folk pointed and stared at him. Under the table, dogs stopped fighting over a bone.

He heard the hiss of swords being drawn, and cursed himself for trusting the lady with the knife. He cursed Veronique for rummaging through his belongings without first asking permission, and taking what he would never have given her. Most of all, he cursed Elizabeth for forcing him into an awkward position. How did he reclaim the knife without hurting her?

"The brooch," she said, her voice shrill.

Out of the corner of his eye, Geoffrey saw a guard edge toward the dais. He fought for the rational, controlled calm that had saved his life many times on Acre's battlefields. This time, he must plan a strategy to avoid bloodshed. "Milady, if—"

"Now."

Her hand trembled, and the dagger jerked the slightest fraction. Warm liquid trickled down Geoffrey's neck. Blood.

Elizabeth moaned, a sound of despair and horror. He sensed the instant her resolve wavered. Lunging to his feet, he grabbed her wrist and slammed it down on the table. Her fingers flew open. The dagger skidded across the oak and clattered onto the floor.

Veronique clapped. "Well done, milord." The guards laughed, sheathed their swords, and the buzz of laughter and chatter resumed.

Geoffrey stared at Elizabeth's down-turned face, hidden by the black veil of her hair. She shook in his grasp, the bones of her wrist jumping like a bird's trapped wing. He heard a sound like a sniffle. Tears? He hoped not. He released her, then strode around the table and picked up the dagger.

With his cuff, he wiped his neck. The wound did not feel more than a scratch.

Veronique hurried to him, and her fingers brushed his jaw. "Does the wound hurt? Shall I bandage it for you?"

Motioning for guards to watch Elizabeth, Geoffrey took Veronique's elbow and led her to a quiet corner. "Give me the brooch."

Disbelief gleamed in her amber eyes.

"You should not have gone through my belongings."

She pulled away, her crimson lips set in a pout. "You never minded in the past. When I needed coins to buy my oils, you told me to take what I liked."

"That does not mean you may claim whatever you wish as yours."

A sly smile curved her mouth, and she ran a finger over the brooch. "I thought you had bought it for me, milord. You promised me a favor after what happened last eve. Remember?"

Fury leapt inside him. He had not promised her a gift wrought from solid gold. He bit back a scathing retort and held out his hand. "The brooch is not mine. Nor is it for you. I will have it."

Her mouth flattened, but she reached to her cleavage and unpinned the ornament. She dropped it into his palm. As she drew away, her nails trailed over his skin, a reminder of a past, wild night of lovemaking. "I did not expect you to concede to her."

He ignored her scorn. "I concede naught." He glanced at Elizabeth, who stood behind the lord's table, the guards flanking her. Despite the watery glitter of her eyes, she kept her head high and met his stare with one of bold determination.

Looking back at Veronique, he said, "We will speak more of this later." He turned on his heel and strode to the table. "Milady, come."

She clasped her hands together. "Before you punish me, I would like my brooch. Please."

He tipped his head to the guards. "Bring her. By force if need be."

Elizabeth's throat moved on a swallow. "I will walk." She rubbed her eyes and, with rigid strides, skirted the table.

Geoffrey stalked across the hall to the stairwell. Children and dogs scampered out of his way. He climbed the winding stairs and threw open the door to the wall walk. The wind whistled, buffeted him and stung his eyes, but he strode to the edge and looked down through the squared crenel to the fields below, where sheaves of wheat dried under the sun.

Light footfalls approached behind him.

"Guards," he said without turning, "stand watch at the stairwell."

"Aye, milord."

He cast Elizabeth a sidelong glance. The wind tangled her hair, blowing it over her shoulders and down her back. She moistened her lips with her tongue, a nervous gesture he had come to recognize. Desire flared, and he forced his gaze back to the fields.

"Why have you brought me here?" she asked. "To throw me over the edge?"

Geoffrey laughed. "A tempting thought." He touched his neck and found the bleeding had stopped.

Her gaze fell to the crimson stains on his cuff. Guilt shadowed her eyes and turned them the color of a winter sky. "I did not mean to draw blood."

"By the morrow, 'twill be a mere scratch. I will accept your apology, milady,"—he met her gaze—"if you tell me why you risked yourself harm for this brooch." He opened his palm, and the gold gleamed against his skin.

She glanced away. Her hands swept up and down her arms, as one did to ward off a chill. "I told you, it belonged to my mother."

"A gift?"

"Aye." Sadness dulled her voice.

He sensed her anguish ran deep. He listened to the wind howl around the crenellated stone like a wounded dog, and waited.

When she spoke, her voice was a raw whisper. "My mother gave the brooch to me on the day she died. She was with child. Her birthing pains had started weeks too soon, and she knew something was wrong." Elizabeth paused. "I saw fear in her eyes. When I asked how I could help . . ."

"Go on," he coaxed.

"S-She told me to fetch the brooch. Told me it was mine. Told me to remember her when I wore it close to my heart. She said she would always love me, even when we could not be together any longer."

A shivered sigh left Elizabeth. "Her hands were so cold. I begged her to lie down and rest. She fell back on the bed, and screamed . . . and screamed . . . the brooch fell into my hand. I could not save her. The midwife could not—" Her words trailed off with a choked sob.

Geoffrey dragged his hand through his hair. He resisted the urge to draw her into his arms. To comfort her with hushed words. To dry the tears which streamed down her cheeks and she brushed away with shaking fingers.

He could not offer her comfort. She was danger, soft and tempting. She had the power to destroy him, if she knew how.

"The babe lived for a day. She was tiny and beautiful. My father was so distraught over my mother's death, he could not look upon his child." Elizabeth sniffled. "I found a maidservant to nurse her. I sat by the fire and rocked her, and held her in my arms through the night. My sister was too weak."

Steeling himself against her torment, Geoffrey touched her shoulder. "I am sorry."

"Are you?"

The words held no challenge, only grief. "I would not have said so if—"

She shrugged free of his grasp and looked at him. "Now will you return my brooch?"

"I cannot."

"You could if you wished." Her wet eyes sparked with blue fire. "You plan to sell the gold to pay for your revenge against my father."

Geoffrey's fingers closed around the gold. The brooch's fastening, sharp as a fang, bit into his palm. "I respect your love for your mother." Bitterness hardened his tone. "Yet your torment is no different to that of a boy who watches his father die."

Her posture stiffened. "You were with your sire when—?"

"Aye."

"You saw my father kill him?"

Geoffrey shook his head and fought a flood of anguish. "I did not see the knight's face, for he wore a helm. Yet I saw his back as he jerked his sword from my father's body and walked away. I dragged my father to a horse. I took him to safety. He died in a rat-infested stable."

Her breath rasped between her lips. "Mayhap 'twas not my sire."

"We both know it was," Geoffrey snarled.

The wind screamed, whipping the hem of her skirt against his knees. She rubbed her arms again. "My father and his army carried out an order from the king. Edouard de Lanceau was a traitor."

"Was he? To my knowledge, my father never abandoned his support for King Henry in written or spoken word, or in deed."

Her face looked pale against her glistening eyes. "You lie. The king would not have ordered a siege unless he had proof."

"Mayhap my father was betrayed."

"Do not twist the truth with falsehoods!" Hair tumbled down over her bodice and the thrust of her breasts, and she flicked it aside with her hand. She glared at him. Tension poured from her like water from an unleashed dam.

Rage burned in his blood. Desire warred with his reason and conscience. Even now, he wanted her. He longed to touch her, to find oblivion in her kisses and sweet body. He cursed his wretched weakness.

"Do you believe all that you are told to be true?" he said, returning the sting of her words. "Would you believe me, milady, if I said your betrothed, Baron Sedgewick, is rumored to have beaten one of his wives so she could no longer walk?"

Elizabeth shook her head.

"He took the Earl of Druentwode's daughter as his third bride. She was a kind, gentle girl who loved music. I was told she lived in fear of the baron until the day she died."

"Nay," Elizabeth whispered.

"I do not know if that rumor is true or a lie. Do you?"

"I care not what the gossips say about the baron. My father is innocent of wrongdoing." Her voice quavered. "He obeyed the king's command when he besieged Wode. He did so because of your father's treachery. *That* is the truth. Do not try to sway me with deceit."

She blazed defiance, determined she was right and he the monster. Easing his hold on the brooch, Geoffrey leaned his elbow on the rough stone merlon. "I remember one night at Wode when my father dined with four or five other lords. I had returned for a visit; for after my eighth summer, my father sent me to the Earl of Druentwode's keep to serve as a page."

"If you aim to beguile me with more falsehoods about my father, you will not succeed," she warned and crossed her arms.

He scowled. "Pray, listen. I left the merriment in the hall to fetch a wooden box I had made under the tutelage of the earl's carpenter. I was proud of my work. I could not wait to show my father."

She made a disparaging sound. "Milord—"

"When I came back down the stairwell, I heard my father shouting. His bellow frightened me as a boy, and I felt real fear then. I crept down to the bottom stair, held my box to my chest, and listened." He swallowed, the moment reviving in his mind. "I heard him condemning a plot to support the king's son and rebellion. My sire refused to take part. He ordered all his guests to quit the hall and never set foot within Wode's walls again. Two days later, your father attacked Wode."

He had shocked her. Her eyes were wide, her mouth agape.

Her cheeks pinkened, and she looked away. "Mayhap you remember what you wish to believe. 'Tis no sin to remember with fondness those who are dead."

"I did not invent my memories. I will never forget my father's face when he strode past me, or his silence when I found him in the chapel later." Geoffrey brushed tangled hair from his brow. "Do you believe I speak false of the treachery? Of my father's words?"

For a long moment, she did not answer. "I cannot pass judgment on what I do not know."

"What could not be proven," he corrected. He had tried, as had the Earl of Druentwode, but had found naught.

She closed her eyes against the gusting wind, her lashes dark against her milk white skin. Geoffrey sensed confusion undermining her anger. Again, he fought the urge to touch her.

His emotions ran high because he had spoken of the past and reopened wounds that bared his soul.

He could not care for Brackendale's daughter.

He did not dare.

"I have no doubt you loved your father," she said, her words hushed by the wind, "as I loved my mother."

"It seems so."

"A bitter irony, milord, that we have this in common."

He nodded. "If I could return your mother's brooch, I would."

Her gaze cooled. "Spare me your gilded lies."

"I do not deceive you."

"Nay?" She whirled, and her skirt flared out around her slender legs. "You know why I treasure the brooch, yet you will not give it back. How foolish that I shared my mother and sister's memory with you. I wish I had not."

Tears shone along her lashes. "Your heart is as corrupt as your father's. I do not doubt his treachery. I do not doubt my father's guilelessness. Nor do I doubt my sire will rescue me and crush this keep into a heap of blackened rubble."

❖ ❖ ❖

De Lanceau's eyes hardened to the gray of chilled stone. Relief shivered through Elizabeth, for the compassion in his gaze had vanished. She *had* to hurt him. She had to reinforce the emotional barricade between them, before she dissolved into a sobbing mess and begged him to wrap his arms around her.

"So be it, milady," he snarled. He turned and walked toward the guards.

Elizabeth turned her face into the breeze and inhaled the scents of wind-scoured stone and wheat. Regret washed through her. Her vision blurred, and she blinked to halt fresh tears. She had laid her heart bare to her enemy, and, God help her, he had understood.

She had shared her grief over her mother's passing with Aldwin and Mildred, but no others. Not even her father, who had changed from the day of her mother's death into a different man. He had shown little outward suffering, but had attacked his duties as though his estates were being overrun by demons of chaos. He had been too busy with demands of the estate to hug her as she wept.

De Lanceau, in turn, had told her of his sire and possible betrayal. Could his words hold any truth?

Nay.

Yet, even if they did, her sire had acted with honor and obeyed his duty to the king.

Voices cut through the wailing wind. Behind her, the door slammed. She turned to find the guards waiting, their expressions impassive.

One man pulled the door open, and Elizabeth preceded them into the stairwell. The air smelled smoky and stale, but the familiar scents revitalized her spirit. They reminded her anew of her captivity, her vow to escape, and her foolishness.

How could she have craved the embrace of her father's enemy? She must find a way out of Branton Keep as soon as possible.

Squinting in the dim torchlight, Elizabeth guided her descent with a palm on the wall, the guards a few paces behind. To her surprise, they did not escort her to her chamber, but to the great hall. Most of the castle folk had gone, and the tables were covered with empty trenchers, ale mugs, and spilled gravy.

A coy giggle drew her gaze to the dais. De Lanceau stood with his hands braced on the marred oak, speaking to Veronique who had claimed Elizabeth's place. The courtesan smiled and offered him a goblet of wine. He took it and drank.

Elizabeth tore her gaze away and wiped her damp hands on her bliaut. She fought a ridiculous pang of jealousy. She did not care what the rogue did with his lover. The fresh air and emotion-laden talk had addled her senses.

Mildred waved from the trestle table. She looked worried. "Milady."

Moving away from her guards, Elizabeth started toward her lady-in-waiting.

Dominic intercepted her and matched her strides. "You are well? You suffered no punishment at milord's hand?"

"None."

He grinned. "Good."

A smile tugged at Elizabeth's mouth. She might have grinned back, if de Lanceau had not straightened and looked at her.

His lazy grin faded. His gaze shifted to Dominic. "'Tis done?"

"Aye." Dominic withdrew a rolled parchment from under his belt, strode to de Lanceau, and handed it over. "I included all of your demands."

Elizabeth halted. "Demands?"

"Your ransom," de Lanceau muttered.

Veronique laughed.

The air seemed to thicken. Elizabeth dragged in a breath, and the tang of burning pitch, drifting from the hearth, burned her nostrils. "Why did you not send it long ago?"

De Lanceau eased the parchment's edges apart and un-rolled the skin. "I wanted to be sure your father missed you, though mayhap he enjoyed relief from your bold tongue."

She ignored the taunt. "What do you demand of him?"

"'Tis not a matter for your concern."

"He is my father."

Geoffrey smoothed a ragged corner with his finger. "You wish to know how I will destroy the great Lord Arthur Brack-endale?" His ruthless gaze locked with hers. "I demand all that should have been mine. Every plot of land, title, and for-tune that I should have inherited from my father, right down to the last bit of silver."

Elizabeth's outrage burned like dry kindling. "He will not agree."

"In exchange for your safe return? Do you not think your father will yield?"

She forced a painful swallow which tasted of bitter re-sentment and fear. "Is that the sum of your demands, or will you kill him too?"

"You will learn that answer soon enough."

"Tell me now."

His gaze clashed with hers. Beyond the furious glitter, she saw resolve not to tell her more than he deemed necessary. "I suggest you and Mildred spend a few quiet moments by the fire." He looked to the end of the table, where Mildred stood arguing with one of the guards. Geoffrey flicked his hand, and the man stepped aside and let the matron pass.

Desperation clawed up inside Elizabeth. "Tell me!"

His mouth thinned. "This is your last warning. Leave us." He pointed to the hearth. "Go, before I decide to lock you back in your chamber."

Elizabeth gnawed her lip. She must know her father's fate . . . yet at the same time, she feared de Lanceau's answer. Imprisoned within Branton's walls, she could not stop his terrible plot for revenge.

Unless she escaped.

Unless he no longer had a pawn with which to barter.

Tension seethed inside her, but she turned and walked to Mildred. Murmurs and the scrape of chairs rose behind her. She glanced back to see de Lanceau and Dominic hunched over the parchment, weighted down at each corner with goblets. Seated beside Geoffrey, Veronique picked at a fresh trencher of stew and looked vexed.

Mildred came to Elizabeth side. The matron smiled before linking her fleshy arm through Elizabeth's. "Do not worry," she said in a low voice. "We shall find a way to thwart de Lanceau."

"Escape," Elizabeth murmured.

Mildred winked. "When the opportunity arises. For now, we will watch, listen, and wait."

While they walked toward the massive blackened arch of the hearth, Elizabeth listened to Mildred chatter. Elizabeth was relieved to hear that despite the days spent in solitude, the matron had not been mistreated in any way. Elena also had brought her meals and helped her dress and wash.

"And you, milady? Have you been treated well?"

Elizabeth nodded. The temptation to blurt out all that had transpired between her and de Lanceau was overwhelming, but she thought better of giving the older woman cause for concern.

They neared the fire. Flames roared over the huge mound of logs and cast an orange glow over the glazed hearth tiles. Several chairs and a side table were lined up before the fire's warmth. Elena sat in one of the chairs, her head bowed over a task in her lap. She cursed and shook her head.

Elizabeth withdrew her arm from Mildred's. "Elena?"

The maid did not look up as Elizabeth rounded the chair. A silk tunic lay across Elena's lap. In her hand she held part of the embroidered hem, damaged by a jagged tear. She jabbed the bone needle into the fabric.

"Ouch!" Elena groaned, dropped the cloth, and sucked the spot of blood on her thumb.

"Elena?" Elizabeth repeated.

The maid glanced up, her eyes round with worry. "Milady. Mildred."

"What is the matter?" the matron asked.

"How will I finish mending this tunic?" Her hands shook, and her face looked pale. Dropping down on her knees, Elizabeth placed a comforting hand on the maid's arm.

"Milord asked me to fix the rip," Elena said with a sniffle. "I have not yet rinsed all the laundry. Mistress Peg asked me to scrub the kitchen floor and chop cabbage and leeks for chicken pies, and I need to see the children fed." Tears welled in her eyes. "I should not complain, but I have much to do and I am tired."

"Let me have a look." Elizabeth took the garment.

"Milady?" Elena whispered.

With gentle fingers, Elizabeth inspected the tear and frayed silver embroidery threads, and mulled the best way to fix them. Her mother had taught her the most difficult embroidery stitches. With care and patience, even the worst rips could be mended.

Her fingers stilled. The tunic must be de Lanceau's. For that reason alone, she should not help repair it. Yet, when she glanced up and saw Elena's tear-streaked face, Elizabeth's reluctance melted. She must help the poor woman.

"The material must be held tighter," Elizabeth said. "Otherwise the silk will sag and be hard to sew. Try to make your stitches smaller. Like this."

Elizabeth pressed the needle into the fabric and took three quick stitches. Her swift, neat work won her a smile from Elena.

Taking the tunic back, the maid tried again. Elizabeth struggled not to frown. Elena's second attempt was better, but her care made her slow. 'Twould take her the entire afternoon to finish the task.

Elizabeth's fingers itched. It had been days since she had embroidered, and she missed working on the orphans' clothes. Focusing on the stitches, pulling the thread just so, and seeing the pattern form on the cloth would be a pleasant diversion.

When Elena's slow progress continued, Elizabeth squeezed the maid's arm. "Go to your tasks. I will finish this for you."

"*You?* Nay, milady. 'Twould not do."

Mildred's chest puffed out like a proud mother hen's. "Why not? She is a fine embroiderer."

Before the maid could utter another protest, Elizabeth curled up in one of the chairs and pulled the tunic onto her lap. Her fingers flew over the silk, each stitch light and deft, and within moments she had mended part of the tear.

Elena stood and glanced at the lord's table. Elizabeth peered around the chair, and saw the men were still bent over the parchment. Dominic looked to be illustrating a point with his finger while de Lanceau nodded, his brow creased into a frown.

The maid shook her head. "If milord finds out—"

Standing next to the hearth, Mildred snorted. "He is far too busy with other matters to worry about a little needlework." She plopped down in an empty chair, folded her hands over her plump belly, and closed her eyes.

Elizabeth had just resumed her work when a shadow blocked her light. She shifted her weight to take advantage of another slant of sunshine, when realization tore through her in a hot-cold tremor.

De Lanceau stood behind her.

"What mischief do you make, milady?" His voice rumbled like thunder.

Clutching the tunic, Elizabeth leapt to her feet. Partway to the stairwell, Elena spun and looked about to faint with fright. Her mouth moved, but no sound emerged.

De Lanceau looked from Elena to Mildred, then at Elizabeth. As he folded his arms across his shirt and quirked an eyebrow, she shivered. "Well?"

Mildred cleared her throat. "Milord, if I may explain."

His gaze did not move from Elizabeth's face. "Aye?"

"Milady offered to help Elena with the embroidery," the matron said matter-of-factly.

"Did she, now?" He snatched the tunic from Elizabeth's hands and scrutinized her stitches. Surprise and admiration lightened his gaze, and his lashes flicked up. "*You* did this?"

"I did."

He swiveled and faced Elena. "Is that so?"

The maid nodded.

"Your work is fine, damsel. Very fine, indeed." His mouth curved into a grudging, lopsided grin.

Elizabeth's breath suspended, caught by a shimmering

magic. His smile held no hint of mockery or malice, but genuine respect. A reverent gleam in his eyes, he traced the embroidery with his thumb. She forced herself to look away.

The matron beamed. "Lady Anne had uncommon skill with a needle and thread, and taught Elizabeth. You were but a scrawny girl when you learned your first stitches, were you not, milady?"

A groan scratched Elizabeth's throat. "Mildred."

De Lanceau chuckled.

The matron tossed her gray braid. "He should appreciate your talent. Many noble ladies embroider, but few have the skill of our dear Lady Anne, bless her departed soul." Her thick brows rose. "Or you, milady. I would wager every good tooth in my mouth that your stitching is the finest in all of England."

Elizabeth blushed. "Mildred."

The rogue's grin widened, and Elizabeth's stomach swooped like one of the diving robins.

"With your talent, he should be paying you to fix that tunic."

An exasperated sigh burst from Elizabeth. "Mildred, cease!"

De Lanceau laughed. "Fret not, milady."

Her face burning, Elizabeth dared to glance at him. His eyes glinted with humor. He bowed his head to her, an elegant, chivalric gesture that made her pulse thump a little faster, and held the tunic out to her.

She hesitated, pretending she did not care whether she finished the task or not, then took it. His smile broadened, and, to her dismay, her blush deepened. She cursed herself for reacting like a giddy girl.

"Milord," Elena said in a hushed voice, her fingers knotted into the front of her bliaut. "May I—"

He dismissed her with a nod. "Resume your duties."

Elena pointed to the silk in Elizabeth's hand. "The tear?"

"Lady Elizabeth will finish the repair since she has the greater skill. If she so wishes," he added.

Confusion and pleasure spiraled within Elizabeth like windblown leaves. He gave her a choice. She looked down at the frayed silk.

Rebellion nagged. She should refuse. He was her enemy, and she owed him naught but hatred. Yet she would rather linger in the hall with Mildred than be cloistered in her chamber.

Nor had she forgotten her vow to escape.

"I will finish it."

"I thank you," he murmured.

The maid curtsied and hurried away.

Brushing a crease from the tunic, Elizabeth turned back to the chair by the fire. De Lanceau did not take his leave. She sensed his stare, and glanced over her shoulder.

Light played over his face and softened the hard line of his jaw. His gaze narrowed, and her fingers curled into the glimmering silk.

Emotion blazed in his eyes, yet she could not define his

expression. Did he suspect her motives?

A strange half-smile touched his lips.

"Milord?"

"You never cease to amaze me, damsel."

His husky murmur sent tingles skittering down her spine. Forbidden heat rushed through her. With shocking intensity, she remembered his lips upon hers, his caress, as well as the regret in his eyes when she told of her mother.

Her legs became unsteady. She dropped into the chair. With stiff fingers, she smoothed out the tunic and yanked the threaded needle into position.

De Lanceau strode away.

❖   ❖   ❖

Geoffrey returned to the trestle table where Dominic waited. He sat, swallowed some wine, and bade Dominic to continue reviewing the last points of the ransom demand, yet Geoffrey's thoughts refused to settle.

He imagined Elizabeth's slender hands moving over his favorite tunic, and the whisper of silk against her fingertips.

Her task seemed intimate, somehow. Or his potent imagination mocked him.

As Dominic's voice droned on, Geoffrey dragged his gaze from the parchment and looked to the hearth. She sat with her lady-in-waiting, their heads bowed in conversation. How she had hated Mildred telling of her embroidery skill. Yet the lady had an exceptional talent few possessed. Her skill deserved more important projects than mending a tunic.

He had such a task.

Painful memories careened into Geoffrey's mind, and he steeled himself against the agony. He had not forgotten and neglected the work, but had saved it until he met an embroiderer with the skill to renew its glory.

Of all ironies, Lady Elizabeth Brackendale had such skill.

A sour taste flooded his mouth and he reached for his wine. She would never agree, not when she understood why. Yet now, more than ever, he wanted the work done.

He would not allow her to refuse.

Shoving his chair back, he rose. Dominic's head jerked up from the parchment, and he looked puzzled. "Milord?"

"I must see to a matter. I will return in a moment."

❈   ❈   ❈

Elizabeth shoved the tunic down on her lap, swiveled in the chair, and glared at her lady-in-waiting. "How could you? Why did you tell that rogue about my mother's skill, and mine?"

"I am sorry." Mildred sighed. "I did not mean to upset you, but I did not think you would mind."

Elizabeth scowled.

"'Tis not so terrible, is it?" Folding her wrinkled hands

together, the matron smiled. "Now he will treat you with the respect you deserve. He seemed impressed by the revelations."

"I do not care to impress him." Elizabeth's tone raised a notch. "You and I are hostages. Have you forgotten we were brought here against our will?"

The warmth vanished from Mildred's gaze. "I have not forgotten. Nor shall I stop trying to find us a means of escape. Yet I will do all I can to protect you. You may be a noblewoman, but all the titles in England cannot save you if de Lanceau decides to take you to his bed."

A gasp parted Elizabeth's lips.

Reaching over, Mildred touched Elizabeth's hand. "I do not mean to alarm you, but we have both heard the stories of maidens held for ransom, who return home with bastards in their bellies."

A log shifted in the hearth. Flames roared, masking Elizabeth's outraged huff. "He would not dare."

"He seems to have treated you with honor thus far, despite his contempt for your sire." Mildred's lips tilted in a saucy grin. "I do believe de Lanceau respects you. Respect, milady, has a power all its own."

A draft blew across the floor, and the fire flickered. Elizabeth shivered. Was de Lanceau's kiss in her chamber the prelude to his ravishing her? She stared down at the tunic and found it wadded into a ball.

"Do not worry." Mildred smothered a yawn with her sleeve. "Keep your wits about you, and all will be well."

"Good advice, milady."

Elizabeth started at the sound of de Lanceau's voice. She had not heard him approach. He stood a few paces away, holding a length of blue silk.

Fighting a blush, she asked, "How long were you listening?"

"I heard no more than Mildred's last words. Should I have come earlier?"

"Harrumph!" Mildred waved a disparaging hand. "You must have more important concerns than our chatter."

"Indeed, I do." Striding closer to Elizabeth, he held out the silk. The tattered, embroidered emblem of a hawk, its wings outstretched for flight, flashed in the sunlight. The faded material was stained and torn almost beyond repair.

She raised her brows. "Another tunic?"

Anger glowed in his eyes. "A saddle trapping. One I have kept for eighteen years."

His words hit her like stones. "Your father's?"

He nodded. "I took it from his horse the night he died. When you are done with the tunic, I want you to mend this trapping. I expect your finest work."

Elizabeth tossed the tunic aside and lunged to her feet. "Never!"

He loomed over her, his face a determined mask. "My destrier will wear it when I ride into battle against your sire. He will know that I am proud to be a de Lanceau, and that I am not afraid to avenge my father."

Rage shook her to her very soul. "I will not."

"You will. I know many methods of persuasion." His gaze smoldered with warning, and he stared at her mouth. "I vow you are familiar with a few."

She was indeed. Her mind and body tormented her with constant reminders. Elizabeth lowered her lashes, refused to let him see her fear. "You are a beast."

His laughter rumbled. "Then you agree?"

A scathing refusal welled in her throat. Yet "nay" was a poor answer when he could force her to yield. If he confined her to her chamber, she might never get a chance to flee. Far wiser to say "aye" and escape him before she finished what he demanded.

Her lips pressed into a line, and she glared up at him with all the fury boiling inside her. "I agree. Not because of your threats, but because you are doomed to fail. Your horse may wear your sire's trapping, but my father will destroy you."

"We shall see, milady."

"Aye, we shall."

He pushed the trapping into her hands and stormed away. His muttered voice drifted back to her, as he spoke with Dominic.

Mildred shook her head. "If I had known he would use your talents in such a way, I would never have—"

"Do not blame yourself." Elizabeth sat back in the chair and set the trapping on the side table. Lowering her voice, she added, "I will not complete it. We will be free before then."

The matron grinned.

Moments later, de Lanceau left the hall, holding the parchment. Dominic walked at his side. As soon as the rogue disappeared from view, Elizabeth exhaled a long breath. Her rigid posture eased.

Mildred soon succumbed to the fire's warmth and dozed with her chin drooping to the front of her gown.

As Elizabeth stitched the tunic, she heard the servants talking, the rattle of crockery as they cleared and scrubbed the tables, the yelp of a dog when it got underfoot. She also learned to distinguish the voices of the two guards by the stairwell, who amused themselves with a game of dice as the day passed. From their rough conversation, she gathered the keep had one well, a gatehouse guarded day and night, and too few horses for their liking, details she tucked away at the back of her mind for her and Mildred's escape.

The fire had burned low when Elizabeth tied the final knot in the thread. Smothering a yawn, she held the tunic up to the fading sunshine and shook out the creases. The embroidery caught the firelight and flashed like a fish out of water.

"'Tis an excellent repair, milady." The matron smiled and looked refreshed after her nap.

"It did mend well." Elizabeth inspected the tiny stitches one last time, pleased herself at how she could not see where the tear had once split the hem's pattern.

Her eyes shining, Elena came to the hearth. "Milady, the tunic looks new again. How can I thank you for helping me?"

Elizabeth covered her mouth with her hand and trapped another yawn. She thought of the agreement Dominic had struck with her that morn which had brought her to the hall, and bit back a disappointed sigh. The rogue had never intended to keep his word.

Shifting in the chair, she eased the cramp in her bottom from sitting so long on a hard seat. With a rueful laugh, she said, "A hot bath would be wonderful."

Elena nodded. "I will fetch it."

Elizabeth almost fell out of her chair. "What did you say?"

"Milord told me to bring a bath upon your request."

"He did?" After their heated words regarding the trapping earlier, she had not expected him to follow through with his vow.

"Lord de Lanceau is a man of great honor. He would never break his word. Not a promise made to a lady."

"How chivalrous," Elizabeth murmured and glanced at Mildred, who arched an eyebrow.

"I shall send the bath to your chamber, milady," Elena said. "I will come and assist you as soon as I have fetched soap, towels, and a basin to rinse your hair." She curtsied and hurried away, murmuring under her breath and ticking off items on her fingers as she went.

At the tromp of approaching footsteps, Elizabeth stood. The guards had come to escort her and Mildred to their chambers.

After anchoring the needle into the remaining thread, she placed both on the table beside the folded tunic. She turned and hugged Mildred. "I will see you anon."

She drew away, but the matron took her hand. "I am glad he granted you the bath. The rogue has a heart, after all."

Elizabeth frowned. "We shall see."

A smile touched Mildred's lips. "I think we shall."

❖   ❖   ❖

Geoffrey met Elena in the stairwell. Head down, one hand flat against the stone wall, she almost ran into him as she descended the spiraling passage.

"Milord." She dropped into an awkward curtsey.

"You are out of breath." He squinted up at her through the smoky torchlight and wished he could read her expression. "All is well?"

"I fetch the lady's bath."

"She has finished the tunic?"

Elena's head bobbed. "You will be most pleased."

He stepped to one side and motioned for the maid to pass. Her footsteps faded as he climbed the last steps, two at a time, to the great hall.

Without breaking his stride, Geoffrey crossed to the empty chairs near the hearth. The garment lay folded on the side table, its design glittering in the firelight.

As he held it up for a better look, a smile tugged at his

mouth. As he expected, the damsel had done well. Swallowing past the tightness in his throat, he let the tunic slide to the table.

His gaze shifted to the trapping, pushed to one side. He rubbed his fingers over the tattered, torn fabric. She resented his demand to mend it, but she had the skill to stitch life back into the cloth, and make the embroidered hawk soar again. He trusted her to make it worthy of his father's memory.

To make it whole.

He lowered his arm and his fingers grazed the parchment tucked into his belt for safekeeping. Today he had learned a great deal about Elizabeth, and also the mother she had adored, a lady who had cared enough about her daughter to spend days teaching her difficult needlework. A vision of Elizabeth's tear-streaked face and anguished gaze flew into his thoughts, and a heavy weight pressed upon his conscience. He forced the memory from his mind.

A child's giggle carried in the hall, and he turned to see a dark-haired toddler dart behind one of the chairs.

"Roydon, come at once." Elena appeared at the top of the stairwell, her cheeks flushed and arms laden with linen towels, rags, and a cake of white soap. "Roydon!"

Geoffrey grinned and pointed to the hearth. "There."

Elena saw him and attempted a curtsey, but the soap tumbled off her pile, followed by two of the towels.

Chuckling, Geoffrey rounded the chair and crept up behind the little boy who was crouched down, watching Elena pick up the fallen items. With a mighty roar, he grabbed the child around the waist and swung him high in the air. Roydon squealed in delight, before Geoffrey set the squirming boy down.

His eyes shone with excitement as he stared up at Geoffrey. "Again."

"Roydon," Elena said in a gentle but firm voice. "To bed with you. I have a lady to tend."

He stuck out his bottom lip. "Mama, 'tis not fair."

Reaching down, she took Roydon's chubby hand in hers and hurried across the hall.

"Elena," Geoffrey called to her.

She halted and looked back at him. "A-Aye, milord?"

"When the lady has finished her bath, bring her to me."

CHAPTER TEN

"The water turns cool, milady. I will fetch you a towel."
Elena set aside the lathered soap and pushed to her feet beside the round wooden tub.

With a reluctant nod, Elizabeth trailed her fingers one last time through the lukewarm bathwater. Candlelight winked off the rippled surface, and the scents of rose, lavender and cinnamon drifted up to her. Elena had poured the fragrance earlier into the bath from a glass-stoppered bottle, and, closing her eyes, Elizabeth savored the exotic essence that reminded her of far away lands.

When she raised her lashes, Elena waited beside the tub. "Please, you must not get a chill."

Elizabeth sighed. After rinsing a soap bubble from her arm, she stood. Water dripped from her hair and body. Shivering, she stepped out of the tub and into the towel Elena held out.

Concern in her gaze, the maid poured a mug of wine from a flask on the table. "Drink. 'Twill warm you."

Elizabeth swallowed a mouthful, glad of the heated glow flowing down inside her.

Once dried, with a towel wrapped around her hair, she took the clean chemise Elena offered. The sheer undergarment was not cut from coarse linen, but fine silk, and felt as light as goose down against Elizabeth's palm.

"Whose garment is this?" she asked, unable to keep the surprise from her voice.

Elena lowered her gaze. "Veronique's, milady."

"Why does she lend it to me?"

"I cannot say."

Memories of Veronique flaunting the gold brooch and her vain hostility whirled through Elizabeth's mind, and she wondered at the leman's motives for being kind. Elizabeth's fingers curled into the silk, and she drank more wine to wash down the bitter taste of indignation.

Dropping the chemise on the table, she said, "I prefer the one I wore before."

Wide-eyed, Elena shook her head. "'Tis a garment fit for your station, milady."

Elizabeth stared down at the gossamer silk and could not hold back a pang of yearning. 'Twould be wondrous to wear such a beautiful garment against her skin, and she could confront Veronique's motives when they were made clear.

"Very well." Elizabeth set down the mug, donned the chemise, and then reached for the green wool. With a hesitant smile, Elena handed her an exquisite bliaut the color of the wild roses that grew inside Wode's bailey. Another of Veronique's garments. As Elizabeth slipped it on, she wondered again what the leman hoped to gain by her generosity.

Elena fastened the gown's ties, stepped back, studied Elizabeth from head to toe, and gave a shy nod of approval.

Elizabeth laughed. She felt like a lady again.

The maid dried Elizabeth's hair by the fire, and tamed it into a braid bound with pink ribbon. She fetched a small, round mirror made of polished steel. "You are beautiful, milady. More so, since you do not require layers of powders and rouges."

Elizabeth stared at her reflection. The eyes that returned her scrutiny appeared wiser and more knowing than days ago. Her face looked slimmer too, mayhap because of the warped metal. But she smiled at her complexion, tinged with pink from the bath's heat, for the bliaut complimented her skin tone.

"You are pleased, milady?"

"I am." Elizabeth placed the mirror on the table. "Thank you, Elena."

The maid beamed. "Milord will be pleased, too."

Elizabeth's smile wavered. She did not wish to hurt the woman's feelings, but she did not care what de Lanceau thought. For the first time in days she felt relaxed, and looked forward to watching the sunset fade into the black velvet of nightfall.

Sipping the last of her drink, she skirted a puddle of spilled water and crossed to the window, the soft wool brushing against her heels. As she drew open the shutters, voices carried on the breeze, children reciting a bedtime prayer.

"I must take you to him now."

One hand gripping the cold stone ledge, Elizabeth faced the maid. "Pardon?"

Panic swam in Elena's eyes. "Lord de Lanceau ordered it. He bade me to bring you to him when you had finished your bath."

"Why?"

"I do not know, milady."

Disquiet pounded in Elizabeth's blood like a drum. Mildred's warnings about ransomed maidens raced through Elizabeth's mind, and she fought for calm. "Tell him I am tired and have gone to bed, and he may speak to me tomorrow."

"A-Aye, milady."

Elena bent and picked up the soap. She was trembling. Did she anticipate a beating? Would de Lanceau punish her, and then send guards to the chamber to see his order obeyed?

Elena was a mere servant, after all, and 'twas her duty to obey the wishes of lords and ladies . . . but after her kindness with the bath, she did not deserve de Lanceau's wrath.

Elizabeth stepped away from the window and set down the empty mug. "I will come. I hope the matter is not important, and I may return here soon."

The maid's eyes shimmered. "Thank you."

When Elizabeth followed Elena into the corridor, the guards straightened away from the wall and fell into step behind her. The passage seemed darker and grimmer than before. The maid led her past rows of hissing torches and into the passage ending at the wooden landing. Despite Elizabeth's sketchy knowledge of the keep, she soon realized the maid led her to the living quarters above the hall reserved for the lord and his family.

To de Lanceau's private solar.

She suppressed a shudder.

A few more steps and the maid halted before two massive oak doors braced with iron hinges bolted into the wood. The doors looked designed for an impenetrable fortress. Elena knocked twice, pushed open a door, and gestured for her to enter. A nervous giggle tickled Elizabeth's throat as she walked inside.

The door boomed closed. The chamber plunged into shadow. Elizabeth whirled and groped for the handle, and her nails scratched over wood. When she found the cold metal ring, it did not budge.

This time, de Lanceau had trapped her in his own cage.

She dropped her forehead against the door and forced herself to breathe. She would not face him with panic screaming inside her like a terrified child. For all she knew, he might ask her a question or two about her father or mending the trapping, and then would let her go.

There could not be many reasons for him to summon her to his solar at night, after a perfumed bath, without a chaperone.

The primary reason that filled her mind was not reassuring.

Elizabeth thrust up her chin. She was the daughter of a strong, respected lord, and she was no coward. She must keep calm and sensible, and see what de Lanceau wanted.

Silence settled around her. Across the room, a fire glowed. Fingers of flame beckoned her, and she headed toward the light.

Her slippers whispered on the wooden floor. Elizabeth held her head high and waited for her eyes to adjust to the solar's dimness. She walked past a large, comfortable-looking bed covered with a silk coverlet and pillows. Opposite were three windows fitted with wrought iron grilles. The chamber must have a magnificent view of the lake and fields in the daylight.

She paused to brush a loose curl out of her eyes and noted the oak table beside the bed, the unlit candles in the sconce on the wall, and, in the darkest shadows, a large wooden chest. The chamber seemed well appointed but not opulent, and well suited to Branton's rogue lord.

As Elizabeth approached the fire, her steps slowed. Two carved chairs were drawn up to the hearth. A table draped with a cloth stood between the chairs, and held a burning candle, a jug of red wine, silver goblets, and assorted sweetmeats on a silver tray. Next to the wine she spied a dish of dried figs, glazed with honey and cinnamon.

Her stomach rumbled. She had not tasted figs in so long—

The solar door slammed behind her.

She screeched. Her hand flew to her throat.

De Lanceau emerged from the shadows and strode toward her. He had shed his white shirt. Another of black wool hugged his shoulders and draped to the thighs of his black hose. He must know he had startled her, but 'twas not laughter that gleamed like gray fire in his eyes.

His strides slowed. His gaze skimmed over her bound hair, down the rose wool, and back up to her hand gripping the back of one of the chairs. "Lady Elizabeth," he murmured.

Her breath burst from her lips.

"I did not mean to frighten you." He picked up the candle on the table, then walked to the wall sconce and lit the tapers and the candles beside his bed. The shadows dissipated into a golden haze. "Better?"

She managed a nod.

"I do not normally light all the candles in the solar," he said, implying he had seen a question in her gaze. "I find the firelight adequate, and the darkness calming after a long day." He crossed back to the table. "I forgot how forbidding the solar can be to those who have not been here before."

His tone was pleasant, but his mild words mocked her fretful thoughts. She would know why he had ordered her here. "Lord de Lanceau—"

"I just came from the hall. As I expected, you did an excellent repair on the tunic."

Elizabeth smothered a startled, pleased smile.

He flicked his hand. "Come. Sit. I promise there are no monsters or ghouls lurking in the shadows." He did not wait for her to reply, or protest, but rounded the nearest chair, lowered himself into it, and stretched his legs toward the hearth.

An uneasy sigh broke from Elizabeth. She did not agree with his comments about monsters and ghouls, but for now, she would do as instructed. She perched on the chair's edge, smoothed the rose wool over her legs, and clasped her hands about her knees. The loose curl sprang back into her eyes and she swatted it away, aware he watched the movement of her hand.

"The gown is to your liking?" His voice sounded husky against the fire's muted roar.

She nodded. "Lord de Lanceau, I must ask. Why—"

"Geoffrey."

"What?"

His mouth twitched. "My given name is Geoffrey. Yours is Elizabeth."

Her hands dampened. "I know milord, but—"

"For this one night, why do we not address one another by our given names? Pretend that we stand on equal ground."

She choked down a gasp. She would never consider a

rogue who intended to destroy her father her equal. Yet until she knew what de Lanceau had planned for her, she would feign ignorance and play along. "Very well . . . Geoffrey."

He smiled. "Now, you were saying?"

Pointing to her bliaut, Elizabeth said, "I do not understand why Veronique was so generous."

"Veronique? Ah, of course. She will miss such a bliaut from her wardrobe."

Elizabeth frowned. Mischief gleamed in his eyes, but she did not understand why. "'Tis a fine bliaut, sewn from quality wool. The chemise is silk rather than linen." She glanced at the logs snapping in the hearth, and her voice lowered. "I am surprised she would lend me such garments after . . ."

"After her scorn this afternoon," he provided.

Elizabeth shifted in her chair and pulled the gown's hem over her slippered toes. "Aye."

"Do not let the matter trouble you." Geoffrey reached over and picked up the stoneware jug. "Wine?"

"Nay, thank you." One mug of wine already tingled inside her, and she must not dull her wits. Yet he had already poured a goblet full and offered it to her. As she took the vessel, her fingers brushed his, but he did not seem to notice.

She curled her fingers against her skirt and sipped. The wine tasted sweet, far nicer than what she drank earlier. She took a large sip. Before she remembered to caution herself, she had downed half. Geoffrey watched her over his goblet's rim, but looked away when a log fell and sparks flew up like tiny, dancing butterflies.

The fire's warmth lulled. Soothed. An odd, companionable silence settled. Beneath lowered lashes, she stole a glance at Geoffrey. Her gaze traveled over his legs outlined by the snug-fitting hose. Horn buttons lined his shirt, and the cloth stretched taut over his wide chest. His muscled physique, sculpted and honed to peak efficiency, revealed his skill as a battle hardened fighter.

A formidable opponent for her father.

Her belly clenched. She sipped more wine, and her gaze shifted up to Geoffrey's angular profile. A day's growth of beard darkened his jaw. Warmth coiled up inside her. He might be a seasoned warrior, but his stubbled jaw proved he was still just a man, formed of flesh and blood. She wondered how his skin would feel beneath her fingertips.

"You are quiet tonight." Geoffrey's voice cut into her musings like a knife through soft cheese.

Elizabeth found his intent gaze upon her. She looked down into the liquid ruby depths of her wine and fought a blush. "I-I was thinking."

"I see." His tone held a trace of humor. Had he noticed her study of him?

"I want to know why you brought me here," she blurted, wishing her voice did not waver. "'Tis not usual for a betrothed lady to meet a man alone in his private quarters." She met his gaze. "I will know your intentions, milord. If you will not answer me, then I wish to return to my chamber."

Geoffrey's fingers tightened around his goblet's stem. A smile flickered across his lips. "You missed the evening meal. I thought you might like something to eat."

Glancing at the food on the table, she said, "That is all?"

He laughed, a rough, dangerous sound. "Not all."

Elizabeth rose to her feet. "Why, then, did you summon me here?" She banged the vessel on the table. Wine sloshed over the rim and stained the pristine white linen . . . and the room swam before her eyes.

"Oh!" She made a frantic grab for the table, and touched Geoffrey's arm.

"The chair is behind you," he said, his voice near her ear. He stood in front of her, she realized through a dizzy blur. As he leaned close and eased her back down to sitting, his earthy, masculine smell filled her nostrils. His prickly jaw grazed her brow. She tried to sit up straight and regain her poise, but her head reeled in a perplexing manner.

"Too much wine," she moaned.

Geoffrey pushed the plate of honeyed figs into her hands. "Here. Eat. You drank on an empty stomach. 'Tis no wonder the floor moves under your feet."

"Sorry." She hated how pathetic she sounded.

He grunted at her apology and sat down. She picked up a fig and bit into it, and found the combination of sweetness and spice delicious. Honey drizzled down her chin. She brushed it away with sticky fingers until Geoffrey sighed and pressed a linen napkin into her hand. Within moments, she finished the plate, and he handed her a bowl of gingered custard and a spoon.

He did not indulge himself, but watched her devour the food. He seemed fascinated. She meant to challenge his stare and the wry grin tugging at his mouth, but first, she would satisfy her hunger. The creamy custard, a little overcooked, dissolved on her tongue and she scooped more onto the spoon, taking care to run it along the bowl's edge to glean every sweet bit.

When she had almost finished, he rubbed his thumb over his mouth. "I suppose I do owe you an explanation."

Elizabeth swallowed her mouthful. Thank God, her head had almost stopped whirling.

"I wanted to satisfy my curiosity."

Wariness crept into her thoughts. "How?"

He looked at her spoon poised over the custard bowl, then at her. "Why did you help Elena this afternoon?"

Elizabeth rubbed her lips together. She had not expected this question. Cupping the bowl between her hands, she said, "Elena was upset because she had many other duties to attend. The embroidery was a simple task for me."

"Elena is a servant," he said in a biting tone.

"What of it?"

His gaze darkened. "She is duty bound to work as long and as hard as I wish. That is her way of life. She was born a villein and worked the demesne fields with her husband until he died in a storm last month."

"How terrible."

Geoffrey stared at the flames. "A tree fell on their cottage and crushed him as he slept."

"I did not know," Elizabeth whispered. At last, she understood the woman's timidity.

"I took pity on Elena and her son Roydon and offered her work in the keep. Yet she is still a servant. Far below your noble caste."

A cold sweat dampened Elizabeth's brow and she shrugged. "I consider her a friend. She has shown me kindness and compassion, and I was glad to help her in return."

His eyes glowed as bright as the candle flame. "Ah," he murmured. "Elena wins greater respect than, say, a gallant stranger who saved your life at the market?"

Elizabeth's stomach did a sluggish turn. Too late, she sensed his careful trap. She set the custard bowl on the table and snatched up her wine goblet. "'Tis not a fair comparison, milord. As well you know."

"Do I?"

Words tumbled from her lips. "You insulted me. You took advantage of your chivalry and demanded a kiss."

"I *demanded* naught. Even so, 'twas not much to ask considering I saved your life." He paused and set his goblet on his thigh. "Tell me, would you have given it?"

A shivered breath caught in her throat. "A kiss?"

"A kiss."

Her gaze darted to his mouth. She could not halt the sinful memories. His lips gliding over hers. His warmth. His taste. "I . . . I cannot say. I did not know you were a lord."

He scowled. Setting down his wine, he steepled his fingers together. "Let us pretend you never discovered my identity. Would you have condemned me to Wode's dungeon because you objected to my harmless jest? Because I teased you about what is natural between a man and a woman?"

Warmth drained from Elizabeth. That morning at the market, he had shocked her with his boldness, and she had spoken without forethought. She felt his verbal snare tighten. "You provoked my anger and—"

"You avoid the heart of the issue," he growled. "Aye or nay?"

"N-Nay."

His breath roared through his lips. She could not tell if he were glad of her answer, or even more furious.

Elizabeth's hands shook. "Is there a point to your questioning, milord?"

"The point, damsel, is I find you puzzling. You flaunt your privileged birthright with annoying haughtiness, yet you also show compassion for a servant who is not of your household, which implies a tender nature. Which is the true Lady Elizabeth Brackendale?"

She stared down at her white-knuckled fingers, which were locked around the goblet. "Does it matter?"

"I find it does." Torment and loneliness threaded through his words. A place deep inside her cried out, and she steeled herself against the foolish empathy.

"I had no reason to withhold my help from Elena," she said, "and would do the same for any servant at Wode. I was taught that lords and ladies should show equal measures of kindness and discipline toward their subjects. Otherwise, they will never win their subjects' best work, respect or loyalty."

Geoffrey nodded. "Wise words."

"My father's words," she said with pride.

Geoffrey's expression darkened. The poignant intimacy vanished like a wisp of smoke. "Your father's." He spat the words like a curse.

Desperate to convince him, to make him see past his hatred, she said, "My father is not the cruel lord you mistake him to be. He is a man of honor and justice."

Menace blazed in Geoffrey's eyes. "With his own sword, your father murdered my sire. I will never forget. Or forgive."

A furious sigh burst from her. "You do not know for certain he cut your sire's mortal wounds. How can you recall what happened eighteen years ago? You were a frightened child, in the midst of a battle."

"Lord Brackendale besieged Wode. He commanded the attack. He gave the orders. The responsibility falls on his head."

"The king's orders!" Her worn patience frayed, about to snap. "My father could not refuse a command issued by the crown. To do so would be treason."

Geoffrey's eyes narrowed to gleaming slits. "Your devotion to your father is admirable, but misplaced. He should have determined, before he led the attack, that my father remained loyal to King Henry, and did not support his intransigent son."

"If there were no justification," she said, her voice as taut as the knot around her heart, "why did the king order the siege?"

"My father was betrayed."

"A theory without proof."

Geoffrey's face, gilded by firelight, hardened with anger. "My father was a powerful lord. His estates covered half of the county of Moydenshire, and he had great prominence in the previous sovereign's reign. I have often wondered if King Henry feared my father's influence."

"If so, that is another reason why my sire is not to blame," Elizabeth said.

Geoffrey's lip curled back from his teeth. "You refer to honor and a lord's duty to the crown. What of greed? I vow like most of the lords in this land, your father wanted his share of the spoils. He would do whatever King Henry asked, including murder an innocent man, to get it."

Elizabeth pushed her empty goblet onto the table. A scream shrilled up inside her. Terrible anguish crushed her hopes of persuading Geoffrey of the truth. How could she reason with a man so embittered, so convinced he was right?

"'Tis senseless to seek revenge for what happened years ago," she choked out. "You cannot change the past. Why can you not find peace within yourself, and forget about Wode?"

Geoffrey lunged with such speed, Elizabeth shrieked.

She slammed against the chair back, her blood hammering in her veins. He gripped the arms of the chair. Ensnared her. Loomed over her. Tremendous anger poured from him.

His breath hissed between his teeth and her forehead burned with the heat of it. "Forget?" he bellowed. "How *dare* you ask that of me? *You* were not there, trying to stop the blood gushing from his chest. *You* were not there when he drew his last breath. *You* did not have to listen as he coughed and gasped and struggled for air. My father was a great man. A man of integrity." Geoffrey's voice cracked. "He was no traitor, and did not deserve to die as one."

"I do not doubt he was a great man," she whispered.

He jerked back a fraction, clearly startled by her agreement, and then glared down at her. She braced herself for more lashing words. Yet his gaze softened. His lips formed a smile tinged with remorse. "Then you understand, milady, why I will take what is rightfully mine. Why I will avenge my father."

Geoffrey's hands fell away from the chair, and he straightened. He crossed to the hearth, braced one hand against the stone wall, and looked down into the fire. Shadows played over his face. He looked tortured, haggard, and . . . human.

"King Richard will never accept your siege of Wode," she said in a hushed tone.

Geoffrey did not stir.

"What you intend is suicide, for my father has the favor of the king. Your attack will be viewed as an act of treason.

The crown will send an army to Wode and reclaim the keep, and you will die in dishonor like your father."

Geoffrey's head tilted. Hair slid down over his brow as he met her gaze. "King Richard has not returned from Crusade. He may be dead. If that is true, his brother John will inherit the throne. The dawn of a new king is the perfect opportunity to secure what is mine." Brutal determination rang in his voice.

"You will seek the favor of John Lackland?" she said.

"I will earn it. I have much to offer in exchange."

"You jest. What can you offer a king that is beyond his sovereign power?"

"Cloth."

She arched an eyebrow. "*Cloth?*"

Nodding, he faced her. "You think me a fool. What if I turned half of Wode's farmlands into pasture?"

"Your villeins would starve." When his lips curved in a disbelieving smile, she snapped, "You have forgotten drought, disease, and plagues of insects. In good years, they threaten the harvests and lessen what is stored for the cold months. In the worst . . ." She remembered the harsh winter seven years ago. "Then, there is naught, for lord or peasant alike."

His smile widened. "Shrewd thoughts, milady, yet I vow I would become a rich man. With that much pastureland, I could raise thousands of sheep. Some would be killed for mutton, but the rest will provide wool. Wool woven into the finest, most sought after cloth in all of England." His eyes glinted. "For a portion of the profits, I vow John Lackland would recognize my birthright to a keep ruled by de Lanceaus for over a hundred years. Well before your father wrested it from us."

"You cannot earn your riches, milord, if you have no means to market the wool."

He chuckled. The disdain in her words did not seem to bother him. "Well said. Yet I have contacts in France and the port of Venice, the center of the silk and spice trades. Good English wool is prized by the French merchants, almost as much as spices and perfumes. Where there is a demand, milady, there is profit."

She swallowed past the ache in her throat. His plans for Wode showed great foresight. He had planned, it seemed, for many years. Unable to school the bitterness from her voice, she said, "You will trade your sword for a merchant's tally stick? You are a hero of the Crusades. A man of war."

He did not even flinch. "I am weary of fighting. When I ride into battle against your father, 'twill be my last."

"True."

His gaze hardened. "My last, because I will triumph. All that I have told you will come to pass."

He moved back to the table, picked up the jug, and offered her more wine. She shook her head.

Elizabeth shut her eyes against a sudden headache. Demand. Profit. Revenge. All of his plans hinged upon her. She was the pivotal pawn, his way to get his fortune and destroy her sire.

Fear cut into her soul. Her father would never agree to de Lanceau's ransom demands. Her father would die before he surrendered Wode. Battle was inevitable. Bloodshed and death loomed like a hideous, fanged specters, and here, snared in de Lanceau's grasp, she was helpless to stop them.

Her heart ached with a pain so profound, she could not bear Geoffrey to see it. Elizabeth pushed up from the chair. Ignoring his brooding gaze, she crossed to the windows and looked out. Thousands of stars sparkled in the sky and reflected back from the lake's glassy surface. How serene the world outside looked, as though war would never scar its beauty.

She sensed, rather than heard, Geoffrey's approach. His hands touched her shoulders, and she stiffened.

"Elizabeth."

Where he touched, awareness blossomed. Her traitorous body still craved him, despite all he had told her. Despite all he intended to do.

With a muffled gasp, she shrugged free of his hold. "I wish to go to my chamber now."

"You have not finished your wine, or the custard."

"I do not want them."

His breath warmed the back of her neck, and stirred the ringlets that had escaped from her braid. She spun around. He stood so near, her hand brushed his sleeve. Stumbling back, she bumped against the cold stone ledge.

A frantic cry warbled within her. She shut it from her

mind. She might be de Lanceau's pawn, but she would not let him intimidate her. Her father refused to yield to a rogue, and so would she. "You may summon the guards now."

"Not yet." His rasped voice sent heat swirling down to her belly, and she swallowed hard.

"'Tis late, milord."

"Mmm." His knuckles brushed her cheek. Then he cupped her face with his hand, holding her captive with a gentle touch. Moving his thumb, he coaxed her chin up, until she stared straight into his eyes. She could feel a tremble weaving through her, and his steely gaze flickered with a hint of regret. "Do not blame yourself for the days ahead, damsel. My battle is not with you."

His tender words rippled through her like water rings spreading across a still pond. How had he known her thoughts? She tried to squirm away, but he did not release her.

"I will not let you kill my father."

Grudging admiration softened his expression. He caressed her cheek. "As you have said before."

"I will stop you."

"You cannot," he whispered without a trace of threat. His free hand skimmed down her side and brushed over her bliaut, near the small of her back.

"W-What are you doing?"

His fingers moved. He had untied her braid. "Such incredible hair," he murmured, and both of his hands threaded through her tresses. "I will never forget the day we first met.

Your hair shone like black silk."

Her pulse thudded with a wildness that excited and ter-rified her. Mildred's warnings echoed in Elizabeth's mind. "Stop. I want—"

"Shh." He pressed his thumb to her lips. His fingers claimed a ringlet and followed its shiny length to where it ended at her waist. "You smell good. Eau de Cypress?"

She shrugged. "Elena poured the fragrance into my bath."

He inhaled a long breath, and then nodded. "I brought the scent from Acre. Once, a woman could win my favor by wearing it."

He leaned closer. His hands spanned her waist and warmed her skin through the gown. Desire rushed through her limbs. She must stop him, before he kissed her. Or she would be lost.

"Do you know how beautiful you are?" he breathed against the side of her face. His breath was a caress against her skin, and heat shot down into her quivering belly.

Reason nagged at her muzzy thoughts. "I must . . . re-turn to my chamber."

He shook his head. "I forbid it."

"Why? What are you going . . . to do?"

His smoldering gaze turned intent. Purposeful. "What I have wanted to do all evening."

His arms went around her waist.

His mouth brushed hers.

Never before had she experienced such a kiss. His lips

came down with the silken touch of a butterfly's wings. He did not aim to possess, but entice. He did not demand she kiss him in return. With each stroke of his lips, he offered an invitation, in an unspoken language as old as the first dawn.

Her body recognized that language. Responded. Her eager lips parted, and their tongues meshed.

Sensation shimmered, sweeter and richer than before. She must protest. Force him away. Her hand came up to push against his chest, but of its own volition, wound into his shirt.

She mewled, a cry of urgent need. Her body pressed against him. Hungry. Hungry . . .

He gasped against her lips. Shuddered. He broke away from her, swearing into the darkness, and pushed her to arm's length.

"Geoffrey?" she whispered.

Breathing like a winded stallion, he looked at her. Fury flashed in his eyes.

She touched her tingling lips, and struggled against an overwhelming sense of loss.

His mouth slanted into a mirthless grin. "You will not sway me that way, milady."

She blinked. "What?"

"You hoped to seduce me."

"Nay!" She jerked out of his grasp like he had slapped her.

His harsh laughter grated like a dagger against stone. "You are quite the temptress, when you put a little effort into your kiss. You would put Eve to shame. How foolish of me, to think you were innocent of such methods of deception."

Tears stung her eyes. "You are mistaken."

"I think not."

The depth of her anguish confused her. This rogue meant naught to her. She should not care whether he believed her or not. "Why would I wish to seduce you?"

"You hoped to find my weakness. To make me soften toward your father." His tone thinned. "Mayhap you thought I might decide to free you. Whatever the reason, I will never yield."

Rage devoured the torment inside her. "You are despicable."

"And you play with fire, damsel. If I so desired, I could take what you just offered me. Here. Now."

Elizabeth shook with fury. And fear. He did not make an idle threat. From the fierce set of his jaw, the rock-hard glare of his eyes, he had spoken true.

Would he do as he said?

"I never intended to tempt you," she said, with far more boldness than she felt. "I came here because you summoned me, remember? I did not choose this gown, or the fragrance Elena put in my bath. Nor do I have the slightest desire to lie with you."

"Nay?"

She sniffed, a sound of acute disdain. "I would rather clean the keep's garderobes than offer myself to you."

"Is that so?" A wicked gleam lit Geoffrey's eyes before his teeth slashed white in the darkness. Did he imagine her tackling the smelly task that even the lowest servants despised?

"'Tis so," she said.

"Such a convincing rejection."

She crossed her arms. "'Tis the truth."

"Careful, damsel, or you might get your wish."

"You would have me clean garderobes?" Elizabeth shot him a withering look. "I think not."

"And I think you tread a perilous path," Geoffrey growled. He whirled away from her, the hem of his shirt billowing, and marched toward the solar doors. His boots thundered on the wooden floor. "Go back to your chamber, before I decide I preferred your earlier offer."

Elizabeth ground her teeth. "I was *not*—"

Geoffrey yanked open the door with such force, it banged against the wall. "Out, damsel. Before I do something we both regret."

CHAPTER ELEVEN

"Up ye get, milady."

Elizabeth opened a bleary eye to see two guards standing beside her bed. One shoved a candle near her face and leered down at her.

Rubbing sleep from her eyes, she sat up. "What do you want? Why do you intrude upon my slumber?"

"Our lord requests ye," said the heavyset guard who appeared enthralled by her dishabille. His eyes wandered over her night shift and she promptly tucked the bedding under her armpits to curtail his ogling.

"He summons me *now?*" Elizabeth shoved hair out of her face and peered past the men to the window. The faintest glow of dawn was visible beyond the shutters' slits. With a groan, she collapsed back on the bed in a tangle of blankets.

"Ye best come with us, milady," said the other sentry.

He nudged his comrade and snickered behind his hand. She glared at the stocky lout, wondering what he found so amusing about her predicament, and in answer he thrust a stumpy finger at the green wool. "Ye are to get dressed."

"Not with you standing there. Await me outside," she said in a firm voice. "I will knock on the door when I am clothed."

The heavyset oaf scowled and opened his mouth, then shrugged and did as she asked.

Elizabeth rose from the bed and shook out the green wool. After her confrontation with Geoffrey last eve, had he decided she no longer needed a maidservant to help her dress? Wretched rogue. Shivering in the draft from the window, she stripped off her shift and donned the plain linen chemise. By some miracle, Elena walked into the chamber at the very moment Elizabeth attempted the ties of the bliaut. The maid set down the meager breakfast of bread, blackberries, and ale, and hurried to Elizabeth's side.

"Why am I summoned? Does he wish me to begin mending the saddle trapping?" she asked as Elena fastened the garment.

"I do not know, milady."

"Your hands are shaking."

The maid held Elizabeth's gaze, then looked down at the floor. "Milord is in a strange mood this morn." Elena urged Elizabeth to the wooden stool near the hearth and, when she sat, began to braid her tresses.

As the ivory comb slid through her hair, Elizabeth

thought back to last eve. Geoffrey had plied her with wine and sweetmeats, told her of his past wounds and future ambitions, and then, of all wicked wonders, he had kissed her. With tenderness. For a fleeting moment, he had become a chivalrous suitor trying to woo her affection. When he had unbound her plait, his hands had been as gentle as Elena's. The memory of his caresses and kisses crept across her skin, and Elizabeth tried to quell her thoughts by brushing a wrinkle from her bodice.

On Elena's instruction, Elizabeth lowered her chin so the maid could secure the braid. Yet the memories persisted like an unsettling dream. The rogue's livid expression and growled words revived in her mind with a wallop. *You hoped to seduce me.*

She frowned down at her clasped hands. She *had* encouraged his kisses—indeed, he had a most tempting and skillful mouth—yet how could he make such an accusation? He had initiated the intimacy. She should accuse him of trying to seduce her.

Annoyance burned the last vestiges of sleep from her brain. 'Twas not her fault he had a temper shorter than a pig's tail.

Her gaze drifted over the beautiful rose wool and fine chemise, folded on the table where she had left them. "Why I must wear this horrible gown? I thought I could wear the clothes of a lady again."

"I do not know," Elena said in a hushed voice. "Milord

was quite specific about your garments."

After downing her breakfast, Elizabeth followed the maid into the corridor. The guards did not take her to the great hall, or Geoffrey's solar, but to the bailey.

As she stepped out of the musty forebuilding, surprise and excitement thrummed in Elizabeth blood. Overhead stretched the robin's egg blue sky. The breeze stirred her gown and teased wisps of hair across her cheek, and brought the smells of horse, damp stone, and blooming wildflowers. A child's voice carried to her, and she saw a boy toss a pail of scraps to the rooting pigs.

Laughter drew her attention to the straw-roofed stables. Geoffrey stood leaning against one of the wooden wagons, chatting with Dominic. Sunlight shot the rogue's dark hair with silver highlights that reminded her of his eyes' gleam when he challenged her to a verbal joust. Her stomach squeezed. How handsome he looked, wearing a leather jerkin, tight brown hose, and leather boots.

The guards ordered her forward. As she walked out of the keep's shadows into daylight, he turned and saw her. His expression turned guarded. "Milady."

She walked past the snuffling pigs and halted before him. "Milord, why did you bring me to the bailey? Am I to embroider outside this day, to better see my stitches?"

Dominic chuckled. She looked into his round, expressive eyes, and he glanced across the bailey. Whatever the secret was, he would not tell her.

"Patience, damsel. All will be clear soon." A mysterious twinkle lit Geoffrey's eyes.

"By the blessed Virgin." At the sound of Mildred's voice, Elizabeth turned. The matron hastened toward her, doing her best not to trip on the hem of a mud-brown bliaut. "Good morn, milady. Milord." She attempted a curtsey. "Lord de Lanceau, pray tell me why you roused me from my warm bed. My old bones do not see daylight until the sun is risen."

Geoffrey answered with a crooked smile.

Mildred's eyes narrowed. "If an old woman may be so bold, what mischief have you concocted for us?"

"'Tis your lady's bidding."

Elizabeth started. *"Mine?"*

"You told me you wished to clean the garderobes."

Horror slid through Elizabeth like chunks of ice. She had indeed made such a rash claim, but had not expected him to believe her every word.

Mildred wailed and slapped a wrinkled hand to her brow. "Milady, what have you done now?"

"I did not say I desired such a task." Elizabeth scowled. "If you remember the circumstances of my comment, you will know I am right."

Geoffrey's gaze clashed with hers. "Our talk last eve made me consider many things. As I told you once before, we have too many tasks for too few hands at Branton. I questioned why I kept two able-bodied women sitting by the fire when they could earn their keep."

Mildred huffed. "Milady mended your tunic."

"That is not the kind of toil I mean."

An angry blush warmed Elizabeth's cheeks. "You hold us hostage. You cannot mean for us to—"

"I regret the garderobes were cleaned two weeks past," he said and straightened away from the wagon. "Otherwise I would have obliged. However, the keep's gardens need tending. You"—he pointed to Elizabeth and Mildred—"will see it done."

Elizabeth tsked. "What a shame, I am not able to mend the saddle trapping. You will have to ride into battle without it."

His insolent smile broadened. "After you have finished your day's labor in the gardens, you will work on the repair." He thrust an iron-edged spade and a billhook toward her. "You may begin gardening now."

"This is madness," the matron sputtered.

Elizabeth stared at the implements, and her fury flared. He expected her to dig up weeds and dirty her hands and clothes like a commoner? She glared at him.

An answering gleam heated his gaze. He expected the refusal on the tip of her tongue.

As she stared at him, standing cross-armed with one eyebrow raised, she forced down an indignant scream. The knave wanted her to protest. He hoped she would throw a tantrum and refuse to cooperate, so he could belittle her in front of his men and have the satisfaction of forcing her to his will.

Elizabeth bit back a smug laugh. If he anticipated an easy victory, he was mistaken.

She accepted the billhook, and her graceful fingers curled around the spade's wooden handle. "Of course, milord."

Geoffrey's face pinched as though he chewed a mouthful of pig slop. "What?"

Mildred gasped.

"Sunshine and gentle exercise do wonders for a lady's figure and complexion. Will there be aught else, Lord de Lanceau?" Elizabeth tilted her face in a gesture of eager compliance.

The rogue looked baffled. His mouth opened, and then snapped shut. "That is all. For now," he added with a snarl.

She beamed. "Lead the way."

He stalked past her, his brow creased into a forbidding frown, and Elizabeth smothered a gleeful whoop. She flipped her braid over her shoulder and strolled off across the bailey after him, carrying the spade like a foot soldier's pike.

"Saints preserve us," Mildred groaned.

Elizabeth followed Geoffrey past the well, the maidservants airing blankets, the blacksmith's shop and roaring fire, to an area surrounded by a wooden palisade. He yanked open the gate, and the iron hinges creaked with disuse. "The garden."

She brushed past him. It must have been beautiful once. Now the vegetation grew in such tangled profusion she could not tell bush from vine, or weed from herb. Insects buzzed.

A straggling rose bush with spent blooms grew across the stone path that started at the gate and vanished into the undergrowth.

Mildred shuffled to Elizabeth's side. "By the blessed Virgin," the matron whispered, mopping her face with her sleeve.

"Which . . . ah . . . patch do you wish us to weed, milord?" Elizabeth asked. A wasp hurtled out of the bushes and, shrieking, she flicked it away.

He chuckled. "You misunderstand. I wish you to restore this garden to its original grandeur."

"*All* of it?"

"Aye." He kicked aside a stone with the toe of his boot. "When you are finished, you will tell me what plants and herbs are here and what I need to purchase."

Mildred's eyes brightened with interest. "Herbs?"

"A former lord of Branton Keep hired a monk from a local monastery to lay out the garden and stock it with herbs. Some were used for medicines. Others were dried or went straight into the cooking." Geoffrey's smile turned wry. "As Lady Elizabeth pointed out at one meal, adding flavor to our food will be an improvement."

"'Tis a monumental task you give us." Elizabeth dropped the spade with a *clank*. "We cannot complete it in one afternoon."

"I give you two."

"Two days?" Mildred snorted.

Geoffrey's eyes glinted like polished silver as he looked Elizabeth. "Two days." He turned, walked out into the bailey, and slammed the gate closed behind him.

The matron plopped down on the edge of a crumbling rockery. "Harrumph!"

After retrieving the spade, Elizabeth uprooted a dandelion by her feet. "The sooner we start, the sooner we finish."

"I am a lady-in-waiting and a healer, not a brawny gardening wench," Mildred grumbled. "This garden is so overgrown it no doubt harbors all kinds of nasty creatures— spiders, snakes, and red-eyed rodents, to name a few. If you ask me, you are better off apologizing to that rogue for whatever he is annoyed about and saving your strength for our escape." She frowned and scratched her head. "What *is* he annoyed about?"

Her cheeks burning, Elizabeth attacked the grass growing between the path stones. Her bruised arm was healing well, and did not twinge with the effort.

She would not fail to meet the rogue's challenge.

Nor did she wish to explain last eve to Mildred.

"Milady?"

Elizabeth cringed at the matron's suspicious tone.

"Since we will be working together all day, milady, I see no better time for you to divulge all the details. Do you?"

❦　❦　❦

Geoffrey halted outside the garden and motioned to the armed sentries who had escorted Elizabeth to the bailey. "Stand guard at the gate. The women are not to escape."

The nodded and trudged over to their posts.

Exhaling a harsh breath, Geoffrey tipped his face up to the sky, and willed himself not to plow his fist into the palisade.

He would not let the damsel win.

He had meant to bend Elizabeth to his will, to teach her that although she tempted him, she would never control him or his deeds. He had expected her to toss her hair and stamp her foot like a spoiled child, or burst into tears. Instead, she walked to the gardens like a woman anticipating a delightful day of picnicking and hawking, even with the spade slapping against her skirt. The lady astounded him.

Admiration and desire battled in his thoughts. He shook his head and strode back toward the keep. Right now, he wanted her out of his sight, rather than sitting within easy glance. He needed a quiet spate in the hall to finalize some important matters, without a black-haired, blue-eyed distraction.

As he neared the forebuilding, Dominic's laughter greeted him. "Well done, milord."

"Well done?" Geoffrey crossed to his friend, who helped a boy draw water up from the well. "The lady made a fool of me."

"Did she?" Dominic's grin was innocent enough, though

the warmth in his eyes proved he knew quite well.

"She will not last. Before the midday meal, she shall be begging to return to her chamber."

As the lad heaved the filled bucket from the well's edge and stomped toward the pig's trough, water splashed onto the ground. The boy could not be more than ten, Geoffrey's own age when his father died. When his life changed forever.

Quelling another surge of fury, Geoffrey looked at Dominic. "My friend, find me a suitable messenger. 'Tis time to send the ransom demand."

✦   ✦   ✦

"If I do not stretch my aching joints, I shall be kneeling for the rest of my living days." With a pained grunt, Mildred pushed up from her place beside a pile of pulled weeds. "I will see what awaits us farther down the path, milady." Without waiting for a reply, she raised her bliaut's hem and trudged into the undergrowth.

Elizabeth set down the spade. The earlier breeze had vanished, and now the sun beat upon her back. Her bliaut and chemise stuck to her body like a second skin that chafed. Why, oh why, had she goaded the rogue?

The garden did not offer any hope of escape. As she had discovered during a quick perusal, the only way in and out was through the gate. The palisade was too high to scale or jump. Moreover, the gnarled plum tree did not grow close enough to the fence to use its boughs to climb over.

"Will you come too?" the matron called. "Spare me from the ticks, snakes, and red-eyed rodents. I recall you once questioned my sense of adventure."

Elizabeth chuckled and started down the path.

As she batted away a bumblebee disturbed by the movement of snarled vines and leaves, Mildred clucked her tongue. "Weeding is not a task for a noblewoman. De Lanceau must be very angry with you for what happened last eve."

"He is a fool."

Mildred's chuckle sounded as dry as the browned rose petals that disintegrated in Elizabeth's fingers. "You told me yourself he thought you tried to seduce him."

"I know naught about seducing a man."

A crow cawed from its perch atop the palisade fence. Elizabeth glanced at it, and did not notice Mildred had come to a halt until she almost walked right into the old woman.

Brushing a cobweb from her sleeve, Mildred glanced over her shoulder. "You need but look at a man with your blue eyes, and I vow he is lost."

Elizabeth felt a strange pang of discomfort, for Aldwin once teased her with a similar remark. At the time, she had dismissed it as a jest.

"You must know how smitten Sedgewick is." Mildred sidestepped the anthill in the middle of the path and resumed her steady plod. "I expect Aldwin is too, and there must be countless others of whom you do not even know."

Loosing a silent groan, Elizabeth wished she had not told Mildred of last night's events. "De Lanceau is not smitten. The last thing I want is more of his attentions." She had only to think of his smoldering, heavy-lidded gaze and her belly flip-flopped in an alarming way.

"He *is* handsome," the matron said with a wistful sigh. "A rogue indeed, but most pleasing to the eye."

"Mildred."

The matron shrugged. "I may be old, but I am not blind."

A blush stung Elizabeth's face. "This chatter is pointless."

Planting her feet on the weed-choked path, Mildred turned around. "I am trying to understand our day of toil. Mayhap you had a reason for your actions last night of which I am unaware."

Elizabeth threw up her hands. "I did *not* try to seduce him."

The healer grinned. "As you claimed before."

"Do you believe that I could . . . that I *would* seduce him?"

Mildred seemed to mull the question, then nodded. "I think you would do whatever you must to stop him from harming your father, or reclaiming Wode."

Elizabeth frowned. "You place a great deal of faith in my abilities as a temptress."

"Milady, you are as sweet and ripe as a summer rose. More than ample temptation for any buzzing bee or hornet." With a swish of her skirts, Mildred spun and walked off down the path.

Elizabeth blinked. She was still struggling to find a

suitable retort when Mildred dropped to her knees beside a leafy plant with yellow flowers.

"Rue." The matron pointed to the spiny-looking plant nearby. "Rosemary. This must have been the herb patch."

Crossing to Mildred, Elizabeth knelt in the carpet of coarse grass. Stringy weeds with pinkish flowers blocked her view, and she tugged at the stems to remove them.

The matron brushed her hand away. "That is sage. A healthy bunch too."

Elizabeth sighed and sat back on her heels. "It all looks like weed to me."

"If you clear the path," Mildred suggested, "I will tend the herbs."

Reluctant to walk back and fetch the spade, Elizabeth tugged on a vine growing over the path stones. It did not budge.

Bracing her leg against a crumbling rock wall, she took the vine in both hands. She gritted her teeth, yanked, and yelped as the roots tore free. She landed on her bottom.

"Milady!" Mildred leapt to her feet. Her mouth gaped, and Elizabeth started to giggle. She could not help it. She must look a sight, sitting in a most unladylike position with her bliaut scrunched up around her knees. Filthy knees, too.

The matron's cheeks turned pink, and then she too laughed.

✺   ✺   ✺

Geoffrey wiped sweat from his brow and urged his destrier under the teeth of Branton's wood and iron portcullis. As he emerged from the gatehouse's shadows, he waved to the sentries calling to him from the wall walk. He had dreaded taking a preliminary tally of the harvest soon to be carted from the demesne fields, but as Dominic assured him, the rains several days ago had been lighter here than on the roads near Wode. The drying crops had sustained little damage. The yield would be higher than expected.

Before leaving the keep, Geoffrey had dispatched Troy to Tillenham with the ransom. He had also sent missives to the few knights under his command, telling them that he would require their military services.

Soon, very soon, he would have vengeance.

Shrugging stiffness from his shoulders, Geoffrey glanced at the guards posted outside the garden gate. They acknowledged him with a nod. He thought to inquire after the damsel when a sound reached him. He frowned, reined in his horse, and listened for the noise that had been dimmed by the bridle's *clink*.

Laughter. It came from the garden.

Geoffrey had not expected Elizabeth's merriment, but he did not mistake her voice, bright, musical, and alluring as a summer breeze. It held none of the caution she used when she spoke to him, and he regretted being denied the pleasure of her laughter.

His fingers tightened around the leather reins. Elizabeth meant naught to him, and he did not care whether she laughed or cried. He had given her a day of work so foreign to a pampered lady she should have wilted from exertion hours ago.

Instead, she laughed.

A maidservant strolled past, carrying a basket covered with a linen cloth. She curtsied to him and approached the guards.

"Wait," Geoffrey said. He slid down from the destrier and took the basket.

The girl looked bewildered. "Cook ordered me to deliver two meals to the garden. Did you not request it, milord?"

Geoffrey patted the maidservant's arm. "I will take the food. Lead my horse to the stable."

The gate squeaked as it swung open, but the laughter did not cease. He headed down the path, foliage hissing against his boots with each stride. A few more steps and he spied Mildred's broad back turned to him.

He slowed. Where was the lady?

His gaze fell to the grass, and he drew a sharp breath. She sat on a broken stone, grinning like a reckless child, her bliaut raised to her knees. Her pale ankles and calves were bared to the sunlight. What curvaceous legs. Desire hurtled through his blood with the speed of an attacking hawk.

His boot hit a half-buried rock, and Elizabeth glanced up and saw him. With a startled cry, she jumped to her feet and brushed shredded leaves from her bliaut.

He cloaked his lust with biting words. "Merriment? Have I not given you two enough work?"

Mildred greeted him with a huff. "You must have seen our progress as you walked, milord—the mounds of weeds, and cleared section of path."

"You have done fair work." As he expected, indignation gleamed in Elizabeth's eyes. He strode forward and presented her with the basket. "When you have eaten, I expect your toil to continue."

Her eyebrows arched. "Or what, milord?"

He scowled. "You would be wise not to tax my patience any further. You would not like the consequences."

She snatched the basket from his hand and set it on the ground. "An empty threat."

Her boldness surprised him. Desire surged again, hotter than before. "Must I remind you of last eve when you tried my fortitude? This time, I shall ensure that you never forget my warnings."

Her glare could have blasted the feathers off a strutting cockerel. "You do not frighten me, and I will never allow you to humiliate me in that manner ever again."

With lazy fingers, he plucked a leaf from her hair. "How will you stop me?"

She flushed and jerked away. "I am not such a fool as to tell you."

"Nay, a fool to challenge me when you know I will win."

Moisture shone on her lips. He longed to kiss her. To appease his fury with her sweet, virgin essence. The most irrational of cravings, to make her his. "Do you doubt my words?"

"Only a fool relishes his victory before he has won," she shot back with a slight tremor in her voice.

He leaned closer. Her eyes widened, and he smiled. "You are the fool. You are but a tiny sparrow, spitting seeds at a hawk who could snare you in his talons and make a meal of you whenever he wishes."

"A hawk?" She snorted. "Nay, you are the ugly wasp, who likes to announce his importance to all around him with his obnoxious buzz. The noise soon becomes tiresome. So much so, in fact, 'tis only a matter of days before he finds himself well and truly *swatted*."

"Swatted?" He grinned. "Ah, damsel, then you had best beware my *stinger*." He watched her face, fascinated by the emotion in her eyes as she pondered his bawdy words, and then understood them.

Her hand fluttered to her throat. Before he could dive in again, Mildred elbowed in between them and nudged Elizabeth behind her.

The matron wagged a dirty finger in his face. "You will cease this crude banter."

"Crude banter?" he repeated in a bland tone.

"Do not pretend to misunderstand me."

He caught Elizabeth peering past the protection of Mildred's plump shoulder, and laughed. "You need not fear for her virtue. She is not appealing covered with dirt, sweat and twigs."

Elizabeth gasped.

Mildred's gaze narrowed. "I warn you, de Lanceau. You had best keep your *stinger* where it belongs—in your hose."

He smiled, turned, and sauntered back toward the gate.

❧   ❧   ❧

Her fingers curled at her sides, Elizabeth watched Geoffrey stride away, light and shadow slanting over his lithe body. Through his taunting, he had admitted his desire for her. He had no right to accuse her of seducing him, when, from what little she knew of such matters, a man gripped by desire did not need further enticing.

He was far more of a threat than she realized.

Mildred touched Elizabeth's arm. "Do not look so grim. He is leaving."

Geoffrey disappeared behind a clump of bushes that stretched out over the path, and a moment later, Elizabeth heard the gate close. She sighed and flexed her hands.

"The sooner we leave Branton Keep, the better, I warrant," Mildred said. She walked over to the basket and removed the linen cloth, and the aroma of freshly-baked bread wafted. "There is wine, bread, and cheese. Here, milady, have a drink. Put color back in your cheeks." As the matron poured wine into a mug and handed it to Elizabeth, she asked, "Were you injured when you fell?"

Elizabeth looked down into the shimmering red wine. "I may have a bruise on the morrow, but 'tis all."

With her foot, Mildred nudged aside the creeper that been so difficult to pull out. She paused, then squatted and fingered the patch of upturned earth and roots. Her face glowed with excitement, and she pointed to the slender plant that had grown in the vine's shade. "Milady, look."

Sipping her drink, Elizabeth moved closer.

The matron gently blew dirt from the plant's waxy dark green leaves and purplish flowers. The pretty blossoms were shaped like a mantle's deep hood.

"Another herb?" Elizabeth asked.

Mildred shook her head. "Monkshood. It might be our way to escape."

ChAPTER TWELVE

"Tell me about the monkshood," Elizabeth whispered, and pushed her needle into the trapping draped across her lap.

Looking down at her hands, the matron cleared her throat and shifted the hose she was mending. Mayhap to get better light. Mayhap to ease a twinging muscle.

Mayhap in warning.

After the evening meal, Geoffrey had sent them to sit near the hearth. They were not alone. Daring to raise her lashes, Elizabeth looked at the trestle table drawn near the fire, where Dominic and Geoffrey sat hunched over a game of chess. Dominic's fingers hovered over the carved walrus ivory pieces as he pondered his move, his brow creased in concentration. The rogue sat with his chin on one hand, drumming his fingers on the table.

Geoffrey glanced up. His fingers stilled. His keen gaze

skimmed over her, and his mouth curved into a little smile. He had looked at her that way when they passed in the stairwell, as the guards brought her in from the gardens. Exhausted beyond words, she had staggered into her chamber to find a bath waiting, an unexpected courtesy he must have arranged and for which her weary muscles were grateful.

Yet she did not for one moment believe the kindness was an apology for his ribald teasing. Nor did she intend to apologize for calling him a wasp.

Dominic slid his rook into the middle of the board, a move which left his queen unprotected. Geoffrey shook his head and looked back at the game.

Elizabeth released her held breath.

"He watches you," Mildred said in hushed tones.

"I know. Keep your voice down, and do not look up."

"Harrumph! 'Tis hard to do when I feel the weight of those gray eyes upon me."

"I know." Elizabeth sighed and brushed a loose thread from her rose wool gown.

Leaning forward, Mildred dipped the hose toward the firelight and pretended to tackle the split seam. "Monkshood is very poisonous," she murmured. "'Tis safest used as a root, ground up with fragrant oils like lavender and rosemary to rub into aching joints and to dull pain. Yet I have, on occasion, mixed a small amount with wine and honey and made an excellent sleeping potion."

Elizabeth tilted her head, intrigued. "Sleeping potion?"

"A few swallows will make a grown man doze like a babe."

Keeping her movements languid, Elizabeth swept a stray lock of hair over her shoulder. Holding up a chess piece, Geoffrey met her gaze. She looked down and resumed her embroidery. "That is all well and good," she said quietly, "but how do we get the rogue to drink it?"

The matron chuckled, the soft sound masked by the hiss and crackle of the fire. "'Twill be easier than you think."

"We cannot tip it into his ale before a meal. In the hall, he never lets us out of his sight, unless we are watched by guards."

"If we get to the kitchens," Mildred said, "we could add it to the jugs to be brought to the tables."

Elizabeth's pulse jolted. "Every grown man and woman in the keep, apart from the few guards patrolling the wall walk, will fall into a slumber."

"Correct."

She envisioned de Lanceau's eyes snapping shut and him slumping face first into a trencher of stew, and smothered a grin. The thought was even more appealing when she imagined his fury at being duped by two women and a few drops of sleeping potion brewed from plants from his own garden.

Caution nibbled the edge off her excitement. "How long does the slumber last? I would never forgive myself if aught happened to Roydon or the other children while their parents were oblivious."

"That is my worry too, though I expect the older ones would look after the younger." Mildred shook her head. "I wish I could remember how long the potion works. I cannot even recall how much monkshood to use, for at Wode, I follow a receipt written out in one of my treatises." Her nose wrinkled. "Pah! If only my brain were twenty years younger."

Elizabeth examined her row of stitches. "We have no choice but to improvise. We must escape."

"'Tis unwise to guess when using poison." Mildred knotted her thread, her voice lowering to a whisper. "I dare not think what might occur if we get the proportions wrong."

Laughter erupted at the chess table.

"'Twould not be so awful to tinker with the mighty lord's constitution," Elizabeth muttered. "He might feel better for it."

The matron's hand flew to her mouth to smother a laugh, but not fast enough.

Had Geoffrey and Dominic heard the cackle?

Elizabeth held up a section of silk and cast the men a sidelong glance. Her fears dissolved like honey in hot wine. Tense and flushed, Dominic complained of foul play while Geoffrey crossed his arms, grinned from ear to ear, and boasted the arrogance of a barnyard rooster.

"There is one obstacle we must overcome," Mildred said.

Elizabeth's gaze flew back to the matron. "Aye?" With gentle strokes, she smoothed the silk with her palm before starting another neat line of stitches.

"We must get access to the kitchens. I cannot brew the

potion without a fire."

"Leave that to me."

"Milady?" Trepidation rang in the matron's voice.

Mildred had a right to be worried, they both did, but with escape near, they must focus on achieving it. Elizabeth winked. "I will stir the rogue's ire, and shall win us scullery work by tomorrow morn."

Excitement tingled over Elizabeth's skin like tiny, melting snowflakes. Her mind half-tuned to the men debating the chess game, she settled back in the chair, tucked her legs underneath her, and concentrated on the silver thread bobbing in and out of the silk. As tired as she was from the day's labor, she no longer minded her discomfort.

Soon, she would be free. Her imprisonment at Branton Keep would be no more than an unpleasant memory.

Soon, she would foil the rogue's plot for revenge and be reunited with her father.

Soon she would face the baron again and the prospect of wedding him. Yet she would confront those difficult days when she had to.

A muffled snore disturbed her concentration, and her fingers paused in mid-stitch. Mildred had fallen asleep. Her head lolled to one side, her mouth drooped open, and the hose lay in a rumpled heap over her stomach. With a tender smile, Elizabeth reached over and pried the needle and hose from Mildred's fingers, and set the garment on the side table.

As Elizabeth rearranged the saddle trapping in her lap,

she yawned. Fragrant logs snapped in the hearth, the sound and heat as comforting as a winter blanket. Fatigue dulled her senses as well as any sleeping potion.

Much later, she sensed the trapping being lifted from her hands. Muscled arms gathered her to a chest that smelled of leather, soap, and summer air. She tried to open her eyes, to rouse her groggy mind, but the effort proved too great.

Her bed ropes creaked as she was laid upon it. A callused hand smoothed away the hair that had fallen over her face, with a touch that seemed almost gentle.

She sighed, and a deep slumber claimed her.

CHAPTER THIRTEEN

Elizabeth opened her eyes and blinked up at the sunlit beams above her bed. Rolling onto her side, she winced. Her shoulders ached. Her legs hurt. Her back twinged when she so much as lifted a finger. Moreover, all her fingernails were split and had a line of dirt underneath them, and her hands bore little resemblance to the smooth, unblemished, lily white ones she possessed only yesterday.

As she levered up on one elbow, she discovered she had fallen asleep without changing into her night shift, and had slept on top of the bedcovers.

Confusion and embarrassment whooshed through her. She did not remember getting into bed without taking off her gown. She could not even recall leaving the great hall.

Where was Elena this morning?

Determined to stagger to the jug of water and wash her

face, Elizabeth pushed herself up to sitting. She groaned. Somehow, she would walk the five paces to the table.

As she sat with her calves dangling over the bed's edge, summoning the energy to step onto the cold floorboards, the door swung open. Geoffrey strode in. He looked refreshed and handsome in his black hose and knee-length russet wool tunic.

The rogue had come to take her to the gardens.

She shot him a mutinous glare, and he grinned. "Good morn."

"Go away."

Geoffrey chuckled as he walked to the window and drew back the shutters, admitting light and gust of cool air. "Elena will be along soon. You slept late, but 'tis a fine morn. The sky is clear, the sun hovers over the distant hills. A perfect day for weeding the garden."

"Must I?" she grumbled, too weary for a show of spirit.

"I gave you two days."

Her patience smarting as much as her strained muscles, she stood. "How long must we continue this wretched charade?"

"Charade?" He raised his eyebrows.

"This . . . this mockery of making me work like one of your servants." She plowed her hand through her mussed hair. "You have made your point. Now leave me be."

His mouth tightened. "I cannot."

She rolled her eyes heavenward. "You could, if you wished."

"Nay, damsel. I have not finished with you."

Her indrawn breath snagged in her lungs. He stared at

her as he had last night in the hall, with a sinful hunger.

Fear, anticipation and sheer curiosity fought to govern her. Forcing her limbs into motion, she crossed to the table, aware of his gaze upon her. Aware of the forbidden thrill snaking through her. Aware of how alone they were in this chamber, whose walls seemed to squeeze closer together.

She fumbled with the water pitcher. "Where is Mildred?"

He stepped nearer. "Dominic is escorting her to the garden, where you will soon be."

Water splashed into the earthenware bowl. "If I refuse?"

"You will serve me in my bed."

Her head jerked up. The jug banged down on the table. "*What?!*"

Geoffrey reached out and caught one of her glossy curls. His gaze scorched her like flame. "I see I must speak plainer, since you are an innocent."

Heat seared her cheeks and throat. Gripping the edge of the table, she faced him. "I understand your coarse words, milord. I will never—"

"Never?" With the barest touch, he trailed his fingers down her cheek toward her lips. Her skin throbbed.

She shoved his hand away. "Do not touch me."

Anger and remorse darkened his expression. "I am shocked by the notion too, yet 'tis the one way I will be free of you."

An icy tremor raked through her to the soles of her feet. "Let me go. When I am gone, you will forget—"

He shook his head. His eyes gleamed like oiled steel. "You claim *I* am the annoying hornet, yet *you* never give me a moment's peace. You are in my thoughts every moment of every day. You taunt me with the memory of your lips. Your skin. Your scent. I do not want you there, yet you persist. I try to ignore you, but I cannot. When I fall asleep at night, you emerge in my dreams, teasing, challenging, your eyes as bright as the stars in the heavens."

His awkward words flew from his lips like a swarm of wasps. Elizabeth's belly tightened. He haunted her in the same way.

"Let me go," she whispered, her tone desperate.

"And forfeit Wode? Never."

"You do not know what you say." Her fingers, locked onto the table, trembled with strain.

Geoffrey laughed, a sound of agony. "I rave like a mad man."

"You are my enemy."

Torment warred in his gaze, and the same emotion clashed within her. Elizabeth's mind flooded with memories of his kiss, touch, and taste. She fought the rush of illicit sensations, and willed her indignant fury to return. Like dry wood added to a dwindling fire, it would refuel her determination to fight him.

The rage did not come.

In its place, came hollowness. Emptiness.

Yearning.

"I cannot change the past, Elizabeth," he rasped.

Her arms ached to curl around him. Her body cried out for his embrace and touch, but she forced a denial between her teeth. "I will not lie with you."

"You did not find the idea so repulsive the other eve."

She sighed. "I did not try to seduce you. Will you ever get that into your addled skull?"

His lips twisted into a knowing smile. "While you scorn me with your tongue, your body weeps for my touch."

"It does not!"

"I will prove it." Before she could dart away, Geoffrey captured her wrists and yanked her against him. Cursing, sobbing, she fought him, but his fingers pushed into her hair, cupped the back of her head, and held her still. His lips covered hers. She pummeled her fists against his chest, but he did not let her go, and he did not relent.

His rough kisses claimed her mouth, to prove him right and her wrong. Pleasure surged. Elizabeth gasped, the sound muffled against his lips. He tasted of blackberries. As her arms slid around him, and her lips melded to his, she despaired of her own weakness.

As her resistance melted, his touch gentled. His fingers, splayed at the small of her back, slid down and cupped her bottom. With a low groan, a helpless sound torn from him, he pulled her flush against his thighs. She moaned at the intimate contact. Tongue to tongue. Chest to chest. Steel to softness.

His breathing ragged, he broke the kiss. With his thumbs, he touched her swollen mouth. "Why do you fight what we both want?" His words shimmered in the air between them, bound her thoughts and desires to his like a silk ribbon.

She gazed up at him. Spellbound. Tempted.

A breeze cooled her arms. Voices floated up from the bailey. Cold reality snuffed the raging need inside her.

How could she desire the rogue who would destroy her father?

She moistened her lips and tasted blackberries. The sweetness soured in her mouth. Mildred was right. His revenge included taking her virginity, and returning her to her father ruined, with a de Lanceau bastard in her womb. Her willing deflowering would make his vengeance all the more insulting.

She squirmed in his hold. "Release me."

His hands remained firm on her buttocks. His breath fanned over her cheek and brushed her lips. "Lie with me, Elizabeth."

"I would rather . . ." She swallowed hard. "I would rather toil in the kitchens all day."

Drawing back a fraction, he squinted at her. "What?"

"Naught is as loathsome to me as working as a scullery maid"—she wriggled in his hold—"except lying with you." When he began to chuckle, she snapped, "I do not lie."

He lifted one hand and trailed his finger along her jaw. His expression shadowed with suspicion. "Why would you make a point of telling me what you hate?"

Her pulse raced like a frantic bird's. If she did not convince him, she lost her and Mildred's chance at freedom.

She must not fail.

Pulling away from his touch, she forced a taunting laugh. "Why? You would not give me a duty so far beneath my station."

"Do not try and trick me, damsel. Do you scheme some kind of plot that requires use of the kitchens, or even plan escape?"

She fought a stunned gasp. Oh, God, she must not betray herself.

Casting him a frosty, resentful stare, she said, "Escape seems to be impossible." She paused for dramatic effect and smiled. "Yet your misplaced suspicion makes me wonder, milord, if you doubt your ability to keep me prisoner?"

He studied her face a long moment, before he grinned and released his hold upon her. "You will never escape me, and I fear you misjudged me. Tomorrow, you will toil in the kitchens. You and Mildred will prepare the midday and evening meals for the entire keep. I warn you, damsel. The food must be palatable, or you will be sorry."

�֍   ✦   ✦

Mildred dug the spade into the herb patch, wiped dirt from her nose, and beamed. Her tone hushed, she said, "Milady, you work miracles. However did you convince the rogue?"

Kneeling before a crumbling rockery bed, Elizabeth shrugged and kept her blushing face from the matron's view. "I challenged him. He reacted as I thought he would." A giggle bubbled in her throat. "You should have seen his expression when he ordered us to do scullery work."

"Pah! You will not laugh like a naughty child when we must make the meals." Mildred plodded closer. "If I may be so bold, how much cooking have you done?"

Elizabeth uprooted a blooming dandelion. "None."

"As I should have expected." Mildred sounded a little concerned.

With careful fingers, Elizabeth nudged aside a spider scuttling up her skirt. "I have helped Fraeda order wine and spices and watched her cook on occasion, but I have not lifted a cauldron, boiled pottage, or chopped onions for stew. Nor, as the lord's daughter, did I expect to."

Mildred sank onto the turned earth and dropped her face into her hands. "We are destined for disaster."

The fine hair at Elizabeth's nape prickled. She raised her head. "You have cooked before, have you not?"

The matron mopped her brow with her sleeve. "Many years ago, when I was married. Long before I entered the nunnery and learned the ways of herbs and tonics. Long, *long* before your father rescued me from those infernal hours of prayer and asked me to be your mother's lady-in-waiting."

Elizabeth blew a relieved sigh. "Thank goodness."

"I cooked for two, milady," the matron pointed out, "not

an entire keep."

"The principles are the same, are they not?" Elizabeth tossed another dandelion onto the huge pile of weeds. "What one does to one quail, one does to fifty."

Mildred clutched at her head. She looked about to faint.

"Why do you look so distraught?"

The matron's throat moved on a loud swallow. "The process is a little more . . . ah . . . complex than you make it sound."

"How so?"

"The quail, if that is what we are to prepare, must be plucked. They must be cleaned, trussed, and . . . and then there is the matter of the fire. The meat cannot sit too near the flame. It must also be basted with fat as it cooks so it does not dry out and become tough and flavorless."

With a loud snort, Elizabeth flicked her braid back over her shoulder. "The rogue cannot fault us for that. We have been eating leather for days."

Mildred's sigh ended with a groan. "I am afraid my skills do not extend much beyond salted pork and roasted chicken."

"Then we will serve pork and chicken."

"Oh, milady." Mildred bit down on her grubby hand.

"Cooking cannot be so difficult." Elizabeth brushed clods of dirt from her bliaut, and then worked a cramp out of her back. "We must convince the rogue we can cook the meal, or we will never manage to escape."

"True." Worry still gleamed in the matron's eyes. "I am

glad de Lanceau will be fast asleep before he has tasted much of our fare."

✤   ✤   ✤

Lord Arthur Brackendale yanked off his helm and dragged his hand through his sweat-soaked hair. Frustration burned inside him like glowing embers. The journey to Tillenham had taken far longer than expected, due to the necessary repair of a splintered wagon wheel, and heavy rains that had flooded parts of the road and forced the convoy to lose a half-day's journey.

He stared at Tillenham's keep looming ahead, a hulking fortress outlined against the crimson twilight sky. The doubt nagging him over the last few leagues settled in his belly like a chunk of limestone. He had not ridden past charred fields or seen clouds of dense smoke. He had found no evidence of devastating fires.

Oaks sighed along the fortress's walls and clustered in fields as far as Arthur could see. Over the stink of his own body and sweaty horse, he smelled drying wheat, sweet as the flowers blooming along the roadside near his destrier's hooves.

The earl's missive was a hoax.

A dog barked in the shorn field to Arthur's left. He turned his head, and saw peasants calling to their bedraggled children. They looked at him, curious, awed, even a little afeared.

He scowled, rage hot in his mouth. They stared at an

old fool.

Aldwin rode up, his horse lathered with sweat. "What now, milord? There are no fires."

"I know." Setting his helm in his lap, Arthur fixed his gaze on the keep ahead. "The earl will answer for his missive."

Nodding, Aldwin fell back and relayed the message to the other knights and foot soldiers. Over the rattle and squeal of the wagons, Arthur heard grumbles. He ignored them. His men would eat and rest when he had the answers he sought, not before.

As they rode up to the keep, a sentry on the wall walk hailed them.

"Lord Brackendale of Wode," he shouted back. "I will speak with the Earl of Druentwode."

After a moment, the portcullis raised enough to allow out a guard in full chain mail. He tromped across the lowered drawbridge, and Arthur spurred his horse forward.

The sentry bowed. "Milord, I regret the earl is not receiving visitors."

Arthur's lip curled. "I will not be refused."

The guard tensed, and he dropped into another bow. "He is very ill. He lies near death, and has done so for almost a week."

Arthur jerked in surprise. Murmurs ripped through the knights behind him. Leaning down, he flipped open his saddlebag, withdrew the missive and tossed it to the guard. "I received this from him several days ago."

The sentry glanced at the document and shook his head. "'Tis not possible."

"Then who—"

Suspicion shattered the lump in Arthur's belly into a hundred shards. De Lanceau.

Arthur's hands clenched around the destrier's reins, until chain mail links dug into his skin. The discomfort sharpened his anger to a lethal pitch. Why would de Lanceau create such an elaborate deception? Why did de Lanceau want him at Tillenham? There seemed no reason unless . . . Arthur sucked in a breath. Unless de Lanceau wanted to lure him away from Wode.

A brutal, invisible fist squeezed Arthur's gut.

"Lord Brackendale?"

With effort, Arthur returned his attention to the guard. The man had not spoken, he realized, but the peasant lad who stood beside the destrier. His smile hesitant, the boy handed up a small bundle, a scrap of black silk bound with twine. "A man brought this for you."

"Man?" Arthur scowled. "He *knew* I would come here?"

The guard's expression turned confused and wary. "Answer the lord's question, boy."

The lad swallowed and looked down at the stony ground. "He told me to expect you. I did not ask questions, milord. He gave me some silver to keep silent until you arrived and"—the boy's face turned red—"he told me 'twas very important."

Arthur turned the object over in his mailed palm, weighing the contents. Round. Heavy. He broke the twine and parted the cloth's frayed edges. In his palm lay a rolled piece of parchment sealed with wax, and a gold brooch.

Elizabeth's brooch.

Anticipating the ransom demand, Arthur ripped open the parchment and read the note. He crushed it into a ball.

"God's blood," he whispered. "Elizabeth."

CHAPTER FOURTEEN

Elizabeth thought the morn could get no worse . . . until Dominic brushed past the grim faced guards and entered the kitchens.

He stopped as though slapped by an invisible hand, wrinkled his nose, and peered at her through the thick smoke around the wall of cooking fires. "What is that atrocious smell?"

"Smell?" Mildred chirped, looking up from a bubbling pot hung low over one of the fires. "Milady, do you note a smell?"

Scowling, Elizabeth leaned away from the chopping block. Dominic chuckled and she shot him a warning glare. How dare he laugh? 'Twas not her fault her green bliaut was splattered with blood, sauces, and vegetable juices. Nor would she apologize for the state of her hair.

"It *could* be the chickens I burnt to a crisp on the spit," she said, raising her hand and counting off options on her fingers. "Or the rotten cabbages I found in the pantry and took the initiative to throw away. Or mayhap 'tis the white sauce I scorched a moment ago when I simmered it over too high a flame. Why do you ask?"

Dominic's gaze fell to the bunch of fresh herbs destined for the cutting board, then slid to the knife by her hand. "Just curious," he said with a grin.

She huffed a breath. "Please take yourself and your curiosity elsewhere. We are busy."

"Of course, milady."

He executed a graceful bow, then strode away to speak to the guards blocking the door to the bailey.

As soon as his back was turned, Mildred joined Elizabeth at the cutting table and started breaking the sage leaves from the stems. "By the blessed Virgin."

"When you suggested we brew sleeping potion," Elizabeth said between her teeth, "you failed to warn me of the stench."

"'Tis the valerian. I did not remember myself, for when I use the braziers in my workshop, I open all the doors to circulate the air." Mildred gave a bright, toothy smile. "'Twas clever of you to burn the chickens to try and disguise the odor."

"The hens scorched by accident, as well you know." Elizabeth grabbed the knife, swept the herbs into the middle of the table, and chopped them with a vengeance, drawing a wary glance from Dominic and the guards.

Mildred touched her arm. "The accident was timely, then."

Elizabeth grunted. Perspiration dripped down her nose. Over the knife's rhythmic *thud*, she heard Mildred lift the lid of the copper pot, and the ladle clank against the side.

"'Tis done."

A smile warmed Elizabeth's lips. "Good. Now, if you will rinse the salted pork we left to soak earlier, we can cook it and set it on the platters."

At last, the meal was ready. Elizabeth dried her clammy palms on a linen towel and forced herself to draw slow, even breaths. Soon she and Mildred would be free.

She was pouring a fresh white sauce, only a little scorched this time, into bowls when she heard Geoffrey's clipped strides. Her pulse jittered. At the same time, a shameful ache reminded her of his body pressed against hers.

Did his tongue still taste of berries?

She shut her mind to the thoughts. She must focus on escape, not on what, in her silly dreams, might have come true.

Geoffrey came to an abrupt halt. He looked through the smoke to where she stood at the serving table, and threw up his hands. "What mischief have you been up to?"

She ignored a nervous tingle. "We prepared a meal, milord, as you asked." With the edge of a cloth, she wiped drippings from the side of a bowl.

He set his hands on his hips. "What did you cook?"

"Salted pork with an herbed mustard sauce."

His mouth flattened, and he strode around the cutting table to peer into the pots over the fires. "You created this amount of mess, not to mention the vile stench, to serve salted pork?" He sniffed the steam over the sleeping potion. "What is *that?*"

Out of the corner of her eye, Elizabeth saw Mildred stiffen.

"'Tis . . . well, a surprise."

"I do not like surprises," he growled. "Not from you. I warn you, do not think to deceive me."

Misgiving shivered through her. She must divert his suspicions, now, before he ordered one of his men to taste the potion and ruined the chance to escape.

Tossing aside the cloth, she planted her hands on her hips and matched his defiant stance. "How could we trick you, with the guards keeping watch? If you must know, Mildred has been most kind. She brewed a special herbal tonic for you and your men. She planned to present it to you when finished, but, of course, you have spoiled that now."

"'Tis medicine?" he asked with the faintest hint of a smile.

"Of a sort." Elizabeth smothered an uneasy giggle. "It eases many ailments, including headaches, stomach pains, and"—she arched an eyebrow—"wind."

"Ah." He grinned. "'Tis good she made some, since we will be eating your cooking."

Dominic and the other guards chortled, and Elizabeth snapped her jaw shut. Let them laugh. Moments from now, they would be snoring into their salted pork as she and Mildred ran to freedom.

The rogue had the gall to chuckle, too. "Dominic, have

the ladies take the food to the great hall."

"With pleasure, milord."

Mildred caught Elizabeth's gaze and tipped her head toward the steaming pot behind them. They had yet to put the potion into the ale.

With brisk strides, Elizabeth walked around in front of the chopping block. Her ploy worked. Dominic's gaze followed her and not Mildred, who hurried to the wooden cask and began filling pitchers with ale.

Elizabeth pointed to the serving table. "Dominic, would you and the guards help us with the platters? They are heavy."

The knight's cheeky grin faded. "Must I?"

Pasting a smile on her lips, Elizabeth looked at him and the other men, who also looked disgruntled. "Please."

"Do not look at me so," Dominic grumbled. "I will summon the serving wenches."

"Lord de Lanceau assigned them other duties today."

With a sigh, Dominic nodded. "Very well. I will help. Yet, if I do not quench my thirst this instant, I will not reach the hall." Leaning past her, he grabbed one of the frothing pitchers Mildred had just set on the serving table, poured a mug, and downed the ale in one swallow.

Elizabeth gasped. The matron shot her a fierce look, then resumed her task, pretending that naught out of the ordinary had happened. Covering her open mouth with her hand, Elizabeth pretended her outburst was a big yawn. The distrustful guards looked away.

Dominic burped and slammed down the empty mug. "Much better. Now, if you will come with me, milord is waiting."

Gnawing her lip, Elizabeth looked at Mildred. Worry shadowed the matron's eyes, but as she came to Elizabeth's side, she smiled. Scooping up two pitchers, Elizabeth followed Dominic out of the kitchens, aware of Mildred behind her and the tread of the guards in the rear bearing the platters.

She entered the crowded hall and her mouth went dry. Men, women, and children awaiting their food and drink looked up at her. Elena waved and a little boy, sitting on the bench beside her, thumped his fists on the tabletop.

Sweat chilled Elizabeth's brow. Fear whined in her stomach. If all went as planned, she and Mildred would escape.

If it did not . . . if aught went wrong . . . Her throat constricted into a painful knot, and she tightened her hold on the ale jugs.

She looked at Dominic. He shooed a pair of dogs out of his way, then walked toward the dais where Geoffrey sat polishing his eating dagger on a table linen. Dominic showed no signs of succumbing to the potion. Under her breath, she prayed the potent brew would not begin working until all the meals were served.

Stopping at a table near the dais, Elizabeth set down the ale pitchers.

Crockery shattered behind her.

She whirled around.

Dominic fell to his knees. The platter lay broken, the salt pork strewn across the rushes. Snapping, barking mongrels converged on the food. Dominic groaned, a sound so horrible, she went numb with fear. He doubled over, clutching his stomach. "Milord," he choked out. "Ale . . . *poisoned*."

A convulsion shook him. His eyes rolled to the back of his head, and he crumpled to the floor.

From a great distance, Elizabeth heard Mildred cry her name. A chair crashed against a wall. Without looking at the dais, she knew Geoffrey had leapt to his feet.

Panic shrilled inside her. She bolted for the stairwell.

Behind her, footfalls pounded.

Her pursuer grabbed her braid. Yanked her back by her hair's roots.

She screamed.

Geoffrey spun her around, her hair twisted around his arm, his face contorted with rage. "What have you *done*?"

Words refused to form on her tongue.

He grabbed her arms and shook her. Hard. "Answer me!"

Elizabeth trembled. "I—"

"You poisoned the ale, aye?" he bellowed. "*Aye*?"

She could not deny him the truth. She nodded.

With an angry roar, he threw her to the waiting guards. He looked at the servants and men-at-arms who knelt beside Dominic's motionless body, whispering and shaking their heads. His gaze narrowed on Mildred. "You"—Geoffrey pointed at her—"will care for him. You will watch over him day and night. You will do whatever is needed to ensure he lives. By God, he had better live, or you will rue the day you were brought to this keep."

His head swiveled. He stared at Elizabeth, his gaze so bitter, so pitiless, she fought a sob. She struggled against the guards' hold, but they pinned her arms to her sides.

"Take the lady to my solar," Geoffrey snarled. "If she tries to escape, lock her in the dungeon."

✤   ✤   ✤

As the guards escorted Elizabeth from the hall, Geoffrey hurried to Dominic's side. The circle of castle folk stepped back, parted, and gave him space to crouch down on the soiled rushes.

Dominic's face looked white as a shroud. His jaw hung slack. Thank God he still breathed.

Geoffrey bowed his head, and his eyes squeezed shut. Rage, guilt, and gut-wrenching fear boiled inside him in a violent tempest. How many times he had awakened in the hospital at Acre, to find Dominic sitting by his bed, a calming presence in Geoffrey's world of physical torment and emotional anguish.

Dominic was the one person Geoffrey trusted with his life. He would not let Dominic die. He had not been able to save his father or his brother, but he would save his friend.

Shoving to his feet, he gestured to the men-at-arms awaiting orders. "Take him to his chamber. Make sure he is comfortable."

Mildred fought the guards that restrained her. "Lady Elizabeth and I did not plan to hurt him or anyone else. You must believe me."

A half-smile twisted Geoffrey's mouth. "You are responsible for his life now, and your lady's."

Concern shivered across the matron's face. "I will do what you ask. Please, milady—"

Geoffrey's jaw clenched. Rage buzzed inside him with a vicious sting. He stared at the wooden staircase which led up to the landing and his solar.

He strode toward the stairs.

❖   ❖   ❖

The silence in Geoffrey's chamber dragged. Arms clasped to her chest, Elizabeth paced before the hearth, slicing through the sunshine and shadows playing across the floorboards. Waiting.

At any moment, he would walk in and mete out her punishment, whatever that might be.

She glanced at the table between the two chairs. Gone were the wine, sweetmeats, and fine linens—the cultured trappings. Today, light gleamed on the scarred wood. Today, she did not doubt she would see the rough side of de Lanceau's character, the part that fed his anger and his thirst for revenge.

Pushing her shoulders back, she resumed her fretful pacing. She must not lose courage. She would face whatever torture de Lanceau ordered for her with dignity and—

The fire popped. She jumped, and jumped again as the chamber doors crashed against the walls. Geoffrey stood outlined in the embrasure. The doors slammed, cloaking him in shadow.

Her trembling legs were as weighty as stone. They refused to move. She waited, frozen, as he stalked toward her. Closer. Closer. He halted a breath away, his eyes flashing pure fury.

He stared at her, his silence as frightening as lashing words. When he spoke, his voice was a cold, dangerous rasp. "What did you put in the ale?"

Elizabeth inhaled through tight lungs. "H—"

"Answer me!" He grabbed her, and his fingers dug into her arms.

"Herbs." She gasped. "Chamomile, valerian, monkshood—"

"*Monkshood*? From the garden?"

Her head jerked in a nod.

"'Tis poisonous." He sounded both incredulous and appalled. "You thought to *kill* Dominic?" His gaze sharpened. "Or did you wish to kill me?"

She shook her head. "We did not mean to harm anyone."

"Then why poison the ale?"

A shuddered breath tore from her lips. "'Twas not poison. Mildred and I brewed a sleeping potion, which we poured into the jugs. We—"

"You planned to escape."

"'Twas all we intended. I promise you."

His gaze raked over her face, and searched her features with such merciless intensity she could not breathe. "What other trickery have you concocted?"

"None."

"You *lie!*" he roared, his breath scorching her cheek.

She squirmed and fought his crushing hold. "I do not!"

With one hand, Geoffrey caught her chin and trapped her so she could not turn away. "I will know all of your deceit, and far more, by the time I am done with you."

A tremor raked through her. "You will punish me . . . here?" Her gaze darted past him to the bed, streaked with sunlight.

His mouth curved into a brutal smile.

"Please—"

"One wicked deed deserves another, does it not?"

Panic shortened her breaths. "Y-You do not understand."

"I understand all too well. The one person in this world that I love as my brother, that I trust above all others, lies unconscious and near death because of you," Geoffrey snarled. "Did you once think of the consequences of your deceit? Did you consider the possible outcome? How much of your sleeping potion might be too much for a man or woman?"

"You dare to call me a murderess?"

"If Dominic dies, damsel, you will be."

"How dare you accuse *me* of such a crime. You, a man who slaughters helpless children."

"I do not kill children." He answered with such quiet conviction she almost believed him.

"You killed Jeremy. Remember?" she said in a tight voice. "Or have you forgotten?"

"Jeremy?" His narrowed eyes lit with comprehension, and he smiled. "Ah, the boy at Wode. He did not die."

Elizabeth choked a breath. "You told me—"

"Viscon caught him on his way back from your chamber, but he did not kill the lad. We locked him in a storage cupboard so he could not warn anyone else."

Her belly hurt. Did Jeremy live? She hoped Geoffrey told her the truth, yet wariness overshadowed her relief. "I do not believe you," she whispered.

"Believe what you will, but I speak true." He released her chin, and his expression darkened. "Tell me, damsel. Did you not realize that even if your plan had worked, even if you had escaped, I would hunt you down? I would find you and make you pay for your audacity."

"Nay."

"Aye," he muttered. "I will start now."

The grim set of his jaw, the determination his eyes, filled Elizabeth with dread. It gusted through her like a winter blizzard, threatening to destroy her last reserves of courage and send her whirling into sheer terror. "W-What do you intend?"

He released his grip on her arms. "Remove your clothes."

"I will not!"

Geoffrey seemed to have expected that answer. He smiled.

The blade of a bone-handled dagger flashed in the sunlight.

Elizabeth shrieked and covered her face with her hands. She tensed, anticipating a sharp pain as the knife pierced her flesh. When cold, flat steel pressed against the side of her neck, she froze.

"When will you learn you cannot fight me and win," Geoffrey murmured. He dragged the blade's icy tip across her skin. It traced the leaping pulse in her neck, grazed the hollow of her collarbone, and fell to the front of her bliaut. His hand moved, once, and her gown and chemise slashed open to her waist.

Elizabeth gaped down at the rent. A deft, clean cut. The knife had left no marks on her skin, which looked pale as snow against the green wool. Panic spiked inside her. She clutched the sides of the material, desperate to shield her exposed skin. Failing.

With a strangled cry, she ran for the door.

Before she had taken three steps, he caught her. His arm wrapped around her waist, and he threw her onto the pillow-strewn bed. Elizabeth landed on her back. Rolled over. Lunged for the opposite side. His hand snaked out and got her ankle. He hauled her back to him like a cat toying with a mouse.

Fear blinded her vision. She clawed. Struggled. Tried to free her leg and kicked out with her other foot. She got him in the stomach. Geoffrey grunted and his grip eased a fraction. With a second, well-aimed kick, she wrenched free. Breathing hard, she dove for the edge of the bed.

He was already there.

Geoffrey caught her wrists in one hand. She tried to jerk free, but he was far too strong, and far too determined that this time, she would not get away. Looming over her, he forced her back on the coverlet. He pinned her hands over her head and, with a triumphant smile, lowered his body onto hers.

Heat sparked where their bodies touched. "Get off me," she spat.

"When I have you right where I want you? I think not."

Elizabeth dug her nails into his skin. He cursed under his breath and exerted more pressure on her wrists, little by little, until with a gasp, she relented.

His breath warmed her temple, and he shifted his weight over her. His body fitted against her breasts, belly, and thighs in a manner that thrilled and alarmed her. His male smell flooded her nostrils. Tempted. A traitorous ache stirred in her belly, and she shivered.

"Surrendering at last, damsel?"

"Never!" Ashamed by her weakness, she arched against

him, writhed and bucked to throw him sideways. She tossed her hair in his face like a weapon.

"I have had enough of your struggling. Cease."

Thrashing, kicking, she got his shin twice, despite his strength and the ease with which he deflected her blows. When she continued to fight, he grabbed her hair. Twisted. Her tresses pulled taut. Panting, she fell back against the bed. Her ripped bodice gaped further open with each breath, and a whimper broke from her. "You are hurting me."

He released her hair, but glared down at her in warning. "Lie still."

"Let . . . me . . . go." On the last word, her voice cracked. He planned to ravish her. He meant to shame and ruin her, and she could not stop him.

The rogue looked down at her . . . and smiled.

As his warm, skilled lips brushed the side of her neck, Elizabeth closed her eyes. Her breaths echoed in the stillness, harsh, painful gasps. How foolish she had been to imagine lying with him in a slow, tender dance of bliss. How foolish she had been to savor his kisses.

Somehow she had to sway him. Somehow, she had to touch his tormented soul and make him see how wrong his actions were.

As his fingers skimmed down to her torn bodice, her lashes flew up. She stared up into his dark, glittering eyes with all the anguish inside her. "Please. Do not."

"I will not have to force you," he said against her cheek.

"Your body is willing."

"Then let go of my wrists."

He laughed, and the chilling sound echoed deep inside her. "I will not, damsel. Not until I have finished with you."

❖   ❖   ❖

Lying over her, Geoffrey felt the violent shudder that rippled through Elizabeth's body. For all of three heartbeats, he hesitated, and looked down into her proud, pale face.

Admiration stirred in his soul. She was brave to try and thwart him, even when she knew he would not heed her pointless words. His mind filled with thoughts of how she had deceived him with the herbal potion, how she had harmed Dominic, and what her cruel father had done years ago, and Geoffrey's wrath blazed like a wildfire.

He had every right to take what he desired.

His palm slid beneath her slashed bodice and cupped her soft, warm breast. Her lips parted on a gasp. Did she, too, feel intense sensation when their skin touched? He had never before felt such exquisite torment. No woman had held such power over his senses, thoughts, and desires. No woman had come so close to touching his soul. Fury and need roared inside Geoffrey, tinged with . . . guilt.

He shoved the unwelcome emotions from his mind. The lady was his hostage. His pawn. He would do with her as he wished.

His fingers skimmed lower, toward her belly's curve. Her flesh tensed beneath his fingertips. She turned her face away, and buried her cheek in the braided tangle of her hair. Her blue eyes glittered. She blinked, but could not hide from him the watery shimmer of tears.

A ragged breath tore from him.

She lay still and silent, resigned to her fate. Her eyes were closed now, and he guessed she blocked out the experience with whatever means were left to her. He had tried to do the same when he lay in the desert hospital. Though he had battled the horrific memories with a mental sword, 'twas a far more difficult fight than he ever imagined.

She would learn that, soon enough.

Her dark lashes fanned against her cheek. He sensed her fear. Helplessness. The shattered pride of a woman forced to compromise when she did not want to yield.

Her lips quivered.

Her desperate plea echoed in his mind. *Please. Do not.*

Revulsion unfurled in him with shocking force. He had never hurt a woman. He had never coerced a virgin to his bed. Never in the lowest moments of his existence had he wanted to commit such a loathsome act.

What kind of beast had he become?

He felt intense shame. Craving. Desire. His shaking fingers curled into a fist against her skin. He did not want to take her in anger. He wanted her eyes open, warm with laughter and shared passion, welcoming him into her body's sweet haven.

The door to his chamber creaked open.

Elizabeth jerked beneath him. Scowling, he raised his head to yell at whoever dared to come in without first asking his permission. He had warned the guards outside that he did not want to be interrupted, unless the matter was of vital importance.

Veronique strolled out of the shadows. When she saw him lying with Elizabeth on the bed, she stiffened. Her eyes flared with shock and outrage, but quicker than he thought possible, her face eased into a smile.

He expected her to curtsey, turn around, and leave. Instead, she walked toward him, her brocaded gown rustling with each of her controlled steps.

Elizabeth squirmed beneath him. His lips thinned, and he wished he could have spared both women this moment of indignity. He glared at Veronique. "I told the guards I did not wish to be disturbed."

The courtesan paused beside the bed. "So you did, milord."

"Why do you ignore my orders?"

Her smile turned cool. "I bring you a missive." She offered him the roll of wax-sealed parchment clasped in her fingers. "'Twas delivered by one of Lord Brackendale's pages. I knew you were awaiting a response to the ransom demand. I thought you would want to see it straight away."

Exhaling a fierce sigh, Geoffrey released Elizabeth's

hands. He rolled off her, got to his feet, and snatched the parchment from Veronique. Behind him, the bed ropes creaked. Elizabeth stumbled away from him, clutching at her ruined bliaut.

Geoffrey broke the seal with his thumb and read the terse lines scribed on the parchment. He laughed. "Damsel, you are not as valuable to your sire as you might believe."

"What do you mean?" Her fingers knotted into the green wool, holding the edges of the slashed fabric together.

"Your father refused to surrender Wode."

Pride and relief glowed in her eyes. "I told you he would never agree to your demands."

"He has challenged me to a melee three days from now, in Moyden Wood."

"A *melee?*" Elizabeth's face turned ashen, and she swayed on her feet.

Her horror touched Geoffrey. Despite her pampered, sheltered upbringing, she knew of the savage mock battles that pitted one enemy against another, without the king's knowledge or consent. He had fought two with the Earl of Druentwode. In the fight's ensuing thrill and blood lust, few warriors heeded the rules of chivalry that governed tournaments. Even fewer considered their opponents' safety. Most weapons were not blunted, a fact, he expected, her father knew as well.

Anticipation snaked down Geoffrey's spine. At long last, vengeance. If he were correct in guessing Brackendale's intentions, one lord would be killed. The other would stand as the dust settled on the maimed and the dead. *He* would be the rightful ruler of Wode.

"You cannot," Elizabeth shrieked. "You cannot!"

Geoffrey shrugged. "'Tis a fair challenge. May the mightiest lord win."

Her eyes grew wide with fear. "My father is no match for you in armed combat. He will die."

"Then he will die," Geoffrey said with cold finality.

Elizabeth's hand flew to her mouth. She ran for the door. He let her go.

❖   ❖   ❖

As the sound of Elizabeth's footsteps faded, Veronique turned to Geoffrey and grinned. "Tsk, Tsk. A spineless wench, is she not?"

"'Tis no concern of yours," he snarled.

Veronique arched an eyebrow. With his hands on his hips, and his lips pressed into a line, he looked less than satisfied with his encounter with the lady. She bit back a smug laugh. Served him right for dallying with another woman.

Frustration and fury surrounded him like invisible armor. Excitement shivered through Veronique. Ah, she loved to soothe his anger. It took skill and patience to transform rage, such a volatile emotion, into unbridled passion.

But she could.

She cast him a teasing pout. With loose-hipped strides, she crossed to him and twirled her fingers into the fine hair at his nape. "You are not pleased I interrupted you, after all?" When he did not respond, she slid her flattened palms down his torso and shoved them up under his shirt.

He cursed. With a teasing giggle, she crushed her body against his while her fingers glided over his bare skin. "Tell me, milord, that you are not angry with me."

He growled. "You disobeyed me. The message could have waited."

Veronique hid a scowl. If she had not entered the solar, he would have sampled another woman's body. She dug her nails into his flesh and covered her rage with a bold, slippery kiss that should have left him enticed and malleable. "Who would see to your needs then?" she murmured. "'Tis clear Brackendale's daughter could not."

His fists snapped round her wrists, stopping her caresses.

"I am no mood for your games," he said, his voice so iron hard, she shivered.

As Veronique stared up into his face, half-masked by shadow, fear prickled in her veins. The night he had returned to bed after leaving her alone, he had not touched her. When she had tried to entice him, he had rolled onto his side and left her cold. Nor, over the past few days or nights, had he invited her to share his bed.

Forcing a sultry grin, she stretched up on the tips of her toes. She would prove he was not immune to her seductions.

He frowned and pushed her away. Turning his back to her, he reached for the wine jug on the side table.

With rigid fingers, Veronique smoothed her gown's crushed sleeve. "A drink first then, to ease you?" she suggested, unable to keep the edge from her tone. Geoffrey must have heard it, too, for his hand froze on the pitcher's handle.

"Go."

"Milord?"

"I wish you to leave, Veronique," he said without facing her. "Close the doors behind you."

"You are *dismissing* me?" As she stared at the unyielding wall of his back, the significance of his rejections crashed down upon her like a crumbling wall. "Why?"

He looked at her, his gaze shadowed with regret. His shoulders raised in a stiff shrug. "I do not feel for you as I once did. I do not want to lie with you. I am . . . sorry."

His words stung. He did not need her. He did want her. Not now, mayhap never again.

Beneath her powders and rouge, warmth drained from her face. He forced her away because he desired the lady.

Elizabeth Brackendale was younger, more beautiful, and her noble bloodlines made her a far richer prize than a poor farmer's daughter turned courtesan.

Veronique's jaw tightened with fury, and her voice shook. "I never expected you to choose Brackendale's daughter over me."

Geoffrey looked at her over his wine goblet, his gaze hard

with warning. "I asked you to leave. Do you ignore yet another of my orders?"

Veronique forced a smile with lips that felt carved from stone. "Nay, milord." She dropped into a graceful curtsey. "I bid you good eve."

She sensed his gaze upon her as she walked across the chamber. How she hated the ache that crushed her heart.

As Veronique hastened down the passage to the musty antechamber she claimed as her private room, her bliaut lashed at her ankles. Her eyes burned, and not from the smoke spewing from the torches. What had happened was all *her* fault, that black-haired, blue-eyed wench's. Veronique remembered Elizabeth's pale limbs entwined with Geoffrey's, and spat an oath into the shadows.

Veronique trembled with rage. Geoffrey was *her* lord. *Her* lover. *Her* warrior. No one had ever challenged her position as his favorite until Lady Elizabeth Brackendale arrived at Branton.

Staggering into the darkened chamber, Veronique slammed the door and leaned back against the splintered wood. She had followed Geoffrey across the continent to this vile, festering, run-down keep because he had ambitions of power and wealth.

After spending two years of her life with him, she would not be denied her share of the riches, or the glory.

She groped for a taper and lit it from the candle beside the straw pallet. Light glinted off the polished steel mirror lying on the bed. She picked it up and looked at her reflection.

The taper flickered, illuminating the wicked smile on her blood-red lips.

If Geoffrey intended to cast her aside, she would find a way to deny him his wealth.

And vengeance.

CHAPTER FIFTEEN

Elizabeth paced her chamber, her slippers tapping on the floorboards. She must find a way to change what was inevitable. Frowning, she turned and walked back the ten steps she had counted out so many times before which brought her to the opposite wall. She had to think. *Think!*

Worrying the end of her braid with her fingers, she spun on her heel. She had to stop the melee. The brutal battle might prove the victor's honor and his right to Wode, but also meant her father's death. She knew that without doubt. Why had he challenged de Lanceau to such a skirmish when he knew he could not defeat a crusading warrior? Why?

Had he chosen the melee because 'twas an honorable death?

She forced a painful swallow. Her gaze fell to the rose wool folded on the trestle table. The melee came about because of Geoffrey's desire for revenge, his quest to seek justice for his father's death.

Geoffrey was not so heartless if he felt such anguish.

He had loved his sire very much, mayhap as much as she loved hers. Even, as he had posed that afternoon on the wall walk, with the poignancy she felt for her mother's death. He, too, knew the anguish of loss. Elizabeth hugged her arms to her chest and blinked away tears. He, too, knew the fear of being alone.

The afternoon sun faded to twilight, and when she next looked out the window, a crescent moon gleamed in the heavens, surrounded by a scattering of stars. An owl hooted in the darkness. Time was passing. Still, she had no answer.

She must stop Geoffrey. She must save her father.

Somehow.

Elizabeth sighed. She could stand the futile pacing no longer. Marching to the door, she pounded on it with her fists and shouted for someone to come. The sentries outside waited until she was almost hoarse before the door opened.

"'Avin' a tantrum, are ye?" The guard eyed her as though he expected the water pitcher to be hurled at his head.

"I must speak with Lord de Lanceau," she said.

"If milord wished to see ye, he would have summoned ye," the sentry grumbled.

"Ask him anyway." She softened her demand with a wide-eyed, plaintive, "Please."

The door slammed in her face.

Determined not to work herself into an anxious fit while

she waited, Elizabeth washed, pulled on the rose wool, and loosened her hair so her curls cascaded down her back. As she smoothed a crease out of her bodice, the door opened. The sentry tipped his head and indicated she was to go with him.

Elizabeth walked into the dark corridor. She prayed that since their encounter, Geoffrey's temper had cooled and also his desire to punish her. If she appealed to his sense of reason, his knight's code of honor, she could convince him there was no advantage to the melee.

Oh, God, she had to convince him. Even if it meant risking his hands on her skin and more of his sinful kisses. Even if meant risking . . . her innocence.

Lie with me, Elizabeth, he had whispered. Those terrifying, thrilling words had torn from him with raw honesty.

Could she save her father's life, by giving herself to Geoffrey?

The guard pushed open the solar door. She stepped in, and the door closed with a *thud*. The solar was shadowed and quiet, as she remembered. Drawing a shaky breath, Elizabeth started toward the hearth.

Geoffrey sprawled in one of the chairs, swirling a goblet in one hand. He stared at the crackling fire, and did not glance up when she neared.

His hair looked mussed. How ridiculous to wonder how many times he had dragged his fingers through it. She expected him to be gloating, basking in the battle victory so certain to be his, but his expression held wariness.

"You dare venture into my chamber alone again?" His gruff voice seemed loud in the room's stillness. He tilted his head and looked at her, and his eyes glinted in the dim light.

She clasped her sweaty hands together. "I am not afraid of you, milord."

"You should be." His thumb brushed away a drop of red wine on the goblet's rim. "If you have come to demand an apology for my behavior this afternoon, you will not get it."

"I do not seek your apology."

"I am still angry, damsel." Distrust echoed in each word. He must wonder why she had dared to enter his solar again and court danger.

Steeling her nerves, she strolled into the shadows painted by firelight. His gaze moved over her unbound hair and the clinging rose wool, and hope sparked within her. Desire still gleamed in his eyes. If he refused to heed her reasons why the melee must be canceled, she still had a chance to sway him.

She paused near his chair. "H-How is Dominic?"

Geoffrey frowned. "Why do you ask?"

"I hope he is recovering well."

He stared at the drop of wine on his thumb, which glistened like blood. "He is awake, but suffering a headache and sour stomach. Mildred has not left his side. She is convinced he would recuperate faster if he drank one of her purgative tonics, but he refuses to have one."

Elizabeth chuckled. "She has great faith in her tonics."

Silence lagged. She fidgeted with her cuff, and tried to

decide the best way to broach the subject of the melee.

He sighed, an impatient sound. "What do you want? Why did you ask to see me?"

"I must speak with you."

"Then speak."

Her legs trembled. She moved to the hearth. The fire's heat, as warm as Geoffrey's caresses, touched her skin and she shivered. "I have come—"

"—to ask a favor of me."

Elizabeth started. She could not deny that was indeed her aim. "How did you know?"

"I guessed." Wry humor warmed his voice. It gave her the courage to plunge ahead and say what she must.

"Milord, I ask that you . . . I want you to refuse my father's challenge."

His bitter laughter filled the chamber. "I am many things, but I am not a coward."

"I did not mean you were." She struggled to keep her tone calm. If she enraged him, she would achieve naught, and she must convince him to halt the battle. "The melee is a fight to the death, is it not?"

He nodded, hair snarling over his shoulder.

"My father is more than twice your age. He is not as strong, quick, or as skilled with a sword. He will die." Her words ended on a whisper. "You accused me earlier of being a murderer. Are you so eager to be one?"

Geoffrey's eyes darkened. He sipped his wine; then he

rested his goblet on his thigh. "My father was an innocent man. Your sire is guilty of taking his life. To kill the guilty is justice, milady, not murder."

"My father is guiltless! He followed orders from the king."

"The melee will decide who is right." His mouth twisted into a mirthless smile. "'Twould please you, aye, to see my head on a pike?"

She pressed her arm across her stomach, sickened by the gruesome image, and shocked by the anguish that swept through her when she thought of him dead. "Of course not."

For the barest moment, surprise flickered in his gaze. Then his face hardened with scorn. "I will not decline your sire's challenge. Naught you say or do will change my mind."

Desperation clawed up inside her like a living creature. His words had sounded so bleak. Final. "Milord—"

"I will not," he growled.

She shook like a leaf buffeted by a gale, about to be tossed over a fathomless pit. Despair threatened to devour her. She braced her palm against the cold wall and sought strength from the solid stone and mortar. "You know the pain of losing a father," she whispered. "You have lived with the agony of losing someone you love, respect, and admire. Do you wish the same torment for me?"

A muscle leapt in Geoffrey's jaw.

"Promise me you will spare my father's life." She pleaded with the depths of her soul. "Please."

Geoffrey raised the goblet to his lips and looked down at

the fire. "I cannot."

Tears welled in her eyes. She should have realized he would never listen to reason or pleas. His anguish had festered for too many years.

Still, all was not lost. Not yet.

One means remained for her to save her sire.

One last chance to sway her enemy from vengeance.

She blinked away the tears. She would have no regrets.

Raising her chin, she met Geoffrey's gaze. With slow, loose-hipped strides, she crossed to him.

Caution flared in his eyes. "Elizabeth?"

A sob jammed in her throat, yet she dropped to her knees before him. The bliaut pooled around her and snagged on the worn floorboards, but she did not care if it never pulled free. She bowed her head, and her tresses fell around her face like a black veil. "I beg of you. Spare my father."

"'Tis not like you to beg, damsel."

Her head jerked up. She fought an angry blush, struggled to find the will to say what she must. "If you spare him, I will lie with you."

"Elizabeth." His voice became a helpless groan. "You must not—"

"I know you desire me. I cannot deny I . . . crave you also." The truth glowed bright in her heart. She would never feel passion for another man as she felt for Geoffrey de Lanceau. "I yield not just for my father," she said, "but for me."

Torment and desire shivered across Geoffrey's face, and

he shook his head. "I can make you no promises for the melee."

"Then I expect none."

"Listen to what you say! You will sacrifice your innocence for naught."

She shivered at the bite in his words, but did not look away. "I yield because I wish to. Because I want this one moment with you that may never come again."

"God's teeth," he whispered, "you are the bravest woman I have ever known." Admiration gleamed in his shocked gaze. He reached out and trailed his wine-stained thumb down her cheek. She did not realize she was crying, until she felt the wet path of his skin on hers. "Ah, damsel, how I wish you wept for me."

His words were soft, tender, and Elizabeth exhaled on a rush. She fought for words to convey the swirling emotions inside her.

He cupped her face with his hand. "Elizabeth, my beautiful, headstrong damsel. I want to love you."

"I am yours."

"Kiss me."

She had never seen such turmoil. Hunger. His need throbbed inside her.

She longed to feel his arms wrap around her, to taste him, to explore him. The yearning—a desire that surpassed the boundaries of past and future to reach pure, elemental attraction between man and woman—was stronger now than it had ever been.

He set the silver goblet on the table. His hand dropped from her face, yet he did not move closer or try to touch her, though she knelt within reach. Mayhap he feared frightening her away. Mayhap he wanted her to reconsider all that she had offered.

Whatever his reasons, they did not matter.

She would not waver.

With a shaking hand, she touched his leg. His wool hose felt smooth and warm beneath her palm, and, edging forward, she closed the space separating them. His hand settled over hers, and tingles shot up her arm. She glanced up to see if he, too, had felt them. He nodded. His gaze smoldering, he plowed his fingers into her hair.

A ragged sigh burst from him, and he leaned toward her. His breath warmed her cheek. A caress. An invitation.

Elizabeth lifted her mouth to his.

The kiss was sweeter than she ever imagined. Her lips feathered over his, explored his sensuous mouth. He tasted of red wine, a tangy, heady piquancy more intoxicating than a sip from the goblet. She kissed him again and drew back.

He exhaled with a gasp, a sound that expressed a deluge of sensations. As she licked her lips, savoring his essence, his mouth hovered close. He raised one eyebrow. When she flushed, he smiled. Anticipation shivered through her. Before she lost her nerve, Elizabeth leaned forward and claimed his lips.

"Damsel," he groaned. Tangled in her hair, his hand shook. She sensed his urgent need, his desire to take control, yet he did not. Instead, he coaxed her with kisses that dared her to seek more. With a sigh, Elizabeth arched forward to deepen the contact, and her belly pressed against his leg. His fingers slid from her hair and, breaking away for less than one breath, he reached down and drew her into his lap.

Awareness assailed her. His thigh under her bottom. His muscled arm at her back. His familiar scent. She trembled, overwhelmed, but his mouth found hers. His lips soothed, teased, and when his tongue eased between her teeth, she gasped. His kisses grew fiercer, more profound, until her pulse hammered and her body arched with wanting.

Breathing hard, Elizabeth drew back. She stared up into his flushed face, into his blazing eyes, and felt an inexplicable sense of incompletion.

"Elizabeth." He nuzzled the hollow of her neck and trailed kisses down her collarbone. "Lie with me now."

His hushed words were not a command, but a request, delivered with such yearning her heart almost broke in two. She snuffed a twinge of panic and regret. She would go to his bed, for she wanted him, as he desired her. If she could convince him not to plunge his sword into her father's heart, she must.

She met his ravenous gaze. "Aye," she whispered.

He answered with a tortured groan and a kiss so brazen, Elizabeth cried out when their lips parted. Cradling her in his arms, he rose and carried her to the bed, her hair brushing the floorboards. His hands gentle, he laid her down on the coverlet. The bed ropes creaked as he stretched out beside her.

His fingers stroked her tresses. He fanned her hair out over the coverlet and pulled a ringlet over her shoulder. She smiled and, spurred by a rush of boldness, pushed her hand up under his tunic.

He tensed. His eyes narrowed in warning, and she froze with her hand pressed to his warm belly. Had she displeased him? She had never lain with a man before. Dismay whirled up inside her. If she had ruined her chance to save her father—

Geoffrey covered her hand with his, and drew it to a buckled ridge along the right side of his chest. A scar. A long, hideous scar. Elizabeth traced the line of marred flesh with her fingertips and bit back a horrified cry. What had happened to him? How had he survived such a wound?

Anguish shimmered in his eyes, and she felt him steel himself for her rejection. With a gentle smile, she tugged the tunic up past his navel.

"'Tis not a pleasant sight," he muttered.

"Please," she said, and pushed herself up to sitting.

He raised up on one elbow, drew the tunic over his head and tossed it onto the floor.

Elizabeth sucked in a breath. She had expected the warrior strength of his physique, but not his godlike beauty, which the scar could never diminish. His skin gleamed like polished bronze. She smoothed her fingers over the swell of muscles and ribs, and marveled at the perfection of the human body. His body.

Geoffrey pushed up to sit beside her. The skin across her breasts tingled, for she recognized the wicked gleam in his eyes. His fingers drifted over her bodice, down to her waist, and as she swayed against him, her eyes closed. He took her mouth in a fiery kiss, reached down and unlaced his boots. They fell to the floor with a *thud*. He did not break the kiss as he unfastened the points of his hose, removed the belt, and stripped the wool from each leg.

His thumb caressed her cheek, and Elizabeth dared to open her eyes. He was naked. Glorious. Her gaze traveled over his body, worshipped each gleaming swell of muscle and sinew. Her fingers burned to touch him. She reached for his thigh, but he captured her hand. His fingers linked through hers and he pressed her back on the bed.

His face taut with need, he leaned over her. His tongue clicked over the sensitive hollow of her throat, then moved to her bodice's edge. How did such pleasure exist in a simple touch? Through half-lowered lashes, she watched him unfasten her bliaut's ties. His hands moved again, down her side, down her leg, to her hem.

When his fingers grazed the inside of her leg, she quivered. His lips swept over hers. He whispered tender reassurances, and pulled her bliaut and chemise to her waist. He coaxed her to wriggle out of them, and then dropped them over the side of the bed.

Cool air kissed her skin. Elizabeth shivered. She lay naked before him, vulnerable as a hatched bird without feathers. The rough hair on his legs brushed against her, reminded her of the different textures of man and woman. With her hands, she tried to hide her nakedness, but he raised her fingers to his mouth and kissed them, one by one.

"You are beautiful," he murmured.

"And you tell a fine falsehood." She gave a shaky laugh. "My cheekbones are too high and—"

"Believe me, damsel, you are exquisite. All of you."

His eyes blazed, and a thrill of wonder and excitement coursed through her. He ran his hand over her hipbone and flat stomach. When the muscles fluttered at his touch, he grinned.

With slow, careful movements, he lowered his weight over her. As he braced his arms on either side of her shoulders, his silky hair brushed her temple. Elizabeth swallowed. Dipping his head, he distracted her with a searing kiss. He teased her desire, taunted her with his hands, lips, and tongue, until her body writhed beneath him.

"Elizabeth," he said in a thick voice. "Are you certain?"

She nodded.

His hardness pressed into her, bringing pressure and stabbing pain. She gasped. His body tensed above her, and she sensed the effort it took him to stop.

"I do not wish to hurt you."

"I know."

His face held such a tortured expression, she drew his head down to kiss him. His lips moved over hers. He kissed her with a soft, muffled apology, and then thrust hard and deep.

He crushed her, everywhere, inside as well as out. She thought she could bear no more, when he whispered her name and began to move. The gentle friction dimmed the pain and brought with it a delicious, slow burn. With each of his strokes, the pleasure intensified.

The smell of his sweat filled her nostrils. His stubbled jaw grazed her cheek. Need heightened, and she whimpered. Groaning, he quickened the pace. She dug her heels into the bedding, matched his thrusts.

Faster.

Faster.

The burn flared before exploding into a single, brilliant flame. She cried out as it engulfed her.

In its fiery wake, Geoffrey roared with pleasure. His breaths became shuddered gasps.

And, when he buried his head against her shoulder, she tasted the tears streaming down her cheeks.

CHAPTER SIXTEEN

In the hazy glow of candlelight, tears shimmered on Elizabeth's face. Geoffrey lay beside her on the coverlet and listened to her breathing slow to a normal pace. He wondered if they were tears of regret, guilt, or worry for what the future might bring.

He shifted the arm curled under his head, but left the other draped over her belly. He sensed her drawing away from him even as his fingers caressed her skin. He did not want the moment to end. Not now. Mayhap not ever.

Leaning over, he kissed the damp curls at her temple. "Are you all right?" he whispered.

"Aye." She wiped away the tears with the back of her hand.

"I did not hurt you?"

With a faint smile, Elizabeth shook her head.

"'Twas not easy to be gentle with you," he said, his tone

gruff. He remembered all too well how her sleek body had molded to him. He had not expected such pleasure when it had been her first time. The damsel had surprised him yet again.

Her soft laughter startled him. "I did not expect you to be gentle. As you once told me, you are not a patient man."

"True."

He saw her hand stretch toward him, but he still flinched when her fingers trailed the length of his scar. 'Twas not a hasty examination, but one of careful study. She seemed to be committing each puckered ridge and lump to memory. He tried to pull away, but she did not let him go.

"Tell me about this," she said.

"Are you certain you wish to know?"

Her blue eyes were moist but steady as they met his. "Aye."

"'Tis not a pretty tale."

Her gaze shadowed. "This wound almost cost your life."

Geoffrey closed his eyes and tried not to heed the tenderness in her tone and touch. No words could express the full extent of his injury—the endless months of agony as his flesh fused, and the emotional torment that accompanied his healing. He wondered at the risk he took telling her. To dig into his past would make him vulnerable. If he gave her insight into the man he once was, he gave her a weapon to wield against him.

Part of him no longer cared.

"You got this on Crusade," she pressed, and linked her

fingers through his.

He nodded. "I still remember the day as though 'twere yesterday."

When she stared up at him, her gaze expectant, he said, "It happened over a year ago, at Acre. The city was still ruled by the infidel. King Richard wanted to free it and the hundreds of Christians imprisoned when the Saracens took control."

"I have heard of Acre," she murmured, interest brightening her expression.

"King Richard and the French king had decided to launch a fierce attack. The city, though, was well fortified and situated by a sea harbor."

"Did they plan a siege?"

"Aye. King Richard and the French king agreed to concentrate forces on the city's gates, which were the weakest point in the defenses. My brother and I were assigned to the division that would swarm inside once the gates fell. King Richard knew of my skill with a sword and placed me at the front, where—"

Elizabeth raised her free hand. "Wait. You have a brother?"

"Had." He could not keep the pain from his voice. "His name was Thomas."

Sympathy softened her eyes. "I am sorry."

"As am I." He stared down at his fingers, joined with hers. In the farthest reaches of his mind, he heard his comrades' coarse laughter, smelled sun-baked sand, and tasted the breeze blowing in from the eastern sea. "The first of our fighters attacked," he began. "The rest of us awaited the king's orders. All of a sudden, we heard a terrible noise behind us, yells, screams, and beating drums. It sounded like the demons of hell had come for our souls.

"Hundreds of Turks flew upon us, shrieking like mad men. Soldiers fled in panic. Even knights, like I, who had sworn fealty to God and King within the hallowed walls of the church, deserted King Richard." He shook his head. "I knew if I ran, I would be no better than the infidel who threatened to bring an end to Christendom. I would die rather than break that sacred oath." A rough laugh warmed his lips. "I doubt I could have done aught else, for the Turks surrounded me."

"Go on," she whispered.

"I had sworn to protect my king," he said, caressing her wrist with his thumb. "I stood at his side and honored that vow. I killed any Turk who came near, as did my brother. King Richard managed to escape to safety. By then the ground was covered with blood and corpses, yet I kept fighting.

"Somehow my brother and I became separated. I found myself fighting beside a man who had joined the king's Crusade to free the holy city of Jerusalem from the Turks."

A startled smile warmed her face. "Dominic de Terre?"

"The same. I saved his head twice, for which he feels indebted to me. As you have seen, I did not survive unscathed."

"What happened?" She sounded horrified, yet also

fascinated. Her gaze dropped to his scar, and he shuddered, remembering.

"Three Turks singled me out. They surrounded me. I killed one, a young man. He was a careless fighter. He must have been the son of one of the other Turks. As he fell, dying, the older Turk screamed and lunged while the other circled to my back. I saw the one behind me raise his blade. I turned and tried to deflect it, but"—he flinched, reliving the pain—"I could not escape the sword that cut my chest."

"Dominic saved me. I do not know how, but he got me to the Knights Hospitallers. He told me my brother died soon after I fell. Thomas had tried to avenge me."

Elizabeth's eyes closed. She seemed to be internalizing his anguish. "How awful."

"I spent months in the Hospitallers' care," Geoffrey went on, the words pouring from him like water loosed from a dam. "King Richard sent a missive in which he expressed his gratitude for my bravery and ceded Branton Keep to me. Yet I held little hope of ever returning to England."

"Why?" Elizabeth whispered.

"The physicians did not expect me to live. I suffered fever and was delirious. When at last I awoke, the physicians told me even if I did recuperate, I would never again be able to hold a sword, a sentence worse than death for a knight." He swallowed. "I wished I had perished and not my brother."

"Oh, Geoffrey." Elizabeth squeezed his hand.

"I grieved for my brother and blamed myself for not protecting him. I had failed. I had not saved my father's life, and had lost my brother as well. Soon, my pain became rage, an anger so intense it gave me a reason to live. I wanted blood spilled for their blood. I wanted vengeance." He tried to steel the bitterness from his tone, but could not. "If your sire had not besieged Wode, if my father had not been murdered, my brother and I would not have joined King Richard's Crusade."

Elizabeth tensed. Geoffrey fought for calm, for the strength to tell her his entire wretched tale, so that mayhap, just mayhap, she might understand. "'Twas a long while before I could sit up, or feed myself, or leave my bed," he said. "I would have gone mad, were it not for the other wounded men under the Hospitallers' care.

"One of them, Pietro Vicenza, was the son of a rich Venetian merchant. He had been returning from the fairs at Champagne when the Turks attacked his wagons laden with cloth. All but he were slaughtered. He had been stabbed and left for dead, but somehow crawled to find help."

Geoffrey smiled. "Pietro entranced me with the riches of the merchant trade. He sat by my bed and told me of the spices his father Marco bought from the Eastern ships that docked in the port of Venice—saffron, coriander, cumin— spices so expensive just a few ounces cost most men a year's wage." Geoffrey's voice softened. "He told me of the jewels, gold, and bolts of cloth. Silks so luxurious, he said, they were the envy of all the courts of Europe. He said 'twas easy for a man with good friends to make a fortune. The idea appealed to me, for without a sword arm, I could not be of use to my king.

"When I was able to leave the hospital, Pietro took me to Venice to meet Marco, his mother, and his three brothers. I learned how to pick out the finest fabrics and barter the best price. I even worked with Marco for a while, lifting barrels and hauling bolts of silks as I strove to regain my strength."

Elizabeth's brow creased into a frown. "What of Dominic? You have scarce mentioned him in your story."

With a chuckle, Geoffrey kissed her cheek. "Patience, damsel. I have not forgotten him. He visited me at the Hospitallers'. The king had dubbed him a knight the day after the Saracens agreed to surrender Acre and hostages. As I said, he felt he owed me for saving his life. He felt he must help me recover."

"As I grew stronger, his visits became more frequent. He encouraged me to work on strengthening my arm. He berated me when I despaired, and boosted my desire for revenge when I did not have the will to live. The day I left the Hospitallers, I could hold the weight of a sword in my right hand, but only for a short while.

"Dominic came with me to Venice. He sparred with me each day, and I grew stronger. The night we saved Marco from a murderous band of thieves, I knew I was strong again. Marco felt so indebted to us he offered us whatever we wished from his stores, whenever we wanted it. To this day, he sends me the best silks off the ships that sail into the port of Venice."

Elizabeth's gaze turned thoughtful. "If you could live as a rich merchant in Venice, why did you return to England?"

With careful fingers, Geoffrey stroked wispy hair from her cheek. "That life was not in my blood. Dominic and I traveled back to England so I could take tenure of Branton Keep, but I knew this fortress would never compare to Wode. I wanted what I should have inherited. What was denied me."

She sighed, and her breath cooled his skin. "You could be happy here. Once you have repaired Branton—"

"I will build a cloth empire in England, but I will have it at Wode."

Her lips tightened. "And revenge."

"Aye, and revenge."

Sadness shadowed her gaze, and she looked again at his hideous scar. "Why can you not see that your desire for vengeance is wrong? You are not a merciless rogue. You—"

He silenced her with a finger to her lips. He laughed, a wicked sound. "I have told you too much. Indeed, I am tired of talking."

She shivered. Her lashes fell, and she covered her breasts with her arms.

A grin tugged at his mouth. She interpreted his words as a dismissal. Did she believe he had grown weary of her? How very foolish.

"You wish me to leave." Her body rigid, she sat up, flipped her hair over her shoulder, and peered over the bed to find her garments.

He caught her around the waist. Tossed her back against the silk pillows. Hovered over her.

"Did I tell you to go?" he growled against her cheek.

"I thought—"

He smothered her words with a kiss, one so blatant a blush stained her cheeks. Her eyes glowed. Her face looked luminous against the black silk of her hair.

"What do you desire now, milord?" she murmured.

Geoffrey grinned. "You."

❖   ❖   ❖

"All is ready, Lord Brackendale," Aldwin said. "The men await your command."

Astride his destrier, adjusting his mail gloves, Arthur narrowed his eyes against the dawn sunlight. He glanced past the squire to the smoking embers and swath of trampled grass, the remains of their camp in the field beside the earl's keep. Aldwin had been efficient, as usual.

The squire's hands curled and uncurled on his horse's reins. His face set in a frown, he turned his horse in tight circles on the dew-laden ground. Arthur shook his head. Since the lad had learned of the ransom demand, he had not stood still. He was impatient to be on the move.

A scowl twisted Arthur's mouth. He felt the same.

He and his men had spent yesterday replenishing supplies from the earl's stores and riding to the far edges of Tillenham's boundaries to rouse the local knights, who had agreed to fight with him in the melee. He would not be defeated by de Lanceau.

Drawing on his simmering fury, Arthur shouted, "We ride!" Thrusting his fist into the air, he signaled his army onto the winding ribbon of dirt road that would lead them to Moyden Wood.

The men behind him rode in silence, their sullen mood matching his. Arthur stared at the fields around him, and bit back a furious bellow. Geoffrey de Lanceau may have succeeded in his deception, but he would learn his folly.

The knights were angry, their tempers thinned by cold, sleepless nights and wretched fare. Of them all, green and seasoned alike, Aldwin had made the fiercest vow that de Lanceau would suffer. The lad saw no honor in de Lanceau making a pawn of one of the fairer sex, and condemned him for not declaring an outright challenge to battle to settle his claim to Wode.

The sun's heat had evaporated most of the morning dew when, on the crest of a distant hill, Arthur spied two figures on horseback. He squinted through his helm's slits. One was a woman clad in a fur-trimmed mantle, the other a man.

Squat, brutish, the ogre looked familiar. Viscon. Arthur's jaw tightened. 'Twas rumored the mercenary had sold his services to de Lanceau.

As the couple drew nearer, the woman's features became clear. Chestnut curls showed at the edge of the mantle, framing a face of such beauty that Arthur's blood ran a little hotter. Yet, as he straightened in the saddle, disquiet rippled through him. Bitterness tinged the smile curving her lush, crimson lips, and ruthless determination gleamed in her amber eyes.

She held his gaze over the last yards separating them. This lady sought him out for a reason. Why did she associate with the vicious, grinning brute riding at her side? Why did she not lower her gaze in respect? Arthur's surcoat identified him as a powerful lord.

His annoyance swelled, for she was bolder still to travel dangerous roads with only one escort. Despite Viscon's reputation, a gang of thieves or bandits could wrest the fine mantle from her back and slash her neck before he had time to draw a weapon.

Arthur ordered the army to halt. As the woman reined in her horse in front of him, sweat beaded his forehead and plastered his hair to his scalp. He took a deep breath, his senses on alert. He smelled flowers. Roses. A lady's scent.

"You are Lord Brackendale of Wode?" she asked, her voice strong in the morning air.

"I am. And you are, milady?"

"Veronique," she answered, her tone husky.

As her slender fingers tightened around her horse's reins, and the mantle's edges parted, Arthur saw the luster of yellow silk. "You are the lady of Branton Keep?" he guessed.

She replied with a throaty laugh.

"She is no *lady*," muttered Aldwin. Arthur knew the slur was intended only for his ears, but the sound carried. Veronique turned her head and glared at the squire, but from one blink to the next, her fury transformed to blatant sexual interest.

As she took a long, thorough look at the lad, Arthur shuddered. "Did de Lanceau send you?" he demanded, reclaiming her attention.

"I come of my own accord. I have a proposal that will benefit us both, milord."

"Return to the cur," he snarled. "I will not barter."

"I suggest you reconsider." She smiled, an angry curl of her lips. "What I intend to tell you concerns your daughter."

❧   ❧   ❧

Elizabeth awoke to soft linen sheets against her skin, a thick feather mattress cradling her body, and sunlight warming her bare shoulders. She stretched her arms out wide. The bed was at least three times as large as that rickety rope thing in her chamber.

She inhaled, and smelled Geoffrey's scent on the sheets . . . and remembered.

With a groan, she slumped back onto the pillow. Opening one eye, she dared to peep over the side of the bed. Her clothes were gone. Glancing toward the hearth, she saw her chemise and bliaut draped—by Geoffrey's hand, she imagined—over the back of one of the chairs.

Memories of her night with him flooded her mind, and her fingers knotted into the bedding. Guilt poked at her like an accusing finger, and, with a firm shake of her head, she forced the remorse aside. She had vowed no regrets, and she would have none. Heat tingled across her skin, still tender from his lovemaking. Why should she feel shame, when their intimacy had been necessary, enlightening and . . . wonderful?

Elizabeth drew the bedding aside, stepped down to the floor, and padded over to the chair. She pulled on the chemise warmed by the fire, and exhaled a long sigh.

Geoffrey was a magnificent lover, his kisses and caresses as sweet as clover honey. Yet she must not succumb to romantic notions of him falling in love with her. They had shared pleasure, sated their physical desire, but in his heart, he did not care for her. He did not love her. Because of his soul-deep hatred of her father, he never would.

She and Geoffrey remained enemies.

But what bliss she had experienced with him.

Indulging in a smile, she ran her fingers through her hair and remembered the boyish grin on Geoffrey's face as he toyed with her ringlets. He had enjoyed learning the secrets of her body, as she had his. After coupling for the second time, he had found comfort in her embrace, for he had fallen asleep with his arms around her.

Odd, how a trust had formed between them by one physical act. An act that had changed her forever—heart, mind, and . . . body.

She twisted around to fasten the chemise. The ties slipped through her fingers, and Elizabeth muttered under her breath. Geoffrey had left her no means to put her clothes back on.

A delicious shiver wove through her. Had he intended to keep her in his solar, awaiting his return for more sensual play?

The fire sparked, releasing the tang of burning pitch, and Elizabeth heard a faint knock. Mayhap Geoffrey had not intended for her to stay in his chamber. He might have sent the guards to fetch her for another day of toil. As the door opened, she clutched at the gaping chemise, but relaxed when Elena slipped inside with a pitcher and wooden board of food.

A blush stung Elizabeth's cheeks. The rumpled bed and her state of undress would tell all that had transpired last eve between her and Geoffrey. Yet the maid did not even look at the bed, but walked straight to the table and set down the fare.

"Good morn, milady," Elena said with her usual timid reserve. "Lord de Lanceau sent me to help you dress." She scooped up the rose wool and shook out the wrinkles.

"Thank you." Warmth blossomed inside Elizabeth, and she could not resist the ridiculous urge to grin. How kind of Geoffrey, to remember her needs.

With deft fingers, the maid tied the chemise then helped Elizabeth don the bliaut.

As Elizabeth perched on the edge of a chair, munching day-old bread, Elena tidied her tresses into a loose braid. "You fare well today, milady?"

"Mmm? Ah, aye. Of course."

"Milord did not punish you too much after what you did to the ale?"

"Nay." Elizabeth fought another blush. What she had been given by Geoffrey could not be called punishment.

"I am glad." Elena exhaled a shaky sigh. "'Twas frightening to see him in such a rage."

"Dominic is recovered now?" Elizabeth asked.

"Aye." Releasing Elizabeth's braided hair, the maid strolled to the bed and smoothed the mussed linens. "Dominic went with Lord de Lanceau to tour the estate today. Dominic refused to lie abed one more day, though milord wished it."

Elizabeth chewed her last bit of bread. "What of Mildred?"

"She weeds the garden. Milord wishes you to work on the saddle trapping."

Elizabeth nodded. She was glad of a day's respite from the gardening and, as she well knew, he could have given her a far more onerous task than the embroidery.

She sat near the hearth in the hall and left her chair once, to eat the midday meal. It seemed strange to dine without Geoffrey's bold presence beside her.

Veronique was absent as well.

As the servants chatted and cleared away the remnants of the meal, Elizabeth returned to her work. The torn silk shifted on her lap, and she straightened it with clammy fingers.

She remembered the shock and loathing in the Veronique's eyes when the courtesan had walked into the solar unannounced. An unspoken rule, that Veronique laid absolute claim to Geoffrey's attentions, had been broken in that moment. Though Elizabeth had resisted him then, Veronique no doubt still held a grudge. The courtesan would hate Elizabeth even more when she learned Geoffrey had spent the night with her in his bed.

Turning the trapping a fraction, Elizabeth began a row of stitches on the embroidered hawk's talons. The needle slipped between her fingers. Had Veronique gone with Geoffrey to the fields? The courtesan enjoyed freedom to roam the keep and its grounds as she pleased. Elizabeth's mouth pinched. Freedom was denied to her. Now, as she embroidered, she was watched by two guards playing a game of dice.

Mayhap Veronique hoped to win Geoffrey back.

Mayhap at this very moment, she kissed him full on the lips. Pleasured him. Ensnared him again in her lover's web.

Jealousy uncoiled in Elizabeth like a hissing snake. She should not care at all about Geoffrey's affairs with Veronique.

Yet Elizabeth could not bear the thought of him making love to the courtesan. Not after last night.

The thread snapped. Elizabeth groaned. She would have

to remove the entire row of stitches and start again. How unfair, that the rogue should be able to rattle her thoughts, when he was not even in the hall.

The servants delayed the evening meal until Geoffrey's return. As the sun's rays lengthened on the walls, Elizabeth heard his unmistakable laughter echo in the forebuilding. Her hand stilled. A thrill of joy and then dread washed through her.

When Dominic and Geoffrey strode into hall, discussing the harvest, she did not glance up. She longed to raise her head and catch Geoffrey's smile, to see his mouth ease into that devastating grin just for her. But she could not bring herself to look him in the eyes. Jealousy chafed like a new wound. How could she look at him, when he had spent the day with Veronique?

As the men's conversation continued, she blew a sigh. Thank the saints he had not seen her by the fire.

The voices stopped. Her relief fled.

Bold footsteps approached. Halted. A broad, tanned hand curled over the arm of her chair. "Damsel," Geoffrey murmured near her ear.

His husky voice sent her pulse pounding with delight. How foolish, that her heart beat so. "Milord," she said, and refused to glance up from inspecting her stitches.

"You have accomplished much today . . ." he said, trailing a finger over the silk.

The slow touch triggered the memory of his hands on

her skin, exploring and caressing. Fierce passion ignited, and she could think of naught but him and the pleasure he had shown her.

He was still speaking. ". . . you have done excellent work."

She shrugged aside her sinful thoughts. "I had no distractions today, milord, to keep me from my work." Though she tried, she could not keep the venom from her voice.

"You are angry with me?"

Her lashes shot up. A curious smile hovered on his lips. His windswept hair curled over the collar of his moss green tunic flecked with dirt and grain husks. He looked rugged, wild, and very handsome.

His gaze dropped to her mouth, a silent kiss. When he handed her a single, bright blue cornflower, her breath jammed.

Did he think she would not know?

She did not take the flower. She stared at her hands clenched into the trapping. "You must take me for a fool."

"Did one of the servants offend you?" His tone sharpened with each word. "Did Elena speak amiss when I sent her to you this morn?"

"Nay."

"Why do you not welcome me with your eyes?" His voice dropped to a purr and he brushed the petals against her cheek. "Did you miss me?"

She answered with an indignant snort.

Geoffrey chuckled. "Ah. You are annoyed because I spent the day away from my bed. And you."

"Cease!" Elizabeth stood and threw the trapping into a heap on the chair.

Geoffrey's eyes hardened. He did not look at all guilty, curse him. Annoyed, confused, and tired beneath the smudges of dust on his face, but not ashamed.

He set the flower on the side table. "I thought that after what we shared last night, you would have softened a little."

"You expect too much."

"Why?"

How well he portrayed his innocence. His cool gray eyes hid a lie well. Elizabeth thought of him pressing Veronique's naked body down in a patch of meadow grass, his hot mouth on her skin, and fought a furious shriek. "You should not ask me why. *You* wished to spend your day with someone else."

"If you mean Dominic, aye, he came with me to the fields, but he always does."

"I do not mean Dominic," Elizabeth bit out.

"Then whom?" He sounded annoyed and frustrated.

"Who else?" Hurt ripped into her. "The woman who throws herself at your feet."

"Veronique?"

"Do not sound surprised."

He frowned. "I have not seen her all day."

"Nor have I."

For a moment, wariness shadowed his features. "She did

not attend the midday meal?"

"Please," Elizabeth muttered. "You need not spare my feelings. I am not naïve. I realize last eve was no more than a meaningless—"

Geoffrey's look of pure fury stopped her. "You know naught. 'Tis not your place to question me, but I swear to you, I did not spend my day with Veronique."

He turned to Dominic, who stood near a trestle table and looked baffled. It seemed the knight did not know of her and Geoffrey's liaison before now. "Find Veronique," Geoffrey said with a growl.

"She 'as gone ta market," piped up one of the kitchen maids, who was carrying in a wooden board laden with roasted hare.

"*What?*" Geoffrey's gaze fell upon the small, dark haired woman who looked about to collapse in a faint. She dropped the board on the nearest table, scattering the dogs at her feet with the loud clatter, and curtsied.

"She left early this morn, she did. Ta buy rosewater."

"Veronique did not send a servant fetch it for her?" His stern, disbelieving tone sent the maid into another curtsey.

"'Twas such a foin day, milord, she decided ta go 'erself. I also overheard her the other week sayin' that the merchant in Branton sold her bad oils. She told me she wanted ta ride to the fair in Haverly ta see if she could buy better there."

"Haverly is a day's ride from here," said Geoffrey.

"Aye, milord." The maid straightened.

"She went alone?"

"Nay. Viscon went with 'er."

Geoffrey's expression darkened. "She knows I despise the man. Why would she—"

"Veronique also knows the roads are too dangerous for a woman to travel alone," Dominic said. "Who better to protect her from thieves and bandits than a skilled mercenary?"

"I do not like it." Geoffrey raked his fingers through his hair. "'Tis not usual."

"Today, much is not usual," Dominic murmured with a wry smile. Elizabeth did not mistake his meaning, and blushed.

"Veronique knows not to test my temper." Geoffrey paced the floorboards. Rushes crackled under his boots. "When she returns to the keep, send her to me."

Dominic bowed. "Of course, milord."

As Geoffrey swung back to face her, Elizabeth stiffened.

"Your jealousy is ill placed, damsel."

She plucked a silver thread from her sleeve. "'Tis ridiculous for me to be concerned with such matters."

"Because of the melee?"

"Because you are my enemy."

A crooked smile teased his lips. "Did you ever stop to think, damsel," he murmured, "I might never let you go?"

Elizabeth forced a laugh. "You jest."

An indefinable emotion flashed in his eyes and vanished on his next blink. "Come, I am starving." He held out his hand to her. The dark haired maidservant hurried past and set the roasted meat, steaming bowls of cabbage pottage, and wine on the lord's table.

Elizabeth looked at his fingers, upturned in invitation. She could refuse, but she did not. She did not want to. His hand closed around hers, and he led her toward the dais.

The warmth of his touch coursed through her.

Bliss . . .

✠ ✠ ✠

Arthur glared at Veronique sitting on the opposite side of the tent, which the men-at-arms had erected in haste by the side of the road.

The woman was as cunning as she was beautiful. She refused to divulge even a scrap of information until she sat in a comfortable chair, ate a decent meal, and drank a goblet of his finest French wine to quench her thirst.

Even Viscon indulged like nobility, though Arthur had denied the scum the privilege of dining in a private tent.

Bees hummed in the clover outside, making Arthur even more aware of the silence within, a silence the wench controlled. Veronique met Arthur's gaze. Her lips spread into a knowing smile, and she ran her tongue along the edge of the silver goblet, catching a drop of wine.

Arthur's patience snapped. He lunged to his feet and almost charged into the corpulent, wheezing knight who staggered through the tent's flap.

"Baron Sedgewick," Arthur said, startled. "I expected to meet you and your army at Moyden Wood. My message—"

"Was delivered as you ordered." The baron grasped his chain-mailed side as though to relieve a cramp. Footsteps sounded outside, and Aldwin appeared through the flap with a wine jug and goblets. "Ah, good. I knew I could count on you, squire."

Arthur frowned. "How—"

Sedgewick poured and guzzled wine with alarming speed. "When the messenger told me of my dear betrothed's plight"—he belched—"and the ransom demand, I followed him to you post haste." He brushed sweat from the end of his bulbous nose and rolls of fat jiggled at his wrist. "Poor, dear Lady Elizabeth."

"So this is the thwarted groom," Veronique drawled.

"Thwarted?" Arthur swung back to face her. "Explain."

"Who is *she?*" The baron's small, glittering eyes wandered up and down Veronique's figure. She had shed the mantle, revealing voluptuous curves encased in silk. A fresh sheen shimmered on the baron's brow.

"Veronique," Arthur said through his teeth. "She is de Lanceau's courtesan."

"*Was,*" she corrected with a smooth toss of her chestnut curls. "Another has taken my place."

"I care not for trivialities." Arthur took a determined step closer. "I have given you food and drink. I wish to hear of my daughter. Without delay. Or I shall have the information flogged out of you."

Apprehension flickered across her painted features, but was repressed by sheer malice. "Be warned, milord. You will not like what I am about to say."

"Tell me."

"Very well. The wench Geoffrey de Lanceau has taken to his bed is your daughter, Elizabeth."

Arthur's breath exploded from his lips. The baron looked about to topple over, but Aldwin reached out and steadied him. The squire looked shocked.

"Why do you test me with falsehoods?" Arthur snarled. Spittle flew from his mouth with the force of his words.

With vexing calm, Veronique sipped her wine. "'Tis not a falsehood."

"Liar! Lady Elizabeth would never lie with de Lanceau," Aldwin shouted, his reddened face taut with indignation. "She is a woman of virtue and beauty."

Veronique's angry gaze fixed upon the squire. "You believe he gave her a choice?"

"God's blood!" moaned Sedgewick. "My dear betrothed, suffering such brutality." He gulped wine, half of it running down his chin and onto his mail and spattering on the ground.

"I witnessed his cruelty with my own eyes," Veronique said. "She wept and screamed and begged him for mercy. He showed her none."

Aldwin gripped the hilt of his sword with such violence, his knuckles snapped. "I will kill him!"

Veronique rose from the chair, her bliaut rustling. She glided toward Arthur, and he tensed. The wench was not finished with what she had come to say. She halted a hand's span away, her sweet fragrance cloying in the confines of the tent.

"I bring you this terrible news," she said, looking up into his face, "because I know Geoffrey de Lanceau. I know how he thinks and what he intends for Wode. I can get you past Branton Keep's gates."

Arthur scowled. Why would she offer to help him? She owed him no loyalty. Indeed, he saw not the slightest hint of integrity in her gaze. "You can get my men inside the bailey?"

She nodded. "'Twill be far quicker than a melee. By attacking de Lanceau without warning—with his hose down, if you pardon the crude phrase—your victory is guaranteed."

"I have already issued my challenge," muttered Arthur. "'Twould be dishonorable not to fulfill the terms of that arrangement."

Her laughter mocked him. "Qualms, milord? You treat de Lanceau with honor when he showed you none? After he deceived you and *raped* your daughter?"

Rage surged inside Arthur like a battle cry. "You are so willing to betray him?"

"For the right cause."

"A price, you mean."

She smiled.

Arthur's mouth curled in disgust. Devious wench. Still, her plan held merit, providing he could ensure she did not deceive him as well.

He motioned to Aldwin. Shaking his head, the squire stormed out of the tent and returned with a small wooden chest. He sprung the lock and raised the lid, revealing hundreds of silver coins bearing the stamped, curly-haired visage of Henry II.

Veronique's eyes gleamed.

"Is it enough?" Arthur asked. With immense effort, he resisted the urge to shake the greedy smile from her lips.

"Aye," she murmured. "I believe 'tis."

CHAPTER SEVENTEEN

"Your move, milady."

Elizabeth looked down at the beautiful inlaid leather chessboard Dominic had loaned her earlier that eve. She had not played the game in months and felt much out of practice. Despite her claim to possess an old and addled brain, Mildred would win this one for certain.

Sighing, Elizabeth propped her elbow on the trestle table, rested her cheek on her palm and studied the carved chess pieces. Geoffrey lounged at the lord's table though the meal had ended some time ago. She sensed his gaze wandering over her. Again. He watched her like a ravenous hawk.

"Good man." He gestured to the coppery-haired musician who sat near the hearth, playing a lute. "Play something merry."

The lutenist chuckled. "Merry, milord?"

Geoffrey banged his goblet on the table, startling Elizabeth and the mongrel curled at her feet. "A song to lift my spirits and ease my loneliness."

Curiosity nagged at her. Tilting her head, Elizabeth cast him a sidelong glance. Geoffrey caught her gaze and stared at her with such scorching heat, she blushed. Did he hope to resume their intimacy this eve? She shook the enticing, wanton thought from her mind and brought her attention back to the game.

The musician's fingers flew over the strings of the pear-shaped instrument and plucked a familiar melody. Elizabeth recognized the song. Her mother had loved to dance to it. Her feet had flown over the floor as if she were weightless.

Sadness weighed upon Elizabeth. Once returned to Wode, she must make sure the orphans' gowns were embroidered and delivered as soon as possible, in honor of her mother's passing.

"You seem leagues away, damsel." Geoffrey's voice came from nearby, and, as he sat down beside her, the bench shifted and squeaked. He leaned forward and his shoulder brushed hers in silent, physical communication.

"'Tis the music. It reminded me of long ago."

"Your mother favored this song, if my memory is correct," Mildred said with a smug grin. Elizabeth shot her a warning glare. Without fail, the matron's tongue wagged after too much wine.

"Harrumph! Do not scowl at me, milady. I do not

intend to become besotted from this rogue's drink."

"I did not mean to remind you of your mother," Geoffrey said, his words soft with apology. His hand closed over Elizabeth's, and, together, they moved a pawn forward into an empty square. As they did so she wondered what had become of her mother's brooch. Would he return it to her now, if she asked?

He stroked his thumb along the sensitive curve between her thumb and finger, and the thought blurred. "Tonight, we shall celebrate some of the joys of life," he murmured. "Will you join us?"

She wet her lips. "Milord—"

He released her hand and snapped his fingers. The lutenist began a new song. A few of the servants started to dance. They linked hands, formed a ring, and stepped and turned. The lute player quickened the pace and pounded out the rhythm with his foot, while another musician joined him and drummed the beat on a tabor.

Dominic approached from a far table. "Will one of you beauties accompany me?"

Elizabeth shook her head.

Mildred pouted and took a big gulp of wine. "I am old enough to have birthed you. I know you do not wish to dance with a crotchety old woman."

"Age brings experience," Dominic said with a crooked grin. "Come, Mildred. Let us show them how 'tis done."

The matron cackled. "You are a charmer." Smiling, she

struggled up from the bench, took the arm he offered and they strolled toward the dancers. As the clasped hands parted, Mildred and Dominic joined the ring.

Geoffrey propped one leg up on the bench and leaned sideways against the table's edge. "You do not enjoy dancing, damsel?"

"'Tis not right to celebrate." Elizabeth sipped her wine, dark and red as blood.

"'Tis foolish to dwell on events that may never happen, or ones you cannot prevent."

He spoke of the melee. Refusing to meet his gaze, to let him see her uncertainty, she watched Dominic and Mildred twirl and dance. The matron's wrinkled face glowed with the effects of wine and good cheer.

"Dance with me, Elizabeth," Geoffrey whispered.

The decision was made for her. At that moment, the dancers separated and Mildred whirled toward the table. She grabbed Elizabeth's hand and pulled her toward the ring.

"Mildred, nay."

"Please, milady. 'Tis most enjoyable."

As the dancers turned and stepped in exact time, Elizabeth found herself drawn into the momentum. The music quickened even more, but she sensed the rhythm and kept pace. The melody hummed in her blood.

She dipped and turned, her bliaut billowing at her ankles. She stomped on herbs strewn in with the rushes, and the blended tang of rosemary, thyme, and meadowsweet rose up from the floor. Her braid came loose and hair tumbled thick and wild about her face. Caught up in the swell of music and emotion, she felt more alive than at any other moment in her life.

Mildred grinned, and Elizabeth laughed. The dance quickened again. Faster. Faster she turned, whirling around in a blur of hair. She dipped, turned, and spun . . . until strong arms pried her from the ring and drew her into the stairwell's shadows.

With a raw groan, Geoffrey pressed her against the cool stone wall. His breath gusted against her brow.

"Ah, damsel. What you do to me." His lips crushed hers in a kiss so intense, Elizabeth's knees buckled.

"I must go back," she whispered, even as she kissed him with equal fever.

"Nay." Geoffrey lifted her into his arms and took the stairs to the solar two at a time. Striding to the bed, he sat her on the edge, yanked off her slippers, and slid her bliaut over her head in one fluid motion. He kissed her until her she gasped and quivered.

His hand slid beneath her chemise.

"Geoffrey," she whispered, "we cannot."

"You belong to me." With gentle hands, he pressed her back on the coverlet.

She shook her head. "Impossible."

"If you do not believe, let me show you." He coaxed her with his mouth, his fingers, and tender words whispered over her flushed skin.

When the tempest consumed her this time, Elizabeth soared with such joy she wished she could hold Geoffrey in her heart forever.

She wondered when the dream would shatter around her.

❈ ❈ ❈

Arthur stood in the tent's entrance and watched Veronique secure a clinking leather sack to the front of her horse's saddle. He had given her half of the silver in the chest. The remainder she would receive at Branton, providing she kept her end of the bargain. She had not liked his stipulation, but with a furious nod, had agreed.

Veronique turned to him. "Till the morrow, milord."

"You are a lady of your word?"

She tittered. "Lady, nay. But I will not fail you. The portcullis and drawbridge shall not bar your way if you arrive at Branton Keep as arranged."

"Do not betray me, Veronique."

Her eyes flashed in the twilight. "You question my trustworthiness *after* parting with your coin?"

Viscon laughed and heaved his body up onto his horse, a roan as ugly as its master.

"I paid a great deal for your help, Veronique," Arthur said and started toward her, his surcoat flapping in the breeze. "You, in turn, offer me no guarantees but your word. You must agree 'tis not much to weigh against a sack of silver." As her gaze hardened, he forced a genial smile. "You will understand, then, why I am sending men to accompany you, to ensure our agreement is met."

Her mouth tautened with anger, and he thought he heard her mask of rouge and powder crack. "You will draw attention to me. Do you think 'twill be easy for me to bribe the guards without de Lanceau finding out?"

"That is why I paid you well. If you cannot fulfill our arrangement, I will have the coin."

"Nay!" Veronique gripped the bag. She looked prepared to gouge out his eyes if he tried to wrest the coin from her. "You may send your escort. Two men, no more."

"Four," Arthur said. He would not underestimate Viscon. This time, Arthur had not bought the mercenary's loyalty. If he and Veronique decided to flee with the coin, 'twould take four able knights to subdue the brute.

"Four," she agreed with a sneer, "but I work alone."

"As long as the deed is done."

"Christ's blood! 'Twill be."

Arthur signaled to the armed soldiers who stood nearby. He picked four of his trusted knights and ordered them to their horses.

"Milord." Aldwin strode over from the fire, buckling on his broadsword. "I beg you to let me ride escort as well."

Arthur shook his head. "There is much to do here before the morrow."

"I must go!" The squire flushed. "Milord, I cannot sit idle when Eliz—milady—is violated by that whoreson."

"I like it no more than you," Arthur said with a growl, "but a rash challenge from you will not free her. You will remain with the rest of the soldiers. Go. Check my sword is sharpened and my horse is rubbed down."

"Already done, milord," Aldwin said.

"Do the tasks again."

The squire's eyes blazed, but he bowed and stalked off toward the horses.

Veronique sat in sullen silence upon on her mount, her curls crushed beneath her cloak's fur-trimmed hood. He sensed her fury, reined in like the animal beneath her. The wench seethed, and from more than his demand to send an escort. She wanted to see de Lanceau suffer. She wanted to watch him die.

Arthur did not envy de Lanceau in the least.

"Can we trust her?" Sedgewick asked in a low voice, coming to Arthur's side. The baron had found a meat pie somewhere and crammed it into his mouth.

"Veronique will do as I paid her."

"My dear Elizabeth." The baron swiped crumbs from his chin with his tunic's sleeve. "The morrow shall not come soon enough."

With a terse command, Veronique kicked her horse toward the road. The sentries followed a few paces behind her and Viscon, and hoofbeats reverberated into the night air until the party disappeared from view. Veronique never looked back, and Arthur did not mistake the slight.

Nor did he miss the anger in Aldwin's eyes as the squire strode past into the tent.

Arthur sighed and turned to the baron. "Will you join me for more wine?"

The tent's opening snapped open and Aldwin brushed by with a woolen blanket, and headed for the tree where Arthur's destrier was hobbled.

"May I drink with you in a moment?" Sedgewick asked, his eyes bright. "There is a small matter I must see to first."

"Of course." Arthur stepped into the stuffy tent which still smelled of rosewater, but after a moment's hesitation, pulled back the flap and watched the baron hasten after Aldwin. Sedgewick's belly wobbled from side to side with each of his furtive steps, and he did not slow down until he caught up with the squire. They disappeared behind the destrier.

What did Sedgewick require of Aldwin?

Mayhap he wished the squire to tend his horse or give it an extra ration of oats. Shrugging, Arthur dropped the flap and reached for the wine. Whatever the baron needed, Arthur doubted the matter was of great consequence.

✠   ✠   ✠

Elizabeth awoke to shouts in the bailey. Blinking to clear the sleep from her eyes, she saw the sky beyond the solar's window was blue-gray. Near dawn. She rolled onto her side, dragging the snug bedding with her, and found Geoffrey had risen. He stood silhouetted against the firelight, pulling on his hose.

A knock rattled the solar's doors.

"Milord!" Dominic's cry sounded urgent. A tremor of unease rippled through Elizabeth. Clasping the bedding, she pushed up to sitting.

Geoffrey shrugged into a burgundy tunic, ran to the doors and yanked them open. Dominic strode in. Alarm buzzed in Elizabeth's veins. His face grim, he wore a broadsword strapped over a chain mail hauberk. The iron helm tucked under his arm gleamed like a bleached skull.

"What has happened?" Geoffrey demanded.

"An army approaches. At least a hundred knights."

Tugging down his sleeves, Geoffrey froze. "A siege! I should have foreseen Brackendale's treachery."

"Father?" Elizabeth wrapped the linen sheet round her body and leapt from the bed. She ran to the windows and looked out.

Dawn's watery light glinted off the conical helms of mounted knights. Foot soldiers trailed through the stubbled fields on the other side of the lake, pikes held high as they marched in formation toward the keep. The rumble of wagons carried like distant thunder. She skimmed the lines of men, trying to recognize her sire, but the head of the procession had already passed from view.

"Why has he come?" Elizabeth whispered, whirling to face Geoffrey. The sheet tightened around her body, restricting her movement. "You agreed to a melee in Moyden Wood."

His mouth compressed to a bitter line. "I did."

"Why would my father bring his army to Branton, then?"

"I have been betrayed."

The dead calm in Geoffrey's voice slammed into her. Fear tore through her—for her father, for herself, and most of all, the rogue who had made her soul and body glow.

"Who would dare to betray you?" she shrieked.

He did not answer. His gaze shadowed, and he looked at Dominic. "Send the women and children below to the storage rooms. They will be safe there. Wake every able-bodied man and order them to the bailey. Double the guards at the gate. No one enters or leaves."

"Aye, milord."

Elizabeth held her breath until the doors clicked shut behind Dominic. She trembled. "Geoffrey, what will you do?"

He strode to the wooden chest against the wall, shoved open the lid, and withdrew a suit of mail armor. "What I am expected to do. Fight."

"You cannot! Please. This must be a misunderstanding—"

He dropped the chain mail on the bed and the iron links settled with a metallic *chink*. "I knew your father and I would face one another in battle, but I did not imagine 'twould be today." He smiled at her, but his expression offered neither tenderness nor comfort. "You do not dance with joy, milady?"

He reached into the chest again and tossed a padded gambeson and sheathed sword atop the mail. "Why not? You have looked forward to your rescue."

Elizabeth shivered and turned her back to him. She could not bear his callous words, not when she remembered the taste of his bronzed skin beneath her lips. It had been wondrous to curl up in his arms, to sleep with her back pressed against his chest, to feel each of his breaths pressing his body closer to hers. She would cherish those moments forever.

"Elizabeth?"

Tears misted her vision, but she blinked them away. She crushed her fingers into the sheet. "How can I be joyous, when this may be the last time I see you alive?"

"A lady like you wants naught from a rogue like me."

She could not stop a sad smile. "Only your heart."

"Ah." His laughter sounded strained. "My heart carved out in triumph and displayed on a silver platter. 'The dark heart of a traitor's son,' the soldiers will cheer. 'Strange how his blood is red like ours.' Shall you also demand my severed head? My steaming entrails? My—"

"Never!" She swung around to face him, her cheeks wet with tears. "How can you accuse me of such atrocious things? How, after all that we have shared?"

He glanced at the rumpled bed. Anguish clouded his gaze, and he shook his head. "Elizabeth, I—"

"Do you believe I care naught for you? That I wish you dead?"

A muscle ticked in his jaw. "With all that stands between us, damsel, 'tis not a fair question. As well you know." He picked up his sword, drew it part-way from the scabbard, and checked the lethal blade.

Desperation screamed inside her. "Do not fight my father." Her words softened to an urgent plea. "I beg you, find another way to resolve your feud."

He sheathed the weapon and dropped it onto the coverlet. "Do not ask me to forfeit my revenge. I cannot and *will not* promise you that. I have waited eighteen years for this fight."

"I could not bear to see you killed." A sob wrenched from her before she could put her hand over her mouth.

Geoffrey bowed his head and cursed. It seemed an eternity before he crossed the few steps between them and gathered her in his arms. He held her in a firm, possessive hug, and she pressed her face against his tunic. "I never thought to hear you say those words," he murmured into her hair.

"Nor did I."

With exquisite tenderness, he smoothed the damp curls away from her face and tilted her chin up, warming her with his sensual smile. "When the siege is over, we will speak of us again," he whispered against her lips.

"Promise?" Elizabeth linked her fingers through his. The press of his strong hands offered reassurance, yet fear roiled inside her like a terrible beast. Despite his brave words, Geoffrey might not live to see another dawn.

"I promise," he said. "With my very breath."

She managed a weak smile. "'Tis not your breath I want to seal your vow, milord."

Half-chuckling, half-groaning, Geoffrey dipped his head and kissed her until her pulse pounded and her knees shook. As he drew back, he brushed away her tears with the pad of his thumb. "No more crying, damsel."

As he stepped away, Elizabeth sniffled and hugged the sheet close to her chest. "What will happen to me?"

He scooped up his gambeson, armor and sword and strode for the doors. "You will be safe here. Stay in the solar," Geoffrey said over his shoulder. "I do not want you harmed."

She huffed a breath. "You cannot expect me to sit idle and wait. I do not want you to die, but I will not allow you to kill my father, either."

"Stay inside," Geoffrey repeated, his tone firm. The door slammed behind him.

Elizabeth ran to the window. The stream of knights and soldiers had passed, but a cloud of dust lingered in the air. Distant shouts and commotion reached her.

She could not twiddle her thumbs while Geoffrey and her father battled.

She would not stay in the solar, alone, and await the outcome of the siege.

Not when Geoffrey's life and her father's were at stake.

Not if she could prevent the bloodshed.

She searched the floor for her chemise, yanked it on, and did not bother to tie the laces. Her hands shaking, she shoved on the rose wool and hurried to the doors. They were not locked.

Three guards stood down the corridor, but were preoccupied lacing another sentry into a battered leather hauberk.

She slipped out into the corridor and hurried away.

"That is the last of the longbows, milord," Dominic said. "The crossbows have been handed out." The knight tossed a quiver of arrows to a young sentry, while Geoffrey passed the remaining pikes and swords to the bleary-eyed servants and men-at-arms congregated in the bailey.

Geoffrey squinted up at the wall walk. A handful of trained archers stood in place, poised to fire upon intruders crossing the moat to scale the outer curtain wall. God above, 'twas a tiny force to hold back a large army. In a booming voice, he ordered more armed men to the wall walk.

The snorts of horses anticipating battle, the jangle of bridles, the tromped footfalls and shouts of trained men carried to him on the breeze. Outside Branton's walls, Brackendale had gathered a formidable force, no doubt with Baron Sedgewick's assistance.

At least Branton Keep was well fortified. Brackendale's men would have to cross the moat, and any soldiers forging through the deep water made easy targets for the archers. If the soldiers made it across alive, they would have to break through the drawbridge and portcullis—

A sound grated down every vertebra in his spine. The drawbridge. Descending.

"God's teeth!" he roared.

Dominic turned, his face white with shock. "The gatehouse," he said above the cries of alarm. "Traitors."

Rage and disbelief thundering in his blood, Geoffrey ran for the looming stone building. The mail hauberk, the repaired armor he had worn in battle at Acre, thumped against his legs and slowed his pace. His chausses lay in a heap beside the bailey wall, abandoned because more important matters had demanded his attention. He could not turn back and put them on.

He reached the gatehouse's entry door. Locked.

Geoffrey pounded his fists on the rough wood and bellowed as splinters dug into his skin. No one answered.

"The wall walk entry," he shouted. Geoffrey bolted up the stone stairs beside the right watchtower with Dominic close behind. He had ascended but a few steps when a hideous roar sounded above him. He glanced up. His belly turned liquid.

Viscon. A drawn sword gleamed in the mercenary's hand.

As he reached for his blade, Geoffrey swallowed hard. He had not trusted the mercenary when he bought his loyalty. Fighting for the enemy, the man was an even more fearsome foe. Garbed in a hauberk of boiled leather, Viscon looked like the county executioner.

Pacing the mercenary along the uneven stair, Geoffrey forced himself to ignore the taunts spewing from the ogre's cracked lips. Geoffrey dodged Viscon's first calculated feint. Grunting, the mercenary lunged again. Their swords clanged. Geoffrey tensed, expecting Viscon to follow with a crushing blow, but, as the sound of metal grinding against metal rent the air, the mercenary leapt back a few steps. He grinned and leered down into the bailey.

Geoffrey dared a sidelong glance. His gut lurched. The drawbridge was lowered. The portcullis was being winched up at an alarming rate. Mail-clad knights and foot soldiers streamed into the bailey and fanned out to confront the soldiers and terrified servants struggling to find swords and don any remaining armor.

Viscon chortled and raised his sword. "I pity ye, de Lanceau."

Eyes narrowed, Geoffrey braced himself for the final attack. He lunged.

His boot hit a raised stone.

He stumbled.

Dominic darted forward. "Pity you, fool." His sword plunged into the mercenary's stomach with the sounds of cracking leather and spurting blood.

His eyes bulging in their sockets, Viscon collided with the wall. He slid to the stair in a crimson puddle. His breath rushed out on a final, rattled gasp. Whispering a few words, Dominic reached over and closed Viscon's eyelids.

Geoffrey blew a sigh. "Many thanks, my friend."

A weak grin tilted Dominic's mouth. "I owed you twice for saving my life. Now, I only owe you once."

Behind them, the archers on the battlements unleashed a hail of arrows upon the army in the bailey. Men screamed. Arrows pinged off shields and helms. Horses whinnied and swords shrieked. As Geoffrey started down the stairwell, the archers fought a concentrated attack from the moat side of the curtain wall. The rain of arrows diminished, and then stopped.

Geoffrey's blood ran cold. The enemy had control of the bailey.

His fist tightened around his sword as one knight, mounted on a huge bay destrier and wearing a silk surcoat, kicked his horse forward and claimed the ground separating the armies. His helm sat low over his face. The nasal guard obscured his features except for his angular jaw and the glint of his piercing blue eyes. Even so, Geoffrey recognized him.

The man who had killed his father.

At last, vengeance.

Geoffrey's leather grip burned his palm. The cry to charge forward, slash, and avenge howled inside him, and he sucked in a slow breath. He must not ruin his victory. He must not give Brackendale any reason to cut him down before the battle between them had been fought. His arm trembled with the immense effort, yet Geoffrey sheathed his weapon.

"Geoffrey de Lanceau," Brackendale roared.

Hands on his hips, Geoffrey strode out of the stairwell's shadows and halted before the destrier. He stood firm as the older lord's gaze raked over him, from his hair to his leather boots.

"You bastard!" Brackendale shouted.

Geoffrey did not flinch.

"Where is my daughter?"

"Safe."

The lord's mouth curled. "*Where?*"

Geoffrey smiled, but did not answer.

With a furious growl, Brackendale reached for his sword. The blade whipped out of the scabbard with ferocious speed. He tilted the weapon at Geoffrey's chest. Warning whooshed through Geoffrey, yet he quelled the impulse to draw his blade, even though the pommel sat close to his fingers.

Brackendale's eyes glittered with warning. "You are surrounded, de Lanceau. I have superior forces, and will not hesitate to demolish this keep, stone by stone, and kill every living thing within it. Tell me where to find Elizabeth. Now. Or I will give the order."

"I thought we were to have a melee," Geoffrey said and raised an eyebrow. "Were you afraid to fight me, old man?"

"How dare you?!"

"Mayhap you feared I would best you." Geoffrey folded his arms across his mailed chest, pretending nonchalance.

"'Twould be ignoble to die by the sword of Edouard de Lanceau's son, a traitor's son, would it not?"

The older lord's mouth thinned. He shoved the tip of his weapon into Geoffrey's mail. The pressure bruised, even through the padded gambeson, but Geoffrey did not step back or acknowledge the discomfort. He would not show weakness, not when a battle lay ahead and he aimed to win.

"Your mockery is far from amusing," Brackendale snapped.

"But true. You attack me with my defenses down. Not a fair fight. Where is the honor in that, Lord Brackendale?"

"You speak to me of honor?" bellowed the older lord. "I see none in falsifying missives."

"True. 'Twas a necessary diversion, though, and it worked."

"You made a fool of me."

"I want Wode," Geoffrey said. "If I thought you would recognize my claim, the ruse would not have been necessary."

Brackendale's sword bit deeper. "Did you also plan to defile my daughter?"

Geoffrey flinched.

Behind Brackendale, a bloated knight on horseback swore. He removed his helm and mopped sweat from his brow. Geoffrey scowled. Baron Sedgewick. How could Brackendale have betrothed Elizabeth to this cruel, pathetic excuse for a man? His jaw hardened at the thought of the baron, or any man, touching her the way he had.

When he saw the woman standing in the shadow of one of the watchtowers, tucking a chestnut curl under her mantle's hood, his scowl deepened. Veronique. He had guessed she betrayed him, but the confirmation stung. She cast him a gloating smile before turning and crossing the drawbridge to join the soldiers guarding the moat.

A harsh grin slanted Brackendale's mouth, as though he had read Geoffrey's thoughts. "You thought I did not know about Elizabeth?"

Rage and anguish blazed in Brackendale's eyes, and Geoffrey guessed Veronique's words had not been favorable or true. "Lord Brackendale—"

"Bastard!" The older lord spat. "You will pay for deceiving me. You will suffer for every wretched moment I wasted riding to Tillenham. Above all, you will pay for dishonoring my daughter."

"I did naught she did not want," Geoffrey said.

Brackendale thrust his sword deeper. "You lie!"

Pain radiated through Geoffrey's flesh. He gritted his teeth and fought the battle yell burning in his throat. He would not attack first.

"You will die like a dog," Brackendale snarled, spittle foaming at his mouth. "Take a good look around you, for 'twill be your last." He whipped his blade up and back, poised to lop Geoffrey's head from his shoulders.

Geoffrey drew his sword.

"Father! *Nay!*"

Brackendale's arm jerked. With an awkward turn of his wrist, he halted the sword's arc and stared in the direction of the piercing cry.

Geoffrey dared to look as well. Elizabeth ran out of the forebuilding, her bliaut flapping about her legs, her tresses streaming out behind her. He would die before he let the baron place a hand on her delicate, scented skin.

She ran to Brackendale's side. "Father."

As the older lord reached down and smoothed her tousled hair, his hand shook. "Elizabeth. Thank God you are all right."

Sedgewick sighed with relief. "Beloved."

Elizabeth did not even glance at the baron. "Father, please," she said, her skin ashen in the sunlight. "No one has to die."

Her gaze turned to Geoffrey, and he steeled his emotions against the distress in her eyes, moist with tears. He flexed his hold on his sword's grip, resenting the sweat on his palms. No matter what he felt for her, he must not allow her to distract him or sway him from vengeance.

His blood buzzed with anticipation. The vow he had shouted years ago, that had branded his soul, echoed in his mind. *I will avenge you, Father. God's holy blood, I will avenge you.*

"Get to safety, Elizabeth," Brackendale ordered in a gruff voice. "You need not witness the fight."

"Please, listen to me."

The older lord placed a firm hand upon her shoulder. "I will kill him first. I will see him dead, for all he has done to you."

Elizabeth's eyes flew wide. "Nay! He—"

"Do as he says, damsel," Geoffrey murmured.

She gaped at him, looking stunned. Wounded. "Geoffrey?"

"Pah! You address this cur by his Christian name?" Brackendale sneered.

"He is as human as you, Father," cried Elizabeth. "You must heed me. Lay down your sword. Let me explain."

Brackendale signaled to two of his knights and, despite Elizabeth's struggles, they pulled her back into his soldiers' ranks.

"Father!" she screamed. "Stop!" The knights held her firm.

Geoffrey shuddered. He hated to hear her distress, but at least she would be protected from any harm.

The older lord dismounted from his destrier, removed his helm and tossed it to his squire. "You want a fight, de Lanceau? You shall have it. We will settle our enmity once and for all."

Expectation tingled through Geoffrey. "Do you think you can best me?"

"I *will* defeat you. When you lie broken and dying, you will watch this keep's walls fall in around you." Brackendale raised his blade and lunged.

Geoffrey leapt aside and laughed. "That is the best you can do?"

Brackendale growled. He thrust again, aiming for Geoffrey's midsection. With a snarl, Geoffrey dodged the blow and sliced his blade upward. Brackendale darted back.

Geoffrey smiled and the battle call rang louder in his blood. Every muscle in his body coiled for attack as he circled. Assessed. Struck.

Metal clanged and shrieked. The swords locked until Geoffrey shoved away. Slashing his blade down, he caught Brackendale full across his forearm. The older lord groaned.

Geoffrey paused, breathing hard. Had he fractured bone? Brackendale staggered. Allowing him just enough time to regain his balance, Geoffrey lunged forward. His sword hit chain mail. The links protecting the older lord's thigh shattered. Blood ran down his leg.

Frantic cries erupted behind Geoffrey. He shut them out. The ambrosial taste of victory flooded his mouth. A growl rumbled in his throat, and he aimed another strike at Brackendale's injured arm.

The older lord jerked his sword up, and the sharp edge skidded across the front of Geoffrey's aging armor. Mail links cracked. Snapped. As the weapon's tip sliced through the padded gambeson and tunic to bare flesh, Geoffrey gasped. He stumbled, feeling the hot trickle of blood. It spattered on his hand.

He saw his father dying. The pool of blood on the dirty straw.

God's holy blood, I will avenge you.

In a haze of agony, he looked up to see Brackendale grinning. The older lord raised his sword and aimed it at Geoffrey's broken mail. Blocking out the pain, drawing upon his fury, Geoffrey leapt forward. Slash after slash, he drove Brackendale across the bailey, parting the crowds of soldiers.

The silver-haired lord grunted, weakening under the onslaught. Geoffrey did not relent. Perspiration ran down his face. Blood dripped onto the ground.

Brackendale stumbled. Uncertainty flashed in his eyes.

Seizing the advantage, Geoffrey lunged forward, just as the older lord regained his footing. The weapon cut across Brackendale's thigh. He cried out. Geoffrey stepped forward, hooked his boot behind Brackendale's injured leg, and shoved him backward.

The older lord crashed to the ground.

"*Father!*"

Geoffrey struggled to shut out Elizabeth's wail and the stinging emotion accompanying it. He raked hair from his eyes and glared down at his enemy, lying dazed at his feet.

Vengeance at last.

With a pained grunt, Brackendale groped for his sword that had skidded beyond his reach. Geoffrey shoved the tip of his blade against Brackendale's neck. Fear darkened the older man's eyes, and anticipation of death.

"Geoffrey, spare him," Elizabeth screamed.

Something twisted deep in Geoffrey's chest.

His soul.

He had dreamed of this glorious moment for eighteen years. With one thrust of his sword, Lord Brackendale would be dead, Geoffrey's father avenged, and Wode free for the claiming.

Geoffrey had anticipated a rush of triumph. Yet he felt no glory. No joy. No exhilaration. His heart constricted with a soul-deep ache. If he killed the man lying helpless at his feet, Elizabeth would never forgive him. She would hate him.

He would lose her.

His hand wavered. He thought of her now, watching the grisly spectacle. He envisioned her tear-streaked face as she waited for him to deliver the mortal blow. He sensed her anguish. He tasted her fear.

God's blood, he did not want to lose her.

Geoffrey flexed his fingers on his sword.

He had no choice.

"Grant me Wode," he said in a voice loud enough for all to hear, "and I will spare you."

Brackendale choked for breath.

"You will also give me Elizabeth, as my betrothed."

Shocked murmurs rippled through the throng around them. The older lord's eyes flared. "Never!"

With deliberate slowness, Geoffrey pressed the blade forward, drawing a streak of blood. A final warning. "I do not want to kill you, but I will. Do you agree?"

Brackendale hesitated, his gaze hard and bitter.

His head jerked in a nod.

"I want your word of honor, as a knight," Geoffrey demanded.

"You have it," Brackendale muttered. He tried to move his bleeding leg and winced.

"I will withdraw my sword, and you will stand and confirm our agreement to all who have witnessed," Geoffrey ground out. "If you betray me, I will kill you. Understand?"

"Aye," the older lord spat.

Geoffrey lifted his blade to return it to its scabbard.

A snap broke the bailey's near silence. In the space of an indrawn breath, he recognized the sound—a crossbow bowstring as the weapon's trigger released.

The bolt whistled like a demon unleashed.

His mind yelled for him to move. It was too late.

The steel-tipped bolt pierced his left shoulder. Mail, flesh, and sinew splintered.

A scream tore from the depths of his soul and shattered his world into a crimson haze.

The bolt's impact sent him reeling back against the stone wall in a spray of blood. The jolt jarred the bolt deeper into his chest.

He screamed again.

Gasping, he stared down at his ruined shoulder. He clutched at the ugly, gaping wound. His numb fingers tried to hold together the broken links of mail and mangled flesh, to staunch the flow of his life's blood.

He sank to his knees.

A figure emerged from the darkness smothering him. A woman with bewitching blue eyes and hair that shimmered like black silk. The woman he loved.

"Elizabeth," he moaned.

Pain flared.

Darkness claimed him.

✤ ✤ ✤

"*Naaaaayyyyyyyy!*"

Elizabeth heard a woman's shrill scream. She did not recognize her own cry until it trailed off and died on her lips.

Wrenching free of the guards detaining her, she ran to Geoffrey's side. He lay crumpled in a heap against the blood-smeared wall, the wooden end of the bolt protruding from his mail. His face was as pale as death. Blood ran down his hauberk and pooled around him on the ground.

She knelt in the dirt and smoothed hair from his brow. Tears streamed down her cheeks and she wiped the wetness away with her sleeve. Her belly clenched into a sickening knot. How could this have happened?

Dominic dropped to his knees beside her. "He lives, milady?" he asked, his voice ragged.

"I do not know," Elizabeth whispered.

The knight took Geoffrey's limp hand and felt for a pulse. "A faint heartbeat. Too faint, I fear." Anguish deepened the worried lines around his mouth. He squeezed her fingers, shoved to a stand, and stared across the bailey. "You bastard!" he roared.

Blinking away tears, Elizabeth followed his gaze to the young man standing against the far wall, holding a crossbow. His golden hair, the hue of corn silk, gleamed in the sun.

Oh, God.

Her stomach lurched. Bile flooded her mouth. She fought the urge to curl over and retch.

Aldwin had shot Geoffrey.

With assistance from several knights, her father struggled to his feet. He glanced down at Geoffrey's prone body and at her; then he leveled his glare on the squire. "What have you *done?*"

Arthur's shout reverberated in the sudden silence. He limped across the bailey, his wounded leg thumping on the ground.

Aldwin stood firm.

"Why did you fire the crossbow?"

"I saved your life, milord." Sweat beaded on Aldwin's forehead.

"Idiot! My life was not in danger."

The squire flushed. "I saw—"

"De Lanceau intended to sheath his sword. You think me a coward, boy?" Arthur bellowed. "You wished to dishonor me before God and all these witnesses?"

"N-Nay, milord."

"Then why did you interfere?"

Aldwin's face turned scarlet. "I—" he said tightly and looked straight at Elizabeth. "I shot him for my lady."

"Nay!" she cried.

"For Elizabeth?" Her father scowled.

"Aye, and I would do so again." The squire's eyes flashed with conviction. "I did it for her tainted honor, and for all the evils de Lanceau forced upon her. I would rather die than see my lady forced to wed that monster. He is not worthy of her virtue, intelligence, or her great beauty. He will never hurt her again."

"Aldwin," Elizabeth moaned. "Nay. Nay!"

Arthur stared at Aldwin. When at last he spoke, his voice shook with rage. "Let it be known Geoffrey de Lanceau is now rightful lord of Wode and all the lands surrounding it. 'Tis an honor he won in battle, before God and witnesses."

"Milord," Aldwin pleaded.

"Get him out of my sight," Arthur barked to the knights behind him. Aldwin was hauled from the bailey, his cries echoing off the stone walls.

Elizabeth looked down at Geoffrey. He had not moved. She held his cool, bloody hand and linked her fingers through his. Her eyes stung. "I will not leave you," she whispered.

A shadow fell over her. "Beloved, 'tis over." At the baron's nasal voice, she felt a dreadful chill. Men-at-arms swarmed around Geoffrey's body, talking and gesturing, and she fought to keep her place by his side.

She clawed at the sweaty hand that encircled her arm and pulled her to her feet. "Please," she choked. "Help him."

"There is naught we can do." The baron's yellowed teeth

formed an ugly grin. "Forget him. He deserves to die."

Elizabeth jerked free of his hold. "I will find Mildred. There is a garden here at Branton. Medicinal herbs—"

"I have sent de Lanceau's friend to fetch her," her sire said and limped up beside her, his face contorting with pain. Blood trailed down his leg.

"Father, we must tend your wound."

"Fear not, I shall live." His eyes softened with a strained smile. "You have a tender heart, Daughter, but do not fret for de Lanceau. He is, after all, a rogue. Sedgewick, pray take Elizabeth from this gruesome scene and see she is well attended."

Fear throbbed inside her. She must not leave Geoffrey to fight for his life, alone. "I will stay."

"Do as I command," Arthur said. "'Tis not a sight for a lady."

A brisk "harrumph" carried above the commotion, and Mildred elbowed her way through the men-at-arms. She looked down at Geoffrey, at the crimson pool by her feet, and whispered, "By the blessed Virgin."

"Can you save him?" Elizabeth asked.

Mildred knelt in the dirt and with light touches, probed the wound. Blood gushed between her fingers, and her mouth pinched. "I cannot say for certain."

Arthur growled, a sound of annoyance. "Take my daughter from here, Baron."

The matron rose to her feet with the sound of popping

joints. "Milord, I have much work ahead of me, tasks that would benefit from a woman's delicate hand rather than a knight's crude fist." Her gaze, bright with meaning, slid to Elizabeth. "Would she be able to assist me?"

Elizabeth squared her shoulders. "I will be glad to help."

Fatigue shadowed Arthur's face. Rubbing his brow, he sighed. "Very well."

As her father hobbled over to the well, assisted by several knights, Elizabeth crouched down beside Geoffrey. She touched his cold cheek, and fresh tears filled her eyes.

She fought the horrible, pressing fear that she had lost the man who had captured her heart and soul.

Forever.

CHAPTER EIGHTEEN

Raising her lashes, Elizabeth stared at the candles flickering on the altar. Laughter, music, and the sounds of revelry floated into Wode's quiet chapel. While she prayed for Geoffrey, the castle folk celebrated her father's safe return and the fact that none of his men had died in the skirmish at Branton. Thirty were wounded, and some had serious injuries, but they would live.

One man at Wode stood to die from the siege.

"Oh, Geoffrey," she whispered.

Her lips trembled, and she pressed her knuckles to her mouth to quell a sob. When she and her father's weary army had ridden up to the keep's gates, she had smiled and waved to the sentries on the wall walk who cheered and clapped. She had bathed, dressed in her finery, and dined in the great hall as her father expected where ale and wine flowed and servants brought endless courses of rich food. Through it all, she had struggled to keep her face a mask of noble dignity. Inside, she was dying.

She linked her icy hands over her favorite blue silk gown, noting with a stab of anguish the folds were a soft gray hue, the color of Geoffrey's eyes as he bent his head to kiss her. She prayed with all the aching love inside her that he would live.

She had done all that Mildred had asked. Elizabeth had watched, horrified but unable to look away, as soldiers cut the bolt from Geoffrey's body and sealed the gaping flesh with red-hot irons heated in the fire. Her head swimming, she had fought not to faint as she helped Mildred apply a poultice of crushed nettles to the burnt flesh.

When Mildred declared Branton's garden ill equipped to deal with a wound of such magnitude, Elizabeth had helped her lay Geoffrey on a crude mattress of straw and blankets strewn in the back of a supply wagon. For good luck, she had tucked the half-mended saddle trapping next to him, and had ridden by his side until they reached Wode.

She might never feel the joy of his lovemaking again.

Tears welled, and Elizabeth blinked them away. She would do all within her power to save Geoffrey, for she could not bear to live without him.

Gathering her skirts, she hurried down the corridor toward her chamber. She passed it and halted at a door father along the passage. Elizabeth made a fist and pounded on the wood.

She knocked again. Why did Mildred not answer?

A muffled exclamation came from inside the chamber, an instant before the door opened and the scent of rose and dill soap floated into the corridor. "Here I am," Mildred grumbled, clutching a towel over her wrinkled bosom and removing one draped over her head. "Can an old woman not have a few moments of privacy?"

When she saw Elizabeth, she started. "Oh, milady, I do apologize." Her gaze softened with concern. "You are crying."

Elizabeth dried her eyes. "Please, I need your help."

"You wish for a soothing draught?" The matron beamed and nodded. "It has been an emotional few days. A touch of poppy and valerian will help you sleep. Come in. I will dress and fetch you a tonic straight away."

"'Tis not for me."

"Who, then?" Mildred's puzzled gaze lit with understanding. "Ah, de Lanceau."

"We must save him. We must."

The healer's eyes misted. Drawing Elizabeth inside, she closed the door. "I left his side not long ago. As I told your father earlier, Geoffrey is so near death, 'twill be a miracle if he lives to the morn, and an even greater miracle if he can swallow even a drop of tonic."

"He will die?" Elizabeth's heart shriveled, dying too.

Mildred shook her damp hair. "I can only help the body to heal," she said, helplessness in her voice. "I cannot mend flesh that is torn beyond repair." She walked over to the linen chest and removed a prim gray wool bliaut.

"I beg you," Elizabeth cried. "Bring whatever ointments you have. Please. We cannot give up on him, not until he is d—" She could not say the awful word.

"As I told the maid who watches over him now, I intended to cleanse his wounds again after my bath." The matron shook her head and smiled. "I must admit, I have developed a fondness for the rogue."

Elizabeth ran and hugged her. "Thank you."

"Thank me when he lives, milady." Mildred pulled on the crisp wool. "If we can keep him alive to the morn, he might have a chance."

✤ ✤ ✤

Elizabeth hesitated outside the guest chamber. Geoffrey lay beyond the stout wooden door. Her father had ordered him ensconced here, in the wing reserved for the privileged guests of the lord and his family. Although the solar now belonged to Geoffrey, 'twas clear her father did not expect Geoffrey to live to assume tenure of Wode.

Quelling a surge of panic, she entered the chamber. The candles on the bedside table sputtered at the draught. Mildred hurried in behind her and shut the door, then spoke in hushed tones to the maid who rose from a chair near the bed. The air in the room was warm, though not stuffy, and bore the odors of well water, pungent herbs, and blood.

Geoffrey lay on the bed near the window, his lean, muscled body stretched out beneath linen sheets and wool blankets. Elizabeth walked to the side of the bed. Her silk gown whispered in the room's stillness.

As the door clicked shut behind the maid, tears flooded Elizabeth's eyes. He looked so pale, paler even than when he lay in the wagon, his profile washed in harsh sunlight. His eyelids were closed, his lashes thick and dark against his cheek. His lips were parted. She leaned over him, hoping to feel his breath on her skin. So very, very faint.

She brushed a lock of hair from his forehead. Fear and terror gripped her, for he felt so cold.

"Mildred," Elizabeth sobbed.

"Hush, milady." The matron set her willow basket on the floor, and it creaked with the weight of the ointments and stoppered bottles. "Come and help me."

"Tell me what to do."

Mildred glanced at Elizabeth. The matron paused a moment, then shook her head. Curling her fingers over the edge of the sheet, she whipped it down to Geoffrey's bare waist. With gentle hands, she removed a second sheet folded across his chest.

Blood stained the linen, and welled past the thick poultice covering the wound. Eyes burning, Elizabeth stared at the magnificent torso that had invited her touch, now slashed and smeared with dried blood and blackened, macerated herbs. Memories taunted her, of his skin flexing and gleaming in the firelight. Of his chest hairs tickling her palm. Of his sweat-slicked skin sliding beneath her fingertips. He was still beautiful, so beautiful. Yet his skin lacked its former luster.

"Are you certain you wish to watch?" Mildred asked, as she worked at the poultice.

"A-Aye."

Even so, when Elizabeth saw the state of the wound, her stomach roiled.

With light fingers, the matron touched the wound. "Mercy," she muttered. "I now understand why the Pope issued an edict to ban the use of the crossbow." She leaned closer and inspected the shattered flesh. "Thank God we had time to seal the wound."

Elizabeth shuddered. For the rest of her days, she would remember the soldiers wrenching the bolt from Geoffrey's limp body. Had he felt pain? Had he felt the blood spurt when—?

"Do not faint," Mildred said in a sharp tone. "I cannot spare the time to cut mint and revive you."

Elizabeth's eyes fluttered open. She had not realized they had closed, or that she swayed on her feet. Straightening her shoulders, she forced her fear to the back of her mind.

Rummaging in her basket, the healer withdrew a small earthenware flask of cooled, boiled water. She added greenish oil that smelled of rosemary and lavender. "Bathe him, milady. Start with the crossbow wound."

Elizabeth took the linen cloth and washed his chest with great tenderness. The water soon turned crimson, but she tossed the bowl's contents into the fire and resumed with fresh water. When finished, she swabbed the grime from his face.

Mildred worked beside her. She rinsed the gaping wound and the slash down his chest with a pinkish lotion. "St. John's wort, betony, and goose-grass to staunch the bleeding and heal," she said, in answer to Elizabeth's questioning glance.

"And that?" Elizabeth wrinkled her nose at the odorous ointment the healer rubbed into the wounds.

"Betony and nettle."

Geoffrey did not stir.

The matron dropped her pot of ointment into the basket. "I must gather ingredients for a fresh poultice, and bring more blankets, too. The fever will start soon."

"Fever?"

"'Tis a grave wound. 'Tis a miracle he still breathes."

"That is a good sign, is it not?" Elizabeth said, clinging to the spark of hope.

Heading to the door, Mildred begrudged a smile. "I suppose 'tis."

Taking Geoffrey's hand, Elizabeth squeezed it to let him know she was beside him, waiting for him to recover.

Waiting to tell him how much she loved him.

She sat on the bed's edge, keeping watch, her fingers cradling Geoffrey's, until the matron returned with fresh nettle leaves. She crushed them using a mortar and pestle and pressed them over the wound.

Sick with worry, Elizabeth rubbed her hands over her arms. Geoffrey still had not stirred, and his breathing seemed shallower than before.

"The fever has started," Mildred said.

Elizabeth scooped up the wool blanket the matron had brought and spread it over Geoffrey, and tucked the edges under the mattress to keep in his body heat.

Frowning, Mildred reached into her collection of bottles and drew out a flask of pale liquid. She motioned for Elizabeth to move to the end of the bed and popped the lid of the flask. "Lift his head."

"What are you giving him?"

"Feverfew and burdock root in wine. 'Twill help control the fever. And," Mildred added with a wry smile, "to dull his pain, a touch of monkshood."

Elizabeth gasped. "Are you certain the quantity—?"

"Not enough to do him harm, I promise."

As instructed, Elizabeth cradled Geoffrey's head in her hands. Mildred forced her finger between his teeth and pried open his jaw. His mouth went slack. With care, she poured in a few drops of the liquid.

The tonic drizzled from the corner of his lips and dripped onto the blanket. "He did not drink it," Elizabeth said.

"He cannot swallow." The healer pressed closer. "Tilt his head a bit more. I will try again."

This time, as Mildred sloshed in more of the elixir, she ran her fingers inside his mouth and depressed his tongue. The liquid vanished down his throat, and she nodded. "There."

Exhaling a shuddered breath, Elizabeth returned Geoffrey's head to the pillow. She trailed her fingers through his silky hair. He had liked that tender caress, most of all after lovemaking. He had once said it reminded him of his mother, of the way she had soothed his stubbed toes and bruises when he was a boy.

"You love him?" Mildred asked.

Elizabeth would not deny the emotion that had rooted deep in her heart. "I do. Very much."

The matron set the flask on the table beside the bed. "I cannot excuse what he has done, but he would have made you a fine husband."

"Not would, Mildred. *Will*."

❖   ❖   ❖

Some time later, Elizabeth admitted two menservants lugging a straw pallet. Both appeared flushed and tipsy. In the brief moment the chamber door stayed open, she noted that despite the late hour, the raucous celebration in the hall continued.

"There, if you will." She pointed to the floor beside Geoffrey's bed. They dropped the bed with a thump, releasing a cloud of dust.

Mildred half-coughed, half-snorted. "You cannot think to—"

"I am," Elizabeth said. With a word of thanks and an authoritative wave, she dismissed the two men. They hurried away, no doubt eager to down more ale.

The matron's brows drew together, and her lips compressed into a forbidding line. "You would be wise to retire to your own bed for a good night's sleep. You look exhausted. Terrible, if I may say so. If aught happens to Geoffrey this eve—"

"—I wish to be here." Fighting the weariness in every joint in her body, Elizabeth looked at Geoffrey. "He is my betrothed," she whispered. "I cannot leave him now, when he needs me most."

She stretched a clean blanket over the pallet and settled herself for sleep. Squeezing her eyes shut, she ignored the straw poking into her cheek and the drafts that skimmed under the shutters and across the floor like a ghoul's breath. In the long, dark hours of the night she lay awake and listened to Mildred's snores and Geoffrey's shallow breathing.

The fire cast indistinct patterns on the stone walls. Unable to drift into slumber, she thought of the first time she woke in Geoffrey's bed, content in his arms, and watched the fire dance on Branton's walls until she fell back to sleep.

She could not imagine life without Geoffrey.

He had become part of her soul.

Rolling onto her side, she stared at his broad hand lying limp atop the blanket, the hand that had wielded his sword and won him all he had desired for so many agonizing years.

As he had wished, he was now the rightful lord of Wode, and he had achieved it without killing her father, for which she would forever be grateful.

How desperately she hoped Geoffrey would not die, after all he fought for lay within his grasp.

She had not told him how much she loved him.

Elizabeth squeezed her weeping eyes shut.

When her eyelids flickered open, daylight shone beyond the shutters. She tossed aside her blankets and leaned over him, and traced his lips with her finger. His breath gusted against her skin.

A joyous cry burst inside her. Had Mildred not said that if he lived till the morn, he might survive?

The matron grunted and, with awkward movements, rose from her mattress in the corner of the room. "He lives?"

"Aye!"

"Do not smile so, milady. His fever is high. Wash him with herbal water while I check the wound. When you are finished, do it again."

As Elizabeth rinsed Geoffrey's face for the second time, a knock sounded on the door. She scowled, for the maids who brought wood for the fire knew not to make so much noise.

She threw open the door.

Bertrand stood in the corridor. "Milady," he said, looking sheepish. "Your sire asks that you come to the hall. Baron Sedgewick has arrived. He wishes to see you."

Elizabeth resisted a disgusted groan. Sedgewick had led

his army back to Avenley yesterday, and she had hoped not to see him again so soon. She would spare him only the briefest moment. Nodding to Bertrand, she said, "I will be there soon."

Pressing the door closed with her palm, Elizabeth glanced down and despaired at the state of her bliaut. She had not changed garments since yesterday, and had not yet sent a maid to fetch clean clothes. The silk bore smudges of Geoffrey's blood and herbs. She had not even washed her face. Yet 'twould be discourteous not to even make an appearance, when her father requested it, or keep him and the baron waiting. She made her way to the hall.

Through the pervasive fog of wood smoke, she saw the baron and her father had pulled up chairs near the hearth. The enticing smells of fresh bread and warmed gooseberry jelly wafted to her.

Sedgewick dropped his roll. "Beloved." He struggled to his feet, licking jelly from his fingertips. His eyes widened at her dishevelment. "You are hurt?"

"I have been tending Geoffrey," she said.

"So your father told me." Sedgewick's smile turned cool. "He says you have not left de Lanceau's side. You and the healer slept in his chamber last eve?"

"We did. He has fever."

"Ah, fever." Sedgewick cast her father a smug, victorious smile. Doubt taunted Elizabeth, but she refused to quaver before this man.

"'Tis amusing, milord?" she asked with an edge to her voice.

"My dear lady." The baron came close and patted her hand as though she were a naïve little child. The lust in his gaze, though, told he appreciated her as a woman. "Many afflictions can take the life of a wounded warrior. Gangrene. Infection. Fever. Do you not agree, milord?"

Her father nodded, looking a little peakish in the morning light. "'Tis so."

"My love, do not look so miserable. You shall not have to wed the bastard after all."

Sedgewick's leering smile brought Elizabeth such a wave of despair, she wrenched her hand away. "I promised Mildred I would help her change the poultice," she lied through clenched teeth. "Good day to you, Baron. Father."

"Wait," her sire commanded.

Elizabeth halted. She turned, forcing her face into a mask of composure. "Aye, Father?"

"There is an important matter we must discuss." His gaze traveled over her and softened. Had he sensed the distress she struggled hard to conceal? "Considering the strain of your ordeal," he went on, "I thought to wait a few days before broaching the topic. Yet since the baron honors us with his presence, and is eager to see it done, we will speak of it now."

Speak of what? her mind screamed. She wished to return to Geoffrey's side, to escape Sedgewick's lecherous stare, but she could not in good conscience be rude to her father. "Of course," she said.

A smacking sound drew her gaze to the baron. He shoved the rest of his roll between his teeth, chewed, and stared at her in a manner that implied she was his prized possession. Her skin crawled. He was vile indeed to look at her that way.

Pushing his chair back, Arthur stood, favoring his wounded leg, and smoothed a hand over his brown wool tunic. "When the baron arrived today, he brought a wagon loaded with barrels of wine. Bordeaux, to be exact. The very best to celebrate his nuptials and his new bride."

"A great kindness," Elizabeth forced herself to say. "'Tis unfortunate we will not wed."

Arthur hobbled forward and took her hands. "Daughter, that is what we shall discuss."

Warmth drained from her face. "What?"

"Sedgewick wishes to proceed with your marriage."

As though from afar, she heard the baron murmur, "I cannot wait, beloved, to make you mine."

Her father's hands curled around hers, steadying her, as tremors ran through her body. "I am sorry if the news is a shock, Elizabeth. As the baron said to me earlier, we cannot imagine the horrors you suffered as de Lanceau's hostage, but Sedgewick assures me he will treat you with kindness. He will do all in his power to diminish your unpleasant memories and be a loving husband."

Her ears rang. She withdrew her fingers and resisted the urge to throw her head back and shriek. Meeting her father's gaze, she said, "I cannot wed the baron. I am betrothed to Geoffrey. You said so yourself at Branton Keep before at least one hundred witnesses."

"Pah! A mockery of an engagement." Her father shook his head. "I am glad 'twill never result in marriage. 'Tis inevitable de Lanceau will die from his wounds. Upon his passing, you will be free from that accursed arrangement and any loyalty you feel obligated to show him." He smiled and looked pleased. "You will be free to marry Sedgewick."

Panic burgeoned inside her. She would never marry the baron. "You do not understand."

He reached out and touched her cheek. "'Tis best—"

"I love him."

"You do?" Arthur chuckled and looked at the baron, who slurped wine from a goblet. "Excellent. Sedgewick assures me you will have every luxury you desire."

"I love *Geoffrey*."

Her words seemed to echo like a clap of thunder.

"You . . . love . . ." Arthur choked a breath.

Sedgewick's mouth fell open.

Pride rang clear in her voice. "I swear it upon my soul."

"You love a traitor's son?" the baron sneered, spitting wine and clots of bread. "He raped you."

Elizabeth's cheeks burned but she refused to back down from his glare and the accusation in his slitted eyes. "He did not."

The baron slammed down the goblet. "Do you deny he stole your virtue?"

"Daughter?" Arthur whispered.

Love for Geoffrey bloomed in every part of her being. "He did not force me. I wanted to lie with him."

"God's teeth!" Anger and dismay darkened her father's gaze.

Elizabeth clasped her hands to steady them.

The baron gripped the back of his chair, his fat fingers white as unopened lilies against the dark oak. "You deceived me?" he roared. "You spread your legs for him when you were betrothed to *me*?" His arm swept over the table, hurling food and wine onto the floor. A dog ran, yelping. The chair followed with a splintering crash.

When he grabbed the edge of the table, her father limped forward. "Baron!"

Sedgewick straightened, his face puffed and red. "I apologize, milord." His jowls twitched. It appeared an immense effort for him to restrain his temper. "A walk will settle my thoughts." Without a backward glance, he strode from the hall.

Elizabeth exhaled. Her body still shook, and she wondered if Sedgewick's rampage would have continued, if her father had not stopped him. The baron looked angry enough to commit murder.

She shoved the frightening thought to the back of her mind. She need not think of him again. He would not wish to pursue the wedding now.

After a tense silence, her father asked, "Did you speak true of your love for de Lanceau?"

"Aye."

"You *want* to marry him?"

"With all my heart."

His gaze softened with concern. "He has not been . . . unkind to you? In any fashion? One that might make you reconsider such a union?"

Elizabeth shook her head. "Why do you ask?"

"'Tis difficult for me to believe." He dragged a stiff hand over the back of his neck. "Veronique—"

"*Veronique?*" she cried.

"Geoffrey's courtesan intercepted us on the road to Branton Keep. She told me de Lanceau forced you to his bed." Her father's mouth turned up in a wan smile. "I paid her to get us through the keep's gates."

"Geoffrey knew he had been betrayed," Elizabeth said. "I am certain what Veronique told you was vicious, spiteful lies."

"'Twas easy to believe her."

Elizabeth stared at the ruined, overturned chair and wine-soaked rushes. "I cannot condone all of Geoffrey's deeds," she said, sickened anew by the baron's violence, "but I do love him. He is a good man. I will do all I can so he will live and be my husband."

"What accursed irony." Arthur's voice broke. "Edouard

de Lanceau's rogue son claims Wode, my fortune, you—all that I hold dear—yet you see him as a hero?"

With her tongue, she moistened her dry lips. "Please try to understand."

"I cannot. I will not forgive de Lanceau as you have, Daughter. I look forward to the day you bring word of his death."

CHAPTER NINETEEN

With a weary groan, Arthur sorted the parchments on the table before him. Too many matters of estate had been neglected during his absence.

He scowled, irritated by his own pricking conscience, for these were de Lanceau's problems now. Yet, with his death imminent, someone had to ensure the keep's affairs and its people were kept in order before discontent stirred another pot of headaches.

Headaches, indeed. Arthur grimaced and massaged his throbbing brow, an aftereffect of yestereve that matched the nagging pain in his leg. He was glad of the quiet hall. Not a soul disturbed him, not even the dogs who lay stretched out by the fire. Thank the saints, not the baron. Composed since his outburst but still rankled, Sedgewick had gorged himself at the midday meal and accepted Arthur's offer of a guest chamber where he could sleep off his meal. And, Arthur hoped, his foul temper.

Arthur skimmed the first grievance, filed by a villein whose leeks had been eaten by a neighbor's sow, and tossed it aside. Leeks? Pigs? How could he think on such matters when Elizabeth's revelations spun through his mind and scattered his thoughts like dry leaves in an autumn gale?

She loved Geoffrey de Lanceau.

Disbelief and remorse jabbed at him like two cantankerous old crones. He had suspected Veronique could not be trusted, yet he had believed her lies. She had manipulated him, the baron, Aldwin, all of them. Aye, she had wanted the silver, but above all had wanted de Lanceau dead and his revenge forfeit.

Arthur shuddered. He wanted de Lanceau's death too. He had wished for it even as he heard his daughter confess she loved the rogue, and longed to be his bride. Part of Arthur felt numbed, betrayed. Was it sacrilege to hope Edouard's son never lived to claim Elizabeth's fair hand?

An image flashed through Arthur's mind, a knight silhouetted against the dawn sky, the young man who had bested him. Arthur recalled the cool calculation in de Lanceau's eyes when he demanded Elizabeth as his betrothed, an emotional blow that proved his ambition to impregnate her and beget a blood claim to Wode and all Arthur owned. Yet was that de Lanceau's motive? Or had something more glimmered in those gray eyes, something Arthur had not wished to recognize before now?

He folded his hands and warmed them with his breath. And what of Aldwin? In different circumstances, his actions might be considered chivalrous. Would he be executed for believing Veronique's slander, and doing what he believed was right? A moral dilemma Arthur did not want to ponder.

A heated argument started in the bailey. A moment later, the forebuilding's outer door crashed open, and footsteps thundered on the stone stairs.

"I tell you again, you are not to disturb Lord Bracken-dale," Bertrand shouted and lunged up the stairs two at a time in pursuit of Dominic, who had reached the top and was stalking across the hall. "If you do not stop, I will arrest you."

"Indeed," Dominic said, his expression savage. "If you insist on throwing yourself upon my sharpened sword, so be it."

As the knight marched toward the table, Arthur pushed himself to standing. Without missing a stride, Dominic dropped down on one knee and bowed his head in a gesture of respect.

Arthur sighed. Dominic seemed to be the most loyal of de Lanceau's men who had escorted the wagon bearing their lord. Since arriving at Wode, Dominic had slept in the stable with de Lanceau's destrier and refused to leave the keep until de Lanceau ordered him to do so, or died.

"Milord, I have come requesting news of my lord and

comrade, Geoffrey de Lanceau."

"Again, I see."

Dominic charged to his feet, shedding bits of straw. "I beg you, do not deny me the truth." His eyes were bright behind a grazing of brown lashes. "Does he live, or is he dead?"

"At present, he lives. Yet his fate remains uncertain."

Relief softened Dominic's boyish features. "I would see him."

"As I told you yestereve—the last time you so boldly demanded an audience—Mildred advised against visitors. She insists de Lanceau's life depends upon it."

"You care whether he lives or dies?"

Arthur scowled at the challenge in Dominic's voice. "I despise de Lanceau. I loathe being responsible for his well-being. I do so because he is now rightful lord of Wode, and my squire committed a rash act and caused him injury."

"And what is being done about this squire?" Dominic asked, his hand settling on the pommel of his sword.

Bertrand reached to draw his weapon, but Arthur stayed him with a flick of his hand. Though Dominic looked irritated, he did not seem a man to attack without due provocation. "My squire's name is Aldwin," Arthur said.

"He—Aldwin—is in the dungeon?"

"For now."

Dominic's curse echoed to the smoke-blackened beams overhead. "You protect him? You believe he will be vindicated from a deed he committed in cold blood, before witnesses? If

Geoffrey lives, Aldwin's life will be forfeit."

Shaking his head, Arthur set his hands flat on the table. "There are other considerations."

"Such as?"

"His reasons for the impetuous act," Arthur snapped. "I, for one, cannot blame Aldwin for being incensed by lies which I believed myself."

Dominic stood very still. "Lies, milord?"

"The courtesan, Veronique, told me de Lanceau bedded my daughter against her will. That he raped her without mercy or remorse."

An indignant laugh burst from Dominic. "You believed her?"

Arthur pounded his fist on the tabletop. Parchments fell to the floor. "Her lies confirmed all that I feared. He held my daughter hostage. He demanded a ransom. By God's holy blood, he wanted to destroy me."

"He did," Dominic agreed. "I will not deny his actions were driven by vengeance, but I promise you, his intentions toward your daughter were noble. Geoffrey is a man of deep passions, but he would never harm a woman. Not one whom he admired." His mouth curved into a lopsided grin. "I believe they were destined to become lovers. They are well matched in strength of will and temperament, and in all the ways that matter between a man and a woman."

Misgiving skittered through Arthur. "How do you know this?"

Dominic grinned. "Have you ever paid homage to a demented boar?"

Arthur shook his head, refusing to digress into metaphor. "Does he love my daughter?"

"That is a question to ask of him, though I expect you know the answer."

Arthur rubbed his aching forehead. Ask de Lanceau how he felt about Elizabeth? Would the humiliations never cease?

"Milord," said Dominic, crossing his arms over his wool jerkin, "what, may I ask, became of Veronique after she told these lies? Is she sequestered at Wode? Enjoying the luxury of this fine keep and your protection?"

Arthur snorted and eased the weight on his wounded leg. "I have not seen her since we besieged Branton and I paid her the rest of her silver. I imagine she has ridden out of Moydenshire and either seeks another lord to cheat, or has booked passage on a ship to the continent to be as far from here as possible."

Dominic grunted. "She is hardly wallowing in guilt."

"Of that, I have no doubt."

Wry laughter gleamed in Dominic's eyes. For a moment, Arthur and he shared a smile.

"Your mouth must be dry from all that blustering," Arthur said after a silence.

Dominic nodded, his gaze wary. "'Tis somewhat parched."

With one swipe of his arm, Arthur launched the remaining documents onto the rushes. Ignoring Bertrand's stunned gasp, Arthur drew out a chair and looked at Dominic. "I am ignorant of what happened at Branton Keep during my daughter's abduction. Indeed, I know little of Geoffrey de Lanceau, but that in his youth he served as page to the Earl of Druentwode. You will enlighten me."

"'Twill take more than one mug of your stoutest ale to quench my thirst, or loosen my tongue," Dominic muttered.

Arthur laughed. "That is a challenge I am prepared to win." He looked at Bertrand, standing beside the table. "Tell the maidservants to bring spiced wine."

"Aye, milord."

Bertrand's strides faded from the hall, and Arthur sat. Despite his overindulgence yestereve, he needed the wine to dull his body's aches and strained nerves.

No sooner had Dominic rounded the table than Bertrand returned.

"What is it now?" Arthur called to him.

Halting, Bertrand bowed. "A rider from Tillenham, milord. He says the matter is urgent."

"*Tillenham?*" The pounding in Arthur's head intensified. "Send him in."

✠   ✠   ✠

Elizabeth jolted out of slumber. She jerked upright. Her calves hit the hard chair rail and with a groan, she realized she had fallen asleep by the fire in Geoffrey's chamber, as she embroidered his father's saddle trapping.

Torn between the mending, which was almost completed, and the gowns for the orphans, she had chosen to finish the task for Geoffrey. The decision was not easy, yet in her heart, she sensed her mother would agree. With each loving stitch that restored the emblem of the hawk, Elizabeth wished for Geoffrey to heal. He must see for himself the trapping's renewed beauty. She hoped he would be pleased.

A hoarse cry shattered the silence. Geoffrey's harsh, frantic breaths echoed in the chamber. "Nay!"

She leapt to her feet. Was he waking?

Setting the trapping on the chair, she ran to his side. His eyes were closed. His hair formed sweaty whorls against his cheeks. As his head thrashed from side to side on the pillow, his neck muscles bunched and corded.

"Father," he moaned.

"Geoffrey?" She clutched his hand.

"He is delirious." Mildred drew the stoppered flask from her basket. "Lift his head. We must give him more elixir."

Elizabeth struggled to part his lips. He fought her, strong despite his injury, and she willed him to cease for a moment and let them help him fight his demons. At last, Mildred managed to pour more of the tonic into his mouth. He thrashed, struggled, then quieted on a low sob and fell into a fitful sleep.

"Will he be all right?" Elizabeth asked.

"I do not know." The matron moistened a linen cloth in

cool water and wiped sweat from his face. "He is fighting, milady. But I do not know whether 'twill be enough."

Buoyed by fresh hope, Elizabeth returned to the chair and resumed her needlework. Yet when her father strode into the chamber a few moments later, without even a preliminary knock, her insides chilled. He had not set foot within the room since Geoffrey had been brought here. Her father had not wished even that small measure of respect upon his avowed enemy.

He looked tired. Grim. Unsettled. A loathsome secret seemed to weigh on his conscience. He carried a crude wooden box marked on the lid by what appeared to be strokes from a dagger.

Where had he obtained such a container? She had not seen it before.

To her astonishment, Dominic entered behind her father. As he closed the door behind him, she set down the trapping and stood. Dominic dipped his head in a gracious nod before he strode to the bed, his face fraught with concern.

"Father?" Elizabeth drew his thoughtful gaze from Geoffrey's sleeping form.

"A messenger arrived not long ago," her sire said. "The Earl of Druentwode is dead."

"Oh, Geoffrey." She thought of his reaction when he awoke and heard of the earl's passing. The news would cause him grief, mayhap even set back his recovery.

"Aye, Geoffrey." Her father's voice sounded odd. Strained.

When she looked at him, puzzled, he pressed the box into her hands. "What is this?" she asked.

"Open it and see."

She set it on the end of the bed. The knife marks on the top were letters incised as though by a young boy's hand.

G-e-o-f-f-r-e-y.

I left the merriment in the hall to fetch a wooden box I had made under the tutelage of the earl's carpenter. I was proud of my work. I could not wait to show my father . . .

An awful tightness gripped Elizabeth's throat. She raised the lid. When she saw the assortment of childhood treasures inside, her gaze blurred. Three feathers wrapped in a swatch of worn linen. A handful of pebbles. A sling shot. A small dagger and a beautiful wooden carving of a hawk with its wings outstretched, the exact image of the hawk on the saddle trapping.

She pressed a shaking hand to her lips.

"The documents," her father said, his tone rough.

There. Flattened against the side of the box. Blinking back tears, she unfurled one of the faded skins with her fingers, noting the broken remains of a wax seal, the terse signature at the bottom, the lines of formal, scribed Latin.

An official document ratified by the crown.

"'Tis dated seventeen years ago," she whispered.

Her sire nodded. "A formal pardon for Edouard de Lanceau."

Her heartbeat suspended; then it slammed against her

ribs. "*What?!*"

"It seems he was no traitor to the crown."

A sob tore from her. "Oh, God!"

With a gentle grip, her father steadied her shaking arm. "The other parchment is a letter written to Geoffrey and signed by the earl. He says he obtained the pardon from the king years ago, but was blackmailed into destroying it by another lord."

"Blackmailed?" she repeated, horrified.

"Aye. As you see, the earl did not burn the document. Instead, he secreted it away until at last he was free to give it to Geoffrey."

"When the earl died," Elizabeth said with a sniffle, "and the blackmailer no longer had power over him." She dried her cheeks with angry fingers. "Who would blackmail the Earl of Druentwode? Who would deny Geoffrey the truth about his sire?"

Her father shook his head. "I do not know. 'Tis unfortunate the earl did not name the lord."

"Why not? Why the secrecy?"

"Mayhap we shall never know." Her sire's gaze moved to Geoffrey, lying still as death beneath the blankets. Dominic knelt by his side, his head bowed.

Elizabeth stared down at the precious parchment and wept. For the past eighteen years, Geoffrey had been haunted by a lie.

Would he live to know the truth?

❖ ❖ ❖

Hugging her arms across her chest, Elizabeth made her way across the shadowed bailey. Overhead, the black sky gleamed with stars and a swollen half-moon, but she kept her eyes on the pitted ground as she walked and tried to make sense of her tangled thoughts.

The cool breeze stung her tear-streaked cheeks and stirred her mantle. What to believe. Geoffrey had insisted that his father's loyalty to the crown never wavered. In the end, Geoffrey was right, her father wrong, all because of a secret someone did not want unearthed.

Head down, she skirted a cat devouring its night's kill and kept walking, her shoes crunching on loose stones. Was it selfish to want Geoffrey to live so very, very much? She would sacrifice all to have him know at last the truth about his sire, to have Geoffrey hold her in his arms again and whisper words of love, as he joined his body with hers.

The night wind gusted, and leaves rustled overhead. Elizabeth looked up, startled, to find she had wandered as far as the garden's giant apple tree. Ahead, moonlight silvered the stone path dividing Mildred's neat, tended vegetable and herb beds, and tempted Elizabeth to linger a little longer.

Nay. She had not meant to go so far and should return to Geoffrey's side. Savoring the tang of lavender in the calming breeze, she turned to go back to the keep.

Hushed conversation drifted to her.

"I want it done this eve," a man said. "Without fail." The familiar nasal voice sent unease racing through her.

Drawing her mantle close to her body, Elizabeth peered around the tree's trunk. Two figures stood beneath the pear tree. The baron had his back to her. The other person wore a voluminous hooded cloak, which concealed all features.

She hesitated, for she had no right to eavesdrop on a private meeting. Yet, as she watched, the baron reached into his sleeve and withdrew a small object. A silver vial.

"Use half. 'Tis more than enough poison to end de Lanceau's miserable life, but this time, I want no mistakes."

Elizabeth clamped her hand over her mouth.

"My payment first," came a woman's voice. *Veronique.*

"Nay. First, de Lanceau dies, and then Brackendale. You have the dagger?"

"Of course I do." Veronique tilted her head, her beautiful face illuminated for the briefest moment. "Are you certain that you will have married the little strumpet by then?"

Sedgewick chuckled. "With de Lanceau dead tonight, there will be no further impediment to my marriage. I shall wed the lady on the morrow. Arthur, stupid fool that he is, will be all too delighted I am willing to save her sullied reputation. He will welcome me with open arms."

"And she with open legs?" said Veronique with a cruel laugh.

"She will accept me. She will have no choice."

Shaking, Elizabeth shrank back against the rough tree bark. Fear slashed deep. She must tell her father.

With a swirl of the cloak, Veronique vanished into the shadows. Sedgewick turned and moonlight shone full on his face. He grinned, a merciless twist of his mouth.

Keeping to the darkest shadows, Elizabeth snuck toward the keep. A pebble rattled under her foot. She cringed.

"Who is there?" Sedgewick called.

Cold sweat broke on her brow, but she kept walking.

"Elizabeth, my love, is that you?"

The baron's voice reached her across the path and clawed at her senses. She should have realized 'twould be impossible to hide from him. Her mind screamed with urgency, even as she forced herself to calm. If he did not suspect she had overheard, he would let her be on her way.

Feigning surprise, she turned and faced him. "Baron?"

He closed the distance between them. "I did not expect to find you out here so late this eve. You are alone?"

A ghastly gleam lit his eyes. The stench of him hit her. He smelled evil. Elizabeth forced her lips into a polite, distant smile. "I told Mildred I would be gone for a moment. I needed a little fresh air. She is expecting me back."

"You left your lover's side for a night walk in the garden?" He smirked, revealing his chipped, stained teeth. "Why, beloved? To soothe your guilt?"

Her brow knit into a frown. "Guilt?"

"You fornicated with him while betrothed to me."

Anger warred with her resolve to stay calm and composed. "Baron Sedgewick—"

"Does that not weigh upon your conscience? Do you not wonder, even for a moment, how the sexual act would be with me?"

A shocked gasp jammed in her throat. "'Tis late. If you will excuse me—"

"Hold." He stepped closer, and his piggish eyes narrowed on her. "I see fear in your eyes."

Over the sighing of the wind through the trees, her pulse thundered. She must not admit she knew his clandestine plans. Fingering aside windblown hair, she said, "I am tired this eve. I bid you good night."

Before she could bolt, Sedgewick grabbed her arm. "You lie with such sweetness, my love. I pray you are as sweet in our marriage bed with your legs wrapped around my thighs."

Where he touched, her skin crawled. Revulsion boiled up in her before she thought to caution her words. "I shall never wed you. Never!"

"Such loyalty to de Lanceau. A pity he will die."

"Murderer!" She gasped at the sudden, bruising pressure on her wrist. Struggling, she tried to free her hand, but the baron tightened his grip.

"So you did overhear. How much? Hmm?"

Denial burned on her tongue, but he would never believe her. She had already condemned herself by calling him a murderer. Now, she must goad him into revealing all of his plans, so that when she got free, she could stop him. "I heard enough to know I hate you."

"As I hate de Lanceau for taking you from me. Aldwin's bolt should have killed him, but the poison will finish the deed." Spittle drizzled from the corner of the baron's mouth and glistened on his chin. "I hope de Lanceau suffers pain in his last moments, just like his father."

"How cruel!"

Sedgewick laughed. "Indeed, the squire said the same when I proposed that he shoot de Lanceau."

"You . . . ?"

The baron studied her face. "That startled you. You thought 'twas Aldwin's idea to fire the crossbow? He soon warmed to my suggestion, though. Once I repeated Veronique's sordid account of your rape and added a few perversions of my own, Aldwin begged to do it."

"Aldwin is a man of honor," Elizabeth bit out. "He would never agree to such treachery."

"To avenge his lady's tainted virtue?" Sedgewick sneered. "Aldwin lives and breathes chivalric drivel. Posed to him in the right way, the task appeared noble. A heroic feat, if you will, with the chance to win recognition from your father. Aldwin is an impulsive, ambitious lad. He was perfect for my purposes."

"Why did you want Geoffrey dead? He had no grievances with you."

"He touched you," muttered the baron. "That in itself

was enough. Yet I expected the battle would come down to a duel between him and your father. I knew de Lanceau was the superior fighter, and I could not risk him claiming Wode." The baron's gleeful, lecherous gaze roved over her bliaut. "Those lands shall be mine. Through you."

She shuddered. "By murdering my father?"

He wagged a plump finger. "*I* will not do it."

"Coward! You shed blood with another's hand." She tried to wrench out of his grasp, but failed.

In the shifting moonlight and shadow, his smile turned brutal. "I do what is necessary to get what I want. Accept it. You *will* be my bride, Elizabeth. When your father dies soon after our wedding, all of his lands will fall under my control. *I* shall wield power in the county of Moydenshire."

"Your logic is flawed, Baron," she said through her teeth. "According to law, only first born male children can inherit."

Sedgewick shrugged. "A few well placed bribes, a discreet murder if necessary, and those holdings will become mine."

Elizabeth trembled. He spoke with such nonchalance. Did he not feel the slightest remorse for having taken innocent lives? How she hated him. "You are a detestable, selfish man."

He jerked her arm, hard, forcing her to stumble. "As I said before, I do what I must."

His smug tone, rife with depraved ambition, sparked a thought in the back of her mind. "Even blackmail?"

His face registered shock. For the barest instant, his

fingers relaxed, and she broke free. Before she had run four steps, he lunged in front of her and blocked her escape. One of his hands clamped on her chin, while the other cinched around her waist and pinned her against his heaving gut. "You are clever, my love." His fetid breath seared her nostrils. "Too clever."

She swallowed the urge to vomit. "Release me, or I shall scream."

With a cruel laugh, Sedgewick forced her face up into the glare of moonlight. He shoved her against the apple tree. "You know too much, beloved. I have been indiscreet with all I have told you. Now I must beat you into silence."

A whimper escaped her. He meant it. She sensed his seething violence, ready to be unleashed. On her.

"You are wise to fear me." His hand at her waist yanked her hair, making her neck arch back at a painful angle. Her tresses snagged in the tree's bark. "With a few good blows, 'twill appear you had a nasty fall during your stroll. Being the devoted husband-to-be, I shall insist on proceeding with our marriage, despite your bruises and broken bones, even if the ceremony must take place at your bedside." His teeth gleamed. "I *will* see the terms of our marriage contract fulfilled."

A scream welled inside her.

His sweaty hand slapped over her mouth. "That bastard may have sampled you,"—he planted a slimy kiss on her exposed throat—"but I shall lay claim to your delectable body. And his babe, if his seed took root."

"Nmmmffff!" She shook her head and fought him, but could not dislodge his hold.

"Did you cry out when he took you?" he said against her ear, and laughed when she struggled. His spit dripped onto her skin. "Did you weep when he tore your maidenhood, or did you moan with pleasure?"

He grabbed her buttocks with both hands, his breaths coming in excited pants.

She screamed.

A sword rasped from its scabbard.

"Sedgewick," a voice boomed through the darkness. "Let her go. Now."

Elizabeth sobbed. "Father?"

He strode from the garden's shadows, moonlight shining off his sword pointed at the baron's chest. More armed men filtered out of the darkness.

Dominic strode forward, his eyes dark with rage. "If Geoffrey were here, he would cut off your bollocks," he growled. "If you do not release the lady, I will take the privilege."

Sedgewick's arms dropped to his sides. He squeaked a nervous laugh. "'Twas a lover's spat, milords. No more."

"Do not heed him," Elizabeth said, massaging her neck, racked by shivers she could not control. "He paid Veronique to poison Geoffrey. He intends to kill you."

"As I heard." Arthur crossed to her side, his weapon still pointed at the baron, and touched her arm. "Are you all right?"

"A-Aye."

The baron chortled and wiped sweat from his nose with his sleeve. "I assure you I did not—"

"I heard all," Arthur snapped. "Part of your account confirmed what Aldwin told me. I spoke to him"—he looked at Elizabeth—"after I left de Lanceau's chamber not long ago."

"Wretched squire," Sedgewick muttered.

Arthur stepped closer to the baron. The tip of his sword met Sedgewick's tunic. "I despise de Lanceau too," Arthur said, "but you are a cruel man indeed to manipulate others to do your evil. If there is any doubt left in your mind, no man of that ilk deserves my daughter's hand in marriage. Most of all, you."

Sedgewick's eyes bulged. "Wait. Milord—"

"Before the guards drag you to the dungeon, I will know why."

"What do you mean?" The baron looked baffled.

"My daughter guessed the common thread in this mess that I could not. *You* blackmailed the Earl of Druentwode."

Sedgewick's mouth pinched.

"Answer me," Arthur snapped.

To Elizabeth surprise, the baron laughed. "Elizabeth's assumptions are wrong. I will not confess to what I did not do, and what cannot be proved."

"On the contrary. The earl sent a box of Geoffrey's possessions to Wode. The earl did not destroy the writ that exonerated Edouard, as his blackmailer demanded, but kept it safe. He also enclosed a letter telling how, fraught with guilt over Edouard's death, he had secured the pardon so that Edouard's sons would not bear the shame of believing their father a traitor."

The baron spat on the ground. "So?"

Arthur's jaw tightened. "I saw your reaction when Elizabeth spoke of blackmail. She was correct in guessing your guilt. Why, I asked myself, would you have wanted the writ destroyed? Why would you wish to keep Edouard's innocence secret? 'Tis clear to me now. You framed Edouard."

Elizabeth gasped.

Fury sparked in the baron's eyes, as though he could no longer maintain he was guiltless. "And if I did? Edouard, the fool, would not listen to me. I risked much to take him into my confidence and ask him to support rebellion. He refused and ordered me—"

"The feast!" Elizabeth cried, remembering. "Geoffrey told me that one eve, his father told visiting lords to leave Wode because they tried to sway him to treason."

Sedgewick's gaze slid to her. "That night, I saw the depth of Edouard's loyalty. I knew he would feel honor-bound to betray me to the king, so I betrayed Edouard first. I shed doubt on his allegiance. I convinced the king to order the siege."

"And I was the ignorant pawn," Arthur muttered.

"*I* wanted the honor of leading the siege. Yet the king chose you, an unknown in his court," Sedgewick said with a scowl. "I knew Edouard, and sought him out during the battle. I had the pleasure of running him through with my sword."

"Oh, God," Elizabeth whispered.

The baron made a sound of disgust. "Was I rewarded for helping the king vanquish a traitor? I asked for Wode. The king, however, granted all of Edouard's properties to Arthur." Sedgewick's eyes hardened. "I was denied what I deserved. I waited for the right opportunity to claim it. When Geoffrey de Lanceau threatened Wode, I seized that chance to realize my desires."

Frowning, Elizabeth said, "I do not understand. How could you blackmail the earl? Why could he not expose you as a traitor?"

Sedgewick grinned, clearly delighted by his own cleverness. "He attended the feast that eve at Wode. For a brief while, he planned to side with the king's son, but in the end refused. That in itself was enough to ruin him. Yet I also learned he sought a pardon for Edouard and intended to prove my duplicity. Using my contacts at court, I had significant documents destroyed. I also pressured the king for the earl's daughter's hand in marriage." Sedgewick smile turned wicked. "The earl loved her very much. With her, I ensured his silence."

"She died not long ago," Arthur said. "That left you free to pursue a betrothal to Elizabeth."

"Without his daughter's safety to consider, and when he realized he was dying," Elizabeth continued, caught up in her father's train of thought, "the earl could at last send the writ to Geoffrey and let him know the truth about Edouard."

A lewd grin tilted the baron's lips, and he held Elizabeth's gaze. "A shame, my love, you had to fall in love with de Lanceau. It would have been simpler for us all to let the past lie."

"Enough." Arthur signaled to his men. "Save your breath for the king's courts. You will need it to convince the jury to spare your head. Till then, 'twill be my pleasure to see you rot in my dungeon."

With a strangled squeal, the baron jerked back and tried to run, but Dominic stepped forward and shoved the tip of his sword against Sedgewick's belly.

Dominic pointed to the keep. "I believe the dungeon is that way." Smiling, he stepped to one side and let the armed sentries haul the baron, kicking and begging for mercy, toward the keep.

Arthur blew out a long sigh. Elizabeth turned to him, tears of gratitude stinging her eyes. "Thank you, Father. Dominic. How did you know I walked in the garden?"

"One of the servants told us she saw you heading across the bailey." Arthur returned his weapon to its scabbard, and clasped her hands. "I apologize for not interceding sooner this eve. As I left the forebuilding, a guard intercepted me and told me he had overheard you speaking with Sedgewick. I ordered him to get reinforcements while Dominic and I made our way to the garden. At first, I did not want to intrude upon your conversation for fear the baron would not finish his confession but then . . ." He raked his hand through his silvery hair. "Then he assaulted you."

Wiping away tears, she said, "I am not harmed."

"I am sorry for being such a rotten judge of character. How could I have thought the baron a suitable husband for you?"

She went into her father's arms and hugged him. "I forgive you. Please, we must find Veronique."

Arthur smiled and nodded. "I will order the keep searched, and will post guards outside Geoffrey's door day and night. If he dies, 'twill not be from the baron's poison."

CHApTER TWENTY

A whispering sound, no more than a rush of air, woke Elizabeth. Her heavy eyelids flicked open to see that the fire had burned low during the night. Her first thought was that Mildred had sent a servant to fetch more wood and rekindle the embers.

The noise came again, louder this time. With a drowsy blink, Elizabeth turned her head. Someone stood at the foot of Geoffrey's bed, staring down at his prone form.

Alarm swept any trace of sleep from Elizabeth's mind. The figure walked around the bed, and stark moonlight illuminated the hooded cloak that brushed the floorboards and caused the soft whisper. The hood slipped a fraction. Chestnut curls gleamed, framing a face so hard it seemed carved from stone.

Veronique!

Moonlight flashed off the silver vial in her hand.

Elizabeth lunged for the bed. "Nay!"

She collided with Veronique. The vial dropped onto the blankets and rolled down past Geoffrey's thigh.

"Stupid!" spat the courtesan. Shoving Elizabeth aside, Veronique clawed at the bedding. She had the vial in her fingertips, but Elizabeth pushed her sideways and sent her crashing into the oak side table. The flask of elixir shattered on the floor. Liquid splashed onto Elizabeth clothes and made the floor slick beneath her feet.

"By the blessed Virgin," Mildred shouted, rising from her pallet, her eyes huge.

"The vial," Elizabeth yelled, struggling in Veronique's grip. "Get it."

"Where? I see no—"

"On the bed!"

Mildred snatched up the vial and hurried to the door. "Guards," she bellowed down the corridor. "Guards!"

An instant later, Arthur burst into the chamber with Dominic at his heels.

"She has a knife," Elizabeth cried. She grabbed at Veronique's wrists, desperate to stop her from drawing the blade. With a cruel laugh, Veronique shoved her away. Elizabeth tripped on the edge of the pallet and sprawled on the floor.

The courtesan whipped the long knife from its scabbard. Elizabeth scrambled to rise.

Turning to the bed, Veronique clutched the dagger in both

hands, raised it high, and plunged it toward Geoffrey's chest.

The blade winked in its downward arc.

Elizabeth screamed.

Dominic lunged for the bed. He slammed into Veronique, knocking her off her feet. The knife tilted sideways, slipped from her hands, and clattered to the floor. Elizabeth grabbed the dagger and pushed up to standing.

Kicking, screaming, Veronique fought Dominic but he soon twisted her arms behind back and held her in front of him, squirming and cursing.

Arthur's smile held genuine admiration. "It appears your skills are not affected by a few mugs of ale, Dominic, or the late hour."

Dominic grinned. "A good thing, too."

Fighting to steady her breath, Elizabeth said, "Were there no guards at the door? Father, you promised."

"They are dead." Her sire glared at Veronique. "I did not pay you enough silver, wench?"

Her crimson lips turned up in a sneer. "The baron offered me coin *and* a keep of my own. His estate in Normandy."

"How fortunate for the villeins of Normandy that you shall never rule them," Arthur said, his voice cold.

She spat at his feet. Dominic propelled her toward the men-at-arms waiting in the doorway. Her shrieks of protest rang in the corridor, then faded into silence.

Elizabeth set down the knife and looked at Dominic, her eyes moist with tears. "If you had not come, Geoffrey might be dead."

"You mean, if I had not plied your father with so much drink he could not deny me another visit." Dominic glanced past her at Geoffrey, and his reckless smile wavered. "In truth, 'twas an honor, and at last, I have paid my debt to him. I hope my friend lives to thank me himself."

❖　❖　❖

Daylight shone in through the shutters when Elizabeth awoke. Her neck felt stiff and cramped from sleeping on the lumpy pallet, but she shrugged away the discomfort.

The baron and Veronique's murderous plans had been foiled. Geoffrey lived. 'Twas all that mattered.

She rose and set more logs on the fire, which had burned down since she refueled it after Veronique's capture. After indulging in a thorough, catlike stretch, Elizabeth smoothed the wrinkles from her crushed gown. She picked up the saddle trapping and smiled down at her deft handiwork. A few more stitches on the hawk's left wing, and the repair would be done.

Taking care to be quiet, she crossed to the bed. Beside it on the pallet, Mildred slept, curled on one side, her mouth relaxed open. A fresh flask of elixir sat in readiness on the side table. The healer must have worked late into the night to brew it.

Elizabeth stared down at Geoffrey. He seemed to be in

a peaceful sleep. His eyelids lay smooth and still, his lashes forming a dark smudge above his cheekbones. His lips were closed but his bottom lip protruded a fraction, and lent a childlike innocence to his slumber.

Stifling a yawn with the back of her hand, she drew a fresh linen cloth out of the willow basket and washed his face. In a feverish fit, he had worked his arms free from the blankets and his hands lay clasped across his chest. Above the linen bandages, his skin gleamed, reminding her again of the bold, muscular beauty of him.

How she hoped that he survived and became strong again. She would not give up hope.

As she worked, the end of her braid brushed his skin. He made a small sound, like a sigh, and turned his face toward her. Elizabeth smiled and leaned over to smooth the tendrils of hair from his cheek.

His fingers brushed her breast.

Elizabeth froze. The movement was so unexpected. Deliberate. Her hand, clutching the wet cloth, hovered in mid-air. She dared not breathe. Had she fantasized the touch? Had she wished with such desperation for him to recover, she had imagined what she felt?

His fingers moved again. A slow, tender caress.

"Geoffrey?" she whispered.

"I had to be sure I was not dreaming," he said, his voice a dry rasp. "Elizabeth, I had to be sure."

She drew back and looked down into eyes that were clear

and gray, and shining with tears.

"Geoffrey!" She smothered him with fevered kisses on his forehead, eyebrows, cheeks, and at last on the fullness of his lips. The kiss slowed and deepened, rich with loving joy.

"I prayed you would not die," she sobbed against his lips.

Pain shivered across his face as his warm, rough hand closed over hers. "I would never leave you, damsel."

She blinked away tears. "Promise me."

"I promise." His gaze shone with passionate conviction. "I love you, Elizabeth."

"As I love you."

She bent to kiss him again. At a muffled snort, she hesitated. Mildred pushed up from the pallet, wiping her eyes.

"I . . . do not mean to intrude, but . . . I am pleased to see you awake, milord."

"I have you and your herbs to thank for it?" Geoffrey asked.

Mildred nodded. "You do."

"Whatever you wish in return, 'tis yours."

The matron gave a proud smile. "Harrumph! Listen to you. Brave words from a man who has much healing to do. I remind you, milord, you are still my patient, and it may take *months* before you are back on your feet."

Geoffrey looked at Elizabeth and groaned. "Months?"

Mildred's head dipped in a curt nod. "If you wish to thank me, you will not disobey when I tell you to rest, or refuse to drink my healing tonics, no matter how foul they look, smell or taste. I cannot bear to see my lady in distress any longer. Agreed?"

He sighed. "Agreed."

"Good." She swept her frazzled gray braid over her shoulder. "Now, I believe I will tell Lord Brackendale the good news. If you have any sense, milady, you will not exhaust my patient with idle chatter. He is still very weak."

The door closed behind her.

A roguish grin curved Geoffrey's mouth, and molten heat flowed through Elizabeth. How she had missed his smile.

"'Tis good advice, damsel," he murmured, as she brushed her lips over his. "My mouth hungers for more than idle chatter."

❀　　❀　　❀

After many savored kisses and cherished words, Geoffrey linked his fingers through Elizabeth's and relished her soft skin against his. Fresh tears scalded his eyes, for she was the one—the *only*—reason he had fought to live.

The pervasive, suffocating darkness had threatened to drown his consciousness, but he had struggled with every last shred of his will to surface in the light and return to her.

"I have much to tell you," she murmured, nuzzling his cheek.

"I remember naught after I was injured." Geoffrey shoved aside the painful memory of that moment which seared through his mind and throbbed deep in his wound. "Are we at Wode?"

Elizabeth nodded, and told him of the squire Aldwin's arrest, how Geoffrey was carted to Wode to be healed, of the baron's manipulation of Aldwin and Veronique's attempted murder.

As Geoffrey listened, his anger flared. "The baron will answer to me." He cursed his infirmity and the bone-deep fatigue that rendered him incapable of storming down to the dungeon, sword in hand, and seeing justice done.

Excitement and a curious sadness shadowed her wet gaze. "There is more."

"More?"

She freed her fingers from his, crossed the chamber, and retrieved a rolled parchment. Uncurling it, she leaned close and held it up for him to see.

"Your hands are trembling," he said. "Elizabeth?"

"Read it," she said, her eyes glistening.

His gaze skimmed the document which bore an official signature, and he forced himself to read. As the meaning of the words permeated his mind, he whispered, "A royal pardon!"

"There is also a letter from the Earl of Druentwode, explaining why he kept the document secret until his death. Oh, Geoffrey, you were right. Your father was innocent. The baron framed him for treachery, and cut him down during the siege."

Rage, anguish, and hatred blinded Geoffrey. "I will kill

him! Bring him here. Now!" The effort of shouting sent acute pain stabbing through his torso. His vision blurred. He gritted his teeth against the mind-numbing agony and tried to rise.

"Geoffrey, stop!" Elizabeth shrilled.

Through the eerie buzzing in his ears, he heard the chamber door open. "Milord!" Mildred's hands were on his shoulders, easing him down onto the pillows as she would a weak child. She pressed a flask to his lips and bade him drink.

Frustration and helplessness ripped into his soul. He cried out in fury, and Elizabeth leaned over him and pressed her tear-soaked mouth to his. Tender, persistent, she kissed, soothed, and coaxed him to set the emotions free.

He could fight no longer. The sobs wrenched from him like that terrible night eighteen years ago, when his father perished. He wept until he was hoarse, and had no more tears to give.

He must have fallen asleep, for when his eyes cracked open, Dominic stood beside the bed, looking down at him.

A relieved smile spread across his friend's face. "'Tis good to see you, milord."

Geoffrey cleared the thickness from his throat. "And you."

Scratching his chin, Dominic tipped his head to one side. "You do look a bit pale, but a few pints of ale would cure that."

Mildred gave an indignant snort. After shooting Dominic a fierce scowl, she snatched up her basket and quit the chamber.

Smothering a grin, Geoffrey watched the healer leave, then glanced at Elizabeth, who sat embroidering near the fire. She met his gaze and smiled.

Pride flowed through him. His life had changed a great deal, and all for the better, because of her. He vowed to spend the rest of his living days proving how much he loved her. "What are you doing?" he murmured.

"Finishing the saddle trapping. Do you not remember?"

"I remember well, but I did not think—"

"That I would still work on it once I was rescued from Branton?" She swept a ringlet out of the needle's path. "'Tis my gift to you. When you set it upon your horse, and ride out among the people of Moydenshire, they will know you are Lord Geoffrey de Lanceau, proud son of Edouard."

Tears dampened his eyes. "*You* are my greatest gift," he said, heating his words with sensual promise.

Her face pinkened, and she resumed stitching. A moment later, she let out a delighted whoop, snapped a length of silver thread, and held the trapping aloft. "Look."

The rips in the silk were gone. Her clever mending could not disguise where they had been, but again, the magnificent hawk glowed on the silk, its wings extended as it prepared to soar.

The trapping was whole again, as he remembered when a boy.

He blinked hard, overwhelmed by gratitude. "Thank you."

Her lips curved in a saucy smile, and she winked. "Later,

you may thank me."

Dominic whistled. "Milord, if I may be so bold as to intrude, the lady and I have discussed a new project. She will begin once she has finished the garments for the orphans."

"Orphans?" Dragging his gaze from Elizabeth's lush mouth, Geoffrey shoved aside fantasies of lusty thank-you kisses.

"She is embroidering clothes for the children in the local orphanage. A special donation to commemorate her mother and sister's passing a year ago. She was working on this when you abducted her."

Guilt wove through Geoffrey. "I see." He looked at Elizabeth, but she was picking threads from her bliaut.

"The new project," Dominic said, "is a banner to honor you."

Geoffrey raised his eyebrows.

Elizabeth looked up and giggled. Mischief warmed her eyes.

Dominic's hand moved in the air as he rendered an invisible picture. "The banner will feature a silver shield on blue silk. In the center, she will stitch a great boar, with its lips curled back in a ferocious scowl."

Geoffrey was not sure whether to laugh or groan. "A boar?"

"A demented boar." Dominic beamed. "A grand idea, aye?"

✤ ✤ ✤

"His strength is returning at a remarkable rate," Mildred said three days later. She stood at Geoffrey's bedside, stirring an herbal infusion into a goblet of red wine. "'Tis not surprising, Lord Brackendale, since he does whatever I tell him and is basking in all the attention."

Arthur grunted. He stood leaning his shoulder against the wall, as far as he could be from Geoffrey in the room, Elizabeth noted. Although news of Geoffrey's awakening had spread throughout the keep, her father had not revisited the chamber until this morn. He did not look at all pleased by Mildred's good news. In fact, his forbidding frown seemed to deepen.

Blankets rustled, and Elizabeth looked over at Geoffrey. He grinned at her, and awareness and happiness swooped through her in a giddy rush.

"How could I not recover," he murmured, "with my betrothed's tender ministrations, and when your medicine is delivered in such exceptional syrup." When Mildred lowered the goblet to his mouth, he took an obedient sip. "Delicious but for the musky aftertaste."

The healer shrugged. "The servants tell me there are ten barrels of this wine in the storage cellar. I cannot imagine a jug or two will be missed."

"You give him the *Bordeaux*?" Arthur growled.

Geoffrey's eyes brightened. "Bordeaux? Mmm."

"That wine cost Sedgewick a great deal of coin," Arthur said, his face reddening. "'Twas for Elizabeth's wedding."

Elizabeth set down the child's chemise she was embroidering. Whatever her father and Geoffrey had still to discuss between them, those matters were best left until Geoffrey's wounds had improved. "Father, please."

Geoffrey's gaze sharpened. "What wedding?"

Arthur shoved away from the wall. "The marriage planned between my daughter and the baron before you chose to wreak vengeance. The one Sedgewick rescheduled assuming you would be dead and buried."

Elizabeth feared to look at Geoffrey and see his fury. Yet when she glanced at him, his expression held understanding.

"You do not like that Elizabeth and I are betrothed."

Hostility flashed in Arthur's eyes. "You may have won Wode, de Lanceau, but I will not stay silent any longer. I am a man of honor. I will respect the agreements made during our fight, but it irks me to see you lord of what was once *my* home, drinking the finest wine in the keep, and being coddled like a hero." He dragged a shaking hand through his hair. "You have taken all from me—my home, my lands, my titles. Is it any wonder that I resent your claim to my daughter?"

Dread clutched at Elizabeth. Before she could try to ease the tense situation, Geoffrey said, "Elizabeth. Mildred. Leave us. I wish to speak to Lord Brackendale alone."

Elizabeth dried her clammy palms on her skirt, put aside the chemise, and stood. Mayhap 'twould be better if her father and Geoffrey settled their differences now. She took Mildred's arm and walked out.

The matron pulled the door shut. "What will they discuss?"

"I do not know." Elizabeth suppressed a shiver. Geoffrey either meant to reconcile with her father, or punish him for his outburst. Yet Geoffrey was still very weak.

Crouching down, the matron pressed her ear to the keyhole. "Harrumph! I cannot hear a word."

"Why do we not walk in the garden? I would enjoy some fresh air. In truth, I will go *mad* if I must stand here and wait."

"An excellent suggestion, milady. A walk will stretch my old bones, and I shall gather herbs for a fresh poultice, too."

Refreshed after a long stroll, Elizabeth and Mildred returned to the chamber. The door remained closed.

Mildred crossed her arms. "'Tis most peculiar."

"I agree." Elizabeth strode to and fro, racking her thoughts for a good reason to intrude. She had just raised her hand to knock when she heard a most unexpected sound. Laughter.

The door flew open. Her father stood inside, his cheeks warmed by a hearty grin and the effects of at least one goblet of red wine, held in his hand. Without a word, he took Elizabeth in his arms and hugged her.

"Father, what happened?" she asked, the sound muffled against his jerkin.

"All is well." He released her from his embrace, and his eyes shone. "I am to remain lord of Wode."

"*You* are? Geoffrey—?"

"—told me all," Arthur said, "of his anguish over his father's death, his desire for revenge, the silk trade, his dreams for my lands . . . but most of all, of his love for you."

She blinked and tried to hold back tears. "What of Geoffrey's desire to reclaim Wode?"

"He ceded the keep and all of my titles back to me, provided he can ship his cloth up and down the river from Branton."

"'Tis wondrous news," Elizabeth cried.

"I suggested he petition the crown for Sedgewick's lands. 'Twould be just for Geoffrey to be granted them." Arthur touched her arm and smiled. "He also told me of the garments you are embroidering for the orphanage. We both agree 'tis an excellent cause. Each year, from this year onward, we will work together to donate such a gift. Whatever you need now so you can finish—cloth, embroiderers, coin—you shall have."

Joy burst inside her. "Oh, Father!"

Arthur grinned. "De Lanceau will make you a fine husband, for a rogue."

Elizabeth hurried into the chamber. Geoffrey lay propped against a mound of pillows. He looked drawn, exhausted, but content. At last, his soul seemed to have found peace.

He smiled, and she bent down and kissed him.

"I could not take Wode from your sire and hurt you," he murmured, his breath brushing her cheek. "I do not think my father would have wanted it, either."

Tears streamed down her face. "Thank you."

His fingers caught hers. "We will be happy at Branton, you and I."

"Aye, we shall." She kissed him again.

Behind her, she heard Mildred's wistful sigh.

Through a haze of bliss, Elizabeth heard her father's footfalls echo out into the hall. "You there," he said. "Fetch another jug of Bordeaux. Fetch a whole case. Be quick about it. We have a betrothal to celebrate."

epilogue

"There." Mildred gave the hem of Elizabeth's bliaut one last tug and pushed to a stand. Her mouth quivered with a watery smile. "Oh, milady."

Elizabeth laughed and twirled around, sending yards of fabric floating in a cloud around her ankles. She felt like a goddess. The air smelled of the apple blossoms crowning the veil over her hair. Shivering with delight, Elizabeth ran her hands down the expensive silk, and remembered Geoffrey's determination to find the right color. Ivory, he had insisted, for the honesty of their love. Pietro, dear man, had searched every ship in Venice until he found it.

She spun again, slower this time, watching the silk shimmer in the sunlight. A pattern of embroidered roses scrolled along the fitted bodice, to which she had pinned her mother's gold brooch. The gown's sleeves were fitted at her elbows and flared to her wrists, paralleling the skirt as it belled out over her hips and fell to the floor. As she turned, the silk rustled. Although she could not see them, Elizabeth heard the *tip-tap* of the slippers Pietro had sent to complement the gown.

Mildred blew her nose. "If your mother—a blessing upon her departed soul—could see you now. You look beautiful."

"I feel beautiful." Elizabeth trailed her fingers over the brooch, which her father had returned to her long ago. Indeed, she felt better than she had in a long time. No bouts of nausea. No hot flushes. No—

A sudden little kick sent her stomach muscles fluttering. 'Twas the fifth month she had not had her flux. She smiled and pressed her palms to her belly's gentle curve. The babe had inherited its father's restless energy.

"'Tis moving?" Mildred asked.

"Aye. Ohhh!"

Chuckling, the healer mopped her eyes. "'Tis a strong son. He will make his sire proud."

The baby kicked again and Elizabeth giggled. "I think he knows how nervous I am."

"If 'tis any consolation, milady, I imagine Geoffrey is as anxious as you."

He *was* nervous, Elizabeth saw moments later, when Mildred and her father escorted her down the winding path toward Wode's parish church. 'Twas odd they should both be so affected by the day. At Geoffrey's bedside months ago, they had exchanged rings in a betrothal ceremony and the priest had published the marriage banns on three successive Sundays. She and Geoffrey had wed in a simple exchange of vows.

Yet he had insisted upon honoring her with a formal ceremony on the church portico in front of plenty of witnesses, followed by a lavish and rowdy feast complete with jongleurs, tumblers, and other entertainers, once he had recovered.

Now, he paced before the crowd of onlookers, his tall form slicing through the streaks of sunlight filtering through the oaks in the church cemetery. A pair of twittering robins darted in front of him, startling him, and Elizabeth chuckled.

The familiar haze of stubble on his chin had gone. His hair shone in dark waves to the collar of his finest black silk jerkin, which complemented his black hose that hugged his muscled legs, and black leather boots.

Elizabeth sucked in a trembling breath and smoothed her veil with her fingers. She could not believe seven months had passed since Geoffrey was wounded. That terrible episode was all in the past now. The injury had almost healed over, leaving but a deep, pitted scar similar to the other one marring his chest. With Dominic's persistence, Geoffrey had regained much of his former strength though 'twould be many more months before he would be able to lift anything heavier than a chair.

In that time, Aldwin had come before Geoffrey to answer the charge of attempted murder. She had stood nearby while Geoffrey listened to the squire's tearful explanation and apology. When finished, Geoffrey had informed Aldwin that his penance would be to swear fealty to him for the rest of his life. 'Twas a decision never once regretted. Aldwin threw himself into his duties and excelled for his new lord.

Elizabeth nibbled her bottom lip. She wished matters had resolved as well with Sedgewick and Veronique. Accompanied by an armed escort, they were sent to the king's dungeons to await trial and punishment, but had somehow escaped. Neither had been seen or heard from since. Elizabeth resisted the urge to worry, for she doubted the baron or Veronique posed any threat to her and Geoffrey's future happiness.

Sidestepping a muddy puddle, Elizabeth looked up at Geoffrey. She loved him more than she ever thought possible, cherished even the simplest of his gestures, like the way he raked his fingers through his hair and with lithe grace, strode back to the priest.

Over the past months, he had proven his devotion to her with his hard work to secure their future. His first shipment of two thousand sheep had arrived at Branton. He left his bed every morn to supervise the construction of a fuller's shop in preparation for the carding and drying of the first shearing of wool that summer. He had also received his share of the returns from the Venetian silk shipments, a profit more than three times his expectations. The coin had not been in Branton's coffers two days before he had spent it to upgrade Branton "to a level of luxury suitable for my beloved wife and babe," he had told her with a tender kiss. Geoffrey had even paid for the modern convenience of piped water.

He seemed to sense her gaze upon him now, for he glanced up. His gaze locked with hers. Still, after all this time, one heated look from him could make her limbs go weak.

The crowd parted with murmurs of awe. Among those gathered, she saw Dominic, Elena and Roydon, waving to her as she approached the portico. She laughed and waved back.

Geoffrey's gray eyes skimmed over her, and his mouth slid into a roguish grin. Elizabeth smiled too, for she saw in his expression all facets of him—the rogue, the confidant, the gentle lover—and knew without doubt she loved them all.

As the priest stepped forward with the gold rings and spoke the first words of the wedding ceremony, Elizabeth also recognized the promise in Geoffrey's smoldering gaze, to cherish her and their children today, tomorrow, and forever.

THE END

Also Available By Catherine Kean:

Dance of Desire

Desperate to save her brother Rudd from being condemned as a traitor, Lady Rexana Villeaux must dance in disguise at a feast for the High Sheriff of Warringham. Her goal is to distract him so her servant can steal a damning missive from the sheriff's solar. Dressed in the gauzy costume of a desert courtesan, dancing with all the passion and sensuality in her soul, she succeeds in her mission. And, at the same time, condemns herself.

Fane Linford, the banished son of an English earl, joined Richard's crusade only to find himself a captive in a hellish eastern prison. He survived the years of torment, it's rumored, because of the love of a Saracen courtesan. The rumors are true. And when he sees Rexana dance . . .

Richard has promised Fane an English bride, yet he desires only one woman – the exotic dancer who tempted him. Then he discovers the dancer's identity. And learns her brother is in his dungeon, accused of plotting against the throne. It is more temptation than Fane can resist.

The last thing Rexana wants is marriage to the dark and brooding Sheriff of Warringham. But her brother is his prisoner, and there may be only one way to save him. Taking the greatest chance of her life, Rexana becomes the sheriff's bride. And learns that the Dance of Desire was only a beginning . . .

ISBN#193281535X
ISBN#9781932815351
Jewel Imprint: Sapphire
US $6.99 / CDN $9.99
Available Now
www.catherinekean.com

SUNBURST'S CITADEL

THERESE NICHOLS

Amid the exotic splendor of historic India comes a sweeping tale of desire and duty . . .

Shamsi, a beautiful but penniless entertainer, is haunted by a childhood tragedy that changed her life. She hides behind silken veils, praying to escape the desires of men. And keeps her secret close to her heart.

Lord Karim, military advisor to the emperor, is bound to put duty above all else, even the desires of his heart. Though he loves Shamsi, his soul-mate, she is destined for another. The man Karim serves. It is not the only obstacle to their union.

Shamsi is Hindu, a commoner. Karim is a Christian nobleman. Shamsi is Rajput; Karim a Moghul. And he hides a secret of his own.

Can love survive the truth? Or will the fire of their passion leave only ashes?

ISBN#1932815619
ISBN#9781932815610
Jewel Imprint: Sapphire
US $6.99 / CDN $9.99
November 2006

A Lost Touch of Paradise
Amy Tolnitch

For the first time in his life, Lugh MacKier, Laird of Tunvegan, finds himself in a battle he cannot win. His precious daughter is dying of the same illness that claimed his wife.

The Isle of Parraba is a whispered legend, a place rumored to be ruled by a sorceress, an isle no one can reach. Yet, legend speaks of a powerful healer as well. Lugh MacKeir, desperate, determines to find Parraba and face its mysterious ruler.

Isobal is the Lady of Parraba, mystical and magical, a woman apart from the world around her. Drawn to something familiar in Lugh's child, however, she reluctantly agrees to help her in exchange for Lugh clearing the blocked entrance to a very special cave.

But the child's illness defies Isobal's skill, and Lugh's task proves more of a challenge than he anticipated. In the end, the secret to saving Lugh's daughter lies in Isobal's ability to open her heart to a brash warrior who has invaded her tranquil sanctuary. She must find the courage to end her isolation, and the wise innocence of a child must lead them all to A Lost Touch of Paradise.

ISBN#193281566X
ISBN#9781932815665
Jewel Imprint: Amethyst
US $6.99 / CDN $9.99
October 2006
www.amytolnitch.com

VANQUISHED
HOPE TARR

"The photograph must be damning, indisputably
so. I mean to see Caledonia Rivers not only
ruined but vanquished. Vanquished, St. Claire, I'll
settle for nothing less."

Known as The Maid of Mayfair for her unassailable virtue,
unwavering resolve, and quiet dignity, suffragette leader,
Caledonia — Callie — Rivers is the perfect counter for
detractors' portrayal of the women as rabble rousers, lunatics,
even whores. But a high-ranking enemy within the government
will stop at nothing to ensure that the Parliamentary bill to grant
the vote to females dies in the Commons — including ruining
the reputation of the Movement's chief spokeswoman.

After a streak of disastrous luck at the gaming tables threatens
to land him at the bottom of the Thames, photographer Hadrian
St. Claire reluctantly agrees to seduce the beautiful suffragist
leader and then use his camera to capture her fall from grace.
Posing as the photographer commissioned to make her portrait
for the upcoming march on Parliament, Hadrian infiltrates
Callie's inner circle. But lovely, soft-spoken Callie hardly fits
his mental image of a dowdy, man-hating spinster. And as
the passion between them flares from spark to full-on flame,
Hadrian is the one in danger of being vanquished.

ISBN#1932815759
ISBN#9781932815757
Jewel Imprint: Sapphire
US $6.99 / CDN $9.99
Available Now
www.hopetarr.com

For more information

about other great titles from

Medallion Press, visit

www.medallionpress.com